The Cowboy Who Called Back

An Older Brother's Best Friend Romance & Small Town Saga

Three Rivers Romance™
Book 5

Liz Isaacson

Reader Note

Hello Fabulous Christian Cowboy Readers!

I'm thrilled you're back in Three Rivers with me!

This is actually two love stories, so I hope you're ready for that. Of course, JJ's and Ruby's is in the forefront, and you'll get to see their mutual pining, mutual unrequited love for one another the most.

But there's another couple here that winds up together too, and I hope you'll love them too!

And of course, the cowboys and their wives and families from the first four books in this series!

We haven't been back to Seven Sons Ranch for a long time, and perhaps this is your FIRST time there! I hope you'll love it as much a I do!

Because one of the Walkers gets a HUGE surprise in this book...

All of my books address real life situations without fear or shame, because I believe we all make mistakes, our Savior suffered for all of us, and we can all repent, be healed, and come back to God.

So are you ready for true-to-life romance, family saga, and the small town goodness you might've come to expect from me?! I hope so! If you're new, you're in for a treat!

xoxo

~Liz

This book's playlist:

Daylight by Shinedown - I LOVE the lyrics for this song! "You saved my life, not once but twice. You keep me free from falling. You saved my life, make it all right. I don't feel like talking. You make sure I always see the daylight."

Mm, yes. This could be for JJ and Ruby, or our own relationship with God.

Give it a listen!

Calum Scott's "At Your Worst" also played on repeat while I worked on this book. It really spoke to my soul for one of the secondary characters, and that bled over into JJ and Ruby's relationship too. I think I'll keep it on my playlist for the next book for sure!

Listen to it!

The Small Town of Three Rivers

Welcome to Three Rivers! There have been three complete series here already - Three Rivers Ranch, Seven Sons Ranch (Walker Brothers), and Shiloh Ridge Ranch (Glover Family).

That's 37 books. Loads of characters. I'm going to list them here, but you don't need to know them all comprehensively for this book. I just know some of you like seeing these amazing small towns and who lives here!

Seven Sons Ranch:

Momma & Daddy: Penny and Gideon Walker

1. RHETT & EVELYN WALKER

Son: Conrad - 27

Triplets: Austin, Elaine, and Easton - 21

. . .

2. JEREMIAH & WHITNEY WALKER
   Son: Jonah Jeremiah (JJ) - 25
   Daughter: Clara Jean - 22
   Son: Jason - 21
   Daughter: Emily - 19
   Daughter: Hattie - 16

3. LIAM & CALLIE WALKER
   Daughter: Denise - 32
   Daughter: Ginger - 27

4. TRIPP & IVORY WALKER
   Son: Oliver - 38 (and married to Aurora Glover)
   Son: Isaac - 27

5. WYATT & MARCY WALKER
   Son: Warren - 24
   Son: Cole - 22
   Son: Harrison - 21
   Daughter: Rachel - 18

6. SKYLER & MALLERY WALKER
   Daughter: Camila - 24
   Son: Sawyer - 22

Son: Gideon - 19

7. MICAH & SIMONE WALKER
    Son: Travis (Trap) - 23
    Daughter: Daisy - 21
    Son: Jensen - 17
    Daughter: Laurel - 15

Coyote Pass:
    Alex Baxter, wife Nikki (twin boys - Shane and Hank, age 4)

Three Rivers Ranch:
    Frank and Heidi Ackerman - patriarch and matriarch. Frank died 15 years ago; Heidi is remarried to Malcolm Rust.

Squire and Kelly Ackerman
    Son: Finn - 36, wife Edith, Theo (son, 6), Bubba (son, 2), pregnant with their third child (in September)
    Daughter: Libby - 31, married to Rusty Jackson
    Son: Michael - 28
    Son: Samuel - 24

. . .

Pete and Chelsea Marshall (Chelsea is Squire's sister, and they own Courage Reins, which is housed at Three Rivers Ranch)

4 sons:

Paul - 32, married to Brielle

Henry - 30, wife Angel, son, Wrangler (6 months) **(Lone Star Ranch)**

John - 26

Rich - 23

Reese and Carly Sanders: They're the admins for Courage Reins, Pete and Chelsea's equine therapy unit at Three Rivers Ranch. They have no children.

Garth and Juliette Ahlstrom (former foreman; vet technician)

Son: Jake - 29

Son: Carson - 26

Cal and Trina Hodgkins (he's the full-time vet at Three Rivers Ranch)

Daughter: Sabrina - 39

Daughter: Abby - 31

Daughter: Olive - 26

. . .

Ethan and Brynn Greene (they own Bowman's Breeds, which is housed at Three Rivers Ranch)
> Daughter: Carolina - 28
> Son: Tyson - 26
> Son: Bryan - 24

Beau Peterson (foreman at Three Rivers Ranch) and Charlotte Wisenhouer
> Son: Walter (11)
> Daughter: Michelle (7)

Bennett and Ellie Peterson (he's a cowboy, she works on the finances on the ranch with Kelly)
> Daughter: Joy - 14
> Son: Jaxon - 11

Tad and Sandy Jorgensen (he's a cowboy, she owns the pancake house in town)
> Son: Nathaniel (Nate) - 26
> Daughter: Helen - 23

Kenny and Taryn Stockton (he's a cowboy, she works for a local online newspaper in town)
> Daughter: Joelle (Jo) - 25

. . .

Jon and Grace Carver (he's a cowboy, she helps Heidi run the bakery in town)

Andy and Lawrence Collins (he's a cowboy, she owns a clothing boutique in town)

Summer and Tanner Wolfe (he's a cowboy, she's a nurse at the hospital in town)

Gavin and Navy Redd - they own their own single-family ranch on the northeast side of Three Rivers

Boone and Nicole Carver (Squire's cousin) - they own and operate the full time veterinary clinic in town

Camila and Dylan Walker (he's a cowboy and an electrician, she owns a plumbing shop in town)

Shiloh Ridge Ranch:
   Lois & Stone (deceased) Glover, 7 children, in age-order: (Lois is now married to Donald Parker)

1. Bear — Sammy, wife

- Lincoln (31), adopted son, married to Misty,
  Dallas (nickname: Diesel, 3.5 / Scout, 5 months)
- Stetson (Smiles, 21), son
- Russell (Rock, 20), son
- Heather (18), daughter
- Sunnie (17), daughter

2. Cactus — Allison, ex-wife / Bryce, son (deceased) //
— Willa, wife

- Mitch (32), adopted son
- Cameron (27), adopted son
- Kyle (25), adopted son
- Charlie (Chaz, 21), son
- Lynn (21), adopted daughter
- Melissa (18), daughter

3. Judge — June, wife

- Lucy Mae (37), step-daughter
- Birch (19), son
- Willow (17), daughter
- Linden (14), son

4. Preacher — Charlie, wife

- Betty (20), daughter

- Hank (18), son
- Daisy (15), daughter

5. Arizona — Duke Rhinehart, husband, living at the Rhinehart Ranch, just south of Shiloh Ridge

- Shiloh (20), daughter
- April (18), daughter
- Dwayne (16), son
- Dallas (12), son

6. Mister — Libby, wife

- Belle (18), son
- Marley (16), daughter
- Hazel (13), daughter
- Brantley (10), son

7. Bishop — Montana, wife

- Aurora (38), step-daughter and married to Oliver Walker
- Robbie (25), son
- Georgia (19), daughter

Aurora and Oliver have 3 children, who are Bishop and Montana's grandchildren:

The Cowboy Who Called Back

- Jewel (11), daughter
- Laramie (Lara, 8), daughter
- Mason (6), son
- Lennon (4), son

Dawna & Bull (deceased) Glover, 5 children, in age-order:

1. Ranger — Oakley, wife

- Wilder (23), son
- Fawn (21), daughter

2. Ward — Dot, wife

- Glory Rose (22), daughter
- Silver (19), son
- Flint (17), son

3. Ace — Holly Ann, wife

- Gunnison (21), son
- Pearl Jo (19), daughter
- Ashton (16), son

4. Etta — August Winters, husband

- Hailey (29), adopted daughter
- Joey (19), son
- Nash and Nellie (twins - 17), son and daughter

5. Ida — Brady Burton, husband

- Johnny and Judy (twins - 23), son and daughter
- Riggs (17), son

- Sonora (14), daughter

Bull and Stone Glover were brothers, so their children are cousins. Ranger and Bear, for example, are cousins, and each the oldest sibling in their families.

Rhinehart Ranch:

1. Dawson, wife, Caroline (son, Colt, almost 3), pregnant with their second child (due in Dec)

Chapter One

"All right." Jonah Jeremiah Walker turned in a circle, taking in the entirety of his cabin in only a few seconds. He'd lived in this same one for several summers now, and being back felt like crawling into a familiar bed and falling asleep comfortably.

His daddy finished putting the groceries in the fridge, and Momma currently stood at the front window, fixing the curtain rod so it hung right. Tate Reynolds assisted her, and the two of them chatted easily.

JJ couldn't believe he was back at Seven Sons, though all signs in his life had been pointing him here for a few years now. He belonged in the Texas Panhandle town of Three Rivers, he knew that.

But a small part of him yearned for an adventure. Time spent outside of his family's expectations, outside of Texas, outside of what he'd always thought his life would be.

You're young, he thought, echoing something his mom had told him loads of times. *You have time to do all kinds of things with your life.*

He saw her loving, appreciative smile in his mind when she'd said it to him in the past, and as she turned from the curtains, he found it on her face again.

"You're all set," she said.

"I can really paint the cabin whatever color I want?" JJ asked.

"We saved it for you," Daddy said. "Since you'll be livin' here for a while now, we figured you could choose whatever you like."

"You've complained about the green in the past." His mother came toward him, and JJ just wanted her to fold him into her arms and tell him everything would be all right.

"I've complained?" He frowned and flicked a look at Tate. "I didn't mean to complain."

Momma and Daddy exchanged a glance, and Daddy said, "We just thought you'd like to choose the color. That's all."

JJ nodded, fighting against his inner grump. Being around so many people for so long tired him, and he needed moving day to be done. "All right," he drawled. "Thank you for helping me move."

Again.

JJ had been back and forth between Seven Sons and Amarillo State College every summer now for four years. Relief painted through him—and he wondered if he could find a paint color titled *relief*—that this was his final move.

For now.

"We'll get out of your hair." Momma cradled his face in her hand, though he stood taller than her now. "Let us know if you need anything." His parents left through the front door, and the cabin had one in the back corner too, that led out of the kitchen to a tiny deck. Down three steps and across a field, and JJ could arrive and his aunt and uncle's place.

Aunt Callie often came in that door with something freshly baked, and JJ's mouth watered for some of her home-made honey whole wheat bread.

He met his best friend's eyes. "Let's get out of here."

Tate grinned at him. "Feeling caged?"

"Here?" JJ threw him a dark look. "Always." He turned for the back door and left, pausing at the railing once he'd gained the outdoors. The Texas Panhandle sun hung low on the horizon, painting the evening sky in a breathtaking array of oranges and pinks.

He scanned the vast expanse of land before him, looking past his aunt and uncle's house to the space beyond. Across the street, where the rolling hills dotted with grazing cattle stood, brought a sense of peace to his soul he desperately needed.

Tate joined him, and he didn't have to say anything. He wasn't entirely thrilled to be back at Seven Sons either, but he hadn't been able to find a ranch of his own that he could afford. His family hailed from Lubbock, but Tate had said on more than one occasion that he would never go back there permanently.

He'd fallen in love with Three Rivers, and he wanted to settle down as a rancher here. But property prices had soared in the past couple of years, and that had shut down his dreams.

For now.

JJ had considered telling him that he could buy every ranch in the Three Rivers area, but something always held him back. At twenty-five, JJ's broad shoulders held plenty of responsibility.

Now that he'd graduated with his degree in equine studies and management, he was no longer just the ranch owner's son; he was about to step into his daddy's boots as the new controller and barn manager at Seven Sons. He'd been groomed for this job his entire life, but that didn't make it any less daunting.

"Lord," JJ whispered, closing his eyes for a moment. "Thank You for this beautiful land and the opportunity to steward it. Guide me as I take on this new responsibility. Help me make my daddy proud."

"Amen, brother," Tate said, though the man didn't know how to whisper. Where JJ frowned, Tate grinned. While he stayed silent, Tate couldn't stop talking. They had opposite personalities, but JJ had always gotten along with Tate extraordinarily well, since the very first day of his very first year at Amarillo State.

Before then, even, as he'd met Tate the weekend before classes had started, as they'd been assigned the same apartment on-campus. They'd lived together since, even here at Seven Sons, and JJ glanced over to his best friend.

18

"How's it feel to be all grown up and important, JJ?"

JJ chuckled, some of the heaviness of his thoughts lifting. He pulled Tate into a quick, brotherly hug. "Feels like I've got a whole lot to learn," he admitted. "But I'm ready for it. How about you? Still annoyed you have to live here with me?"

Tate nodded, leaning against the deck railing. "Yeah, I'm over that. Your daddy pays real good, and I can save up for my own place faster than working anywhere else."

Words piled in JJ's throat, admissions about how much money he had, confessions that he could buy any of the ranches Tate saw online, offers to fund his best friend's dreams. He swallowed against them, because such a thing would need to be discussed with Daddy first, as JJ's money had been gifted to him at age twenty-one, but he didn't have complete control over it until he turned thirty.

Everything had to be done inside a trust, and JJ honestly didn't want to add one more thing to his mental and physical load right now.

As they stood there, soaking in the evening sunshine, JJ's mind wandered to Ruby, Tate's younger sister. The thought of her made his heart skip a beat, and he immediately chastised himself for it.

Ruby was off-limits, plain and simple.

Her close relationship with Tate dictated as much, and besides, she was probably off living her big-city dreams now that she'd graduated from college too.

"You okay there, Jay-J?" Tate's voice broke through his

reverie. "You looked like you were a million miles away for a second."

JJ forced a smile, guilt gnawing at him for his wayward thoughts. "Yeah, just thinking about all the work we've got ahead of us." He started down the steps. "And they didn't paint the cabin?" He scoffed as Tate's boots sounded on the steps behind him. "That wasn't for me, trust me."

Tate laughed, the sound free and loud and filling the sky. "You *have* complained about the green every year, brother. Just admit it."

JJ would do no such thing. He just wanted to see his horses and steal from their gentle spirits. As they walked toward the stables which sat out past the homestead, the storage shed, and the barn, Tate's phone rang.

He pulled it from his pocket, took a look at it, and scoffed before shoving it away again. JJ's interest piqued, but he didn't ask who'd called. Tate obviously didn't want to talk to them, and JJ thought it might be his on-again, off-again girlfriend from Amarillo, Frieda.

Tate's expression darkened, and he let out a heavy sigh. "It's Ruby. She's been calling me non-stop, but I'm not in the mood to listen to her whine."

JJ had never once thought that Ruby had whined about anything, but she wasn't his younger sister. He'd thought that plenty about Clara Jean, his younger sister, so he simply kept his mouth shut. He could listen to Tate complain and disagree with him silently.

His opinion of Ruby wouldn't get tarnished, that was for

sure. JJ had had a crush on her since the moment he'd met her, four years ago now.

Four. Long. Years.

Time to move on, he told himself. Now that they didn't have to see each other daily, he might be able to. She'd graduated this spring too, and she had an internship-that-could-become-a-job in San Antonio as part of her interior design degree. He'd been real happy for her when she'd gotten it a few months ago, though it had made his heartbeat sing with sadness.

Truth be told, the pang in his chest still existed. He'd dated other women, but nothing serious, and JJ told himself that once he found his real feet under him at Seven Sons, he'd find someone to date.

All of his friends here in town had found someone, and JJ really wanted it to be his turn. Of course, none of his cousins besides Oliver had gotten married yet, and his momma's words rang through his head again.

You're young.

Tate's phone rang again as they went past the shed, the big, bright, obviously recently painted, red barn came into view. Around the other side of it, the American flag waved, and JJ craved the sight of it. Somehow, it made him feel safe, and protected, and loved.

"Stop callin' me, Ruby." Tate ran a hand through his hair, frustration evident in his voice. He swiped the call away again, while JJ's heart played like a jackrabbit in his chest.

"Come on," JJ said, pushing Ruby out of his mind, hopefully for the last time that evening. "Let me show you the new breeding stock we just got in. Daddy's real proud of 'em."

As they walked toward the stables, JJ tried to focus on the task at hand. He pointed out the improvements they'd made to the ranch over the past year—the upgraded irrigation system, the expanded cattle pens, the new fences along the highway.

"You've done all this?" Tate asked, seemingly impressed.

"Daddy involved me in everything in the past year, though I was still in school." JJ came to a fence that contained a pasture with a couple of horses grazing in it. "He's not going to just hand over Seven Sons in a single day."

JJ didn't even want him to.

"He trusts you, though," Tate said. "That's huge."

A surge of pride moved through JJ with Tate's words. "He seems to, but I've still got a lot to learn." He had dreams to add more horses to Seven Sons, but he hadn't spoken those out loud to anyone yet. Not even his father.

They had space for another stable that could house twenty horses, and JJ wanted to bring horse breeding to Seven Sons Ranch. It was the only thing he got excited about lately—besides Ruby, of course—but now that he'd determined they could only be friends—and long-distance friends at that—he only had the horses.

Tate clapped him on the back. "If anyone can do it, it's you. You've always had a way with horses and cattle that the rest of us only dream of."

JJ nodded, because he did communicate with animals in an extraordinary way. "Let's go see the flag."

He started along the fence, soon leaving that pasture behind, the corner of the barn they needed to round only a few paces away. Just then, Tate's phone rang again.

A yell filled the air.

JJ's boots brought his body to a stop as a bull came charging around the corner of the barn.

Tate had his eyes on his phone still, his head down. How he didn't hear the thundering hooves, JJ didn't know. Couldn't comprehend.

JJ's instincts kicked in, and he stepped forward, his voice low and soothing as he tried to calm the charging bull.

He should've known better. Bulls couldn't be soothed. They weren't horses.

"Tate!" he yelled as he dodged out of the way. Two cowhands came flying around the corner of the barn, ropes in their hands.

But things moved too fast. Time didn't slow just because JJ wanted to save his best friend.

"Tate," he called again, and the bull seemed to know who JJ was trying to summon. He huffed and trotted toward JJ's best friend just as he lifted his head.

He didn't seem to catalog what was happening, at least not fast enough.

"Move!" JJ yelled. Or maybe he didn't. Maybe the warning only screamed silently through his soul.

Because Tate didn't move.

The bull did, and it caught Tate in the chest, butting

him backwards in a violent move that stole JJ's very breath from his body.

JJ watched, horrified, as his best friend in the whole world hit the ground hard—without even trying to catch himself.

He didn't move, and JJ didn't think.

"Tate!" JJ yelled, rushing to his friend's side as the other cowboys whistled and clapped and yelled at the bull to hopefully distract it from charging again.

Tate lay motionless, a small trickle of blood coming from somewhere on his head.

"Tate, can you hear me?" JJ had no idea where to put his hands, and Tate didn't move a millimeter. JJ's heart pounded in his chest, and thankfully, his daddy held mandatory first aid and safety training every year.

JJ had always found it a tad ridiculous, but that training kicked in as he pulled his phone out with shaking hands. He dialed nine-one-one, rattled off the situation, and where they were on the ranch.

"Stay on the line with me," the woman said, and JJ said he would.

He glanced over his shoulder to find Orion on the phone, probably with Daddy, and the bull moving away in the distance, still free when he shouldn't be. But at least he wasn't over here, continuing to cause problems.

"He's still breathing," he told the operator.

"An ambulance has been dispatched," she said. "They're only six minutes away."

Six minutes felt like six lifetimes, and JJ nodded. After

taking a deep breath, JJ picked up Tate's phone, which lay near his hand, as if he'd been able to hold onto it as he'd flown through the air.

He found Ruby's name sitting there, the last incoming call, and silently praying that he'd have good news for her once they got to the hospital, he tapped to call her.

"Lord, give me strength," he whispered. "Help me find the right words." Because then she'd have to give them to the rest of Tate's family.

The phone rang, but Ruby didn't pick up. JJ's mind raced. What would he say to her? How could he tell her about Tate's accident without frightening her too much? And how could he push aside the feelings that threatened to overwhelm him at the thought of hearing her voice?

He looked at Tate, his best friend's face still slack, as Bobby came skidding to his knees beside JJ. "Nothing?"

JJ shook his head, both because no, Tate had not stirred at all—and Ruby had not answered her phone.

Chapter Two

Ruby Reynolds paced the small living room of her soon-to-be-former student apartment, her phone clutched tightly in her hand. The room held a mess of half-packed boxes and piles of clothes, a physical representation of the chaos her life had become.

Sunlight streamed through the dirty blinds, highlighting the swirling dust motes in the air and casting long shadows across the worn carpet.

She glanced at her phone again, willing it to ring. She'd called Tate three times now, and every time, it had gone straight to voicemail. Ruby was probably annoying him, but she didn't know who else to turn to.

Her internship, the one she'd been counting on to launch her career and provide her with housing, had fallen through at the last minute. Now, the future didn't hold excitement and promise after four long years of schooling.

It didn't hold an internship with one of the best interior design firms in Texas—one that came with an additional twelve weeks of schooling and an apartment in a beautiful neighborhood in San Antonio.

"Nowhere to live," she drove home to herself as she collapsed back on the couch. She didn't even own that—she literally only had clothes, knick knacks, and a couple of boxes of household goods to her name.

"Come on, Tate." Her fingers hovered over the call button once more. "Pick up, please." Desperation choked her, making her tongue swell and her eyes fill with tears. The thought of calling her parents and admitting defeat made her stomach churn. They'd been so proud when she'd landed the internship, and the idea of crawling back to Lubbock with her tail between her legs absolutely would not come to fruition.

Ruby closed her eyes and took a deep breath. "Lord, I know You have a plan for me," she whispered, her voice trembling slightly. "But right now, I'm feeling lost and scared. Please, give me strength and guidance."

Her eyes popped open, and the only thing Ruby knew to do, the only safe place she had, was to talk to Tate.

She refused to call him again, though. Frustration bubbled with complete feelings of self-loathing, and Ruby bent over and pressed her forehead to her knees.

"Tate Reynolds, I swear if you're ignoring me on purpose, I'll...." She trailed off, not sure how to finish the empty threat to an even emptier living room. She loved her brother dearly, but sometimes his laid-back attitude drove her crazy. Especially now, when she needed him most.

Just as she was about to throw her phone across the room in exasperation, it rang. Ruby's heart leapt, practically knocking into her skull she sat up so fast.

Tate's name sat on the screen.

"Finally," she said as she looked at the four letters of his name. She wanted to swipe on the call and forgo the hello and go straight to chewing him out for ignoring her calls. But a louder, more devilish part of her wanted him to know what it felt like to get sent to voicemail.

She thought of him on the beautiful Seven Sons Ranch, in the gorgeous small town of Three Rivers. He'd spent every summer there these past few years, living with and working alongside his best friend, JJ Walker.

Her pulse quickened, and a familiar flutter winged through her stomach.

JJ, the cowboy she'd been secretly crushing on for years. It was silly, she knew. He'd always seen her as Tate's annoying little sister, the woman who'd gotten separated from her family on a campus tour, gotten scared, and couldn't communicate.

He didn't know that it was only around *him* that her tongue tied itself in knots. And her heart hadn't gotten the message that they couldn't have JJ. Tate had told her more than once how "weird" it would be for him if Ruby dated one of his friends. So she'd never tried to send any signals to JJ, never flirted with him, never said or did anything to indicate the slow-burning embers she harbored for him.

Ruby's mind raced with images of JJ—his tall, muscular frame silhouetted against the sunset as he worked on the ranch—a picture her brother had unknowingly tortured her with last summer.

His easy smile that never failed to make her knees weak whenever he opened the apartment door and said, "C'mon in, Ruby. Tate's in the living room."

The way his eyes crinkled at the corners when he laughed, though that sure didn't happen a whole lot. Still, he smiled when someone brought cookies to the apartment, and whenever he mixed Sprite with orange juice and offered her some too.

She could almost smell the leather that seemed to come with his skin, and the fresh scent of hay that always clung to him after his classwork in the stables.

Tate's call went to voicemail, and Ruby startled out of her thoughts with the silence.

She'd never known what to do with her feelings for JJ, so she'd ignored them. And life's paths had diverged for them anyway, and in the end, Ruby didn't have to decide. JJ now lived in Three Rivers, miles and miles from where she sat in her student apartment.

Ruby ran a hand through her tangled hair. "You're twenty-three years old, Ruby. Stop thinking like a lovesick teenager." But even as she chastised herself, she couldn't help but let her mind go down the forbidden path with JJ Walker on it.

She flopped back against the couch, surrounded by the

remnants of her college life. She closed her eyes, trying to will away the stress and uncertainty closing in around her. She wasn't sure if she dozed or just zoned out, but she jerked to attention and sat up when her phone rang again.

It buzzed against her thigh, and she fumbled it as she tried to pick it up. Again, Tate's name sat there, and Ruby set aside her immaturity and swiped on the call. "You're so busy you can't answer my calls?"

"Ruby," a man said, decidedly not Tate. "It's JJ. JJ Walker?"

Ruby nearly dropped the phone. "JJ?"

"I'm so glad you answered." Concern laced JJ's deep voice, and she imagined it to be for her. Intellectually, she knew it wasn't—and the fact that he'd called from her brother's phone clicked into place in her head.

"What's wrong?" She jumped back to her feet, her nerves shouting at her.

"There's been an accident." JJ spoke in a calm, even tone, about the way he did everything. That, or he growled his thoughts, as he wasn't exactly one to fill the world with sunshine. He'd always been kind to her, though, and she knew his grouchy exterior could be broken fairly easily.

"Tate's hurt." More voices came through the line, then shuffling, and JJ said, "No, he hasn't woken up," which only sent Ruby's pulse through the roof.

"Tate is unconscious?" she asked. The blood drained from her face, pooling somewhere in her stomach, making her sick. Her earlier irritation with her brother evaporated instantly, and she started looking around for her car keys. "Where are you? What happened? Is he okay?"

"He got...hit," JJ said. "The paramedics just arrived, and they'll take him to the hospital here in Three Rivers."

"I'm on my way," Ruby said, already heading for the door. "Text me the details. I'll be there as soon as I can."

As she rushed out of her apartment, Ruby's mind whirled with emotion. Worry for Tate consumed her, pushing aside her earlier problems. She should call her parents, so they could pray, and Ruby did that from the car.

"I don't know, Daddy," she said. "JJ called from Tate's phone. The paramedics had just gotten there."

"I'll call him," her father said, and Ruby set her teeth together.

"He said he'd text me updates." Ruby looked down at her phone in the cup holder. "I haven't gotten any yet." She had no idea how far Seven Sons Ranch sat from the hospital in Three Rivers.

Her dad didn't say anything, and that fueled Ruby's worry. "We can pray," she said, her voice tiny among the vast road in front of her. "I'm on my way, and I'll text you the moment I'm there and know anything."

"Of course you will," her dad said. "We'll pray here, and we'll wait for more news."

Ruby and Tate had two younger siblings, and both of her parents worked. Getting all of them from Lubbock to Three Rivers wasn't something easily done, and Ruby prayed, "Lord, bless Tate that he'll be just fine. That he'll wake up and be okay, so Mama and Daddy don't have to come."

The drive to Three Rivers blurred by, with JJ only texting once that they'd arrived at the hospital, and Tate had woken up in the ambulance. *They took him back in the ER*, he'd said. *I don't know much, but I'll text you more when I do.*

Ruby's knuckles shone a bright white on the steering wheel as she navigated the unfamiliar roads in Three Rivers, her phone dictating to her where to turn. Another text from JJ arrived, the buzz of her phone sending a jolt of fear and anticipation driving through her.

They moved him to a room, he said. 235. *You can come up when you get here.*

"Turn right," her GPS said. "And your destination will be on the right."

Ruby peered that direction as she turned, and yep, there sat the hospital. She had no idea how to get up to the second floor, where the patient rooms would be. "Hospitals have information desks," she reminded herself, and she parked near the Emergency Room entrance, because she could see a door leading inside.

JJ hadn't texted again, and he hadn't said if Tate was awake, had broken bones, nothing. Her adrenaline raged through her, and tears pricked at her eyes as she tried to grab her purse and realized she'd left it at home.

"Great," she muttered, swiping at the tears that dared to escape. She turned off the car and headed inside. Her eyes didn't seem to work, and frustration filled her when she got on the first elevator she saw and realized it only went up to the fourth, fifth, and sixth floors.

She went back down and got on another elevator, only to get right off again. Tears flowed down her face freely now, and an elderly man coming off the elevator took pity on her and touched her elbow. "Where are you trying to get?"

Ruby sniffled, her voice always stuck way down in her belly when she got emotional. "The second floor," she managed to squeak out.

"You need the elevators across there." He indicated the bank across the foyer, and Ruby looked over to them. They bore no signs or anything for her to know that, and she wanted to light the place on fire.

"Thank you," she managed, feeling foolish and angry at the same time. She practically ran across the rotunda and stabbed at the button to call the elevator. When it arrived, she shot forward, only to be greeted by a family getting off.

Impatience stroked through her, but she turned her face away and wiped at her eyes. She didn't want to run into JJ as a total mess, and she certainly wouldn't be able to get anything past Tate. He'd probably laugh and joke and ask her what she was so upset about.

She made it to the second floor, and a huge, triple-wide door waited for her. She had to cross through a waiting room to get there, and as she stepped that way, JJ rose from a chair, his tall frame unfolding into all of his gorgeous glory right in front of her. Her heart betrayed her at the sight of him, even as worry for Tate threatened to overwhelm her.

Without thinking, Ruby changed course and threw herself into JJ's arms. She buried her face in his chest, inhaling his familiar scent of leather, and hay, and cool water falling over a ledge as sobs wracked her body.

His strong arms enveloped her, and for a moment, Ruby felt safe, like nothing could hurt her as long as JJ held her against his pulse.

"Shh, it's okay," he murmured, his lips brushing against her hair, practically touching her earlobe. Her cells sizzled at her. "Tate's going to be fine. The doctors say he has a concussion and some problems with his ribs, but he'll recover."

JJ's mouth ghosted over her cheek, not quite touching her, but leaving a trail of warmth from his breath in its wake. "It's all going to be okay, Ruby. Okay? It's going to be okay."

Standing there in JJ's arms, feeling the solid strength of his body near hers, and the tender brush of his lips against her skin, Ruby believed him. Despite everything going wrong in her life—her uncertain future, Tate's injury, her waiting parents—Ruby felt like maybe, just maybe, everything really would turn out okay, simply because JJ said so.

As she pulled back slightly, Ruby looked up into JJ's handsome, filled-with-concern face. His dark eyes broadcasted warmth and something else she couldn't quite define. For a moment, she allowed herself to imagine what it would be like if JJ saw her as more than just Tate's little sister. What would it be like to be held by him like this every day, to be loved by him?

He didn't step back, and he didn't drop his hands from

holding her. They seemed locked in that moment, and Ruby wanted it to go on forever.

Her mind buzzed at her about something she'd come here to do, but in this moment, Ruby did the most un-Ruby thing of her life.

She kissed JJ Walker square on the mouth.

Chapter Three

JJ Walker had been through some tough situations in his life—cattle stampedes, wild storms, long days in the saddle that left his muscles aching for days—but none of it compared to the sheer shock that hit him when Ruby Reynolds pressed her lips to his.

For a split second, the world stopped spinning. The maddeningly silent hospital waiting room, the enormity of his thoughts, the worry about Tate's condition—all of it vanished. Only Ruby existed.

Her hands gripping his shirt, her lips soft and warm against his, and her breath mingling with his in a way that made his heart feel like it wanted to jump right out of his chest.

He couldn't move. Couldn't think. All he could do was feel.

And wow, did he feel it.

Almost as fast as she'd touched him, Ruby pulling back with wide eyes, her cheeks flushed in an incredibly attractive way. Her lips still hovered dangerously close to his, like she wasn't sure if she should apologize or kiss him again.

JJ tried to catch up to the situation, tried to remind himself of all the reasons this shouldn't have happened, couldn't happen, wouldn't happen.

But his heart? His heart had other plans.

It raced in his chest like it had been running a marathon, thumping so loud Ruby could surely hear it. A part of him—one he'd been trying to bury for years—wanted to pull her back in, to kiss her again, and again, and again, until all the tension between them melted away. Until everything made sense.

JJ swallowed hard, his mouth suddenly dry though the taste of her lip gloss had worked its way inside. "Ruby," he managed to say, his voice rough.

He realized his hands rested on her arms, and he pulled them back, let them drop to his sides. He took a step back, putting some much-needed space between them, though every cell in his body screamed to close the distance. "I'm sorry," he muttered, unclear why he had to apologize.

Probably for kissing her back, he told himself, because he'd definitely done that.

And she knew it.

Her pretty eyes, wide and full of something JJ couldn't name, flickered with uncertainty. She stepped back too, stumbling slightly over her own feet—where she wore her trademark Converse, these a bright blue—as her hand came up to her mouth like she couldn't believe what she'd just done.

"I—I didn't mean to...." She trailed off, her voice shaky, her gaze darting around the waiting room like she'd disappear as fast as she'd arrived.

JJ's pulse pounded in his ears, the silence between them growing heavier by the second. She offered him a smile, and his heart did a funny little pirouette that made him frown.

"How is he?" Ruby breathed out heavily, put more distance between them, and looked past him to the entrance to the hospital rooms on this floor.

His stomach held only knots, and his brain kept conjuring up what it felt like to kiss her. She'd ruined him in less than five seconds, and JJ honestly didn't know how to move forward now.

"He's, uh, resting?" JJ sounded like he was guessing, and he reached up and removed his cowboy hat. "I was waitin' on you. We can go back. Then you can see him, call your parents, all that." He cleared his throat and side-stepped away from her instead of moving into her to get to the hallway leading onto the floor.

As they crossed the waiting room, he buried his feelings the way he'd been doing for seemingly ever.

"JJ, I didn't mean to," she said, her voice stronger now. She darted in front of him and stood her ground, looking at him like he could be the only thing keeping her grounded in this chaotic world.

Impossible.

Was that a flicker of...hope in her gaze?

Doubly impossible.

"It's okay," he said, his voice softer than he intended.

"You won't tell Tate, will you?" She looked over her shoulder. "He's...." She let out a shaky laugh. "Honestly, I think he has a big ole cowboy crush on you." She faced him again, her pretty hazel eyes lit up from within. "He told me you were off-limits."

JJ's eyebrows went up, because Tate had never given him any rules when it came to Ruby. He knew his best friend wouldn't approve, simply by listening to him talk about Ruby and who she'd dated throughout college.

"You're...you were just worried about Tate. It's been a long day, and you're upset." The out made it easy for both of them to brush away the kiss, to pretend like it had happened in a moment of weakness, a moment of panic.

He watched as she closed everything down, as a figurative pair of shutters slid into place, hiding her feelings from him. "Yeah," she said airily. "I'm upset." With that, she turned toward the doors and led the way through them.

She muttered something else under her breath, but JJ could barely walk and think at the same time, so he didn't even try to understand what she'd said.

His mood worsened with every step he took, Ruby's fruity perfume wafting back to him as they went. The Lord had just played a terribly cruel trick on him, and JJ had no idea why.

He'd worked hard in college. Gotten good grades. Graduated while doing an internship at a local ranch and working with his father through weekly online meetings at Seven Sons Ranch in his senior year.

He'd had a few girlfriends in college, but nothing serious. He'd treated them well—really well. There simply hadn't been any sparks that lasted longer than a couple of months.

Now, walking behind Ruby, she seemed to be sending off showers of sparks, whole fireworks that exploded through JJ's bloodstream, and pure fire that licked through him, whispering dangerous things like, *You don't have to tell Tate.*

And, *He's not in charge of your life. Or Ruby's.*

And, *No one would have to know.*

Which was an absolute laughable thought. JJ even scoffed out loud at the ridiculousness of such a secret relationship. One, he lived on the ranch where he'd grown up, and just because his mother didn't sleep downstairs anymore didn't mean she wouldn't know about JJ's secret crush within seconds of seeing him with Ruby.

"Tate Reynolds?" Ruby asked, bringing JJ back to the present. "He's not in his room."

"They took him for x-rays," the nurse at the station said. "He'll be back in about twenty minutes or so."

It was that pesky "or so," that irritated JJ. Nothing in a hospital only took twenty minutes.

"He's awake, though?" JJ stepped next to Ruby. "He was asleep when I left him."

"He's awake." The nurse stood, a pile of folders in her arms. "Not happy about it, but awake." She grinned and nodded to the room just across from the desk. "You can wait for him in there."

A small—tiny, microscopic—space JJ had already been in. The bed barely fit, and the only other seat was a narrow recliner. He swallowed hard, not sure he could go into that room with Ruby and not kiss her again.

"Okay," Ruby chirped like she hadn't kissed him five minutes ago. "Thanks." She exchanged a glance with him, then turned to enter the room.

JJ didn't really see how he could get out of doing the same, and then his phone rang. Pure relief sang through him, almost like a choir of heavenly beings from above. Oliver's name sat on the screen, and everything tight inside JJ's chest collapsed.

He swore under his breath, which caused Ruby to turn back to him. "What is it?" she asked, hurrying back to him.

JJ swiped on the call as he met her eyes. "I forgot I was supposed to babysit my cousins tonight." He lifted the phone to his ear and turned his back on Ruby. "Ollie, hey."

He hated that he'd just used this mistake to get away from Ruby, but he honestly felt like God had realized what a predicament He'd put JJ in, and that he couldn't handle it.

"You'll never believe this, but Tate got hit by a bull," he said. Behind him, Ruby pulled in a breath. "I'm at the hospital with him right now."

"Oh, no," Ollie said at the same time Ruby strode around him.

Her eyes flashed dangerously now. "He got *gored* by a bull? You didn't say that."

"I'll call my mother," Ollie said. "It sounds like you've got a lot going on."

"I'm sorry," JJ said, and he could've been speaking to Ollie or Ruby. No matter what, the call ended far too soon, and JJ stood there with his device at his ear for a few extra seconds just because he could.

As he lowered the phone, Ruby folded her arms and cocked her eyebrows. "A bull, JJ?"

He glanced left and right, looking for an escape. Ruby wasn't having any of it. "You better start talking right now, Mister Walker."

That brought his eyes back to hers. Irritation spiked through him, mostly because his heart mooned over how gorgeous she was when angry. He reached out and grabbed her hand. "Come on," he growled as he pulled her into the empty hospital room and practically slammed the door closed behind them.

He certainly couldn't be having this conversation out in the open, where anyone walking by could hear. Everyone in this blasted small town knew his parents, as his mother's family owned and operated one of the biggest grocery stores in the area.

His daddy attended ranch owner meetings and had even sat on the City Council for two years. Guaranteed anything JJ said could—and would—get repeated.

He paced over to the window that stretched a few feet tall and only gaped a handful of inches wide. His thoughts tangled and spun, and he couldn't see a way out of this. He turned to face Ruby, who'd stayed over against the door, pressing against it like she was afraid of him.

"We were just walking around the ranch," he said. "A bull was loose, and we didn't know it, because we're not on the ranch-wide messaging system yet. You had just called Tate—" He cut off when she sucked in a breath, her eyes going wide.

JJ cleared his throat and pressed on. "He didn't see the bull. He didn't move out of the way. I couldn't get to him fast enough." JJ could still see every—single—moment in slow motion as it ran through his memory.

"He didn't get *gored*," he said, his voice almost a growl. "The bull charged at him and head-butted him in the chest." Pure guilt ripped through him, and JJ turned away to look out the window. "I'm sorry, Ruby. I'm sure my daddy will pay for all of his medical bills."

She came closer, her shoes making soft sounds against the tile floor. She didn't touch him as she arrived at his side in the tiny window bay, but every cell in his body reacted anyway.

"And while we're being fully honest," he said, feeling reckless and wild and so ready to unburden himself of this secret. "I wish that kiss wasn't a mistake." He stared out into the twilight, wishing the darkness could cover him too. It would make this confession so much easier.

"You wish that kiss wasn't a mistake?" Ruby asked, her voice a timid whisper.

JJ shook his head, still unable to look directly at her. "I like you, Ruby," he said simply.

"Well—" She blew out her breath, emitting a frustrated sound with it.

"Tate's never told me I can't go out with you." He turned to face her now, praying with everything he had that he could take this day and make it something more than the day he moved back home and watched his best friend get hurt.

And he really had nothing to lose. Ruby didn't live here. She'd be on her way to San Antonio within the week, and he'd text her updates of her brother's recovery. Maybe he could flirt with her a little at the same time.

That sounded good. Safe.

"So...." He lifted his hand slightly and caught her fingers with the very tips of his. On the second try, he slid his palm along hers and held her hand. "Maybe if we're ever in the same town for longer than a couple of days, we could go to dinner."

He shrugged like it meant nothing if they couldn't, but really, JJ thanked the Good Lord Above for a breastbone, as his currently concealed the harried thumping of his heart.

Chapter Four

Ruby had no idea what to say. Dinner with JJ Walker sounded like a dream come true, and she opened her mouth to suggest they grab something together tonight when the door opened and voices filtered into the room.

She turned away from him, stepping out of the alcove where she'd wandered, and found Tate being wheeled back into his room, bed and all. "There you are," she said, pure relief rushing through her so strongly her vision blurred.

She rushed toward Tate, who shook his head. "I'm hurt, Ruby. Don't touch me."

Barely managing to stop herself, Ruby dodged out of the way too, so the nurses pushing his bed could get him turned around and in position. That forced her back to JJ's side, and his warm, strong fingers brushed hers, held on, and then let go, all in a single breath.

The touch felt forbidden. Naughty. And oh-so-exciting.

She had the man's phone number, and she could text him anytime she wanted. What she'd say, she wasn't quite sure yet, but she wasn't going to let him ask her to dinner and leave him without an answer.

"You two are family?" the male nurse asked.

"I am," Ruby said, cutting a look to JJ that didn't land for long. "He's fine to stay."

"He's my best friend," Tate said, his voice tired. He leaned his head back against the pillow and closed his eyes. "He's gonna have to take care of me, so tell him everything."

The nurse picked up the chart. "The doctor will be in to talk to you soon." Of course. Nurses didn't give diagnoses.

"Define 'soon,'" JJ growled, taking a protective step forward.

The nurse looked up. "He's in the room next door," he said. "Probably five or ten minutes." He finished writing on the chart and plunked it back into the slot at the foot of Tate's bed. "We'll bring dinner by in about a half-hour."

The female nurse smiled at Tate as she finished hooking him up to everything. "There's a cafeteria on the first floor," she said. "They're open until nine, and if you order food to the hospital, they'll only take it to the information desk. You have to go pick it up there."

"Okay," Ruby said. "Thank you." She hadn't thought about eating until JJ had mentioned dinner, and now her stomach roared like she'd done it a great wrong by starving it for so long.

The nurses left, and Ruby moved to Tate's side. "Are you okay?" She wanted to crawl into bed with him and listen to his heart beat against her ear, the way she had as a little girl when the storms came to the Texas Panhandle.

"I'm tired," Tate murmured without opening his eyes. "The lights are so bright."

"That's the concussion," JJ said, and he squeezed behind Ruby to turn the lights down in the room. He dimmed them, and Ruby's eyes took a moment to adjust.

"We'll stay with you until you fall asleep." Ruby glanced at the single recliner in the room. "Mama and Daddy will want a report."

Tate's eyes opened, and it took him a few moments to focus on her. "Wait until the doctor comes. Then you can call them."

"We'll go grab dinner after you eat," JJ said, but he didn't even look at Ruby. "I can stay with you tonight."

"No," Ruby said quickly, and that brought both her brother's and JJ's eyes to hers. "I'm his sister. I'll stay with him." She hadn't even brought her purse with her to Three Rivers, and pure foolishness ran through Ruby. She didn't have another pair of clothes. Nothing.

Her pulse started to whiplash through her body, making her breathing become labored. "I...I'll have to go back to Amarillo tomorrow, and you can sit with him while I go figure things out with my apartment and my stuff."

"You're moving to San Antonio this weekend," Tate said. "Go do that. I'm fine here with Jay-J."

Ruby had always wished she could call JJ by the nickname Tate did. She'd never done it, and she wasn't going to start tonight. She sank onto the edge of the recliner, deciding it was her turn to confess everything.

"I lost the internship," she said, her voice thankfully coming out evenly. "That's why I was calling you so much. I just found out this afternoon." She looked down at her hands, everything from before JJ's call slamming into her again.

"They don't have a position for me." She drew in a breath that lifted her shoulders a few inches. They sank back down as she exhaled. "No apartment. Nothing. I have to be out of my place in Amarillo on Saturday, yes."

Ruby looked up, first at Tate, who laid there, his eyes wide. Then she switched her gaze to JJ, and he'd lowered his head so much that the brim of his cowboy hat concealed his eyes. That so wasn't fair, but JJ had never played very fair when it came to what he did to Ruby's pulse.

"But I don't have anywhere to go."

"So you'll come here," Tate said.

Ruby double-blinked once, then twice. "What?"

"You can be my nursemaid," he said with a smile.

"How hard did you hit your head?" Ruby asked. She looked over to JJ, who now stood at the end of the bed, frowning down at Tate.

"Where is she going to live?" he asked.

"With me," Tate said, his gaze moving slowly to meet JJ's. They seemed to have a silent conversation Ruby didn't understand, because Tate blinked as he realized something. "Oh, I live with you."

"Yes, you do," he said slowly.

Ruby didn't like the way he wouldn't look at her, because she couldn't seem to pry her eyes from him.

Tate didn't offer any solutions, and JJ sighed like he'd just been told there would only be vegetables in the cafeteria. "I'll text my parents," he said. "Maybe there's an extra spot on the ranch somewhere."

"Maybe in the homestead," Tate said. "Or your aunt and uncle's place."

"No," Ruby blurted out again. She looked from JJ to Tate and back. "I...can't live with your aunt and uncle. I'll see what I can find here in town."

"Everything is really expensive," Tate said, his voice fading to a whisper as his eyes closed again.

"We'll work it out," JJ said, his phone out and in his hand. His thumbs flew over the screen, and Ruby swallowed, trying to find the right thing to say, to do. Nothing came, and she cursed her lack of life experience.

She'd found her on-campus apartment with the help of Tate and her mother. She honestly had no idea how to even look for an apartment, especially in a town she didn't know at all. She felt like she sat on needles, and she had no idea how she'd sleep here.

In her cutoff shorts and oversized sweatshirt. Without a purse—or her contact case or glasses.

Sudden tears pressed into her eyes, and Ruby ducked her head. Thankfully, the door opened and the doctor entered at the same time she sniffled. When she looked up, she found JJ's eyes glued to hers, barely moving out of the way as the doctor reached for the chart.

"Howdy, folks," he said with plenty of boister to his voice. "I'm Doctor Baker. Let's see what we have here." He studied the chart, then moved over to Tate and checked his eyes, listened to his heart, and looked at the IV.

"You've got yourself four broken ribs, my friend." He smiled like this was a great thing. "And five others that are fractured or bruised, and one of them has been popped out of position."

"No wonder I feel like I've been run over."

The doctor chuckled, and he started writing something on a small pad. "They'll have you here overnight and on pain meds. I'll write you something for when you go home, because I hate to say it, but you're going to be in some pain for a while." He looked at Tate, then JJ, then Ruby, where his eyes held. "Ribs take a very long time to heal. You're his sister?"

"Yes, sir." She got to her feet, using the movement to quickly wipe her face clear of the hint of tears. "I'll be here to take care of him when he goes home."

"Good," Doctor Baker said. "He's going to need that." He flipped a page on his prescription pad. "The concussion is a Grade Three, because you passed out. He was out...." He returned to the chart. "For twenty-one minutes. That's a long time. Your vision is blurred?"

"Yes, sir," Tate said.

"You've likely got a coup and a contrecoup concussion."

Ruby had no idea what that meant, but she quickly opened her phone and started typing. She could look things up later, and she'd want to tell her parents.

"What does that mean?" JJ asked.

"The coup is a concussion at the site of impact—the back of the head." The doctor looked at JJ. "You said he fell backward and didn't catch himself?"

"That's right," JJ drawled. "He was knocked out before I could even get to him."

Ruby hadn't heard that either, and desperation combined with a dangerous cocktail of frustration. She kept typing notes, adding some of the things he'd told her about the bull from earlier.

"So the brain hit the back of his skull," Doctor Baker said. "And then it rebounds. So that's the contrecoup—the front of the brain hits the front of the skull. So he got it in two places. The coup is responsible for the blurred vision—and that needs to be monitored." He glanced over to Ruby, who nodded in an exaggerated way but didn't take her eyes off her phone as she continued to type up notes.

"The frontal lobe most likely has some damage too, and those symptoms range, because the frontal lobe governs behavior, decision-making, and emotions."

"No wonder I feel like crying," Tate said, his smile bright and quick. Ruby almost rolled her eyes, though she was used to Tate's perpetual positivity.

"He might be a bit of a bear in the next few weeks," Doctor Baker said, once again focusing on Ruby. She'd paused in her note-taking, and she met his eyes.

"Okay," she said. "I'm used to him being a grouch to me."

"That is not true," Tate said.

"You wouldn't even answer my calls this afternoon," she shot back. Then she smiled sweetly at the doctor. "See? I can handle him."

Doctor Baker smiled. "I can see that. I'm going to have the nurses print you up a bunch of information on how to deal with a concussion patient."

"Thank you," Ruby said. "I'll call my parents and tell them everything." She nodded like she'd been taking care of Tate for her whole life when the opposite was true.

"How far away are they?" Doctor Baker asked casually. "You guys here for college?"

"We just graduated," JJ said. "All three of us. Tate and I are workin' the ranch. Ruby's...." He trailed off, and that about summed up Ruby's whole life.

Dot, dot, dot.

"I have some time to come help him," she supplied in the resulting silence. "My parents live in Lubbock."

"So not too close, but not too far."

"My whole family is here," JJ said.

Doctor Baker grinned at him. "That they are, JJ."

Ruby shouldn't have been surprised that the doctor knew JJ, but she was. Tate had told her his family was well-known in Three Rivers, but she'd never been here, never witnessed it.

"My sisters will be all over us," JJ said with plenty of disdain in his voice. "Trust me, he'll be well-cared for."

"If Clara Jean makes her chicken Alfredo lasagna, can I have a concussion?" Doctor Baker joked. "Just a mild one, but that lasagna is worth it."

That got JJ to crack a smile, and seeing such a glorious thing on his face made Ruby's whole chest warm from the inside out. "My grandma sells that lasagna at the grocery store now."

"Does she really?" Doctor Baker pulled out his phone and started typing. "I'm telling my wife that...right...now." He grinned after he'd sent the text. "Okay, boys. Tate, my friend, you have to be here overnight, okay? We'll do some more tests in the morning to see how the concussion is, and the nurses, well, they're going to want you to move around."

"I can't move around," Tate said, his attitude suddenly dark. "How many ribs does a person have?"

"Is this a real question?" the doctor asked.

"Yes," he barked.

"Twenty-four," Doctor Baker said.

"And how many of mine are injured?"

Doctor Baker glanced at the chart. "Ten."

"I'm not moving around," Tate said sourly.

"Tate," Ruby said.

He turned his glare on her, and even though he blinked to do it, she closed her mouth. "I get one day after being bull-butted to stay in bed."

Ruby looked at the doctor, who watched Tate for another few moments. "If you don't get up and show them you can walk around tomorrow, they won't discharge you."

"That's tomorrow," Tate said without missing a beat. "Isn't dinner almost here?"

"We have a diet plan for people with Grade Three concussions," Doctor Baker said, once again meeting Ruby's

55

eyes. "While he's here, they'll give him only those approved foods. I'll get that printed for you too, so you know how to feed him at home."

The enormity of care Tate needed settled onto Ruby's shoulders, pressing her back into a seated position on the recliner. "Okay," she said.

The doctor clapped his hands. "All right. Dinner should be here soon, and I'll come by in the morning too, to see how you are." He grinned like they'd be meeting up for a fun brunch date. "Good to see you, JJ." He stretched his hand out and shook JJ's. "Tell your family hello."

"Will do."

The doctor smiled and nodded his way out of the room, and Ruby looked to JJ too. Surely he'd know what to do.

He took a deep breath and looked at Tate. "Brother, you have to do what the doctors and nurses say."

"Tomorrow," Tate growled at him.

JJ looked at Ruby. "You wanna go call your momma? I can stay with him while he eats, and then I've got to get something."

"Me too."

"We can go try the cafeteria," he said, his dark eyes suddenly glittering.

Ruby nodded, the tears pressing into the backs of her eyes again, so she ducked her head and headed for the exit. Everything would be fine if she had her purse, and she couldn't believe she'd left her apartment without it.

She couldn't even go buy contact solution and a case or a fluffy blanket that would make this night in a hospital room recliner so much better. She shoved those things aside and paced down the hall, trying to calm her storming emotions.

After all, she couldn't call her parents while crying—and she had a lot more to tell them about than just Tate's ribs and concussion. And she certainly didn't want to sit down across from JJ, no matter if it was just in a hospital cafeteria, with tears in her eyes.

If this was going to be their first, clandestine date, she didn't want any trace of water on her face. So she drew in a deep breath, paced off of the patient floor, and found a quiet corner so she could call her parents and tell them everything.

She could figure out everything else after that—including her newly complicated relationship with JJ Walker.

Chapter Five

J J sank into the recliner, his phone full of messages. Both his momma and daddy had texted separately, as well as in a group message, as had Clara Jean, Grams, and Conrad. JJ shouldn't be surprised, but it felt like a huge wall of water had just hit him. His chest tightened, and he told himself, *Just read one message at a time.*

His parents wanted to know how things were going, what the official diagnosis was, and when Tate might be able to come home.

Grams said she'd started a pot of her hamburger stew, and she'd have it—along with her delicious dilly-herb rolls—at his cabin in a couple of hours. He didn't want his grandmother to work too hard on his behalf, but trying to stop her was trying to make gravity push things up instead of down.

Clara Jean was at the grocery store, where she worked full-time, and she wanted to know if JJ needed anything. *I can come to the hospital,* his sister had said, and JJ experienced a massive flash of love for Clara Jean.

Conrad, who had bought their granddad's farm a few years ago and currently worked the land and lived in the house with Grams, had offered his support also. *My farm is small, so if y'all need help at Seven Sons, I'm there, brother.*

He sent a quick text to Conrad—*Thank you. I'll keep you updated.*

Then to Grams—*You're the best. I'm starving right now, but Tate's gonna be here overnight, but we'll be so grateful for the food tomorrow!*

He glanced over to Tate, who looked so peaceful as he slept. JJ's mind flowed to Ruby, and he'd seen the way she rubbed her eyes. He hadn't seen a purse, though she could have a backpack or bag in her car.

Something inside JJ told him that Ruby didn't have anything in her car. He'd be buying her dinner in the cafeteria—which was just fine by him—and she had nothing for her contacts. The recliner where he sat was fine for a few minutes, but sleeping in it?

And she'd been wearing a pair of jean shorts and a sweatshirt. He had no idea if she had a tee or tank on underneath, but JJ wanted her to be comfortable overnight and tomorrow.

"She needs clothes," he muttered to himself. His thumbs started flying, and he tapped out a whole list of things for Clara Jean, explaining about Ruby and how he didn't think she had anything for the next twenty-four hours.

He straightened after sending that text, only having his

parents left to deal with. A sigh slipped out of his mouth as he thought about Ruby. He didn't care if Clara Jean knew about his feelings, but at the same time, he did. Because Clara Jean adored Tate, and she'd definitely tattle on JJ's feelings for Tate's sister.

So she can't know, JJ thought, re-reading over his text though it had already been sent. He could deny everything should Clara Jean think his text indicated feelings for Ruby in any way. It was hard for him to tell, because he knew how he felt about the gorgeous redhead who'd left the room only a few minutes ago.

Drawing in a deep breath, JJ turned his attention to his parents. They'd started a group message with the three of them, and JJ figured he could answer there and save himself some time and energy.

He detailed everything that had happened since the moment he'd left the ranch in the ambulance, and he sent text after text until they'd gotten all the news.

So you're staying overnight? Daddy asked.

Ruby is going to, JJ said. *Tate's dinner is coming soon, and then Ruby and I will go grab dinner, and then once she's settled here, I'll head back to the farm. Or Conrad's.*

If he slept at Conrad's house, he'd be twenty minutes closer to the hospital should Ruby or Tate need him.

Are his parents going to come? Momma asked.

I don't know, JJ said. *Ruby stepped out to call her parents. I'm sure they'll work something out.*

"All right," a woman chirped in an overly bright voice, causing JJ to look up from his device. "Time to eat." She held the door while another nurse entered the room carrying an enormously wide tray. Everything on it sat covered, and while JJ couldn't see what it held, it sure smelled good.

His stomach roared, and he got to his feet to push the recliner back so the nurse could move the rolling table into place. "Tate, brother," he said. "You gotta wake up and eat."

His best friend's eyelids fluttered, and the nurse practically yelled, "Come on, Mister Reynolds. Dinner is here."

Tate opened his eyes then, and he didn't look happy or awake. He blinked a couple of times, then looked at JJ. "Jay-J."

"Dinner's here," he said again. "You gotta eat, bro. Remember you're in the hospital?"

Tate frowned at him. "Of course I remember I'm in the hospital. My body hurts like the devil."

JJ grinned at him. "Are you hungry?"

"Yes." Tate looked like he might try to push himself up a little straighter, but pain streamed across his face.

"I got you, Mister Reynolds." The nurse picked up the remote that lifted the bed. "Once you finish eating, we'll go for a walk."

"No, we won't." Tate glared at her. "I told the doctor I wanted until tomorrow."

"Let's see how you feel after you eat," JJ said quickly, shooting a look over to the nurse. She wore a nametag that read Mindy, and while JJ didn't know her personally, she looked semi-familiar.

The second nurse slid the tray onto the table and started taking off lids. A bowl of brothy soup sat there, and JJ wasn't sure it had anything solid in it. Tate wouldn't be happy about that. JJ couldn't remember the last time Tate had voluntarily eaten soup, if he ever had.

A couple of pieces of toast sat on a plate, but they'd be cold and soggy, JJ knew that.

Orange Jell-O, and JJ's heart started to pound. This wasn't a meal. Tate would not be happy with this "food."

"We've got herbal tea," the nurse said. "But your caffeine needs to be limited. You can have chicken broth if your throat is bothering you."

"My throat is bothering me," Tate said as he surveyed the tray of food in front of him.

"You've got an IV in," Mindy said. "So you're getting the liquids you need. We're starting you on food slowly."

"I'll say," Tate said crossly, and JJ wanted to jump in and smooth things over again. He bit his tongue, and simply watched the nurses. "This is all I get?"

"You have a lot of broken ribs," Mindy said in her same perky voice. "If you're hungry later and you've tolerated this well, we can get you more to eat."

Tate picked up a spoon. "Okay."

Mindy nodded, and JJ did his best to smile at the nurses as they left. He sat back down and watched Tate eat.

"Where did Ruby go?" Tate asked after he'd taken one bite of soup. He didn't flinch or grimace, so it must not be too bad.

"She went to talk to your parents," he said.

"They won't be able to come."

"No?"

"My mom can't leave her class the last month of school." Tate lifted a piece of toast, frowned at it, and bit into it. No crunch, so JJ's assumption had been correct. "And Daddy's right in the thick of planting. No way he can leave the farm."

JJ swallowed, because he'd heard Tate talk about his parents and their jobs in the past. Farm work did consume a man from dawn until dusk, and he had no idea how teachers did anything during the school year.

Dealing with a major injury had not been on JJ's summer to-do list. He'd already been dreading the amount of work he had in front of him at Seven Sons this year, and that was with Tate at his side.

Now, Tate wouldn't be able to help JJ with anything. Not for months, at least.

"It's fine," Tate said dismissively, like he didn't care if his parents came. Of course he did. "Ruby doesn't have that internship anymore, and she said she'd come to the ranch and help." He took another slurp of soup.

"That reminds me," JJ said, his tone definitely darker as he returned his attention to his phone.

Ruby is going to need to come stay with Tate, he told his parents. *That cabin isn't for three, especially when one of them is a woman. Should I plan to move back into the homestead?*

He swallowed hard, because coming back to Seven Sons Ranch had been hard enough for JJ. So moving back into the house where he'd grown up?

He so didn't want to do that.

Brayden just left for a place in Missouri, Daddy said. *So*

Cody's in the cabin next to you and Tate alone. We could get you moved in over there.

Relief rushed through JJ, though he didn't really want to live with Cody either. He was a new hire Daddy had brought in around Christmastime, so JJ didn't know him at all. He told himself that he'd moved an hour away to college to live with three men, only one of whom he knew.

Rich Marshall had graduated this past week too, but instead of returning to Three Rivers and the ranch where he'd grown up, he'd taken a job at a ranch a few hours south in the Hill Country.

In so many ways, JJ envied him, though Rich had been nervous to pack up everything he owned and drive away from the apartment in Amarillo by himself. JJ hadn't had to do that.

Okay, he told his parents. *I'm sorry about all this.*

Hey, it's not your fault, Momma said.

Bulls get out, Daddy said. *Accidents happen.*

Tate is really hurt. JJ looked over to his best friend, pure guilt infecting him.

Before his mom or dad could answer, a text from Clara Jean came in. *I'm here with all the stuff you asked for.*

JJ got to his feet. "Clara Jean is here," he said. "I'm gonna go meet her."

"Okay," Tate said. "I would kill for a hamburger. Did she bring one of those?"

JJ grinned at him. "I doubt it, but maybe we can smuggle one in tomorrow."

"If I'm here tomorrow, someone might really die." Tate

didn't look like he was kidding, though that was more of a JJ thing to say.

"No deaths while I'm gone," JJ said, raising his eyebrows as he turned back to Tate. "Promise me."

"Yeah, yeah." Tate took another bite of his toast, and JJ ducked out of the room. Clara Jean pushed through the triple-wide door before JJ had taken two steps, and he continued to meet her.

"Thank you so much, sissy." He hurried toward her to relieve her of some of the bags she carried, one of which had a blanket bulging out of the top of it. Once he held most of the bags, he wrapped Clara Jean in a hug. "I appreciate it."

"How is he?"

"He's hurt real bad." JJ cleared his throat and stepped back. "Come say hi. Maybe you can sit with him while I go grab dinner."

"Sure," Clara Jean said. "I like Tate."

JJ's boots grew roots while Clara Jean continued toward the room. "But you don't like, like-*like* Tate, right?"

His sister turned back to him, her dark hair spilling over her shoulders in dark ringlets. JJ saw her for the first time as a really pretty woman. The same age as Ruby. And Tate was his age.

Horror washed through him while Clara Jean's smile spread across her face. "No, JJ. I like him as a friend."

"Clara Jean."

She looked past him as he turned around to find Ruby coming into the hallway too. She barely looked at him as she went by to hug his sister. "It's good to see you again."

Clara Jean hugged her and said, "You too." They separated and she grinned at Ruby, holding up the bags. "I got everything."

Ruby looked at the bags as JJ approached, making a triangle-huddle. "What's 'everything'?" She eyed the bags in JJ's hands too. "What's going on?"

He so didn't want to have this conversation in the hallway, in front of Clara Jean. Or at all. He looked over to his sister, who likewise watched him, waiting for the explanation.

"I got a few things to make your overnight stay more comfortable," JJ said as easily as he could, which meant his voice came out slightly strained. "Let's take it into the room. Tate's eating, and Clara Jean is going to sit with him while we go grab something from the cafeteria."

He nodded toward the door, and thankfully, Clara Jean turned that way and started walking again. He met Ruby's eyes, noting with his quiet cowboy observation skills that she'd been crying.

That so wasn't okay, but JJ couldn't take back the past three hours. He couldn't fix this for her, but he could make it easier, and he hoped the things he'd asked Clara Jean to bring would do exactly that.

She moved to follow Clara Jean, and finally JJ did too, praying that the next hour would take him and Ruby on a new trajectory in their friendship...where he could hold her hand, kiss her, and take care of her.

Chapter Six

R uby took in the enormity of items as Clara Jean kept
unpacking them from the plastic grocery sacks. She
caught sight of a bottle of contact solution, a contact case, a
three-pack of fuzzy socks, a new sweatshirt, the softest-
looking blanket in the world, and more.

Then JJ put his bags on the side-counter and removed
more items. Chocolate-covered cinnamon bears—her
favorite comfort candy. A six-pack of mini cans of ginger ale
—her favorite soda pop. A couple of bottles of orange juice.
A pack of sweet mint gum.

A pillow. "You sell pillows at Wilde and Organic?"

JJ bent his head to look at her out of the corner of his
eye, but Clara Jean turned the full wattage of her smile on
Ruby. "Yeah, we have a whole home goods section of the
store. It's amazing." She lifted the light gray blanket. "This is

my favorite blanket. I have one I use every night when I'm reading."

She grinned, and while Ruby had only met her a couple of times when she'd come to Amarillo for something with JJ, Ruby did like her a whole lot.

Ruby looked at JJ as he turned and handed Tate a neck pillow. "Maybe this will come in handy tonight."

Tate grinned, which meant something considering his current health situation. "Thanks, brother."

Brother.

Ruby swallowed and looked at JJ's smile. It filled the whole room with light, and Ruby's heartbeat picked up speed from that simple grin. He looked at her, and his countenance dimmed slightly.

"Is the rest of this for me?" she asked, moving over to the counter and taking in the sweatpants she hadn't seen yet.

JJ inched to her side as Clara Jean went around the end of the hospital bed to the recliner. She pulled it right up to the side of the bed and started talking to Tate.

"Yes," JJ said quietly. "I didn't see your purse or a backpack, and I wasn't sure what you had for tonight and tomorrow."

Ruby looked at him, pure electricity flowing between them and making her blood sizzle. "I ran out the moment you called."

JJ nodded, the brim of his cowboy hat very nearly kissing her forehead. "You hungry?"

She picked up the cinnamon bears. "I might be okay with these."

He grinned and took them from her. "This is candy," he said. "It's for after dinner."

"Have you ever eaten in a hospital cafeteria?" JJ asked, and pure joy filled Ruby when she realized he was *flirting* with her.

"No, sir," she said, giving his coyness right back to him. "But there's a first time for everything."

"Yeah," he said. "Let's go see how bad it is." He turned toward Tate and Clara Jean. "We're going to go grab something in the cafeteria. You guys okay here?"

"Just fine," Clara Jean drawled like a true Texan. Tate, who'd just put his last bite of toast in his mouth, nodded.

JJ put his hand on the small of Ruby's back and turned her easily. Her legs felt disconnected from her body, but she managed to get them to move in the direction of the door. It seemed like the world watched her and JJ, and Ruby didn't breathe until the huge door leading onto the floor closed behind them.

The waiting room loomed in front of them, and JJ came to her side and took her hand. "Is this okay?" he murmured in that low, sexy tone she'd only heard him use with horses and dogs.

She couldn't speak either, because she was holding hands with the focus of her years-long crush. She nodded, and JJ looked at her, pure concern in his eyes.

"Because if it's not...." He pulled his hand away so fast, she couldn't catch it to keep it in hers. "I get it." He reached to push the down button to call the elevator. "Did you talk to your parents?"

"It's fine, JJ," she said.

He wouldn't look at her, and frustration moved through Ruby. "I'm going to be in town for longer than a couple of days."

"Yeah, I know." He pocketed his hands, which fueled her irritation.

She stepped over to him and slid her hand through his arm. "You said you liked me."

"I do."

"You said you wished the kiss wasn't a mistake."

"I did."

"It's been an hour." Ruby's chest stormed, and she hadn't had very many boyfriends. She was only twenty-three years old, and she didn't know how to handle this situation. "Have your feelings changed?"

"No," he whispered.

Ruby's pulse started to settle. "Thank you for getting me the stuff I need for my contacts, the clothes, the cinnamon bears." She leaned her head against his bicep, this elevator the slowest thing in the world.

"You're welcome," he said.

"Is this a date?" she asked.

"Do you always ask so many questions?" JJ ducked his head toward her, and she caught a hint of a smile as she looked up at him.

"Yes," she said. "I need to talk through things. Surely Tate's complained to you about this."

He full-on grinned now. The elevator finally chimed as the car arrived. He led her onto it, and once the door had slid closed, sealing them inside alone, he said, "I'd like it to be a date, but it's the hospital cafeteria, so I'm fine if you'd rather postpone our first date until another time."

Ruby sure did like the sound of "our first date," and her smile felt a bit stretched and maniacal to her. "I think it's kind of romantic."

JJ chuckled, and the elevator spit them out on the first floor. He led them off it, and Ruby kept the fact that she'd gotten lost in the small-town Three Rivers hospital to herself. She let JJ navigate them down long, sterile hallways until they reached a set of double-doors that marked the cafeteria.

Inside, he paused for a moment, assessing the situation. It seemed to be pretty easy, with a clearly-marked station for trays, and then a buffet-line spread of food around three walls in a large part of the room. Two more bars ran down the middle of the area, with three check-out registers.

Then, dozens of tables and at least a hundred chairs surrounding them filled the space. Several others had gotten their food already, and as Ruby looked back to JJ, he lifted his eyebrows.

"There's other people here," he said.

"It doesn't smell like rotten food," she added.

He grinned and took her hand. At the tray station, he handed her one and said, "You go first. Get whatever you want."

And Ruby did exactly that. She loaded her plate with three kinds of salad—macaroni, sweet pea, and a green salad with ranch dressing—before moving on to the main dishes.

Someone stood at this counter, and she asked for the meatballs, mashed potatoes, and brown gravy.

She took two rolls, and then she reached the dessert buffet. Apple pie, peach pie, chocolate cake, strawberry shortcake, and a variety of cookies. She took the peach pie, the strawberry shortcake, and then tipped two chocolate chip cookies onto her tray, because another plate wouldn't fit.

JJ said nothing as they checked out, and she went over to a table near the windows though the sun had set at least a half-hour ago. She still wanted the feeling of openness, and she couldn't get that with a cinderblock wall beside her.

Warmth emanated off the window on her left, and Ruby pulled the plate of pie off her tray first.

"Going straight to dessert, huh?"

"It's my favorite thing about being an adult." She grinned at JJ, barely feeling old enough to be living on her own, despite her four years of college. Her smile faded fast, and she ate her first bite of pie, trying to figure out how to talk to him. "Listen," she said once she'd swallowed.

If there was something JJ did extraordinarily well, it was listen. He raised his eyebrows at her and forked up another bite of the spaghetti and meatballs he'd picked up.

Ruby fidgeted in her seat, but she didn't know Tate's arrangement with JJ. And she had a little bit of money, but not much. Not enough to live on for the summer without a job. "I need a job," she said. "I can help with Tate a lot, of course, but maybe I could get a job overnight or something."

She could sleep when she was dead, right?

Ruby barely forced another bite of pie into her mouth. JJ finished his food and wiped his mouth too. "I'm sure money won't be a problem," he said.

"You're sure?" she asked around her mouth of dessert. She searched his face, trying to find some tell, some information he hadn't shared with her. She finished chewing and swallowed. "Tate's not going to be able to work, JJ. We won't be able to pay rent, or—"

"He wasn't going to pay rent," JJ said coolly.

Ruby's eyebrows went up. "When you were living with him, right? But what about now that I am?"

"It's fine," JJ muttered. "He got hurt at our ranch." He focused on his noodles and sauce, and that bothered Ruby. She couldn't read him very well when he looked right at her let alone when he didn't.

"We'll have to eat," she said. "Pay for utilities. Gas to town, doctor's appointments, all of that."

JJ lifted his head enough for his dark, glittering eyes to meet hers. They held plenty of danger, and he held very still as he watched her. Five seconds, then ten, and Ruby finally looked down at her pie and scooped up another mouthful.

"My family has plenty of money," JJ said. "I'll talk to my parents, but I'm sure we can provide whatever you guys need until Tate is back on his feet for good."

Ruby nodded, a sense of relief threading through her gently. At the same time, it didn't solve her lack of employment long-term. "I can work on the ranch," she said. "Maybe not as much as Tate, and I'm not as strong as him, but I worked my family farm my whole life, and I can do a lot."

"I'm sure you can, princess." He immediately ducked his head, but shock poured through Ruby.

"Princess?"

He lifted one shoulder in a kind of shrug and said, "Yeah, you're like my Scarlet Princess."

Scarlet Princess.

His Scarlet Princess.

"I don't mind Scarlet," she said. "But I'm going to veto the princess part."

JJ started to chuckle, the sound almost like the hum of a dishwasher before she realized what it was or where it came from. His laugh grew and grew, and oh, Ruby sure liked the deep, throaty sound of it as it filled her ears, then the whole cafeteria.

She grinned and finished her pie while he settled down. "What can I call you?" she asked.

That got him to quiet all the way. "Me?"

"Yeah, Tate calls you Jay-J. Is that allowed?"

He blinked at her, a blank expression on his face.

"I don't want to use the same thing my brother does," Ruby mused, enjoying his confusion too much. "I mean, he's your best friend, and we didn't want that kiss to be a mistake." She pulled her main dish in front of her, not quite used to saying such bold things. Heck, she barely *thought* such things.

JJ coughed and reached for his soda pop. He popped the top and took a drink to settle himself. Then he poured the lemon-lime soda into a glass, filling it only half-way. He topped that off with orange juice, and that only made Ruby like him even more.

He took a long drink of his mixed juice and when he set the glass down, he finally looked at her. "You didn't want the kiss to be a mistake either?"

"I kissed you, didn't I?"

"You said it was a mistake."

Ruby had said that. She took a bite of dinner, thinking through how to answer. Then she said, "You know what? Yes, it was a mistake, because it didn't happen under the right circumstances. But...if it did, then, well, then it wouldn't be a mistake."

"Tate is going to be unhappy," JJ said. "And he just got hurt on my ranch, and—" He blew out his breath in a frustrated way and started twirling up his spaghetti into another bite. "Maybe this is a bad idea."

Ruby hadn't known Tate cared who she dated. And why should he? Didn't he want her to be happy?

"Maybe he just needs to warm up to the idea," Ruby said, thinking of one of her favorite movie quotes. From My Big Fat Greek Wedding, when the ladies make a plan and then make it seem like her husband came up with it.

The man is the head, but the woman is the neck. And she can turn the head any way she wants.

"Let me work on him," she said.

"Work on him?" JJ cocked one eyebrow. "What does that mean?"

"I'm not sure." She smiled at him and cut her meatball in half. "Now, tomorrow, I'm going to have to go back to my apartment and get all my stuff. My dad and sister are going to meet me to help me load up."

"I can come."

She shook her head, as much as she wanted to drive with JJ for an hour—both ways—to Amarillo and back. "You're going to be here with Tate."

"Oh, sure."

"I should be back by late afternoon. If they release him before then, I'll meet you at the farm."

"It's a ranch," JJ said with a smile.

Ruby rolled her eyes. "Fine, the ranch. I'm assuming I can put it in my GPS and find it?"

"I'm sure you can," he said.

"You'll keep me updated on Tate throughout the day?"

"Yes, ma'am."

She shook her head again. "No, not ma'am."

"I've called you that before."

He had, yes. But for some reason, it bothered her now. "That was before," she said.

"Before what?"

"Our first date." She finished her meatballs and mashed potatoes. "And a cowboy's scarlet princess doesn't want to be called *ma'am*." She picked up her cookie and took a bite, almost daring him to challenge her.

She didn't truly expect him to, and JJ chuckled again as he shook his head. Then he said, "Okay, Scarlet," almost under his breath. Ruby still almost swooned on the spot, and she had to remind herself not to be so obvious.

She'd already said way too much, and she didn't need JJ to have any more ammunition than she'd already given him.

"Now, we just have to make it through the next twenty-four hours," she said, offering him the other cookie. He took it and broke off a piece.

"And pray for Tate's speedy recovery," he added just before he popped the treat into his mouth.

Yes, Ruby definitely needed to pray for fast healing for Tate, because he so wasn't a good sick person. At the same time, she hoped he'd take all summer to get better...because then she'd get to have more time with JJ.

Chapter Seven

JJ smiled at the photo Ruby sent him, then quickly turned his phone over and placed it face-down on his thigh. "Your daddy is helping Ruby get moved out right now," he said to Tate.

"Great," Tate said in a deadpan. He didn't move his gaze from the TV mounted to the wall. He'd lost so much of his zest for life, and JJ could admit he wanted to get out of this hospital too.

"I'm sure the doctor will be back soon."

Tate grunted, and JJ retreated back into his own thoughts, the way he'd done plenty of times in college too. Usually, he was the grumpy, silent one while Tate tried to coax him out of his shell.

With that thought, JJ pocketed his phone, which he'd already silenced so Tate wouldn't demand to know who was texting when Ruby messaged him. She'd definitely sent him more messages than would be considered friendly, and that still surprised him a little bit.

The fact that she'd been harboring feelings for him downright shocked him if he dwelt on it too long. And he'd fixated on her so much last night after leaving the hospital, he'd barely gotten any sleep.

"Come on," he said, getting to his feet. "Let's go take another walk."

Tate looked at him with daggers in his eyes. "You're not my nurse."

"Tate, brother," JJ said. "This is gonna be our reality for the next several months. Are you going to be so...irritable for that long?"

"No," Tate barked. "Besides, when you were in a bad mood, I just let you be in it."

"Yeah, but that's me." JJ grinned at him. "I'm not sure you've ever been like this for longer than a couple of minutes."

"Whatever." Tate looked back to the dog show playing on TV. It was from last year, so he certainly couldn't care. "I was in a bad way for a week when I failed that biology class."

"Yeah, but I only had to see you after class." JJ extended his hand toward him. "One lap around. It'll at least pass the time, and you're still on the good meds."

"Did you find out if the pharmacy has my pills ready yet?" Tate pinned him with his green-eyed glare. "Because I'm not leaving until I've got those."

"I got a text five minutes ago," JJ said coolly. "We're literally waiting for Doctor Baker to sign your release papers." Then, JJ planned to take Tate through a drive-through burger joint on the way back to the ranch.

He didn't want to shove him off on Ruby, but JJ hated sitting around inside all day. How he'd survived college was a sheer miracle. Oh, and God had led him into a major and field of study that had taken him outside to the stables, where he could work with horses and his hands. That had played a big part of his survival.

He prayed for an increase in patience now as he looked at Tate. "I know you hate being inside as much as me. I'm sorry about—"

"It's not your fault." Tate cut him off with the harsh words and a sigh. He reached for the remote and turned off the TV. "I can't stand you trying to be the cheerful one." He made no move to get out of bed though. "Help me up, Jay-J. Let's go for your walk."

"When we get to the ranch, it'll be nice to walk outside," he said. "We can just go to the hives and back."

"By the time we get to the ranch, I think I'll be exhausted," Tate said as he carefully moved his legs so they hung over the side of the bed. "I'm so tired right now."

JJ steadied him with both hands in Tate's, and he held very still while Tate got himself to his feet. He groaned in a pitiful and painful way, panting afterward. "My word, why did God give us ribs if they could hurt this bad?"

JJ didn't want to tell Tate that without his ribs, that bull would've butted his heart and lungs, so he said nothing. He simply waited for Tate to find his balance, and when he let go of his hands, JJ let his arms fall.

When Tate got tired enough, he'd hold onto JJ's arm, but for now, he made his own way toward the door. He didn't move fast, and he barely picked his feet up, which reminded JJ of his grandfather in his later years.

He'd died a couple of years ago, only about eight months after Conrad had bought the farm and moved in to help their grandparents. JJ had liked his cousin's plan, because all of Grams and Gramps's sons still had families, but they'd needed help.

And Conrad could offer that help.

He was the oldest in his branch of the Walker Family too, and he had three younger siblings—triplets Austin, Easton, and Elaine. Uncle Rhett and Aunt Evelyn didn't have a farm, and Austin had gone into law enforcement and worked in Amarillo.

Elaine worked at a preschool here in Three Rivers, and Easton ran all the physical facilities operations for the town of Three Rivers. He was a bit of an odd duck, and his job allowed him to deal more with buildings and spaces than people.

JJ had stayed close to them all, as his daddy and Uncle Rhett were very close and spent a lot of time together. Uncle Liam's girls had left town years ago, both of them down in San Antonio living good lives.

Uncle Wyatt's two oldest boys had gone into the rodeo already, with their third son finishing up his college degree next year and their only daughter about to graduate from high school next month. Word in the Walker family was that Aunt Marcy and Uncle Wyatt would then move to Montana to be with their older boys, as both Warren and Cole lived and trained there.

"Jeremiah," Tate said, and JJ looked up from the white tiles on the hospital floor. He glared at him. "There you are."

"Sorry, were you talking to me?"

"For the past ten minutes," Tate said. "I hate it when I finally realize I've been talkin' to myself."

"Sorry." JJ gave him a smile, because no, it wasn't the first time JJ had tuned out on his best friend. "What were you saying?"

"I asked what the plan was once I'm discharged. You love your plans."

"Burgers," JJ said without missing a beat or ribbing Tate back about how spontaneous he tended to be. "Fries. Milkshakes. Then the ranch. Trust me, everyone will come to us. I'll get you set up in your cabin, make sure you can get on and off the couch, in and out of bed, all of that."

He exhaled heavily, wondering when Ruby, her father, and her youngest sister would arrive. "Then, I've got to move my stuff in with Cody, so Ruby will have room for her things when she gets here."

Tate grunted, and JJ figured he'd have more to say soon enough. Grunting usually indicated as much with Tate. So JJ kept his voice silent as Tate shuffled along, and as they rounded the corner, with the nurse's station coming up on their right and Tate's room on the left, his friend drew in a breath.

JJ tensed too, hoping Tate wouldn't say anything about Ruby. He'd been hiding his feelings for years, and hopefully, he could continue to do that for right now. He hadn't kissed Ruby last night, but he had held her hand all the way back to the second floor.

Once they'd stepped out of the elevator, he'd put an acceptable distance between them, and Tate had been asleep again when JJ and Clara Jean had crept away, leaving Ruby to stay overnight with her brother.

"I can't just live on your ranch," Tate said, his voice low and dark. "And now Ruby's there too? We can't pay for the rent."

"Room and board is part of the work on the ranch," JJ said easily, a measure of relief welling up in his stomach.

"I won't be working on the ranch, JJ."

JJ's vocal chords froze, and his mind seemed to break right in half.

"And Ruby certainly won't be. She's an indoor cat, JJ. We'll be lucky if she's not covered in bug bites or poison oak before dinnertime."

JJ burst out laughing. "I'm sure that's not true," he said between chuckles. He sobered, but his smile stayed on his face. "She said she could help on the ranch."

Tate scoffed, then half-laughed. "How much time did she spend outside in college?"

"How would I know that?" JJ asked. He'd paid attention to Ruby, of course, but he didn't want Tate to know that.

"Not much," Tate said. "I'll tell her she'll have to get a job."

"She doesn't need to do that." JJ rolled his neck as he pushed open Tate's hospital room door.

Tate stopped and leaned against the doorframe. He panted and sweated and held JJ's gaze. "We can't just live on your ranch for free, and neither of us will be working for the ranch."

JJ swallowed, because the heavens had just opened and it sounded like God Himself was screaming from above. *Tell him.*

He cleared his throat. "Go in the room," he said, his voice scratching his throat.

Thankfully, Tate must've seen something in JJ's eyes, because he limped past JJ. He followed him inside and let the door close. He pressed his back against it, arguing with himself—and with God.

They're going to find out soon enough anyway, he told himself.

They'll be angrier if you don't tell them.

And Clara Jean can't keep her mouth shut.

Back and forth he went, and when Tate turned and looked at him, JJ opened his mouth. "My family is really rich," he blurted out. "Heck, *I'm* really rich. So don't worry about the rent or the work. I can pay my daddy if he says anything, which I seriously doubt he'll do."

Tate blinked at him, and he should be calming and cooling, but he continued to breathe roughly.

"We'll pay all the hospital and doctor's bills too," JJ said. "You got hurt on the ranch. We have insurance for that."

"Insurance," Tate repeated.

If that was what he wanted to focus on, fine by JJ. His phone rang and someone started to enter the hospital room at the same time. The door hit him in the back, and JJ got out of the way as the doctor entered.

"Oh, you're up," Doctor Baker said jovially, like he'd just arrived to a great party where there'd be fabulous food.

JJ quickly swiped away Conrad's call, so he could listen to the doctor. He could call his cousin back when they finished.

"I've got your discharge papers right here." The doctor held them up triumphantly. "You're free to go, and we got word that all the prescriptions are ready downstairs." He looked over to JJ. "I suppose you're the lucky recipient of this paperwork. I trust you can get it to Mister Reynolds's sister."

"I sure can," JJ said, taking the thick packet of paperwork. The top sheet listed Tate's name, with his injuries right below that. His dietary restrictions had been lifted, according to the paperwork, and his treatment was walking and pain management.

Rib injuries really just needed time and rest to heal, and JJ prayed they all wouldn't be at each other's throats by the time Tate got better.

"All right, then," Doctor Baker said. "You, cowboy, are good to roll."

JJ grinned, but Tate rolled his eyes. "I'm not even dressed."

"I can send Mindy in to help with that."

"No way," Tate practically yelled. "I can get dressed

myself." He shot a look over to JJ, and since they'd lived together for the past five years, JJ had a whole conversation with him. He nodded to the doctor, who left, and then JJ put down the packet and went to help his friend with his T-shirt.

* * *

An hour later—it had taken at least twenty minutes to get Tate downstairs and into a pick-up truck—JJ turned onto Seven Sons Ranch for their second major homecoming in as many days.

"Oh, boy," he muttered as he took in the number of trucks parked in front of the homestead. "Everyone's here."

"Great," Tate said.

"You have a concussion." JJ glanced over to him. "The papers actually say you have to avoid loud situations and crowds."

"You must have a permanent concussion then." Tate grinned at him, because he did love people. He loved talking and laughing, and he didn't care if he knew everyone in the room when he first walked in. He would before he walked out.

JJ was his opposite in a lot of ways, and they both knew it was JJ who didn't want to deal with the whole Walker Family Welcome Wagon.

He drove past the double homesteads, past Uncle Micah's place on the left, and past the barn. The row of cabins came into view, and JJ swore right out loud. "Look how many people are here."

Uncle Rhett's truck, Conrad's, Austin's, Easton's, Ollie's, Finn Ackerman's. As he slowed and stopped, JJ realized they'd left him and Tate one space in front of their cabin. Lincoln Glover waved at him and pointed as if JJ couldn't see it, and Alex Baxter—another man from the luncheons and date nights JJ had attended sporadically over the past several years—approached.

JJ had no choice but to openly dis him or roll down his window. He did the latter and said, "What in the world is goin' on?"

"Everyone heard about Tate." Alex stepped up onto the runner on JJ's truck and peered past him. "Heya, brother." Alex flashed a smile, about all he ever did. JJ liked him, because he was serious and no-nonsense and yet still friendly, fun to be around, and personable.

"Hey," Tate said. "So you called in everyone?"

"This is the work of Conrad," Alex said. "He's got tables set up in the field behind the cabins, and he put down those big tiles they use to make the dance floor in the park for the summer dances so you'd have something flat and even to walk on."

"Wow," Tate said, meeting JJ's eyes. "Guess I'll have to go for a few minutes at least."

"We got burgers," JJ said. "Not enough for everyone."

"I've already eaten mine," Tate said.

Every excuse JJ could think of vanished.

"It's Saturday," Alex said. "Beautiful weather after some

rain. I think my wife is just glad to get the twins out of the house finally." He chuckled, dropped to the ground, and joined the other cowboys waving for JJ to pull into the reserved spot.

Henry Marshall did, his wife Angel at his side. They both wore smiles the size of the sun, and JJ really wished he'd have been warned about this homecoming.

Then he remembered Conrad had called him. JJ had never circled back to his cousin, and he put a smile on his face for Dawson Rhinehart, his brothers Brandon and Duke, and dutifully pulled into the parking space to a deafening round of applause.

"This is ridiculous," he muttered as he rolled up his window. "I mean, I'm glad you're alive, but—"

The roar of the noise came inside, cutting off JJ's words, as Daddy opened Tate's door. "All right, son," he said. "Take it real slow now."

Pure irritation shot through JJ when someone opened his door too, as if he couldn't do it himself. When he turned, he met Conrad's eyes. "Have you lost your mind?"

Conrad grinned at him, tipped his head back, and laughed. "Yeah, about." He pulled JJ out of the truck and hugged him. "We've all been really worried, JJ. You're not a great go-between."

"I'm not a great go-between?" He stepped away from the truck and slammed the door.

"You haven't texted any of us this morning," Conrad said good-naturedly. "We've all been here for a half-hour, and I called and texted everyone when I finally saw your pin move off the second floor of the hospital." He grinned at JJ and paused at the corner of the truck.

JJ stopped next to him and took in the scene. "This is a nightmare in real life." A sign with Tate's name on it ran from corner to corner of the cabin they'd moved into yesterday. The scent of sugar and roasted beef hung in the air, and JJ thought freshly cooked food would be better than the hamburger he'd gotten twenty minutes ago, though it was a mushroom Swiss, which was his favorite.

No matter what, his plans to get Tate settled and his stuff moved out—then he'd retreat to Aunt Callie's and raid her freezer for some of Uncle Liam's homemade ice cream—had just been blown up.

Because this?

He'd never get out of here.

"Don't stand over here, glowering." Momma came around the front of the truck and hugged JJ. He sank into the embrace, because he loved his momma so much.

"I'm not glowering."

"Your friends won't even come over to say hello," she said as she pulled back. "They're worried they'll lose a limb."

"I talked to Alex," JJ said, watching as Daddy carried a tray with at least three pies on it through the crowd.

"Come eat," Momma said. "You too, Conrad. He's not mad."

"Oh, I'm mad," JJ said. "But I think a really big piece of chocolate banana pie will cheer me up." He took a couple of steps with Conrad and his mother. "And then, I expect everyone here to help me move my stuff into the cabin next door."

"Oh, that's done," Momma said. "Your friends came to do it, so be sure to *be nice* to them."

"I'm nice," JJ said under his breath as he approached Link and Finn. He hitched his smile in place. "Hey, guys." He stepped into them as a pair and hugged them simultaneously. "Thanks for moving my stuff this morning."

Chapter Eight

R uby's impatience boiled over every other second, and no amount of deep breathing and long bouts with her eyes closed could calm her.

And she couldn't drive with her eyes closed anyway. But she really wished Natalie didn't need the solo driving hours, because Ruby would rather have her in the passenger seat than her father.

She'd thanked him fifteen times for coming to help her, though Ruby probably could've cleared out her belongings by herself. She didn't own a bed or any furniture of any substance, and everything she owned fit in a laundry hamper or a box.

It would've taken longer, but she could've done it.

Now, she had her father telling her not to drive so fast, and that only made Ruby want to press the accelerator to the floor, just to get there quicker.

"Natalie can't keep up," Dad said, and Ruby looked out her side window and closed her eyes for a moment.

When she opened her eyes, she checked her rearview mirror. "Natalie is right on my tail," she said. "She's fine, Dad."

"We have an uncovered load in the back of my truck."

"Dad, there's four taped boxes." Ruby tossed a look over to him. "What are you so worked up about?"

He sat rigidly, and he kept checking the rearview mirror too. He swallowed and then finally relaxed. "We haven't heard anything about Tate today."

"I was with him this morning," she said easily. "JJ texted to say they left the hospital right when we finished taking the boxes out." Then, they'd had to stay and clean her bedroom, the bathroom, and part of the kitchen.

Two of her roommates still lived in the apartment, but the landlords had check-out procedures, and she, Nat, and Dad had done the required work. Then they'd left Amarillo, and Three Rivers sat about sixty or seventy minutes away.

Her heartbeat throbbed in her neck as she wondered how long it would take JJ and Tate to get to the ranch.

"He's okay, Daddy." She wasn't used to reassuring her father, and the new role felt like someone draping an icy blanket over her shoulders. He usually gave her the confidence boost she needed, not the other way around.

"Are you going to be okay in Three Rivers?" Dad zeroed in on her now, and she didn't like the scrutiny.

"I'll manage," she said.

"It's a ranch, Rubes."

"I know that, Dad. It's right in the name of it." She flashed him a smile she hoped would convince him she'd be okay. "I can handle Tate."

"It's hard taking care of someone who's not well," Daddy said. "Your mother can come as soon as school is out."

"Okay." Ruby swallowed and buttoned up her bravery. "Daddy, I don't have an internship in San Antonio, so I—"

"What do you mean?"

"I mean they called me yesterday and told me they didn't have the funds for five interns. Only three. And I was the last one awarded, and they were really sorry, but I didn't have an internship or an apartment."

She spoke the words in a rush, hardly believing that phone call had come only yesterday. So much had happened since then.

Her lips tingled, almost like they had an independent memory of their own and had suddenly remembered kissing JJ.

"So what are you going to do?"

"I'm going to accept it as God's hand in my life," she said. "He made it possible for me to be available to help Tate this summer." She glanced over to him. "I know Mom is doing that summer school, Daddy. I know I'm not going to be as good as her, but Tate's not going to die."

"She said she can get out of the summer school."

"And I'm saying she doesn't need to." Ruby didn't want to carry her parents' problems, but she knew her mom didn't teach summer school for fun. She did it, because they needed the money. "Tate will tell her the same thing."

Daddy looked out the window, and his silence spoke volumes. Ruby basked in the discomfort for a few seconds, and then she let it simply...fly away. She reached to adjust the volume on the radio, and with it playing, she sped up a little bit.

He didn't say much on the rest of the drive to Three Rivers, and Ruby smiled at the first farm she saw on the outskirts of town. "This is a cute little place," she said. "We're going to be fine here, and once Tate is all healed up, I'll start looking for another interior design job."

She glanced over to him and smiled. "And he'll find the most perfect farm or ranch—probably here—and buy it, and he's going to be so happy." She'd heard Tate talk about finding his one small operation and running it, just like their father.

He simply didn't like Lubbock, and the farm there wasn't exactly profitable. Ruby wasn't sure what her parents would do with it once Daddy got too old to take care of it himself, and maybe one of her younger siblings would take it over.

"Yeah," Daddy said.

"Maybe he'll get a job at a boarding stable," Ruby said, filling the silence with her voice now. "Or maybe he and JJ will start one." How, Ruby didn't know, as Tate didn't have much money, and JJ sure seemed to be on the path of taking over his father's ranch.

She couldn't believe she felt any spark of excitement at all to be driving into another small Texas ranching community, but it flared to life within her chest and sent light and heat out to the very tips of her fingers and toes.

She suspected JJ had something to do with that—a lot to do with that—but Three Rivers seemed so...green when Lubbock was always so drab. Or brown. Or beige. Any of those adjectives would've worked.

Ruby turned right and skirted around the bulk of the town, going by a couple of communities on her left as farmland stretched on the right. She passed a big landscaping company, then made a left, went past a really cute mechanic shop, and made another right.

This road became a highway and seemed to be leading away from the town of Three Rivers. She checked her phone and saw she simply stayed on this road for another thirteen minutes.

Then she'd make a left, and she'd arrive at her destination—Seven Sons Ranch. Her pulse turned into a jackhammer, and it didn't stop as she completed the drive and turned onto a well-kept gravel road with plenty of big, beautiful buildings on it.

"Wow," she said, taking in the one, two, three homesteads she could already see. Barns. Sheds. Other buildings that ranches must need for something. The bluebells had only just bloomed here, and a whole field of the bluish-purple flowers stretched in front of her.

The red poppies of Texas spread all along the fence, and she turned around the corner and moved between one of the houses and two of the others. The picture of the "strip-mall sheds" JJ had sent came to life in front of her, and Ruby knew she needed to go past those.

She did, everything here seemingly perfect, from the huge oak trees, to the emerald green lawns, to the cloudless sky.

Another house came into view directly ahead, but she turned right to enter the parking area in front of the row of six of the cutest cowboy cabins Ruby had ever seen in her life. "This is it," she said, noting that her father hadn't said a thing.

Several trucks had been parked in the gravel in front of the cabins, and Ruby eased to the last one and pulled her car in. "Is Natalie going to back in the truck?" Alarm bells rang through Ruby, because she could still barely back up a vehicle.

"No. Just stop here, and I'll get out and do it."

Ruby was already stopped, and her dad got out to go help Nat with the truck. She got out of her car and took her first deep breath of the air here at Seven Sons.

And it smelled good.

She turned in a full circle, and when she faced the cabins again, the most glorious sight in the world greeted her.

JJ Walker, in the flesh.

He came down the steps of the last cabin in the row, his eyes on them as he moved. When he reached the ground, he looked up, his face bright with a smile. "You made it."

Ruby wanted to squeal and dance over to him, wrap her arms around him, and breathe in the scent of his cologne, his skin, and his pure cowboy goodness. Instead, she cut a look over to her younger sister and then turned her attention back to JJ.

"The GPS led us right to it," she said as she approached him slowly. She glanced left and right. "This place is huge, JJ. You didn't mention that."

"I'm sure I did." He paused a couple of feet from her, clearly not sure what to do with his hands—or himself—either.

"I can see four houses if I turn in a circle." Ruby did that again, catching sight of the big barns and stables back behind the closest homestead. "And all these cabins. And look right there—there's a pasture with horses in it. They're so cute."

JJ chuckled and said, "I'm pretty sure no one has ever called those horses cute."

"Just those ones or any horse?" She grinned at him, knowing full-well her flirtation would be fully detectable to her sister. Hopefully to JJ too, but Ruby swallowed in an attempt to take things down a notch.

"We're a working ranch," JJ said, still grinning. "The animals here work, princess." He stepped past her then, putting one hand on her forearm and branding her as he moved past her. "Hey, Todd."

Ruby turned and watched him shake her dad's hand. They'd met before, of course, as Tate had brought JJ home for weekends on occasion.

"This is a nice place, JJ," Daddy said.

"Yeah." JJ sighed as he surveyed the ranch to the north

of the cabins. "It's great." He clapped his hands together, which startled the serenity hanging in the air. "We just finished a massive coming-home party for Tate, so he's resting, but I saved y'all some food."

JJ moved to the tailgate and picked up a laundry basket with Ruby's comforter and bedding in it. "You guys can eat while I bring things in, if you want."

"Let's unload," Daddy said, deciding for them all. "Then we'll stay for a bit." He glanced over to Natalie. "We have to get back tonight."

"Oh, you're not staying?" JJ asked over his shoulder as he walked toward the cabin. Daddy picked up Ruby's stick vacuum and her dirty clothes basket—which she'd stuffed with her towels and a couple of pots and pans—and followed him.

"No," he said. "I have to get back to the farm."

Ruby watched the pair of them climb the seven or eight steps to the tiny porch and then as they went inside, not even realizing Natalie had settled to a stop right beside her. She sighed, and Natalie giggled.

"How long have you liked JJ?" she asked.

Ruby sucked in a breath and spun toward her sister. "I don't—I don't like JJ."

Natalie looked at her with their mother's green eyes, her eyebrows lifting straight up. A couple of seconds passed, and then she returned to her resting expression. "Okay, you don't like JJ."

She turned and picked up a single box that probably only weighed a few pounds. "But you should probably get better at hiding it if you don't want anyone else to know." With that, she followed the men, her solo box no burden at all.

Ruby turned to the truck too, her heartbeat thrashing for an entirely different reason now. She had to go inside and put her life together in this cabin. Tate would be living with her.

Tate, who'd once told her, *I just don't see you with a cowboy, Rubes. Especially not someone who relates more to horses than people. Nah, you need a...a sportscaster or something.*

She'd laughed and questioned him. *A sportscaster?*

He'd chuckled too and lay next to her on the bed, where she'd been after her break-up with her last boyfriend. She'd harbored feelings for JJ then too, but she'd dated Davy for seven months before he'd broken up with her.

She'd sobered and asked him, *What if the cowboy was JJ? Or Riley? Or someone you know, who's good and smart and all that?*

Nah, Tate had said. *You can't date any of my friends or roommates. That would be...weird.*

Ruby climbed the front steps, the past conversation with her brother humming through her, the volume of it growing with every step she took.

What was weird was being here, on JJ's ranch, to take care of her brother. She entered the cabin, expecting more of the same high-end stuff she'd already experienced here. She wasn't disappointed as a bright living room with a couch, loveseat, and coffee table in it greeted her.

The kitchen sat at the back of the house, with a table pushed against the wall on her right. The hallway went out of the kitchen to the left, and Dad and Natalie came back that way, now empty-handed.

They dodged into the kitchen to get out of her way, and Ruby continued down the hall with her makeup kit on top of a box labeled *pictures*.

JJ came out of the room in the back right corner of the house, and since he had nowhere to go, he ducked back into it so she could enter with her load. "I got it," he said when she did, and he took the box from her. "The room comes with a bed and a desk, and we can just put this here for now."

He slid the box onto the desk, then turned back to her. With her hands empty, Ruby didn't know what to do with them, and she ended up tucking them in her back pockets.

JJ glanced toward the open doorway, then back to her. "It's great to see you." He grinned at her, stepped into her, closing the distance between then, and swept his big, warm hand along her waist.

His lips skated across her cheek, sending fire through her whole face. "I'll go get some more of your stuff, okay? I'm glad you're here." He left, and Ruby turned in another full circle, trying to get her bearings.

She spotted the laundry basket with her bedding, and she lunged toward it. Once she got her room together, she'd feel more settled. Dad and Nat would leave, and Ruby would see Tate, and JJ would go to his own house, and Ruby wouldn't have to work quite so hard just to exist.

She'd just finished stretching her fitted sheet over the mattress when her phone chimed with the ringtone she'd assigned to JJ. She pulled her phone from her purse and turned her back on the doorway, just in case someone came in.

Coffee in the morning? he'd asked. *Cowboys get up early, but Tate will sleep late, so we might have a few minutes together, just the two of us.*

"Just the two of us," she murmured, her fingers hovering above the screen as she tried to figure out what to say.

"Clothes," Nat said, and Ruby tucked her phone away as she turned to face her sister. She spotted a closet on the same wall as the door, and she stepped over to it. "I'll put them in here."

"Thank you, Nat." Ruby finished making up the bed and then more boxes got piled on top of it, and after only ten minutes, everything she owned had been brought inside.

JJ brought in her car keys and handed them to her. "I got the food out."

"Yes," she said, sort of blurting the word at him.

He cocked his head and studied her. "Yes? To the food?"

Ruby gathered her wits and stepped into his personal space the way he had hers. "To coffee, cowboy." Then she went to get something to eat, because she was positively famished.

Chapter Nine

JJ leaned against the porch railing of his cabin, watching the first hints of dawn streak across the Texas sky. The cool, crisp air carried the scent of dew-covered grass and distant hay fields, horses and...his cologne. So maybe he was trying too hard. After all, he never spritzed around cologne to simply go work on the ranch.

He took a deep breath, savoring the quiet moment before the ranch came to life, before the world woke up. His gaze drifted to the cabin next door, where he'd left Ruby and Tate last night. He'd helped his best friend into bed, and Ruby had tucked him in, promised him a cup of hot chocolate, and walked JJ to the back door.

He could admit he'd thought about kissing her for real, but Aunt Simone and her youngest daughter, Laurel, had been finishing up the clean-up from the party. So he'd ducked his head, muttered something about seeing Ruby in the morning, and he'd waved to his aunt and cousin as he went down one set of back steps and up another.

Next door, a soft yellow light flickered on, and his heart quickened. He'd been looking forward to this moment since he'd texted Ruby yesterday. Maybe for years. A cafeteria date and stolen coffee sipping by the dawn's early light. He wasn't sure if he was hitting any homeruns in terms of dating, but he couldn't exactly show up on Ruby's front porch and whisk her off to the most romantic date in the world.

Number one, he lived in Three Rivers, Texas, and number two, Tate would fillet the skin from his bones, bruised and broken ribs or not.

He lifted his mug to his lips and took a slow sip of coffee, feeling the buzz already starting in his stomach. Or maybe that was the promise of seeing Ruby this morning. No one loitered out in the pastures and fields between the cabins and his aunt and uncle's front yard, and he located the beehives to the northwest and watched the gray light lighten by degrees.

Finally, the back door next door creaked open, and Ruby stepped out, her red hair cascading down over her shoulders. She wore jeans and a light purple sweater with short sleeves, looking both comfortable and beautiful.

JJ's breath caught in his throat, and he lifted his mug to silently toast her, then indicated he'd run and get her a cup too. He did that, his fingers shaking slightly as he prepped her coffee. She waited outside on the tiny back porch, and JJ squeezed himself into the space with her with a, "Here you go, Scarlet."

"Thank you." She took the mug and wrapped her fingers around it for a brief moment. "I'm going to sit." She moved over to the top step and settled down. JJ followed, handed her his coffee so he could sit, and then took it back.

"Sleep well?" JJ reached up with his free hand and adjusted his cowboy hat. "That bed is fairly new."

She snuggled a little closer to him, her hip pressing into his and her coffee cup balanced on her far knee. "As well as I could with Tate snoring like a freight train."

JJ chuckled, taking her coffee and setting it on the next step down so he could hold her hand. Such a simple gesture made his whole world take on new meaning, and he loved the way his skin sizzled and vibrated where hers touched it. His thoughts raced for several moments, and then he calmed.

"It's good that Tate slept okay," he said. "I was worried he'd be callin' you all night for things."

"I stayed up pretty late," she said. "And checked on him before I finally went to bed."

He nodded into the brightening horizon. "I forgot you're a night owl."

She yawned. "Yeah, so that makes early-morning coffee dates difficult."

A rush of humiliation streamed through him, and he handed her the coffee again. "Sip that, princess. You'll be awake before you know it."

She took a sip and leaned her head against his shoulder,

like she wasn't strong enough to hold it up herself. Like she needed him. "This is perfect."

A sudden round of nerves moved through him, rendering his mind blank and his voice mute. Why couldn't he think of anything to say?

"I'm worried about how today will go," Ruby whispered.

"You are?"

She nodded against his bicep, and she remained quiet enough that the morning calm settled over them again. Finally, she said, "I just don't know what to do with him all day."

"Mm." JJ squeezed her hand. "He's not good just sitting around."

"I read through some of his care packet," Ruby said. "I'm going to make him walk three times a day; two naps—one in the morning and one in the afternoon. Then there's showering and getting dressed. He doesn't move very fast, and everything takes forever. This might be his whole day."

"It might," JJ said. "And you know, Rubes, he's not a toddler. He can stay in the cabin by himself while you go do something else."

She took another sip of her coffee. "True."

"So when he's bothering you, you leave," JJ said. "Text me, and I'll come sit with him."

"Thank you, Jay-J."

He loved his nickname spoken in her pretty voice, and he liked the soft, special way she sighed. "This place is beautiful. So different than our place in Lubbock."

"You get good sunrises there too." He bumped her in

what he hoped was a playful way. "You just never get up early enough to see them."

"Sunsets are just as beautiful," she said. "And we'd be facing the right direction."

Too many eyes at night, JJ thought, but he kept it to himself. A few more minutes passed, and golden light started to seep into the day. The other cowboys would be up soon, and JJ's blissful bubble would pop.

"Listen, I'm real sorry about your internship this summer. I'm sure this isn't what you had planned."

She gave a mirthless laugh. "Not even close."

His heart skipped a beat. "If there's anything I can do to make it easier, you let me know, princess."

"This is nice," she said, squeezing his hand.

"It's too early for you," he said. "But it can be a standing date. If you get up, you come over and have coffee with me. If you don't." He shrugged the shoulder not touching Ruby and didn't say anything else. He held no grand illusions that she'd show up every morning, but a cowboy could hope and dream, right?

"What are you going to do about your job?" he asked.

She drew in a deep breath and lifted her head. "When Tate is all healed, I'll look for something."

"You wanted an adventure in the city," he said.

"Well, Three Rivers is bigger than Lubbock," she said.

JJ chuckled, knowing Three Rivers was not the big city adventure Ruby had been hoping to have. "Can I tell you a secret?"

"You have secrets?" She pulled in a breath that truly

sounded scandalized. "JJ Walker, you better spill them all right now."

The way she flirted with him sent an electric thrill through every muscle in his body. JJ took a moment to enjoy it, then contain it, and then he said, "I kinda crave an adventure too. I didn't leave home right after graduating high school. Then I went an hour away to college, and now I'm back. It feels really sort of stale."

Ruby gave him the courtesy of not jumping in immediately to reassure him, and he wished he could get closer to her somehow. "You did that mission trip to the Dominican Republic," she said. "You've at least been on an airplane."

"You haven't?" he asked.

"Not yet," she said, and he heard the smile in her voice. When he turned to look at her, he found it sitting prettily on her face too.

"Well, now I know what to get you for your birthday," he said.

She laughed, clearly disbelieving that he'd ever do that. But JJ's mind started working through getting her the plane ticket she needed to have an amazing adventure. He couldn't help the fact that he saw himself with her, enjoying somewhere tropical, or maybe they could visit the mountains and go hiking to a crystal clear blue lake.

Or the city, he thought. Ruby didn't want a small-town life. She wanted something grand.

That thought made his mood turn slightly sour, because all he had to offer her was small-town Three Rivers, with a big ranch on the south side of it.

"Sometimes I wonder if running this ranch is really what I want, or if it's just what's expected of me."

Ruby leaned forward and looked back at him. "What would you do if you could do anything?"

JJ hesitated, then said, "I've always dreamed of starting a horse breeding program here. High-quality stock for racing, show jumping, that sort of thing. But it's a big investment, and I haven't said anything to my father."

Ruby's eyes sparkled like the gem she was. "That sounds amazing. You're so good with horses."

Her enthusiasm warmed him, and for a moment, JJ let himself imagine a future where Ruby worked at his side, supporting his dreams and making her own come true too. But reality crashed back as the ranch began to stir around them, with Brant coming out onto his back porch three houses down the row.

"I should get going," JJ said reluctantly. "Horses won't feed themselves."

Ruby nodded, understanding. As they stood, she surprised him by stepping close and placing a soft kiss on his cheek. "Thanks for the coffee, cowboy. Let's do this again soon."

"I'll always be waitin' on you, Scarlet." He tipped his hat at her as she handed him her coffee mug and then headed back to her cabin. His cheek tingled where her lips had touched, and he waved to Brant and Lawson as they went by. With a deep breath, he turned to take the dishes back into the cabin, Ruby's kiss giving him an extra spring in his step he hoped would last all day long.

* * *

JJ finished feeding the horses in the section of the stable where he'd been assigned. It was the Sabbath, and that meant his daddy had scheduled only essential chores. It also meant his parents would expect him to be ready to go to church by nine-thirty.

For whatever reason, JJ didn't want to go this morning. Probably because of the craziness of the past couple of days, and he wanted this Sabbath to be a true day of rest.

He finished washing up in the barn sink, and then he moved over to the clipboard that hung by the entrance. With an operation as large as Seven Sons, jobs had to be marked off so they didn't get done twice, and so everyone knew they'd been done at all.

"There you are."

JJ looked up from the sheet at the sound of his daddy's voice. "Morning, Daddy." He finished noting that he'd fed the horses in stalls twenty through thirty-nine, and that he'd cleaned them out. He rehung the clipboard and turned to hug his father. "Are we still meeting today after church? Over wings?"

"I've got them in the oven now," he said. "Then we'll crisp them up in the air fryer after church."

JJ's heartbeat blipped through his body. "I think I'm gonna skip services today."

Daddy pulled back and studied JJ's face. "You are?" He swept his fingers across JJ's forehead, right below where his cowboy hat sat. "Are you feeling okay?"

"I'm actually really tired," JJ said. "Too much peopling yesterday."

Daddy grinned. "Conrad wanted you to know we care about you and Tate."

"I know." JJ stepped out of the stable and into the morning sun. It cleansed him, and he did love working outdoors more than anywhere else.

"Budd has the horses out over here," Daddy said, and he led JJ around the front of the stable. Sure enough, several horses dotted the large paddock there, grazing on the late spring grass.

JJ's eyes landed on Midnight, a sleek black mare who was one of his favorites. He approached the paddock slowly, him and Daddy sauntering in the silence, and then he snapped his fingers.

All the horses looked up, and Midnight wasn't the only one who started for him. Wisdom whinnied as she trotted over, and JJ chuckled at her and said, "You missed me, didn't you?"

The horses kept their ears forward as they came right up to the rail. Some farms and ranches used electric fences to keep their animals back, but Daddy didn't believe in such things. So the equines came right up to the rail and leaned against them, all of them getting their big, heavy heads close to JJ's.

"Hey there, beautiful," he murmured to Midnight, running a hand along her neck. The horse nickered softly, leaning into his touch. Wisdom huffed, and a couple of the other horses darted away. So their pecking order hadn't changed much.

"You wait your turn," he said to the gray spotted horse he remembered his daddy bringing to the ranch like it had happened yesterday.

"I want to talk to you about something," he said to his father. "When we meet this afternoon."

"That's why we're meeting," his father said. "Unless you want to give me a hint, and then I can take it to church with me."

Sometimes his father did need time to mull over a problem or just to have time to think through things before coming up with how he truly felt. JJ had seen his mother give his daddy a "heads up" about something long before Daddy had to deal with it, and that had helped him do so in a better way.

"I want to add another stable to Seven Sons," JJ said. "A stable and a herd, actually."

Daddy said nothing, but he pulled in a deep breath through his nose.

"A breeding stable," JJ said. "For show horses. I met a couple of women who train them at college, and MariLynn says there's a big need for them."

"I'm sure," Daddy said quietly.

"And I think it would be awesome to have a herd of longhorn cattle here," he said. "I knew this man in college— Timlan Shepherd, and his family has made a living raising and selling longhorns for a couple of generations now."

"Longhorn cattle?"

"Yep." JJ pulled his hand away from Midnight and stroked Wisdom's neck. "They sell them for slaughter, the way we do our beef cattle. Or just to other farms and ranches who want a herd. I want to get some breeding stock with amazing genetics, and have a high-end herd."

"For fun."

"It would be fun, yes," JJ said carefully. "But I'd sell them, I think. Not sure about going the production route. We have beef cattle for that."

Daddy put his foot up on the bottom rung of the fence and stroked Wisdom's nose. "We sure do." He at least sounded contemplative, and JJ couldn't ask for much more than that.

He had sketches of the ranch property, and he knew he could keep a longhorn herd on the land they already had. But—he cleared his throat. "I want to buy the Adair property."

Daddy's gaze flew to his, his eyebrows up. He didn't have to say anything to say a whole lot.

"It's up for sale," JJ said simply.

"It's been up for sale for eight months," Daddy said. "It's too expensive."

JJ cocked his head. "Is it, though?" The familiar sense of peace and belonging he felt whenever he came home to Seven Sons filled him. This was where he belonged, he knew. But maybe there was more for him than what had always been here.

Maybe he could expand the ranch, as well as the operations on it. Or maybe he'd buy the Adair property—which came with it's own house, barns, stables, and outbuildings, and run his own ranch.

Alex Baxter did. Finn Ackerman too. Link Glover and Dawson Rhinehart worked their family land—and JJ could do that too. Henry and Angel worked and managed a huge boarding stable outside of Amarillo, but it was theirs.

JJ wanted something that truly belonged to him, and only him.

His father looked at him thoughtfully. "You've really been giving this a lot of thought, haven't you?"

"Yes, sir," JJ said, suddenly thinking of a future where he didn't live right next door to his momma and daddy, and where he could build a future and a life with a pretty scarlet-haired princess for a wife.

"Well, I best be headed in," Daddy said with a groan as he lowered his foot. "How was Tate this morning?"

And just like that, the reminder that JJ had obstacles keeping him from the future that seemed to take shape so easily here on the ranch brought him back to solid ground.

"Good," he said lightly. "I mean, I didn't talk to him or anything, so I'm assuming...." He also didn't tell his father he'd coffee'ed with Ruby, and he told himself he hadn't lied. He hadn't spoken to Tate. Neither had Ruby. JJ was totally assuming his best friend was good that morning, and after he dropped his daddy off at the homestead so he could get to church with Momma, JJ set his sights on Cabin Row so he could go find out about Tate for himself.

Chapter Ten

Ruby yawned loudly as she stretched her arms above her head. The sun had already started to seep through the blinds, and she'd heard Tate's bedroom door squeak open about thirty seconds ago. Just the fact that he could get out of bed by himself testified to how much he'd already improved.

One short week. That was how long Ruby had been in Three Rivers, and she padded across the room in three strides and opened her bedroom door too. The water in the bathroom ran, and she wasn't surprised that Tate had left the door open.

She'd griped at him enough this week about it. A flicker of surprise made her blink, because he'd actually done it. The scent of minty toothpaste and men's body wash mingled together, and Ruby didn't hate it. She didn't understand how Tate could brush his teeth in the shower—the water was hot and he couldn't rinse his mouth properly—but she didn't have to do it.

"Are you thinking of going to church today?" she called from outside the bathroom, where the hall dead-ended. Her bedroom sat to the right, his to the left.

"Yeah," he said. "It'll be my morning walk."

"Okay, I'll go make coffee." Ruby turned to do that, thinking through this past week. It had been a whirlwind of activity, each day blending into the next in a haze of helping Tate get dressed, helping Tate get down the steps to the path, walking with Tate, listening to Tate talk about what he could be doing that summer, making meals for Tate. Tate, Tate, Tate.

Ruby loved her brother, and they'd always gotten along really well. But perhaps she needed the rest and respite of church as well. "You need to get off this ranch," she muttered to herself.

Seven Sons was a ranch a cut above every other she'd ever seen, that was for sure. But she still felt a little trapped here, despite the wide open fields, the stretching sky above, and the endless pastures. The place still had fences, and they felt caging to Ruby.

She'd only had a few more stolen moments with JJ. The man had come to his family ranch to work, to start the transition to take over for his father. He didn't have very many minutes to simply walk along a paddock, chitchat with a horse, or stroll hand-in-hand with Ruby while the sun went down.

She'd joined him for early-morning coffee one other

time, but other than that, she'd only seen him fleetingly. He came over in the evenings, but Tate dominated most of that time.

With the coffee dripping, Ruby scrambled eggs and set English muffins to toast. When she finished breakfast, and Tate still hadn't arrived in the kitchen, she threw a look down the hallway. She'd been helping him get dressed every morning, changed into his pajamas at night, and anything else he needed. Putting on his boots was especially hard—for both of them.

"Tate?" she called, because he had gotten up and into the shower by himself this morning. "For the *first* time," she muttered. "He's not well, Ruby."

She left the hot eggs and muffins and went down the hall. Tate's bedroom door had been closed, and she rapped on it smartly. "I'm coming in." She did just that, bracing herself for what she might see.

Tate sat on the hard chair they'd moved to his desk from the kitchen table. He looked up at her, his face a bit white. "Whoa, whoa, whoa."

She rushed into the room and knelt in front of him, trying to find the problem just by looking. He had bruises up and down his torso, a couple of them disappearing into the towel he wore around his waist. Otherwise, he didn't wear anything, and Ruby's hands hovered a few inches from his skin.

"I think I just moved too fast," he said, his breath coming in short spurts. "I just need to sit here for a minute."

She glanced over to the desk, where his array of medications sat. "Did you take these?" She'd asked Clara Jean to bring them a pill case from the grocery store, and Ruby had doled out his medication a week at a time so she didn't have to think so hard three times a day.

Tate's head swiveled toward the orange pill bottles too, but it didn't move fast. "Yeah," he said. "I think so."

Ruby got to her feet. "You think so?" She picked up the case, and yes, Sunday's morning pills were gone. "You need to eat." She set down the case. "Let me go get your breakfast."

"Rubes," he said weakly behind her, but Ruby dashed out of the room.

She returned only half a minute later, the fork making irritating metal sounds against the plate. "Eggs and muffins," she said. "I'll go get your coffee." She slid the plate onto the desk and turned to leave again.

A sense of being completely underwater hit her as she entered the hall, and Ruby struggled to breathe. She couldn't kick up. Didn't even know which way was up.

She stifled a sob as she ran into the kitchen, ducked around the corner, though Tate couldn't and wouldn't follow her, and pressed her back into the refrigerator there. *Breathe in,* she told herself. And she did.

Breathe out.

She managed to do that too. In and out, and she kept her eyes pressed closed. But she'd seen the dark circles under Tate's eyes this morning, the way he'd only moved his head. No way they could go to church.

Someone knocked on the back door, and Ruby's eyes

flew open. JJ entered the cabin in the next moment, and he froze when he saw her plastered against the fridge. Then he strode toward her, not even bothering to close the door behind him.

"What's wrong?" He searched her face, something fierce and protective entering his gaze. "Where's Tate?"

"Bedroom," Ruby whispered. "He's fine, just...."

JJ reached out and cradled her face when she didn't go on. "Are *you* okay?"

She pressed into his touch now, letting her eyes drift closed again. "Yeah," she said. "I just got overwhelmed there for a second."

"I'll go check on him." JJ dropped his hand, gave her another long look, and then stepped by her and down the hall calling, "Tate, brother? You decent?"

"I'm fine," Tate called back, and he did sound better.

Ruby moved over to the second plate of food and split the eggs. She set another muffin to toast, then took the plate to Tate's room. "Breakfast, JJ?"

He'd taken a spot on the end of Tate's bed, facing her brother. He barely glanced over to her, and Ruby shouldn't let that hurt. But it did. "No, I'm fine," he said. "My momma's makin' cinnamon rolls this morning."

Ruby nodded, suddenly not hungry at all either. She left without another word, and she heard the lower voices of JJ and her brother as they picked up their conversation.

It was ridiculous to feel left out. They'd been friends—best friends—for five years. Ruby sat at the kitchen-table-for-one and put a cold bite of eggs in her mouth. The new

English muffin popped up, and Ruby did the same to go slather it with butter.

She ate that instead of the eggs, and in fact, she scraped everything else in the trash, then went down the hall and into her bedroom. She closed and locked the door, not that she thought Tate or JJ would come barging in. Even if Tate couldn't get to church today, Ruby could.

She needed to.

Something ached in her soul, and she didn't know how to soothe it. She stood in front of her closet and stared, her mind feeling sluggish and slow. In that moment, she wasn't sure how long she could live on this ranch, in these conditions.

She sure seemed to be losing mental capacity by the minute.

So she quickly pulled out a floral sundress and shimmied out of her pj's and into that. She could step into some sandals, brush her teeth, and refluff her hair with the blow dryer in less than ten minutes. Which gave her time to sit down at the small desk in front of the window and open her design book.

She loved sketching out a room, arranging the furniture in exactly the right spot for flow of traffic and energy. She'd lovingly pasted or stapled in fabric samples, color patterns she loved, and photographs of paint and flooring.

As she flipped through the front half of the book, her inspiration started to vibrate, and by the time she reached a blank page two-thirds of the way back, Ruby had a pencil in her hand.

A concept for a farmhouse living room took shape on the paper in front of her, stolen and sketched right from her mind. This would definitely be a farm-chic type of design, and she shaded in the cow spots on a rug in front of the fireplace.

The light brown leather furniture would speak to the saddles and boots the occupants wore and used, with light blue on the walls to bring the sense of the sky indoors. Paintings of flowers and ranch landscapes would cover the walls, further solidifying the country features and making the house feel like a home.

Her mind flowed into the kitchen of such a house, and she envisioned a dark brown granite for the countertops, all of it flecked with white and gold. No stainless steel. No way. This kitchen would have black matte appliances, with pale yellow cabinetry to match the gold in the counter and brighten the darkness from the fridge and dishwasher.

Ruby could just see it, one space flowing into the next, with a dining room there too. A proud table for twelve stood ready at all times, for the large cowboy family who'd gather for Sabbath Day meals on a day exactly like today.

"Ruby," JJ called, and she blinked a couple of times to get back to reality.

She sat at a plain white desk, nothing grand like granite anywhere in sight. She blinked again. "Yeah," she said as she got up to go unlock and open the door.

"We've got to go in about fifteen minutes," he said, and he now wore a white shirt and tie, with a black pair of slacks, black cowboy boots, and a stunning black hat. His tie was pale pink, the only stitch of color on him, and Ruby could only stare at him. "Are you coming? It's fine if you don't want to."

JJ's eyes raked down to her bare feet and quickly rebounded back to hers. He swallowed—hard. "I can take him off your hands for a couple of hours."

"I want to go," Ruby said, her voice a bit robotic. "I just need to finish getting ready."

"I'll start him toward the car," JJ said. "Can you drive him? My sisters want to come with me this morning." He gave her a smile, and Ruby couldn't say no to him. She wouldn't anyway.

"I'll be out in ten," she said, and JJ nodded, backed out of her doorway, ducked his head in the most adorable way, and turned to go down the hall. He hadn't touched her, and a flutter of sadness winged through her heart.

When she went outside, she found Tate waiting in the passenger seat of her car, and JJ hugging his youngest sister just before she climbed up into the backseat of his truck. He tipped his hat to her, said nothing, and rounded the tailgate to get to the driver's seat.

"Hey," she called over to him, then jogged that way. Clara Jean rolled down her window, her smile sunny and bright. "I don't know where the church is. I can follow you?"

"Oh, sure," Clara Jean said, glancing over to JJ. She looked back at Ruby. "I'll make sure he doesn't leave you in the dust."

"I'm not a racecar driver," JJ said dryly, and Ruby grinned at his sister.

She got behind the wheel of her car and glanced over to her brother. "You sure you're up for this?" she asked, concern coloring her voice.

Tate nodded firmly. "I'll be fine."

The drive to church was quiet, with Tate closing his eyes before they'd even driven off the ranch. He made soft, almost indistinguishable noises when she hit a bump, and he kept his grip on the overhead handle tight, tight, tight.

JJ kept his promise and didn't leave her in the dust, and Ruby finally pulled into the church parking lot just down the street from the cute mechanic shop she'd passed when she'd moved here. The white-washed building charmed her at first sight, the tall steeple reaching toward the sky, the flower beds bursting with color along the walkway, and everyone headed toward the building in their Sunday best.

JJ came around to help Tate out of the car, and Ruby couldn't help but admire the gentle way he supported her brother. She fell into step beside them as they made their way into the church, making sure to keep Tate between her and JJ.

His sisters flocked to her side, and Ruby grinned over to Clara Jean as the young woman laced her arm through Ruby's. She said nothing, but such a simple gesture sure made Ruby feel like she belonged in this group of people.

Inside, the pews had already started to fill, and she simply followed JJ's sisters onto the pew he found for them. To her surprise, he sat next to her and left the end for Tate.

"If you need to get up, tell me," JJ said. "I can take you home anytime."

"I'm fine, JJ," Tate growled out of the side of his mouth, and Ruby hid her smile. She turned her attention to the Walker girls, who twittered and giggled over something on Clara Jean's phone.

"If there's too much noise back here," a man said, and all four of them looked to JJ's daddy. He wore a stern expression. "You know what? Give me your phones." He held out his hand as his daughters started to protest. "Then come sit with me and Momma."

His wife waited one row down, a very serious look in her dark eyes.

"We'll be so quiet," Hattie, the youngest, said. She tucked her phone under her leg.

Jeremiah Walker surveyed his daughters, gave Ruby a withering look, then swept his gaze past JJ and Tate too. "If I hear *anything* I don't like, I'm coming back here to get you. Think how embarrassing that will be."

"Yes, Daddy," Clara Jean said.

"We'll be quiet," Hattie promised again. The middle daughter, Emily, simply nodded somberly.

"JJ," Jeremiah said.

"They'll be quiet," he said, glaring down the row of his sisters. When his gaze came back to Ruby, his eyes softened slightly. But he looked away quickly, and his parents moved down a few rows and sat with his aunt and uncle.

They didn't have any kids with them either, and Ruby leaned over to Clara Jean when she could've just as easily done the same to JJ. "Who are they sitting with?"

"That's my uncle Rhett and aunt Evelyn," Clara Jean

whispered. "Oh, and there's Aunt Simone and Uncle Micah. Simone and Evvy are sisters."

The new couple had two teens with them too—a boy and a girl—and they looked back to where Ruby sat with JJ's sisters. The girl leaned over to her mother, and then Simone looked behind her. She nodded, and the two teens came to sit with them, sliding in down by Hattie on the other end of the row.

"That's my cousin Jensen," Clara Jean explained. "And Laurel." She waved with just her fingers, keeping her hand below the pew, to her cousins.

The service began, and Ruby let herself get swept up in the warmth of the pastor. The hymns reminded her of Sunday mornings back home in Lubbock, and she snuck a glance at JJ during the first one, just to see if he sang.

He did, his eyebrows going up as he met her eye. She smiled and shook her head, then focused on the hymnal in front of her again.

Everyone sat as the pastor stepped up to deliver his sermon, and she couldn't be completely sure, but it definitely seemed like JJ sat a little closer to her now.

"Today, I've been wrestling with the Lord about our topic," the pastor said. Ruby didn't know his name, and it didn't matter. He had a loud, calm voice, and he looked out to the sea of people in front of him with confidence. "So much so, that I called my sister and told her she'd need to speak this week."

Ruby watched as a pretty woman climbed the steps to the stage and crossed toward him. Something electric moved through the congregation as she arrived at his side, and she leaned into the mic. "So I prepared a sermon too," she said.

"And it turned out." Her brother looked at her.

"Who are they?" Ruby whispered to Clara Jean.

"Patrick Knowlton," Clara Jean whispered back. "And his sister, Willa."

"We prepared messages on the same topic," Willa said with a laugh. She sobered quickly, though, and Patrick moved to the side. "The topic today isn't a light one. We shouldn't laugh about it, but it is a message of hope, love, and peace."

"And getting to know God the Father and His Son, Jesus Christ," Patrick added. Surely they'd practiced this to get the timing and delivery just right. But Willa watched Patrick, and when he didn't say anything more, she edged in front of the mic again.

"Pain," she said. "Is not something we seek out. No one wants to be hurt, not emotionally, physically, mentally, or otherwise. In fact, our bodies and minds are wired to warn us of pain and keep us away from it."

Patrick moved forward. "But I have felt more and more these past few weeks, that it is through our pain that we draw closer to the Lord. It is in our moments of mighty struggle that we truly come to know Jesus Christ and understand the depth of His sacrifice for us."

Ruby nodded along with Willa, finding beauty and truth in their words. She thought about Tate's accident, about her own disappointment with losing her internship.

Perhaps she could—and should—find a greater purpose to it all.

"When we suffer," Patrick continued. "We gain a deeper appreciation for all that Christ endured for our sake. Our pain becomes a pathway to gratitude, a means of connecting with our Savior in a profound and personal way."

"We get to know Him," Willa said. "In a way we can't otherwise."

Ruby had never thought about pain and suffering in that way before. She glanced over to Tate, hoping to see a similar reaction, but was startled to see his jaw clenched tight, his eyes stormy.

Before she could say anything, Tate stood up, struggling and wincing as he did so. Without a word, he glared toward the pastors at the front, turned, and started to limp out.

"Tate," Ruby whispered at his retreating back. "What are you doing?"

Ruby started to rise, ready to follow him, but a hand on her arm stopped her.

"I'll go," Clara Jean said softly. "You stay here."

Ruby hesitated, torn between her duty to her brother and her desire to respect his obvious need for space. Finally, she nodded, sinking back into her seat as Clara Jean slipped out after Tate.

She looked at JJ, who hadn't spoken nor moved. He too wore concern in his eyes, but he shook his head. "Clara Jean's good at talking to people when they're upset."

Ruby's nerves screamed at her, but then JJ slipped his

fingers between hers, tugging her hand down onto the bench between them so no one could see.

He looked straight forward, as if nothing was happening, and Ruby did the same. After a minute or two, she finally allowed herself to draw comfort from his steady presence and the warmth of his skin against hers.

Oh, how she loved holding his hand.

She marveled at how natural it felt to be at JJ's side like this. She found herself imagining a future where this was their normal—Sunday mornings at church, sitting with friends and family, his hand warm in hers.

The sermon ended, and they stood to sing. Ruby glanced toward the back of the chapel, but she didn't see Tate or Clara Jean.

JJ checked his phone and tilted it toward her. His sister had said, *I'm taking Tate back to the ranch in your truck. I hope y'all fit in Ruby's car.* He leaned toward her, and with the hymn already going, she had to get really close to him so he could speak and she could hear it.

The scent of his skin, his shampoo, that cologne, nearly sent her back to the pew with how weak her knees got. "I'll send my sisters with my parents," he whispered right in her ear, his lips practically grazing her earlobe.

She straightened and nodded, every fiber of her being now vibrating for a different reason.

The sermon ended, and chaos ensued. JJ did send his sisters and cousins back to his parents and aunt and uncle. He then stepped out into the aisle, creating a gap for Ruby that she filled. He kept his hand on her hip as she left the chapel and then the building.

The crowd opened up then, and JJ removed his touch. She led the way to her car, and she felt strange to get behind the wheel while he took the passenger seat.

The bright Texas sunshine now heated the day, and Ruby didn't hesitate to get the car started and the air blowing. "Do you think they really went back to the ranch?" she asked, unable to keep the worry from her voice. "Tate needed to get out of there."

JJ squeezed her hand reassuringly. "Knowing Clara Jean, she probably took him for a drive. Sometimes it's easier to talk when you're not face to face, you know?"

Ruby nodded, trying to take comfort in his words. "I just... I don't understand why he got so upset. The sermon was beautiful."

JJ sat quietly for a moment, his thumb tracing gentle circles on the back of her hand and sending chills through her bloodstream. "It was an interesting sermon. I've never heard anything like that before."

They waited in her car, hand in hand, watching as the other churchgoers filtered to their cars and tried to get out of the lot. Ruby found herself leaning slightly into JJ's solid presence, drawing strength from him.

"We can probably go now," JJ said after several minutes. He turned to face her, his eyes soft with an emotion Ruby didn't dare name. For a moment, she thought he might kiss her, right there in her car, in the church parking lot. Instead, he brought their joined hands up to his lips, pressing a sweet kiss to her knuckles.

"All right, Scarlet? Let's go see where he ended up."

Chapter Eleven

Tate Reynolds stormed out of the church, his ribs protesting with every angry step. The pastor's words echoed in his head, fueling a fire of frustration and disbelief that threatened to consume him.

Pain brings us closer to the Lord? What a load of—

"Tate, wait up!"

He recognized Clara Jean's voice but didn't slow his pace. He couldn't face her right now, couldn't bear to see the concern in her eyes. She'd been nothing but kind to him since the accident, and he didn't want to snap at her. Plus, he didn't want her to see him like this—angry over a sermon. He'd already been humiliated and embarrassed about his current condition, and while he couldn't believe he'd caught feelings for JJ's younger sister, he had.

Oh, how he had.

But Clara Jean didn't give up easily. She caught up to

him at the edge of the sidewalk, slightly out of breath, a big field of grass in front of them. "Where do you think you're going?"

Tate stopped, more out of necessity than choice. His ribs were on fire, and he already regretted his hasty exit. Plus, uneven surfaces made walking even more difficult and painful.

"I don't know," he admitted through gritted teeth. "Away from here."

Clara Jean studied him for a moment, her expression unreadable. Then she nodded, as if coming to a decision. "Come on," she said, fishing her car keys out of her bag. "Let's go for a drive."

Not a purse. He'd never seen Clara Jean with a purse. This bag had been dyed bright blue, purple, orange, and white, and it had fringe hanging from the bottom of it. It totally fit Clara Jean's retro, almost granola, vibe, and Tate was semi-surprised he knew that much about her.

Of course, he'd listened to JJ talk about Clara Jean a lot. He'd met her loads of times over the past few summers, and heck, he'd had his crush on her last year. So he reminded himself she wasn't a stranger to him, and he could get in a car with her.

Still, another part of Tate wanted to refuse, to tell her to leave him alone. But a larger part, the part that ached for company even as he pushed people away, made him nod and follow her to JJ's truck.

As they pulled out of the parking lot, Tate stared out the window, watching the familiar buildings of Three Rivers blur past. Clara Jean didn't speak, didn't push him to explain his retreat from the chapel. The silence should have been uncomfortable, but instead, Tate found it oddly soothing.

They drove for about fifteen minutes before Clara Jean turned onto a dirt road that Tate didn't recognize. A few minutes later, she pulled to a stop at the edge of a small lake. The water sat very still, reflecting the clear blue sky and surrounding trees like a mirror.

"Where are we?" Tate asked.

"My secret spot," Clara Jean replied with a small smile. "I come here when I need to think, or pray, or just...be."

She got out of the truck, and after a moment's hesitation, Tate followed. He appreciated that she didn't come around and baby him, hold his arm to steady him, or even ask him if he needed help. She simply waited at the front corner of the hood, gazing at the lake, until he joined her.

The air entered his lungs easier here, and Clara Jean glanced over to him, then took his hand in hers. She said nothing with her voice, but her eyes screamed questions at him.

Is this okay?

Can I hold your hand?

Do you even want to hold mine?

Tate squeezed her fingers, hopefully answering everything she needed answering.

Oh, JJ was going to kill him. Kill him dead, right where he stood.

Tate swallowed as Clara Jean stepped down the path

that led to the water's edge. There were no benches here, but people had set up stumps to sit on, and Clara Jean moved along the side of the lake to a fallen tree that felt about a chair level.

"Can you sit on that?" she asked.

"I have no idea." Tate hated that he wasn't whole. Hated it with his whole soul.

Clara Jean sat first, and Tate lowered himself gingerly onto the log beside her, wincing as his ribs protested. He breathed out, as he held his breath to do anything he thought might hurt. And everything he did hurt.

Dragonflies danced over the surface of the water, and Tate further felt the ire drain from him.

"You didn't like the sermon," Clara Jean said, no question mark in sight.

"I did not." He looked at her then, really looked at her. Her brown eyes shone with concern, no judgment in her expression at all. Just patience and understanding. Something in Tate's chest tightened, and it had nothing to do with his broken ribs.

"I just...." he began, struggling to find the words. "I couldn't sit there and listen to that pastor talk about how pain brings us closer to God. How it's supposed to make us more grateful." He clenched his fists, feeling the anger rise again. "It's so stupid. Pain is just God's way of reminding you that you're human."

"It's okay to be angry, Tate," Clara Jean said. "God can handle your anger."

Tate scoffed. "Yeah? Well, maybe I can't handle His

silence. Where was He when that bull charged at me? Where is He now, when I can barely get out of bed without feeling like I'm being stabbed?"

The words poured out of him, all the frustration and pain of the past week spilling over. "I'm supposed to be working, saving up for my own ranch. Instead, I'm stuck relying on charity from JJ and my little sister. How is any of this bringing me closer to God?"

He wanted to throw something, and plenty of rocks sat at his feet. He could see moms and dads bringing their kids here and teaching them how to skip the stones over the surface of the lake. Tate just wanted to grab as many as he could and launch them straight into the water while he bellowed out his frustration.

But to get a rock, he'd have to bend over. And bending over was something Tate couldn't do.

"He could heal me," he said miserably instead. "But He won't."

God could've saved him. But He hadn't.

And why? So Tate could live in perpetual pain while ten of his ribs healed?

Clara Jean sat quietly, her gaze fixed on the lake. When she spoke, her voice carried thoughtfulness. "You know, we all fasted and prayed for my Gramps that he'd get better. But he didn't. He died the next day."

Tate blinked, caught off guard by the sudden change in topic. "I...I'm sorry."

She nodded, a sad smile on her face. "For a long time, I was so angry at God. I couldn't understand why He'd let it happen when we did everything right. I prayed and prayed for answers, but all I got was silence."

"What changed?" Tate asked, finding himself drawn into her story despite his own turmoil.

"Time, mostly," Clara Jean admitted. "And a lot of conversations with my momma or daddy or Grams. But mostly, I think I just...chose to believe. To have faith that God is in charge, even when it doesn't make sense. Even when we're in pain and He could save us from it."

She turned to face him, her eyes intense. "The pastor wasn't saying that God *causes* our pain, Tate. He was saying that God can *use* our pain, if we let Him."

Tate shook his head, frustration bubbling up again. "But why? Why does there have to be pain at all? If God is all-powerful, why can't He just...fix things?"

Clara Jean scooted closer, turning her shoulder into him slightly. She hesitated, and then leaned into his chest gently. With some difficulty—and yes, an arc of pain that ran down the back side of his ribs, he lifted his arm and put it around her. Holding her.

The touch sent a jolt of fire through Tate, momentarily distracting him from his anger. Because this wasn't painful fire. This was the flame of attraction.

"I don't have all the answers," she said softly. "I don't think anyone does. But I do know that the pain we have to go through can make us bitter, or it can make us stronger. The choice is ours."

Tate looked down at her, feeling a mix of comfort and

guilt. He shouldn't be enjoying her touch this much, shouldn't be feeling this flutter in his chest.

"I don't know how to choose strength right now," he admitted, his voice barely above a whisper. "I feel...lost. I'm useless, and that makes me angry."

Clara Jean squeezed his hand. "I'm sure you feel that way. Doesn't mean it's true."

Tate nodded, not trusting himself to speak.

"And I think what Pastor Knowlton and Pastor Glover were trying to say is that when we're in these valleys of pain and fear and darkness, we can turn to the Savior for relief. For light. And when we do, we'll come to know Him in a way we wouldn't be able to otherwise."

"Yeah," Tate said, his mind opening a little more now that he wasn't so irritated. "Like I'm getting to know you in a different way because you brought me to this lake."

"Sure, like that."

They sat in silence for a while, the gentle lapping of the lake against the shore the only sound. Tate found himself acutely aware of Clara Jean's presence in his arms, of the warmth and shape of her in his life. And he liked it. He really liked *her*.

"Can I ask you something?" he finally asked, breaking the silence.

"Of course."

"How do you do it? Keep your faith, I mean. Even when things are hard."

Clara Jean considered him for a moment, something so bright in her dark eyes. So alive. "I guess I'd say I try to look for God in the little things. In the kindness of friends, in my big, loud family who I love, in the beauty of a place like this." She gestured to the lake before them. "In the strength I find when I think I can't go on."

She turned to him, a small smile on her face. "And sometimes, I see Him in people like you, Tate."

"Me?" Tate asked, surprised. He uttered a dark chuckle. "I'm not exactly a shining example of faith right now."

"Maybe not," Clara Jean said. "But you're honest. You're not pretending everything's fine when it's not. That takes courage."

Tate shook his head and looked away from her pretty eyes. "I don't feel very courageous."

"Courage isn't about not being afraid," Clara Jean said. "It's about facing your fears, your doubts, your pain, and choosing to keep going anyway."

Tate nodded slowly, letting her words sink in. For the first time since the accident, he felt a glimmer of something that might have been hope. "Thank you," he said softly. "For coming after me. For listening."

Clara Jean smiled, and Tate's heartbeat rippled at him like someone had skipped a stone over it. "Anytime, Tate. That's what friends are for, right?"

Friends.

Right. Tate pushed down the pang of disappointment at the word. He had no right to hope for anything more, especially not with JJ's sister. He straightened so she would too, and when she did, her eyes widened.

"I mean, we're not friends."

"We're not?" he asked.

Clara Jean wore panic in her expression now. "I mean, we are. But we're—we're—uh, more than that too, right?"

Tate's heart raced. He opened his mouth to respond, but no words came out.

Clara Jean rushed on with, "I mean, I want to be. You seemed—maybe you were just being nice." She got to her feet, which jostled the log and had Tate scrambling to catch his balance.

"I know it's complicated," she said, pacing away from him. "You're JJ's best friend, and I'm his sister, and you're still healing. If you don't feel the same way, or if you're not ready, I completely understand."

Tate's mind whirled. Not ready? What would he need to be ready for?

Talking to JJ, his mind shouted at him.

"Clara Jean, I..." he began, then stopped, unsure how to continue.

She sat back down and squeezed his hand gently. "It's okay. I get it."

Tate didn't, but he didn't want to admit that. He already felt like a complete doofus with her, questioning how she kept her faith and not being able to do much more than sit— and even that took a lot of effort.

He looked at her, saw the mix of hope and vulnerability in her eyes, and he knew he couldn't leave things unsaid. "I'd love to go out with you," he admitted quietly. "But I'll have to run a few things by JJ first."

Clara Jean's eyes widened slightly. "He's not as overprotective as you might think."

Tate shook his head. "I know exactly how JJ is." He sighed out another round of frustration, this time aimed at himself. "I've brought this on myself. I told him Ruby was off-limits." He smiled ruefully. "He made some joke about how all of his sisters were too."

She tilted her head, studying him. "Why would Ruby be off-limits to JJ?"

"I don't know. She was dating this guy at the time, and all she did was talk about him. I joked about what it would be like if that guy was JJ, and I had to listen to Ruby go on and on about him. We laughed." He smiled now. "I said I never wanted him to date her, because it would be weird."

Even now, he thought that. His vision blurred as he simply stared at the horizon past the shiny lake. "It's like... she's my sister, and he feels like my brother."

"So do I feel like your sister then?"

"What?" Tate blinked away from the reflection in his eyes. "No, of course not."

"I can talk to JJ," Clara Jean said. "He doesn't scare me."

Tate grinned at her, suddenly feeling flirtatious and fun again—like his old self. "He's been away at college for too long then," he teased. "Because he's terrifying if you do something he doesn't like."

She scoffed and waved her free hand. "Please. I've seen him cry over a splinter."

Tate tipped his head back and laughed, and laughed, and laughed. And dang, that felt so good.

At the same time, it sure did hurt, and he cut the sound off. "Don't make me do that," he told her. "It hurts."

"Yeah, it hurts so good." She grinned at him, and Tate realized he'd have to face whatever came his way. Right now. Tomorrow. In the future.

And with JJ.

He leaned forward, glad when Clara Jean made the decision that much easier by meeting him halfway. He slid one hand up the side of her neck to cradle her face, and he touched his mouth to hers.

Oh, you're in so much trouble, ran through his mind.

And he was. Because kissing Clara Jean made him start to fall, and he realized the only way he didn't crash and burn here was if JJ gave him a parachute.

He broke the kiss before it went too terribly far, and he ducked his head. He didn't apologize, because he wasn't sorry. The way Clara Jean didn't retreat, but breathed in with her cheek still against his told him she'd liked the kiss, so he didn't have to ask.

"We should get back to the ranch," he whispered.

"Yeah." Clara Jean stood first, and this time she did offer Tate her hand. He took it, and they made their way back to the truck slowly.

She drove gingerly back to the ranch, back to the cabins, where Ruby's car had been parked out front. Clara Jean pulled in next to it and picked up her phone. "Oh, shoot. My momma's called three times." She threw Tate a panicked look and added, "I'll come by and see you later, okay?"

"Yeah, okay, go."

She flew from the truck, and Tate watched her run across the pastures and lawns separating Cabin Row from the homestead. A mix of emotions swirled within him. Hope, fear, excitement, guilt. He knew he had a lot to sort out – with God, with JJ, with Clara Jean. But for the first time since he'd woken up in the hospital, he felt like maybe, just maybe, things might turn out okay.

Taking a deep breath and holding it, Tate got out of the truck and turned toward his cabin. In that moment, Ruby opened the front door, and she and JJ spilled out onto the porch, clearly waiting for him. Clearly worried about him.

"Hey," he said, trying to sound casual. "Sorry about earlier."

Ruby flew down the steps and wrapped him in a gentle hug. "It's okay. Are you all right?"

Tate nodded, his eyes meeting JJ's over Ruby's shoulder. His best friend's expression was unreadable, and a pang of guilt gonged through Tate. He needed to talk to JJ, to explain about Clara Jean, to clear the air. But not now, not with Ruby here.

"Yeah, I'm okay," he said, pulling back from Ruby's embrace. "Just had some things to work through."

JJ nodded slowly as Tate climbed the steps. "Clara Jean help you sort things out?"

Something in JJ's tone set off a warning buzzer inside Tate's mind, but he couldn't identify why. Did he suspect something? Tate swallowed hard, feeling like he stood on the edge of a precipice.

Then he said, "Yeah, she's a very good listener."

JJ grinned at him and gestured him into the cabin. "That she is, brother. Now, I'm glad you walked out, because it allowed me to simply get these ribs from my parents and bring them over here. Now we don't have to eat with the entire family."

"They're *your* family, bro," Tate said as Ruby closed the door, sealing the three of them in the cowboy cabin together.

"Yes, and I'm tired." JJ speared Tate with a look. "So come eat, and then it's naptime for everyone."

"No argument from me," Tate said, glancing over to Ruby. She watched JJ, and Tate's gaze flew back to him too.

Oh, boy. Had they been talking about him?

Of course they have, he told himself. But something else nagged at him, especially when he looked back at his sister and she still only had eyes for JJ. She finally looked at him, and he raised his eyebrows.

Ruby smiled and said, "I'm going to take my nap outside, in one of the hay fields like we used to do as kids."

Tate chuckled and said, "It's hot today, Rubes."

"We're Texan," she said back. "I can handle the heat."

"Your funeral." Tate took the plate of food JJ had made for him and shuffled over to the table. While he usually liked a crowd, he could admit that a quiet lunch with just his sister and his best friend sure was nice too.

And it would be even better if Clara Jean were here.

Suddenly, Tate couldn't wait to be alone with JJ so they could talk.

Chapter Twelve

JJ leaned against the stable door, watching the sun climb over the horizon. The ranch was quiet, save for the occasional nickering of horses and the rustle of hay as they moved in their stalls. He'd been up since before dawn, unable to sleep, his mind a whirlwind of thoughts and emotions he couldn't seem to quiet.

He'd made coffee, whispered with Ruby, swept her hair off her face, the quality of it between his fingers like magic still in this moment. He'd brought more caffeine out to the ranch with him in the form of an energy drink, because he had a long day ahead of him.

"A long, good day, Lord," JJ said to the wispy clouds in the sky. "Bless me to have quick hands this morning and to be on time for my appointment later today, and then bless me to get everyone's opinion at the luncheon today."

He couldn't wait to sit down with the men who ran

ranches around Three Rivers, and he'd asked Conrad to come with him to all the appointments today, mostly because his cousin could keep JJ on schedule.

Plus, he was a good friend and a good sounding board. He'd bought their grandfather's farm, and JJ had no experience buying anything more than gas and groceries.

"If that farm could be good for me," JJ said, continuing his out-loud prayer. "Will You please let me know? And remember, I'm not that great at feeling things. You've got to *tell* me—and the louder the better."

"Heya, JJ."

He turned to find Uncle Skyler walking toward him. He lived in the other homestead here on the ranch, and he'd bought into the operation here almost as equally as Daddy. He and his wife, Mal, had raised their three kids here, and both of their sons still lived at home and worked the ranch.

JJ would eventually run it with Sawyer and Gideon, and he grinned at his uncle and clapped him in a hug. "You're up early," he said.

"I heard you were takin' off this morning," Skyler said. "I wanted to talk to you, and I wasn't sure I'd see you if I didn't get out here early enough."

"Here I am," JJ said, his pulse vibrating in his chest. "What did you want to talk about?"

"The Adair property."

Walls flew into place around JJ's heart and mind. "I'm sure you've talked to my father about it."

"Of course."

"I know it's a bit above market value."

"It is."

JJ finally turned toward his uncle again. "Then what do you want to talk about?"

Skyler studied the sky for a few more beats of time, and then he said, "The Dewey property."

"Dewey?" JJ frowned, the name not coming forward in his head. "I don't know where that is."

"It's across the west highway," Skyler said.

"The only thing for sale down here is the Adair's farm," JJ said.

"But the Dewey's are getting older," Skyler said. "And I think it would be...neat to have Seven Sons run east to west across that highway."

"Your boys could live out there."

Skyler nodded, his earlier joviality gone. "Your dad thinks I'm crazy."

"Daddy doesn't like buying jeans if they're not fifty percent off," JJ said dryly.

Uncle Skyler burst out laughing then. "He so doesn't."

"Well, it's not his money, and I'm not in control of my trust yet, but Daddy just has to co-sign."

"Will he?"

"We're going to look at it today." JJ swallowed, because he'd really been trying to listen to God, and buying the land next door had always felt right. He wouldn't have to go through months of construction, and he wouldn't have to live here on his childhood ranch while he took over.

"He's having all of us for lunch at my house afterward."

"Of course he is," JJ said, though he hadn't known that.

He supposed he was talking to his friends-who-felt-like-family about the land purchase too.

"We all love Seven Sons."

"I do too," JJ said, not sure if Uncle Skyler was implying anything different.

"The Glovers bought up all the land around them," Skyler said. "It's a good strategy, and if we wait until market value on that land, we might-could lose it." He shrugged one shoulder. "And honestly, JJ, I think you're the only one who could get your daddy to buy that land."

He thought about the conversation he'd had with his father a couple of weeks ago, the very first weekend he'd returned to town. Daddy really didn't like spending more than necessary on anything, which was one of the reasons he had so much money.

"He wants you to be happy here," Skyler said.

"I am happy here," JJ said. "I came back, didn't I?" Irritation and frustration combined within him. "I don't understand why anyone thinks I wouldn't do what would make me happy." He pushed away from the doorway and finished his energy drink. "Are you going out to the orchards with me to check on the apples?"

"All boys go through a bit of a transition when they become men and decide to step into their father's boots," Uncle Skyler said. "Both of mine have, and I think your daddy is just now experiencing it with you."

He fell into step with JJ as he moved away from the stables and toward one of their equipment sheds. This one held ATVs, and they could ride out to the orchards on the north side of the ranch.

"Are you workin' with that new stallion when you get back?" Skyler asked. "Later this afternoon."

JJ grinned at him. "Yeah, you wanna come out and watch?" He nodded to one of the ATVs and went past it to another one.

"Of course I do," Skyler said. He straddled the ATV and started it, the roar of the engine filling the shed. He backed out while JJ climbed on, and then he followed his uncle. He'd just cleared the shed when he caught sight of Ruby, and he let off the gas and came to a stop.

She wore a pair of blue jeans and the sexiest cowgirl boots he'd ever seen. She wore a pale orange tank top with white butterflies on it, and JJ had lost the ability to breathe completely.

"Hey," she said as she reached up to tighten her ponytail. All that dark hair with the reddish tint gleamed in the sunlight, and JJ wanted to feel it between his fingers again as he kissed her mouth. Those pink shiny lips. Maybe even as he slid his lips down that slender column of her neck.

He'd had a few girlfriends in his life, and he knew exactly what he wanted to do with Ruby.

"You coming?" Uncle Skyler called as he circled back on the ATV, and JJ blinked at him.

"Yeah." He looked at Ruby again. "We're going out to check the orchards. Did you want to come?"

"Can I?"

He nodded over his shoulder. "Climb on, Scarlet."

She did a hop, skip, and partial run as she neared, and then she launched herself onto the seat behind him. This wasn't a four-wheeler built for two, and Ruby snuggled in close and wrapped her arms around JJ. He did his best to tame his smile, but one look at his uncle told him he hadn't done a good enough job.

He went by him, and Uncle Skyler moved out to the side of him, both of them knowing how to get to the orchards quite easily.

Ruby whooped and released her hold on him, laughing as he drove them northward on the dirt road. "This is great," she called above the noise and wind.

"Don't you have ATVs at your place in Lubbock?" he asked.

"Yeah, but we never got to ride them for fun."

This wasn't for fun either, but JJ did enjoy himself immensely as he drove out to the orchards. He parked first and waited for Ruby to get off the back, then he followed her.

"What are we doing here?" She gazed up at the trees. "I didn't know you had orchards."

"There's so much you don't know," he said as Uncle Skyler pulled in.

"So a ranch tour seems fitting," Ruby said, giving him a flirtatious smile. She toned it down as his uncle arrived. "What are you guys doing out here?"

"Checking the crop," Skyler said. "Then the fences. JJ will note any slash we need to get cleaned up, and then someone will come do it."

"You?" Ruby asked JJ. "And what's slash?"

"It's debris left behind after a harvest," JJ said. "Sometimes just whatever falls out of trees. Old pine needles or whatever. All of it creates a huge fire hazard, so we like to keep the orchards clear."

"We've had fires here before," Skyler added, which was true. He exhaled heavily. "So, let's see what we've got."

JJ grabbed the clipboard from the back of the ATV, so he could make notes, and he nodded for Ruby to go ahead of him and after his uncle. "And I might come do it," he said. "Whoever gets assigned will come clean up whatever needs to be cleaned up."

"If you come, can I come with you?" She took a deep breath of the morning air. "It smells good out here."

JJ grinned at her and let his fingers brush hers. "Let's come have dinner out here one night."

"You tell me when, cowboy, and I'm yours."

"Any questions you have, you let me know," Jerry Bozeman said. He stood in front of the farmhouse on the Adair property, and JJ gazed at it alongside his father and his cousin. "The house is original to the farm," Jerry said. "Built in 1906, but updated with central heat and air. It's had two additions built on, one of the left there, and one out the back. It was fully redone about seven years ago, with fresh paint, carpet, flooring, and fixtures."

JJ had seen the pictures, and while not every piece of the

ranch shone like the North Star, he could move in tomorrow and be comfortable.

"Porch is nice," Daddy said.

"The landscaping is exquisite," Conrad said. "Grams would love these flowerbeds, the shrubs, the big trees." He grinned at JJ, ignoring Daddy's tension. He moved forward first, and JJ knew it had been a good idea to bring Conrad.

"Come on," his cousin said. "We don't have much time, and this place has three barns and three stables we've got to walk through."

"Besides the house," JJ muttered as he followed his cousin. The front porch of the house spanned the whole width of it, and it faced east—perfect for sunrises. Such a thought warmed JJ's soul, and he felt something very loud and very right inside his heart.

It was God, telling him in no uncertain terms and with the loudest voice JJ had ever heard, that he was walking into the place where he belonged.

He didn't dare to hope that perhaps he could find a way for Ruby to join him here. They were still very new—so new JJ had not taken her on a proper date nor kissed her the way he would a girlfriend. He had no idea if he'd lose Tate as a friend if he ever confessed his feelings for Ruby.

Everything in that part of his life had been put in a blender and liquified, but as JJ walked through the foyer with its two-story-tall ceilings and plenty of natural light into a living room he could certainly be comfortable in, this one thing was certain.

Thank You, God, JJ thought as he took in the dark hardwood floors and the bright white quartz countertops in the kitchen. *Thank You for talking loud enough for me to hear.*

He still wanted and valued his father's opinion, but Daddy would keep it to himself until they finished the tour, until he'd talked it all out with his brothers and Momma, until JJ could get back to the ranch that night and meet with him.

He also couldn't wait to tell his friends and soon-to-be fellow ranch owners about this place, and JJ pulled out his camera and started taking pictures.

After all, he'd want to show them to Ruby at some point too.

"Wow, look at this back deck," Conrad said, and JJ jerked his attention in that direction. It faced west, and all he could think was, *What a perfect place to sit and watch the sunset.*

With that thought in his head, and God's words still ringing in his ears, JJ made a promise to himself to talk to Tate about his interest in Ruby soon.

Very soon.

Chapter Thirteen

Finn Ackerman surveyed the sprawling backyard, watching Edith reach over their son's head to open the door of her she-shed. Bubba then waddled inside, nothing cuter than the walk of a two-year-old. He smiled, then turned back to the farmhouse where he'd lived with his wife for the past several years.

Soon, Edith would bring their third child into the world, and Finn had been praying with every ounce of his being that the baby would be a girl. Edith wanted one to go with their pair of boys, and if she got her wish this time, perhaps she wouldn't want another baby.

Finn loved his children to bits and pieces, but they were already outnumbered in wits and whining by their six-year-old and their two-year-old. With the addition of the baby, they'd be outnumbered physically too.

Inside, he grabbed the lighter for the grill and stepped

back out onto the deck. They'd screened it as one of their major home improvement projects, and four fans moved the air around in the fall, winter, and spring.

This late in May could definitely be considered summer, but Finn still wanted to use the outdoor space for today's luncheon. Their numbers had grown, and the larger area and bigger table simply worked better than trying to corral everyone inside.

He lit the grill and tossed down the lighter before returning to the house to get the protein, paper plates, plastic utensils, and potato salad. Trip by trip, he got everything outside where they'd eat, and he'd no sooner done that when someone knocked on the front door.

"Just me, brother," Alex called as he entered.

"Outside," Finn said, already heading that way and expecting his brother-in-law to follow. Alex did, and Finn added, "Text everyone to come around back, would you?"

"Yep." Alex pulled out his phone to do just that, and Finn put the burgers on the grill. They hissed and sizzled right away, and he quickly closed the lid to maintain the heat.

"Let's get things set out," he said, moving the burger toppings to the folding table, where he and Edith usually served from when they entertained.

"Drinks," Link called as he came around the corner of the farmhouse-slash-cabin. Dawson Rhinehart came with him, and he carried a huge bag of popcorn. Those could only be bought at the movie theater, and Finn grinned at his friends as they came up the steps and onto the deck.

"It's not game night," Finn said, moving over to Dawson and giving him a one-armed hug. "You didn't need to bring anything."

"You said a side dish," he said. "Popcorn is a whole grain." Dawson chuckled as he pulled back, and Finn appreciated him and Link for coming to these luncheons when their drive took a significant chunk of their day.

Finn knew, because when Link hosted, he had to make the same drive. And Dawson lived further south than Link. Both Shiloh Ridge and the Rhinehart Ranch sat as far south of Three Rivers as Legacy—Finn's place—did north of it.

But these meetings meant something to all of them, and it wasn't about the food.

"How's Caroline faring in the heat?" Finn asked.

"About as well as Edith, I suppose," Dawson drawled. Both women were pregnant, with Edith due in September and Caroline due with her and Dawson's second child in December. He'd just made the announcement at last month's luncheon, and it was still too early for them to know the gender of the baby.

They had one little boy, Colt, who'd be three years old in a couple of months, and Finn loved it when someone hosted family night and he got to see his cowboy friends with their wives and children. The luncheons were just for ranch owners. Their game nights were for couples, and everyone found a sitter for their kids.

And a couple of times each year, someone—usually Misty or Nikki—organized a family night, where everyone got together to eat, chat, play, and spend time together.

Nikki, Alex's wife, loved planning parties, and she'd designed and asked Alex to build a "play barn" at their ranch. He'd done it too, and it provided a good space for children and adults alike.

Link and Misty, of course, had amazing family facilities at Shiloh Ridge, and Finn never complained about going there. Their barn could be rented for weddings, and they had a great fire pit area with plenty of picnic seating too.

"Hey-o," Henry called, and he and Angel crossed the lawn hand-in-hand, with Paul right beside them. Finn loved his cousins, glad they'd both found the right place for them.

Angel didn't have their baby with her today, though she'd brought Wrangler for the past few months, since he'd been born.

"Who'd you get to take the baby?" he asked as they joined everyone on the deck and Paul set down the bags of potato chips he'd been carrying. He and Brielle had been married for a bit longer than Henry and Angel, but they didn't have any children yet.

"My momma." Henry grinned, pulled Finn into a hug, and added, "Doing burgers today?"

"I'd eat a hamburger for every meal if I could," Finn said, his own smile infusing him with joy. "And I bet your mom is loving her day now that she's got Wrangler."

"Your mom was there too," Henry said as they separated.

"My mom would move in with us if I'd let her," Finn said, not a drop of sarcasm anywhere.

Henry laughed, and Finn took a quick headcount. Then

he focused on the meat, quickly flipping each burger with practiced ease.

Libby hadn't arrived yet, and neither had the Seven Sons cowboys—JJ, Tate, and Conrad. As far as Finn knew, they were all coming.

"Morning glory," Link said, his focus on his phone. "My son is going to be the death of me."

Finn chuckled, because he'd definitely felt like that before. "What's he gotten into now?"

"Misty just sent me a picture of him laying down in the mud." Link looked up from his phone. "I get my childhood was a bit different, but I *never* would've done that."

"Which one?" Dawson asked, peering over Link's shoulder.

"I have more than one son who'd lay in the mud?" Link practically screeched.

He did have two sons—a rambunctious three-and-a-half-year-old named Dallas, and a five-month-old named Scout. Since the Glovers gave a lot of their children nicknames, everyone called Dallas Diesel, and Finn hated to admit that the name fit. The boy literally never stopped, except, apparently, to lay in the mud.

The burgers finished, and Finn pulled them from the grill and flipped off the flame just as JJ led the way around the house. He didn't move fast, and Conrad flanked him on one side while Tate walked on the other.

And he actually looked like he was walking now, not shuffling or limping.

"Hey, hey," Finn called. He quickly set down the

burgers on the table and covered them with aluminum foil. "Did you see Libby out there?"

"She just pulled up," Conrad called from under his enormous white hat. He was one of the only men who could pull off the look, in Finn's opinion, and he grinned as the younger men came onto the deck. He hugged them all, being extra careful with Tate.

"You're lookin' good, brother," Finn said, clapping him on the shoulder.

"I think I've turned a corner," Tate said. "Thanks for having me. I know I'm not really a ranch owner, but—"

"Yet," JJ said over him. "But you will be." He gave Tate a grin, and the two friends bumped fists.

"Sorry I'm late," Libby called as she hurried across the lawn toward them. She'd married a cowboy she'd met in Oklahoma just before she'd taken over the family ranch for their daddy, and Finn loved his half-sister with his whole soul.

He greeted her with a hug at the top of the steps too and held her tight. "Hey, you."

"Mm." Libby embraced him back and smiled as she pulled away. "Edith said I could have the boys tonight. Is that still happening?"

"If she said you can have the boys tonight, then you can have the boys tonight."

Libby grinned from ear to ear. "Rusty and I will ride over and get them after dinner." She clapped her hands together. "I'm so excited."

"Do I get a clue as to what you guys are planning for my birthday?" Finn asked.

"Absolutely not." Libby gave him a scandalized look and then stepped over to Angel and Alex, who were talking about the fields they'd just finished planting.

Finn had set planting and agriculture as their topic for today's luncheon, and they'd spend plenty of time talking about it while they ate. They also always found a few minutes for personal news, though Finn wasn't sure who would have any today.

He clapped his hands now and called, "Let's eat." He uncovered the burgers and went through the line first, filling his plate with potato salad, potato chips, and yes, even a little buttery popcorn. He took a seat at the big table which took up half of the deck, and listened as others talked while they got their food.

Once everyone had sat down, Finn finished his sour cream and cheddar potato chips and said, "Let's go around and do personal news."

No one jumped right in, and eyes flickered from one person to the next. He caught Tate elbow JJ, who glared back at his friend. "Might as well go," he said.

"He's right," Conrad said. "Maybe you'll be the only one."

"Fine." JJ Walker cleared his throat, his dark gaze darting around the table. "I'm going to buy the Adair farm. It's adjacent to Seven Sons, and it'll expand the ranch."

Silence settled over the table, and only when JJ finally let a smile crack his face did everyone respond. Some cheered, Link whistled, and Finn applauded along with Angel and Paul.

JJ's face turned red, and Tate nudged his best friend in a playful way. Conrad grinned and grinned too, and it sure was good for Finn's heart to see JJ making his own way in the world.

Not that there was any shame in taking over an operation from the previous generation. Heck, Libby had done it. Angel too. Link and Dawson and now JJ. But they each had their own way of doing things, and they each had so many lessons to learn that could only be done through their own personal experience.

"Anyone else?" Finn asked before he took another bite of his burger. He didn't have any news—everyone knew Edith was due in a few months and that they weren't learning the gender of the baby until it was born.

Link and Misty had just had a baby, and that seemed to be the majority of their news now that so many of them were married. Dawson and Caroline had announced last month, and Henry and Angel had a small baby still. Alex and Nikki had been very blessed to get the twins at all, so Finn didn't expect them to have any baby news.

That left Paul and Libby, and both of them shook their heads.

Of course, personal news didn't have to be babies, and Finn smiled at Conrad. "You seein' anyone?"

Conrad chuckled and shook his head. "I wish." He looked over to Tate and JJ, but neither of them volunteered anything more.

"We're a real boring bunch," Finn said, and that got a few laughs.

"Just livin' life," Henry said. "I mean, we're getting a puppy in October. Does that count?"

"Absolutely it does," Dawson said. "Have you ever had a puppy?"

"Of course I have," Henry shot back.

"Say goodbye to sleeping then," Link said good-naturedly.

"I already don't sleep through the night," Henry said, glancing at Angel. "That's why we decided to get a puppy."

"*You* decided, baby."

That sounded about right, and Finn grinned at his cousin. Henry did love dogs. Maybe not as much as horses, but Finn certainly couldn't judge him. He and Edith had three dogs and her meowing cat. Plus all the horses, chickens, goats, and sheep. So if Henry wanted a puppy, the man could have a puppy.

"Mitch is gonna move home this fall," Link said. "I think that's news, and I'd love him to come to our luncheons."

"That's great news," Finn said, his voice getting drowned out by the others saying similar things. Link grinned and nodded like he was the one doing amazing things. Mitch had earned a Bachelor's degree and then a Master's at a deaf college in Virginia.

Word at the cowboy luncheons was that he wanted to come back to Three Rivers and open a school for the deaf. Or a facility to help deaf people and their families. No matter what, he'd been working hard to achieve his dreams, and Finn always admired that.

A rush of gratitude flooded him, because he knew that sometimes hard work wasn't enough. Sometimes a man needed good timing. He needed to be in the right place at the right time. His daddy had taught him that if he did good and worked hard, he'd be met with the opportunities he needed.

And of course, he had to rely on God too.

"Tell us how you are, Tate," Finn said.

JJ swung his attention to him too, and they exchanged a glance. "I'm good," Tate said, his voice a bit tight and a bit too airy. "I can do a little bit around the farm now. Here and there."

"He feeds the chickens," JJ said, his grin huge. Finn smiled too, because Bubba's job on the farm was to feed the chickens.

"Hey, I get the honey from the hives for your aunt too," Tate said good-naturedly, and Finn did like the man. He prayed he could find the right piece of land for him when the time was right.

"So, how'd planting season treat everyone?" Finn asked, looking around the table as he moved the conversation to business.

"We had a bit of trouble with our irrigation system," Libby said, leading them out. "But we managed to get it sorted out just in time. I'm a little worried about how dry it's been, though. If we don't get some decent rain soon, we might be in for a rough summer."

Nods of agreement rippled around the table, with Dawson adding, "We've been looking into some drought-resistant crops, just in case. Caroline's been doing a ton of research on it."

"That's smart," Paul chimed in. "We've been thinking about doing something similar at Courage Reins. The therapy horses need good grazing, and if the pastures dry up, we'll be in a tight spot."

JJ leaned forward, his interest piqued. "What kind of crops are you looking at, Dawson? I've been thinking about diversifying a bit myself."

As Dawson launched into an explanation of various drought-resistant grains and grasses, Finn couldn't help but notice the way JJ seemed to be hanging on every word. An intensity rode in the younger man's eyes that hadn't been there before.

This sparked a lively discussion about various dry farming techniques and water conservation methods. Finn listened intently, making notes on his phone, because drought was a very real issue that could affect every farm and ranch in Three Rivers. Conversations like this made these gatherings so valuable—the sharing of knowledge and experience that could make all the difference when times got tough.

"Well, I've got to get back," Alex said, and Finn wasn't surprised at all to find the clock sitting right at one-thirty. They did try to keep this luncheon to ninety minutes, because they all had very busy lives.

"Yep," Link said, tossing down his paper towel. "Me

too." He stood and started to clear his place. Finn got up and did the same, holding open a big garbage bag for everyone to toss in their trash.

"Thanks so much for coming," he said, lifting his voice to hopefully be heard by everyone. *And thank you, Lord, for leading me home and giving me these good men and women to learn from. To rely on.*

To love.

Finn had never considered himself overly emotional, but his heart swelled and swelled with love for his cowboy brothers, for Angel, and for Libby. As they left one by one or in the groups they'd come in, he prayed all would go well for their spouses, their families, their loved ones, and that all their hopes and dreams could be realized.

And while he knew God didn't always answer prayers in the exact way Finn wanted him to, he absolutely knew God answered every prayer uttered by one of His children.

Chapter Fourteen

Conrad Walker stepped out of his truck, the Texas sun beating down on his broad shoulders as he surveyed the fields across the street from the grocery store in Three Rivers. There'd been a lot of growth in town in the past couple of decades, but somehow, this farmland had not been touched.

Of course, he knew Aunt Whitney's family owned a lot of it, and that her brother stocked the produce section from the harvest of such fields. The lot on this side of the road buzzed with its usual mix of shoppers getting their groceries, and Conrad joined them.

Grams had made him a list of things she needed for the week, and while Wilde & Organic had online shopping, Conrad didn't mind a slow evening of pushing a shopping cart around, choosing the cantaloupe he wanted, and buying too much gum at the checkout.

His mind lingered on the luncheon from earlier this week. He'd checked his well, as well as the forecast, and while summer was just heating up, there had been no indication of rain in the next fortnight. He didn't have a terribly huge plot of land to keep up with—he'd bought his grandparents farm from them just before Gramps had died.

That had turned out to be a huge blessing, because then Grams didn't have to be alone, and Conrad didn't have to run every change and improvement he wanted to make past his grandfather.

He'd gone to school for a couple of years, just long enough to learn how to do online trading, and he managed his own wealth, his grandmother's, and his siblings' when he wasn't out on the farm planting, watering, feeding the herd of miniature donkeys, or harvesting.

He had no beef cattle, but a half-dozen horses to take care of too. Thirty-four mini donkeys. Fifty acres of land and crops. Barns, stables, sheds, and outbuildings.

He loved it almost as much as he enjoyed sitting in front of the computer and writing down decimaled numbers as he kept track of stock prices, read predictions, and did financial research on publicly traded companies.

He was very much the bespeckled accountant of the family. Quiet. Reserved. Didn't like the spotlight. Couldn't make a joke if his life depended on it.

But he was dependable in other ways. The work always got done. He always showed up. "Always," he muttered to himself, feeling very much like what his younger brother had been calling him for years—dry toast.

JJ had put in an offer on the Adair's property, and it had been accepted. Conrad was going out with him, Tate, Ruby, all of JJ's siblings, and all of Conrad's that night.

Right after he got this shopping done.

Conrad couldn't help but feel a mix of pride and a twinge of...something else. Envy, maybe? He pushed the thought away. He was happy for JJ, truly. His cousin had worked hard and deserved this chance to expand. He'd asked Conrad for advice every step of the way.

But a small part of Conrad couldn't help but wonder when his own big break would come.

Or maybe he'd just manage his family's money and a mini donkey herd for his entire life.

Somehow, it felt wasteful. Like God expected him to do more with his money, more with his mind, more, more, more.

But what, the Lord had never said.

Conrad had asked, and God had simply left the door wide open for him. It could've led anywhere, and that honestly made Conrad shrink back and not take a step at all.

A blonde woman rounded the end of the aisle as Conrad entered the store, and he dang near tripped over his own feet. "Chloe?" came out of his mouth before he could stop it.

But she'd already swung her cart into the next aisle over, and he couldn't see her anymore. It couldn't be her anyway. Just a figment of his tired mind, after a long week of heat, cleaning stalls, and being around other cowboys who seemed to have everything Conrad should.

He did want a wife and family. He was trying, no matter

how much he chuckled and ducked his head whenever Grams asked him about going out with someone.

He'd dated Chloe Downard for a little over a year, until she'd left town to go help her sister in Dallas. She'd just had twins, and their mother was confined to a wheelchair and couldn't help much.

So Chloe—his blonde, beautiful, and very serious girl-friend—had made the move to help her.

Conrad had tried to stay in touch with her. Texts, video calls, and he'd even bought a plane ticket to Dallas once. He'd never used it, because Chloe had ended things with him very decisively before he could.

The slash she'd left on his heart throbbed even now, and though Conrad had been using the TwoCents app to talk to a few women, he couldn't honestly say any of them had intrigued him all that much. Certainly not enough to get cologned up on a Friday night after a long week on the farm and go out with her.

In fact, such a thing sounded like torture to Conrad.

Maybe Grams is right, he thought as he picked up the bagged Ceasar salad she wanted. *Maybe you need to get out of your comfort zone more than you have.*

No maybe about that.

He'd read on TwoCents that one of the best places to meet women was at the grocery store. But no one looked his way for longer than three seconds as he picked up the grape tomatoes, then a bunch of bananas, and then a twenty-pound bag of potatoes.

He filled his cart with the things he wanted and needed,

everything Grams had put on her list—plus a bag of her favorite potato chips—and headed for the checkout. Friday night seemed to be the new Saturday morning, and Conrad didn't even try to find the shortest line.

He simply picked one and got behind a woman wearing a long cardigan with her skinny jeans and ankle boots. He did find it odd someone would wear a sweater in Texas when the calendar would flip to June next week, but it wasn't any of his business how someone else dressed.

The line edged forward, and then it became the woman's turn. She moved to the side of her cart and began to unload it. Conrad looked up from his phone, trying to decide if he had time to send an email, or if he better put his phone away and get ready to check out.

The woman's cart wasn't even half-full, and Conrad tucked his phone away and looked at her.

His lungs sucked in the biggest gasp of air they ever had. Then that air all came out as he said, "Chloe?" for the second time that day.

She looked at him, a quick glance that stuck immediately. She straightened, the bottle of cream in her hands going completely still.

His brain blitzed, telling him the woman he'd seen when he'd first arrived had been wearing a dress. So it hadn't been Chloe.

But this woman certainly was.

"Hello, Conrad," she said, breaking the tether between. She twisted and put the cream on the belt, then reached for the jar of peanut butter in her cart.

That was it? Hello, Conrad?

His face heated, and Conrad moved up to the other side of her cart. "Did you move back here?" he asked, not quite daring to hope.

So much of Chloe called to him, and yes, he'd been devastated when she'd left town and broken up with him. But they had...secrets in their past too, and Conrad had worked hard to air those out, make them right, and move on with his life.

Seeing her again...he wanted to go right back to the man who'd done things with a woman he shouldn't. His twenty-eight-year-old hormones still wanted her, and his heart and mind demanded answers.

"I'm not back in town," she said.

Conrad bent to pick up her loaf of bread and the package of sliced ham. "You're not? Who are the groceries for then?"

Chloe gave him a withering look, then something else entirely covered her expression.

Fear.

She swallowed and glanced over to the cashier, who was still ringing out the customer in front of them. The belt held all it could, and she stood there with a six-pack of Trix yogurt in her hand, waiting for more space.

Suddenly, she wouldn't look at him, and Conrad wanted to raise his voice and make her—something he never did.

"I need to talk to you," she said, her eyes flying around the store now.

Conrad looked around too. "Okay, I'm standing right here."

"Not right here," she said.

Nothing made a whole lot of sense, and Conrad cast a look back to his grocery cart. It would take at least ten minutes for him to check out, and then five more to get to his truck and get all this loaded. And he had ice cream, butter, and other meltable items that needed to get put in the fridge or freezer.

"How long are you in town?"

"Just until Sunday," she said. The belt moved forward and she put down her yogurt.

To his great shock, tears slithered down her face. "I was —I've tried to call you so many times."

Conrad swallowed now, because Chloe's voice had pitched up into the range of a cartoon character, and the woman scanning groceries looked down to both of them. Of course Conrad knew her. He was a Walker, and it seemed everyone in town knew his family.

Tanya's eyes widened, and Conrad wanted to turn Chloe away from her. She sniffled now though, her makeup running with the tears. So Conrad put the groceries in his hand on the belt too, then moved down to Tanya. "Do you have any tissues?"

"Yes, sir." She swiped them up from the shelf under her monitor. "You need some help? Your aunt is upstairs today."

Conrad's pulse went wild in his chest. "No, ma'am," he said. "I'm fine." He was, but as he returned to Chloe, he realized she wasn't. The tears gave that away, but the fact that she couldn't stop crying.... Conrad had never seen her like this before.

"I have to go," she said as she took the tissue. And before he could protest or even ask what she meant, she pushed past him, leaving her cart and all her groceries, went around the front of the checkstand, and down the one next to them.

It sat closed, and by the time she exited from it, she was running. She went into the bathroom, leaving Conrad to stare dumbly after her.

"You better go after her, honey," Tanya said in her momma-Southern drawl. "Todd, go get that cart, and put Conrad's groceries on the belt."

Conrad fumbled in his back pocket for his wallet, and he moved back to Tanya. "I'll pay for hers and mine. Pick any card in there."

"Yes, sir." Tanya smartly took the wallet, and Conrad wiped his hands down the front of his jeans as he walked toward the restrooms. The cashier said something else behind him, but he couldn't catch what, and then he came face-to-face with the women's restroom.

Was he really going to go in there?

Yes, shouted in his head. He didn't think it was his voice, nor Tanya's. His mother had been the voice in his head for his entire life, but this didn't sound like her either.

"I'll close it for you, Conrad," Todd said, and Conrad looked at the man. He now held a yellow cleaning sign that would ensure that once Conrad went into the ladies' room, no one else would follow.

He couldn't hear a sniffle or any crying from inside, but

that voice once again boomed through him. *Get in there, Conrad. She has something to tell you.*

It had to be God, and Conrad had worked so hard to get back to a place where he could have God's hand in his life. So he took a deep breath, prayed, *If I shouldn't go in here, stop me right now*, and took the first step.

No one stopped him.

Chapter Fifteen

C hloe Downard locked the bathroom door behind her and pressed her back against the cool metal door. Her breaths came in shallow, rapid bursts, her chest heaving with the weight of the tears she'd been holding back for months. Maybe a year.

Maybe longer.

Maybe since the moment she'd found out she was pregnant with Conrad Walker's baby.

"This wasn't how this was supposed to go," she whimpered. Had he not noticed that everything in her cart was either for a child or one of his favorite things? Probably not. He'd barely looked away from her, and Conrad probably didn't care about fruity yogurt or even the peanut butter bars she'd planned to make—his favorite treat.

As if she could wow him with her baking skills and then

say, "Oh, by the way, you have a daughter I never told you about."

The very idea made a fresh round of tears flow down her face.

She wasn't supposed to see him like this. Not here, not today, and certainly not in the middle of Wilde & Organic, with a cart full of groceries she couldn't afford to pay for.

She had rehearsed this moment a hundred times in her head—what she'd say, how she'd say it, where he'd be, and what she'd be wearing. But none of those practiced words had made it past her lips. Instead, she'd fled like a scared rabbit, leaving Conrad standing there with that dumb-founded look on his face.

Chloe clamped her hand over her mouth to stifle a sob, her body trembling with the effort. She had to pull it together and get back out there. She owed it to the little girl who was currently staying with Chloe's aunt, blissfully unaware of the storm brewing around her.

She squeezed her eyes shut, trying to block out the noise of the bustling grocery store outside the restroom. But all she could see was Conrad's face. His eyes—those same kind, steady brown eyes that had once made her feel like every-thing in the world would be okay—had been wide with shock.

And why wouldn't they be? She'd ghosted him two years ago, cutting off all contact after she'd gone to Dallas to help her sister.

She left the stall and grabbed the brown paper towel already hanging from the dispenser. She held it under the faucet, glad when the water came out ice cold. Sniffling and hiccuping, she managed to clear the makeup from her face.

Her shoulders shook violently, but everything froze when the tall, dark, delicious cowboy Chloe had once loved entered the restroom.

The women's restroom.

"Chloe," he said, his voice soft, strangled, strained.

Their eyes met in the mirror, and she spun to face him, quickly wiping her nose with the paper towel and then leaning to toss it into the trash can.

This is for Sarina, she thought. Her daughter deserved better than Chloe could give her. And Conrad had a farm and all that money....

She'd wrestled with herself—and with God—over this. She knew she could've called Conrad at any point and told him about his daughter, then asked for money. He'd have given it to her. Heck, he still would.

"What's going on?" he asked.

"I—" she started. "You—when I went to Dallas, I was pregnant."

Conrad's mouth fished open, his eyes widening so far, she thought they'd pop right out of his head. "What?"

"The baby is yours. Well, she's two years old now." Chloe didn't even try to fight the tears. She just let them come out. "I can't—can't take care of her. I've tried, but my sister is getting a divorce, and her twins aren't much older than Sarina."

She hated that this story flew from her lips in a bathroom in a grocery store. Never, ever had this been where Chloe confessed everything to Conrad. Never.

But she'd started, and she couldn't stop now.

"She needs me. Mama moved to Dallas about six months ago, and she's worse than ever. None of us have any money, and—"

"I can give you money."

She shook her head. "No. I mean, yes, I know you could. But what really needs to happen is one of us needs to work. I have a nursing certificate, and I can take care of my mom, my sister, and her twins, but I can't do it if I can't work."

Conrad said nothing, his eyebrows pulling down into a very unhappy expression.

Chloe's whole body shook. "I love her. I do. But I can't take care of her, and I know you can."

Her sister's mental health had deteriorated rapidly since her husband of only four years had told her he'd met someone else. Her momma's mobility had gone from bad to worse, and she was very nearly bedridden at this point.

"I tr-tried," she said, sobbing now.

"Okay." Calm, cool, confident Conrad stepped into her and wrapped her in his arms. "Okay, Chloe. It's okay."

Nothing was truly okay. What kind of mother first, never told the father about their daughter, and second, showed up two years later and dumped her on him?

This is what's best for her, she told herself. And it was. God had told her it was. Her sister, her momma, her aunt. She had no support system—she was all of their support system.

And Conrad had family coming out of every street and house in Three Rivers.

Sarina deserved to know her father, to have the kind of stability Chloe couldn't provide anymore.

That was why Chloe had made this tiring and worrisome drive to Three Rivers. Not to rekindle anything with Conrad—Lord, no. But to give Sarina a chance at the life she deserved.

A life Chloe couldn't give her.

"Where is she?" he whispered.

Chloe listened to his steady, strong heartbeat, wishing with everything inside her she'd made different choices. But some things couldn't be undone, even if she was sorry.

"My aunt Diane has her." She stepped back and gestured haphazardly toward the grocery store beyond the bathroom. "I was buying all the things I needed to make you your favorite treats, and then we were going to come over."

His dark eyes blazed with an energy Chloe had once loved. Now, it only burned her, reminding her of how good he was, how he would've never concealed something like this from her.

He glanced toward the exit, then extended his hand toward her. "Come on. I'm sure our groceries are ready."

Chloe didn't care about the groceries, but she threaded her fingers through Conrad's, touched by his kindness and care. He led her toward the exit of the restroom, then paused. "Yes, can you get a hat, maybe?"

Someone else said something, but Chloe hid behind Conrad, though she had no right to use him like that. Several seconds later, Conrad turned toward her and handed her a ballcap.

"Just stay right by me," he murmured, and then he stepped out of the bathroom. Two grocery store workers stood there, each with a cart of bagged and ready-to-go groceries. They started walking, with Conrad keeping Chloe as far from the rest of the store as possible.

Outside, the sun still blazed, as it was summertime in the Texas Panhandle, and they still had plenty of daylight left. She took a deep breath, her face feeling crusty and crackly.

"Where are you parked?" Conrad asked, his hand in hers tightening.

Chloe lifted her head and scanned the lot. "To the right."

Conrad slowed and paused while the clerks continued with the carts. "I'm not sure what to do, Chloe."

"What do you mean?"

"I don't want you to get in your car and drive away," he said, his voice firm. "I might never see you—or my daughter —again. So I want you to go get her carseat, and I'd like you to come with me."

She thought about her car, but she didn't argue. "Okay," she said, and she led him over to her SUV. It took her a couple of minutes to get the seat out of the back, and then Conrad easily took it from her.

He led her to his truck, where the last of the groceries got loaded in the back. The door slammed, and the last man there nodded to Conrad and took his cart with him.

Conrad put the carseat in the back without buckling it in, then opened the passenger door for Chloe. He wore a look somewhere between anger and irritation, and she couldn't blame him for that.

She got in the truck. As Conrad closed the door and walked around the truck, Chloe sat there in the suffocating heat, everything in her life crystal clear. She felt like the eye of a great hurricane had finally arrived, and she knew exactly what to do and what to say.

Then Conrad opened the door, breaking that silence, that pure serenity, and got behind the wheel. "I don't know where I'm going."

"We're at the Star Eight," she said.

Conrad nodded, and of course he'd know where the hotel was. They drove with only the sound of the air conditioning blowing.

Chloe's heart rolled around painfully. He was going to see his little girl in less than ten minutes.

"When's her birthday?" he asked.

"February twenty-fourth."

"When did you know you were pregnant?" He looked at her, then quickly back out the windshield again. "Did you know when you left?"

She shook her head. "No. I found out about three weeks later." She wrung her hands together. "I'd already ended everything. Told you not to contact me again. I'd deleted your number from my phone."

"Numbers aren't hard to get."

"I know." Tears leaked out of her eyes again. "I know, Conrad. I'm so sorry."

His jaw jumped, and he didn't repeat what he'd said in the bathroom—that everything would be okay. "Did you even try?"

"Yes," she said, her voice breaking. "I did. I tried to get in touch with you. I've typed out so many messages."

"Telling someone they have a child is not something you message them on social media," he clipped out.

"I know that. That's why I never sent the message."

"I had a right to know." He gripped the steering wheel. "You left me here, right when I was trying to fix so many things."

She nodded, because they'd been on shaky ground during that time.

"I told you I'd come with you."

"I didn't want you to—and I didn't know I was pregnant when I was here."

"I thought you'd left, because I'd said we'd—we shouldn't sleep together anymore. That it was wrong."

She nodded, because that was also true, and she couldn't deny it.

"I asked you to marry me."

She pressed her eyes closed. "I know."

"I just want to make sure we're all living the same story," he said, making the last turn that would get them to the Star Eight. "Because I was in love with you. We should've gotten married before being together. I knew that; you knew that.

I've been working on fixing that mistake for *three* years now."

Chloe hadn't had time to even think about that yet. She didn't know what to say, so she kept quiet.

Conrad scoffed and pulled into the hotel parking lot. "How is this going to go?"

"I don't know."

"What was your plan?"

"I was going to bring her to your farm," she said, her stomach vibrating in the worst way possible. "I've brought all of her clothes and toys. Her favorite stuffed animals and her blankets she loves."

"You were going to leave her with me on Sunday."

"Yes." Chloe whispered the word, so ashamed.

"Well, let's just do it today," he said, peering at the hotel. "I can call my cousin and he'll go get your car. We'll get her and take her to my farm. My grandmother is there, and she'll be able to help me." For one brief moment, he looked absolutely terrified, and then the strong, confident cowboy returned.

"I'm sorry, Conrad," she whispered, her voice trembling. "I'm so, so sorry."

He nodded slowly, his jaw tight. "I want to meet her."

Chloe's stomach churned with a mixture of fear and relief. She had known this moment would come, but now that it had arrived, she wasn't sure she was ready for it. She wasn't sure *he* was ready for it.

She dropped out of the truck, sure her legs would give out. They kept her upright, and she walked into the hotel.

She'd gone through so many things in the past few years, and she almost disengaged from herself as she went down the hall and held the keycard to the reader. The lock released, and Chloe entered the room.

Her mother's sister turned from the window, her expression serious. "He's with you?"

"I ran into him at the grocery store." She found Sarina laying on the bed, watching the cartoon playing on the television. Her face lit up when she saw Chloe, and that made a brand new kind of sob rip through her.

"Mama," she said, and Sarina didn't say a whole lot. A few things, like "Mama," or "cheese," or "juice."

Chloe went straight to her and picked her up. Her dark hair mirrored Conrad's, as did the shape of her chin and the way she was so agreeable. "Hey, baby girl." She knew Conrad had entered the room, because his big presence couldn't be contained in such a small space.

"Hello, Diane," he said in his cowboy twang. Then he turned his full attention to Chloe and Sarina. He looked only at the little girl, and Chloe saw the moment he accepted she was his.

"Do we need to pack up anything?" he asked, glancing around. "You guys can stay with me on the farm too, until Sunday. That might make things easier."

"Nothing about this is easy," Aunt Diane said.

Chloe simply cried, because she couldn't imagine getting in her car on Sunday morning and driving away without her daughter. But that was what she'd planned to do.

"No, of course not," Conrad said. "I called JJ. He's going to meet us here in about twenty minutes. He'll go get your car and bring it to the farm."

Chloe nodded and pulled in a tight breath in an attempt to get herself together. "Yes, let's pack up the room." She glanced over to Aunt Diane, who wore her disapproval openly. But she'd made the trip with Chloe and Sarina, because no one else could.

She stepped toward Conrad, squeezing her daughter tightly. She hoped he'd tell Sarina how much she loved her. "Baby, this is your daddy, and you're going to go with him now."

She sniffled as she transferred Sarina from her arms to Conrad's. He stared at the child like she was an alien, and she blinked up at him with her long lashes.

"Hey, baby," he whispered, and he placed a kiss against her cheek. "You're sure a pretty little thing." He looked at her, pure anguish in his expression.

Then he said the very best thing in the world—the one thing Chloe had prayed for, even when she had no right to ask God for anything.

He said, "I love her already. I'll take care of her."

Chapter Sixteen

Penny Walker sat in her favorite chair in the living room, a pair of knitting needles clicking softly in her hands. The early evening sunlight streamed through the wide windows, casting golden hues over the well-loved furniture. Her husband Gideon had picked out the empty armchair on her right a decade ago, back when they'd moved onto this farm. She could almost hear him sighing as he sat down and said, "Time for *Wheel of Fortune*, love. I'm gonna get the bonus round this time."

But Gideon wasn't here anymore. He'd gone to be with the Lord three years ago, and though Penny had found peace in her faith, there were days—like today—when the emptiness weighed a little heavier on her heart.

She paused, looking at the family Bible open on the small table beside her. A well-worn bookmark lay in the Psalms, where she often turned for comfort. Today, it seemed God had been quieter than usual, and Penny wasn't sure if her attention span had shortened, she couldn't hear Him, or because He was waiting for her to be still.

She adjusted her reading glasses, paused her knitting, and looked out the window. "I miss you, Gideon," she murmured, wondering when Conrad would be back with the groceries. He was then going out with his cousins and siblings, and Penny would likely be in bed before he returned home.

The sound of tires crunching on the gravel driveway drew her attention, and Penny rose from her chair. Her knees creaked, the old joints not what they once were, but she made her way to the front door with purpose. The screen door squeaked as she pushed it open, and she stepped onto the porch just as Conrad brought his truck to a stop.

A blonde woman rode in the passenger seat, and Penny studied her, trying to call her name forward. She definitely knew her, and she watched as both Conrad and the woman got out of the truck and turned to open the back doors.

"Hey, Grams," Conrad called, but his usual joviality didn't shine through in the words. She expected him to emerge from the backseat with the reusable shopping bags she'd sent him to the store with.

Not a dark-haired girl.

Penny's heart squeezed, and she pressed a hand to her chest as the truth flowed through her mind. "Dear Lord," she whispered. "Bless me with strength."

Because she knew she was looking at Conrad's daughter. Her great-granddaughter.

Her eyes flew to the blonde woman, who did carry the groceries Penny had expected to see in Conrad's arms.

Conrad's eyes locked with hers, and Penny saw the turmoil written all over his face. He came forward now, and he said, "Hey, Grams," as he came up the wide porch steps.

The woman followed behind, her face pale and drawn, her eyes red from what Penny guessed had been a lot of crying. She looked exhausted, like she'd been carrying the world on her shoulders for a while now.

Her grandson reached the porch and paused only a pace from Penny. "This is Sarina. She's my daughter." He looked over to the blonde while Penny took in the lighter eyes of the little girl—those had come from her mother. But the dark hair that curled along the ends, and the shape of her chin, the way she smiled at Penny when she smiled at her—that all came from Conrad.

He needs you.

The words made her heart stop. She'd been longing to be reunited with Gideon, and she knew she was becoming a burden to her sons, their wives, and her grandchildren. She'd been questioning how much longer the Lord would make her stay here.

Now she knew why she hadn't been taken home yet.

"Do you remember Chloe?" Conrad stepped back as Chloe came upstairs. "She's Sarina's mother. Remember we dated a few years ago?"

"Of course," Penny said, relieved to have the woman's name. "Come in, come in." She hurried to open the door as they both had their hands full of girls or groceries.

Chloe entered first, her head down, a ball cap concealing her face. Conrad gave Penny a shaky smile as he entered the house. "JJ's going to bring Chloe's car. I ran into her at the grocery store, and we have some things to unpack."

Penny continued into the kitchen, where Chloe had hefted the grocery bags. She said nothing as she left, presumably to go get more bags.

"Conrad," Penny breathed as he set the little girl on the counter and stayed close, holding her so she wouldn't fall.

"I know, Grams," he said quietly. "Yes, she's mine. Yes, I was sleeping with Chloe. No, I didn't know until a half-hour ago." He glanced toward the front door. "My parents are going to lose their minds."

Penny wanted to step in and reassure him that he didn't have anything to prove to his parents. To any of his aunts or uncles. To anyone.

She held the words back as she started to unpack the groceries. "It'll be a lot to explain," she said.

"I've been working so hard to get back where God wants me," Conrad said miserably. "This feels like I have to start all over again. Publicly."

"Well, maybe you will," she said matter-of-factly. She'd raised seven boys who'd come along in only six years, and she didn't even know how to sugarcoat things. "But maybe you won't. Maybe this is just the final step you needed to take in your healing, and the Lord knew you couldn't do it until you knew about her."

"Maybe." Conrad brushed his fingers along Sarina's hair

in such a loving gesture. "I have no idea how to take care of a two-year-old."

Chloe re-entered the house, more grocery bags in her arms. "JJ is here," she said, and Conrad turned that way, pulling in a breath. Chloe wept openly, and Penny wanted to wrap her up into a tight hug and tell her it wouldn't always hurt like this. "My aunt wants to go straight to her room."

She cut a look over to Penny. "Conrad said we could stay here."

"Of course," Penny said without missing a beat.

"They're just staying tonight and tomorrow night," Conrad said, picking up Sarina again. "Then they have to get back to Dallas."

Penny's heart crashed to the floor. "So we only get her for a couple of nights?" She stopped pulling out cabbages and carrots and went to take the little girl from Conrad. He eased her into Penny's arms, and she snuggled the little girl.

"No, Grams," Conrad said. "Chloe can't take care of Sarina anymore. She's going to—she's my daughter. I'm going to raise her. She's ours for...forever."

Penny dang near dropped Sarina. "Forever," she repeated. She looked back at the girl who watched her with sober eyes. "Come sit with me, baby."

"She named her Sarina Penny," Conrad said. "She's got the birth certificate, and I'm not listed, but we can get it changed."

"Okay." Penny sank into her recliner and settled the precious little girl on her lap. "Hi," she whispered, her voice so soft and so kind. "Can you say hi?" She smiled with as much energy as she could muster.

The little girl watched her for one second, and then she smiled too. "Hi."

Penny barely heard her, but the sound was enough to melt her heart completely. She reached out and gently touched Sarina's cheek. "Well, aren't you just the most beautiful little thing I've ever seen?"

Sarina said, "Hi," again, and in that moment, Penny knew. She *knew* that God had brought this little girl into their lives for a reason. That this was her purpose now, to help Conrad navigate this new chapter, to help him heal, to help him raise his daughter.

"How old are you?" she asked, curling the girl's fingers around hers.

Sarina held up her hand, then used the other one to put down all but two fingers.

"Two," Penny said, vocalizing it for the child. Activity whirled around her, but she held Sarina in her arms, humming and protecting her from the stress of the adults in her life.

"Okay, that's all of our bags," Chloe said. "All the groceries."

"Grams."

Penny looked up at JJ, who stared at the little girl on her lap. "Oh, hello, darling. I didn't know you were here."

"Holy cow." JJ wore wide eyes as he looked at the little girl and then Conrad.

"Yeah," Conrad said.

"It won't be new for long," Penny said. "JJ, this is Conrad's daughter, Sarina Penny." She looked at Conrad. "Take her, Conrad. I'll put away the groceries."

He took the girl and Penny got to her feet with the help of JJ. "Come help me."

JJ did, and the farmhouse felt stuffed with tension and silence. "Grams," he finally whispered as he handed her a bag of oranges.

"Conrad is going to need all of our love and support," she said. "Chloe's not staying in town."

"I'm so sorry," the woman said, and Penny hadn't even realized she'd come into the kitchen. "I never meant for it to be like this."

Penny reached out and took her hand, squeezing it gently. "Life rarely turns out the way we plan, dear. But you're here now, and that's what matters."

Chloe nodded, tears slipping silently down her cheeks. "My momma needs so much help, and my sister...." She shook her head. "You'll tell her every day that I love her, right?" She looked over to where Conrad had put the child on the floor with a pink blanket and a blue stuffed elephant. He held the remote control in his hand, and he flipped through channels, trying to find something the little girl would like.

"We'll tell her," Penny promised. "I'm really sorry about your family."

Chloe wiped her eyes and nodded. "It's just a lot, and I can't give her what she deserves."

"You're welcome here any time," Penny promised, her

heart full but heavy. There was so much to unpack here—so many questions, so much hurt—but right now, she needed to focus on making sure they all felt welcome. The rest would come in time.

"I don't deserve that," she whispered. "But thank you." She drew in a shaky breath and looked over to Conrad and Sarina. "I think I'm going to go lay down for a few minutes, if that's okay."

"Totally okay," Penny said, wondering when Chloe had slept properly. She couldn't imagine a situation that was so bad that she'd give up her child, so things must be really terrible.

She left the kitchen, and Penny and JJ finished putting away the groceries. Then they joined Conrad in the living room. He too looked dejected and completely overwhelmed, exhausted. The situation likely hadn't sunk all the way in yet—but it would tomorrow morning when the little girl woke up and needed breakfast—and he'd have to get it for her.

"I know this is a mess," he said. "I've made some big mistakes, haven't I?"

Conrad had always been a good man, but yes, he'd made mistakes, just like anyone else. The important thing was that he'd been working to fix them, to repent. And now, God had given him this new challenge—a challenge that would test him, but also one that could bring him closer to the Lord.

"We all have," Penny said gently. "But God's grace is bigger than our mistakes. You're going to do right by Sarina."

"I'm really angry at her," Conrad whispered. "And that feels like just one more thing I need to repent of."

She couldn't tell him not to be angry, so she simply took her chair again while JJ settled on the loveseat. Conrad reached over and pulled Sarina into his lap, his gaze softening as he looked down at his daughter.

Penny watched the way his face changed, how the tension eased slightly, the way his shoulders seemed to relax now that Sarina was beside him. He was already falling into the role of father, and Penny knew that with time, he would be a good one.

"I'm going to need help," he admitted quietly, his eyes meeting hers. "I don't know the first thing about raising a little girl."

Penny smiled, her heart swelling with love for her grandson. "I'm right here, baby."

He nodded, his jaw tightening as he fought back the emotions swirling just beneath the surface. Her heart ached for him, and she wanted to fire questions at him about what he planned to do to tell the family about this child.

Rhett and Evelyn....

You'll help them.

God once again reminded her that she'd been kept here to help her whole family through this trial, not just Conrad. And in doing so, she would find healing of her own. She would renew her faith and strength.

She would find purpose again.

Chapter Seventeen

"Ｗhat's on the agenda for today?" Ruby asked as she poured herself a cup of coffee. Tate sat at the kitchen table, his own mug in front of him as he swiped on his phone.

Her brother looked up, his eyes sharpening as he focused on her. "Think I'll head out to check the fences in the north pasture. JJ mentioned there might be a weak spot that needs mending."

"So that'll be your morning walk," she said. He wasn't strong enough to ride a horse or control an ATV, and that had to be a good hour-long walk.

"I'm going to drive," he said. "But I'll be walking around a bit."

"You can't pull the fencing tight."

"Thanks, Doctor Reynolds," he said sarcastically. "Cody's coming with me. JJ's signing the papers on the

Adair place this morning, and then we're going to work with that pair of mares."

Ruby stirred in a spoonful of sugar, debating with herself over whether she should say the words in her mind or not. In the end, she had to report to her parents that she'd done her best with Tate. "Be careful with the horses, okay, Tate?" She looked up and into his eyes, pleading for him to understand she wasn't trying to smother him. She simply worried over him.

"I will, sissy."

Ruby nodded and took a sip of her coffee, already feeling fluttering and scattered. Her relationship with JJ had been complicated these past few weeks. Stolen moments of tenderness, hand-holding, and quick chats interspersed with long stretches where they barely saw each other. JJ had been working himself to the bone, and Ruby couldn't shake the feeling that he was avoiding her.

Why, she had no idea. She hadn't even kissed him again.

"Oh, Whitney just texted," Tate said, oblivious to Ruby's inner turmoil. "She invited us to the homestead for lunch today. You going?"

Ruby nodded, grateful for the distraction. "Yeah, I think I will. It'll be nice not to have to cook."

"What are you doing today?"

She took a moment to swallow another mouthful of coffee. "I'm going to finish up my sketch, look through the job boards in San Antonio, text Mom and Dad about how you're doing, and then I'm going to update the agricultural binder with the notes JJ left for me. That should get me to lunch."

"Cody asked about you again," Tate said with a smile. "He said you two are going to be working in the stables together this afternoon."

Ruby turned away from her brother so he wouldn't see the distaste on her face. "Yeah, he's teaching me to clean out the stalls."

"He's sweet on you."

"He's way too old for me," Ruby said.

"Yeah, maybe," Tate said thoughtfully.

Ruby's heartbeat flounced through her veins. "What if he asks me out?"

"Maybe you'd like him," Tate said as he got to his feet, the chair scraping the tile.

"And that would be okay with you?" She glanced over to Tate, feeling like she'd just stepped out onto a tightrope.

"I mean, I wouldn't care, I guess," Tate said.

"What if I went out with Austin?" They'd been out with some of JJ's cousins, to the movies, to restaurants, to Conrad's to hang out, especially now that he had his daughter full-time.

Boy, that had blown up the Walker family, that was for certain. To Ruby, it was just one more thing that took JJ from her, as he'd been spending more time with Conrad on his farm with all the mini donkeys, and the Walkers had had a family meal for four or five nights in a row—that she and Tate were not invited to.

"You like Austin?"

"No," Ruby said. "I'm wondering if you'd care if I go out with him."

"I don't care who you go out with," Tate said, coming to her side. Something swam in his eyes, but Ruby couldn't quite read it.

"No?"

He shrugged. "Not really." He dumped out his coffee and set the mug in the sink. "I mean, you and JJ would be super weird for me, but other than that, I don't care." With that, he moved to the back door, plucked his hat from the hook there, and said, "See you later, Rubes," before he left the cabin.

Ruby stood at the sink, trying to figure out how to breathe. *You and JJ would be super weird for me.*

Tears pricked her eyes, because it hardly seemed like there was a her and JJ anyway. Maybe she should flirt with Cody this afternoon, see if she could get a date with him.

Ruby drifted back to her bedroom and the desk where she worked. Dozens of sketches and fabric swatches—the beginnings of design ideas she'd been working on in her spare time—covered the surface, and she ran her fingers over a particularly beautiful piece of blue paisley brocade.

Nothing like this would go in a farmhouse, but it would make a lovely couch for a doctor's office or a waiting room at a law office.

Despite the uncertainty of her situation, she couldn't help but feel a spark of excitement at the thought of creating beautiful spaces again. The morning passed quickly as Ruby lost herself in her designs. She found three new jobs to apply for, but she didn't have time to do it right now. She marked them, called her parents, and headed outside to get over to the administrative barn to update the records with JJ's notes.

Before she knew it, her stomach growled, reminding her that she'd been invited to the homestead for lunch. She finished the last entry in the agricultural binder, made sure she had her phone, and set off across the sun-drenched fields.

The Walker family homestead was a beautiful old farmhouse that had stood for generations. As Ruby approached, she couldn't help but see it with a designer's eye—the potential for updating while still preserving its classic charm. Her fingers itched to sketch, to bring her vision to life.

As she walked, she wondered if JJ had been invited to lunch today, and if so, if he'd be there.

Her nerves shouted at her as she approached the back deck, where a couple of ranch dogs lay panting in the shade. Ruby loved golden retrievers, and she took a moment to crouch down and give them both a scrub.

The sliding glass door opened, and Whitney Walker, JJ's momma, stepped outside. She wore her jet-black hair back in a ponytail and an apron over her clothes. "Hey, Ruby. C'mon in."

Ruby followed Whitney into the spacious kitchen, where JJ's youngest sisters, Emily and Hattie, set out paper goods for lunch. The mouthwatering aroma of freshly baked bread hung in the air, and the familiar scent and sounds of a busy kitchen reminded Ruby of her family in Lubbock.

For a powerful moment, she missed her parents so much, though she'd just spoken with them that morning.

"Hey, Ruby," Emily said, and she stepped over and hugged her. Hattie did the same, and Ruby sure did like them. They'd all done such a good job of making her and Tate feel like they belonged here at Seven Sons Ranch.

She didn't see Clara Jean, or Tate, or JJ, and she faced Whitney, though JJ had said his daddy often manned the kitchen and fed the family. "What can I do to help?"

"Nothing." She smiled at her. "We're almost ready. I'm just pulling the mac and cheese out now."

Ruby's phone chimed, and she checked it, because this sound was for a job board. "Oh," she said. "A new interior design job has come up."

"Interior design?" Whitney asked.

"Yeah." Ruby looked up. "That's what I do. Or, I mean, I graduated in interior design. I had an internship in San Antonio that fell through."

"Oh, right," Whitney said. "JJ mentioned that."

"You should see her sketches, Momma," Emily said. "They're really good."

Ruby smiled at her, because she had shown her binder to Clara Jean, Emily, and Hattie. JJ's sisters were so nice, and Ruby really felt like she could be friends with them for a long time.

Just then, Clara Jean came into the house with Tate hot on her heels. The two of them laughed and laughed about something, interrupting all happenings and conversations in the kitchen.

"What's so funny?" Whitney asked coolly, and Clara Jean seemed to realize for the first time that she and Tate weren't alone.

"This video Tate showed me," Clara Jean said without missing a beat. Her face did hold more red than perhaps the Texas weather would give it, and Ruby studied her brother while Clara Jean went to wash up at the sink. She immediately started talking about the family garden plot, which she tended to, and her sisters engaged in that conversation.

Ruby edged closer to Tate. "You are going to be in so much trouble if you date JJ's younger sister."

"We're not dating," Tate said out of the side of his mouth, his eyes still glued to Clara Jean.

"Why can't you look away from her then?"

It took another few seconds, and then Tate tore his gaze from Clara Jean and looked at Ruby. A slow flush crawled up his neck, and Whitney saved him from Ruby's cocked eyebrows as she said, "It's time to eat."

"Is JJ coming?" Tate asked, voicing Ruby's question as he moved away from her.

"Yes, he said he'd be here," Whitney said. "Ruby, I want to sit by you and talk about your interior design."

"You do?" She went with Whitney into the kitchen while the others picked up plates and started filling them with food. "About what?"

Whitney gazed around her house—the kitchen, the mudroom off to the side that led into the garage, the expansive dining room, the living room, and then a hallway that ran toward the front of the house. Ruby certainly hadn't seen more than that—oh, and the half-bath off the kitchen—but she'd seen the house from the outside.

Jeremiah and Whitney had five children too, and JJ had told her he'd never shared a room. So the house must have plenty of bedrooms, maybe even another living space upstairs.

"This place needs a refresh," she said, a smile coming to her face. "Jeremiah's too tired to do it, and I can stage photographs, but I'm terrible at decorating a room."

Ruby blinked at her, sure her ears had malfunctioned. "You want me to...design your house?"

"Maybe just this back room," Whitney said. "Is that something you can do?"

"Of course," Ruby sputtered. "I mean, yes, of course." She turned in a full circle, seeing the space for the first time all over again. "I'd start at the front door, and make sure the energy flows from there to here."

Whitney smiled at her. "There's an office up front too. Three bedrooms down the hall. Two more baths that way too."

Ruby gaped at her. "You want me to do the whole thing? Or just the main living areas?"

"Oh, are you talking about redesigning the house?" Clara Jean asked, her plate overflowing with pulled-pork-topped mac and cheese. "Did you ask her to bring over her binder?"

"Not yet," Whitney said.

"It's amazing," Clara Jean said. "She has some real cowboy stuff, Momma. I think you'd like it."

Ruby's face heated, and she smiled heartily at Clara Jean. "Thanks, Clara Jean." She focused on Whitney again. "I mostly did home spaces in college, though I've got a bit of commercial experience too."

"Are you taking on clients?"

Ruby's mind blanked. "I mean—I guess?"

"Maybe we could fit it in around your care of Tate."

"She barely does anything anymore," Tate said from the table, where he'd clearly been listening in.

"Hey," Ruby protested. "I do all the cooking, cleaning, laundry, dishes. And you're messy and dirty at the end of every day."

He just laughed, which about summed up Tate. Flustered, Ruby looked back to Whitney. "I could probably do it, sure. I'm helping JJ keep up with some clerical stuff on the ranch, and I work on my portfolio, do a few things for Tate and I, and look for jobs."

"I'd pay you," Whitney said.

Ruby started to shake her head no, then it turned into a nod. "I mean—we live here for free."

Whitney flashed a look over to the table, where Tate sat with all three of her daughters. "That's part of Tate's wages."

"Well, I—I—" Ruby didn't know what to say. She had not planned on opening her own design studio. She'd planned to get on with a firm, a place where clients would come, and she'd be assigned to them. Sure, she knew how to source materials, and she absolutely believed in her ability to put together an amazing space, but....

"Put together a proposal for me," Whitney said with a smile. She picked up a paper plate and handed it to Ruby. "It would be nice to keep you around a little longer, and this job might just do that."

"How long would a job like this take?" Clara Jean asked as she returned to the kitchen island where Ruby had been standing with Whitney. She picked up the bottle of ranch dressing and looked from her mother to Ruby.

"The whole first floor?" Ruby scanned the parts of it she could see. "Several months, at least."

"Then you won't be so stressed to find another job," Clara Jean said.

"Or be so worried about finding another internship," Tate added.

Clara Jean smiled at him—there so was something happening between them—and took the ranch dressing back to the table.

Ruby watched them for a moment, but nothing seemed *too* friendly as they chitchatted and passed the ranch back and forth. She looked back to Whitney, who also had her narrowed eyes on her daughters.

"He's mostly just a flirt," Ruby said quietly as she dug the serving spoon into the mac and cheese.

"My younger girls have always had a crush on him," she said. "This thing with Clara Jean is new...."

Ruby didn't know what to add, and her mind had so many other things to stew over. She knew her time at Seven Sons had always been temporary—at least, that was what she'd told herself. But the thought of staying for several more months, of putting down roots here...it stirred something deep within her, a longing she hadn't even realized she'd been harboring.

She joined the others at the table, and Hattie asked, "What theme are you going to go with for the farmhouse?"

As the conversation erupted into excited chatter about color schemes and furniture arrangements, a sense of purpose settled over Ruby.

Whitney had just given her an opportunity to prove herself, to create something beautiful in a place that was quickly becoming dear to her heart, to have a piece in her portfolio that hadn't been staged for a class or a workshop.

For the first time since losing her internship, she felt like she stood back on solid ground instead of quicksand.

The sound of the sliding door getting slammed back into place brought their conversation to a simmer. JJ strode into the kitchen, his hat in his hand and a sheen of sweat on his brow from the midday sun.

Ruby's breath caught in her throat at the sight of him, her heart doing that familiar flip in her chest.

"Hey, y'all," he greeted them, his eyes lingering on Ruby for a moment before darting away.

She felt the weight of that gaze, the unspoken tension that had been building between them for weeks.

Whitney beamed at her son, hopefully oblivious to the undercurrents between her and JJ. She didn't want to be as obvious as Tate and Clara Jean. "JJ, you'll never guess. I've just hired Ruby to redesign and redecorate the homestead."

Ruby watched JJ carefully, expecting—hoping—to see

the same excitement in his mother's voice reflected in his eyes. Instead, she saw something that looked unsettlingly like dismay flash across his face before he schooled his features into a neutral expression. The sight sent a chill through her, dousing her earlier elation.

"Is that so?" he said, his voice carefully even. "Well, that's... that's something." He kept his head down as he washed up at the kitchen sink, then turned his back on all of them as he picked up a plate and started dishing himself some lunch.

His sisters went back to chatting, and Ruby listened to them without participating. Her earlier elation at being asked to do a big job deflated like a punctured balloon.

Why wasn't JJ happy for her? She'd thought he'd be happy to have her staying on at the ranch a bit longer. The realization that he might not want her here sent a wave of hurt washing over her. She hadn't gone over for coffee as often as she'd like, what with the hour being so early.

They didn't get to work together much on the ranch, and JJ had not found a way to take her out just the two of them to get off the ranch. They hung out with his siblings and cousins in a group, stealing touches and glances and exchanging texts.

Ruby wanted more, but now she wondered if JJ did. Perhaps he'd reconsidered his feelings for her.

As she ate, Ruby found it increasingly difficult to focus on the conversation around her. JJ stayed uncharacteristically quiet, responding to everyone's questions with mono-syllabic answers. Every time Ruby glanced his way, she found him staring intently at his plate, as if it held the secrets of the universe.

He finished first somehow, got up, and said, "I have to get back out there."

Something inside Ruby told her to *go with him. Don't let him walk away like this.*

So while she could hear her momma's voice telling her to stay and help Whitney clean up, thank her a bunch more times, and then finally slip out to do her stall cleaning with Cody, she got to her feet too.

"I have to make a phone call," she said, and she darted down the hall and out the front door while JJ made his exit out the back.

But with such a wide open ranch, Ruby could hurry around the side of the house and catch him—hopefully in the shade—to find out why he'd just put more distance between them when he'd learned she'd be on the ranch for longer than originally planned.

So she did just that.

Chapter Eighteen

JJ marched across the deck, then the lawn of the backyard, his boots making angry noises though he walked on grass as he made a beeline for the barn. His mind spun like a tornado, and he forced himself to breathe slowly, to keep the storm inside controlled rather than exploding outward.

Ruby would live here at the ranch longer than he'd anticipated, longer than he'd planned for. And working intimately with his momma and daddy?

His fingers curled into fists.

He'd thought they were on the same page—that the time she spent living here, with Tate as her roommate, was temporary, that they'd eventually be able to move into a more normal rhythm of dating. He wanted to pick her up at her own place, take her somewhere special, and not have to worry about running into Tate every time he reached for her hand.

But now? Now, she was practically embedded as a friend in his life, in his family, at *his* ranch. He did not want to be just friends with her. And with Tate still recovering and Ruby spending so much time around him, JJ couldn't shake the feeling that he was being boxed out of his own future.

He pulled his cowboy hat lower over his eyes and cursed under his breath. The sun was unforgiving today, but not nearly as brutal as his own thoughts.

Coward.

He'd known for weeks he needed to talk to Tate about his feelings for his younger sister. Things had gotten hectic on the ranch and with the purchase of the land next door, and well, JJ had reasoned he had more time. He'd put off the conversation, because he didn't want to have it.

But really, it was because he was afraid.

Afraid of losing Tate as his best friend. Afraid of causing a fall-out between Ruby and Tate. Afraid of admitting out loud to the strength of his feelings since he and Ruby spent so little time together. Afraid of everything.

He was a coward, blindly praying and hoping everything between him, Ruby, and Tate would magically work out.

But things rarely worked themselves out. He knew that. Ranching didn't work that way—neither did life. If he wanted something, he had to go after it. He had to fight for it, even if it meant getting his hands dirty and risking everything.

Conrad and his little girl flitted across JJ's mind, and he'd really admired the way Conrad had handled the stunning news that he was a father. He'd told his parents with his head high. He'd called a whole-family meeting—which Daddy had cooked for—and told everyone in the family. Anyone who couldn't make it, he'd texted. So everyone in the Walker family knew his situation.

They knew he'd done things with Chloe he shouldn't have done. They knew his life now sat on a completely different path than it had two weeks ago. They knew his situation and could offer help, *because* they knew.

JJ kept everything bottled tight, and he honestly felt like he might explode at any moment.

"JJ." Ruby's voice cut through his thoughts, sharp and breathless. He stopped abruptly but didn't turn around.

Of course she'd followed him. She never let things go, and a part of him loved that about her. She was relentless in the best way, but right now, he simply wanted to stew through a plan to talk to Tate.

"Thank you for waiting." Her voice sounded closer now, and the gravel crunched under her feet as she hurried toward him. She arrived, clearly out of breath, and JJ so didn't want to have this conversation in the sun.

He took a deep breath and raised his eyes to meet hers. Pure hurt lived there, and JJ regretted scarfing down his food and running out. Her cheeks flushed red to match the undertones in her dark hair, and she searched his face in a way that made his heart ache.

"Do you really have to get back right now?" she asked.

He shook his head and took her hand in his. Something screamed at him that Tate could potentially see them, but JJ decided he didn't care. Maybe that was a solid plan—simply start dating Ruby openly and let Tate deal with his feelings on his own.

"Let's find some shade," he said, and he led her around the corner of the barn and into the shadow of the American flag on the other side. Relief painted through him, though the air still held plenty of heat. Ruby said nothing, and JJ wanted to start talking anyway. He wanted to explain the intricacies of his feelings so she'd understand.

"I miss you," came out of his mouth. He ducked his head and pulled her into his arms. She fit there easily, and JJ took a long breath of her skin, her hair, her clothes.

"You seemed upset about me staying here longer."

"I am," he said, and she stiffened in his arms. "Because I want to pick you up for a date without your brother knowing." He touched his lips to her shoulder, and she shivered. "I want to drop you off and spend some time kissing you goodnight without him seeing us on the doorbell camera."

Ruby wrapped her arms around him and held on too, and JJ sure did like that. It made him feel wanted and desirable, and he didn't get to feel that way very often.

"You and him living together makes me feel like I'm in a straitjacket." He lifted his head and looked at her, really looked into the depths of those pretty hazel eyes. "I can't be your boyfriend the way I want to be."

"I talked to him about it."

His eyebrows went up. "You did?"

"I mean, a little bit. He said it would be 'super-weird' but you know what? He can get used to super-weird." She wore a sharpness in her eyes JJ really liked.

"I'm going to talk to him," JJ said.

"And you're moving soon."

He blinked at her. "I am moving soon."

"So we won't be living in the same place," she said. "And I can come over to your house." She smiled up at him. "No Tate."

"I've been trying to protect him," JJ said, his voice quieter now, more desperate. "I've been trying to protect *you*."

She reached up and ran her hand down the side of his face. JJ leaned into the touch, glad she hadn't fired back at him that she didn't need him to protect her. Super glad she hadn't called him a coward.

"I'm going to kiss you now," JJ murmured. He lowered his head and swept his cowboy hat from his head when it bumped against her forehead. His eyes drifted closed only a moment before he touched his lips to hers, and that beautiful, blissful fire burst through him at that first contact.

She'd kissed him in the hospital, weeks and weeks ago, but that had only lasted for a couple of seconds. And she'd been crying.

She wasn't crying right now, and he reveled in the

feeling of her hands sliding up his chest and around to the back of his neck. She kissed him back, and JJ lost all track of time, of movement, of everything.

All that existed was Ruby and kissing Ruby and finding a way to spend way more time with Ruby.

A loud, harsh gasp entered his ears, warning him that he wasn't alone with Ruby. It still took him another moment to stop kissing her, and then he turned toward the source of the sound, effectively protecting Ruby behind his body.

Clara Jean stood there, her eyes as wide as dinner plates.

JJ's heart sank all the way to the soles of his feet and kept on going into the ground. "Clara Jean." He looked toward the corner of the barn closest to the house.

Ruby emerged from behind him and slid her hand into his. He tilted his head down to look at her, almost desperate with the need to kiss her again.

"I was—" Clara Jean took a deep breath. "My uncle said we could go out to the orchards, and I thought you might want to go."

"I don't want to go out to the orchards," JJ said.

Ruby squeezed his hand. "She was talking to me."

"We can pick some apples and take them to the store." Her eyes came back to JJ's, and he glared at her. Clara Jean shifted her feet and looked toward the corner of the barn too. "Uh, there's something else."

"Something else?" JJ growled.

Clara Jean moved toward him with long, sure strides now. "Are you and Ruby dating?"

He lifted his chin. "Yes," he said boldly.

"Does Tate know?"

"Not yet."

"He's coming back out," Clara Jean said. "He just moves slower than me."

"Great," JJ said like he'd tell his best friend he'd kissed his sister right there in the shade of the barn.

Clara Jean swallowed and darted a look over to Ruby. "I kissed Tate."

JJ opened his mouth to respond before he'd truly heard and comprehended what she'd said. Beside him, Ruby sucked in a breath and gasped out, "What? When?"

"That day after church." Clara Jean lifted her chin too, and JJ saw so much Walker in her. "We've sort of been texting and stuff secretly."

"There you guys are," Tate said, and all eyes flew to him —even Clara Jean, who had to spin around to do it. Ruby started to withdraw her hand from his, but JJ held on tighter. She looked at him, and JJ shook his head in two short bursts.

"What's going on?" Tate asked, his eyes narrowing as he frowned.

Clara Jean fell to JJ's other side, and JJ stared at his best friend and begged God silently to give him the right words.

About the same moment that Tate noticed JJ and Ruby's entwined fingers, JJ said, "I like your sister."

Tate's eyes flew to his.

"I like your sister a lot, and we're seein' each other."

"If that's weird for you, oh well," Ruby added.

"I told them about us," Clara Jean said.

Tate looked over to Clara Jean, his mouth dropping open. "You did? What did you say?"

"I said I kissed you that day you left church."

"Well, that's just not true," Tate said with a frown. He came further into the shade, and JJ tensed, not sure what his best friend would do. "I'm pretty sure I kissed you."

"You did not," Clara Jean said, and JJ rolled his eyes. "We met halfway."

"Okay, stop," JJ said. Watching the two of them flirt was downright painful, and he released Ruby's hand to go meet Tate. They stopped in front of one another, and JJ searched Tate's eyes, trying to see and feel and know everything his friend did.

"I like her," JJ said quietly. "I'm going to do my absolute best not to hurt her."

"It's weird," Tate said.

"Maybe as weird as you kissin' Clara Jean," JJ said.

Tate grinned. "I like her."

JJ raised his eyebrows, waiting for the second half of that. When Tate didn't say it, he said, "Go on."

"I'll do my best not to hurt her."

"Your *absolute* best," JJ said.

"My absolute best."

"You know what?" Ruby practically yelled. "I don't need anyone's permission on who I date. I can go out with whoever I want."

"Same," Clara Jean said.

JJ grinned at Tate, and Tate grinned back at him. Then

he opened his arms and grabbed onto his best friend, clapping him in a hug.

"Love you, brother," Tate said.

"Love you too." JJ stepped back and looked over his shoulder to Ruby. She stood with her arms folded and one hip cocked out.

"I'm going out to the orchards," Ruby said as she stalked forward. "Will you please tell Cody that I won't be able to help him muck out the stable this afternoon?"

JJ raised his eyebrows. "Who am I going to get to muck out the stable then?"

Ruby gave him a sickeningly sweet smile he wanted to kiss off her lips. "Please. Like he needs my help."

"He obviously does," JJ said.

"Yeah," Tate added.

Ruby glared at him and rolled her eyes. "Come on, Clara Jean." She stalked out of the shade and around the corner of the barn, Clara Jean hot on her heels.

"I'll call you later, CJ," Tate called after her, and JJ blinked at him.

"CJ?" he asked.

"Clara Jean," Tate said, and JJ tipped his head back and filled the sky with laughter.

Chapter Nineteen

Ruby stood on the tiny back deck of the cabin, her heart fluttering in anticipation as the sun continued to sink into the horizon. The light from it cast a golden hue over the ranch, making everything look like it had been dipped in honey.

She'd spent the better part of the day going over the farmhouse design plans Whitney had asked her to work on, but her mind kept drifting back to JJ. Their first real date—the kind where he'd pick her up, just like she'd always dreamed—loomed only a few minutes from now, and she couldn't help the nervous excitement bubbling in her chest.

She glanced down at her outfit for what felt like the hundredth time—her favorite floral pantsuit, with a wide, white belt cinched around her waist. The soft blush pink with big, splashy flowers across it complimented her hair and skin tone, and made Ruby feel feminine and flirty and like she'd put in a lot of effort. It wasn't too fancy, but it wasn't casual either. It felt like the right balance for a first date with a hot, handsome cowboy on a warm Texas evening in mid-June.

"It's almost down," Tate said as he came walking toward her.

She focused on him instead of the sunset. "It has at least another hour," she said.

"JJ's not here yet?" Tate raised his eyebrows as he reached for the railing and then stepped up. He did little things like that that showed her he wasn't all the way healed yet.

Ruby shook her head. "The turkeys got out, and he had to chase them down." She smiled at her brother. "Then his daddy called, and then he ran inside to shower."

Tate joined her on the deck, the two of them filling it right up. "Where's he taking you tonight?"

"I'm not telling you."

"Oh, come on." He grinned at her. "I won't bring Clara Jean to the same place."

"Yeah, because she's working tonight." Ruby gave him a dry look and focused on the sunset again.

Tate leaned his forearms against the railing, then immediately straightened. "Nope, can't stand like that."

"Go shower and go to bed," Ruby said. "You've been working too much this week."

"Maybe," he said, and coming from Tate, that meant she'd spoken right. He turned and went into their cabin.

Ruby gave the sunset one more smile and then followed him into the air conditioning.

"You can get dinner?"

"Conrad is bringing out pizza," he said. "His aunt is going to take Sarina for a couple of hours."

Ruby nodded as Tate set about making coffee. She knew he could take care of himself, but she'd been doing it for the past several weeks, and she still worried about him. His recovery had been slow, and he still had painful and frustrating days, but today, he seemed more relaxed.

They hadn't talked about her and JJ much, and she'd only brought up Clara Jean once. Of course, it had only been a few days, and while JJ said the summertime on a ranch meant watching the hay grow, he'd been wrong.

Or maybe he ran a different kind of ranch, because the work here never seemed to end—and he wanted to add more stables and more horses to it.

"Are you nervous?" Tate asked.

"No," Ruby said.

"Then why do you keep combing your fingers through your hair?"

Ruby dropped her hands to her sides. She hadn't realized she'd been playing with her hair, which she did do when she got nervous.

He grinned, leaning back into the countertop. "You like him."

Her stomach did a little flip at the truth of that statement. "I do like him," she admitted softly, almost to herself.

Her hands came up to fiddle with her hair again, and Ruby forced them back down. "What about you and Clara Jean?"

"Yeah, I like her," Tate said, his voice pitching up in a forced-casual kind of way.

"You haven't asked her out," Ruby said.

"Not every relationship is made of fancy dates in big trucks," Tate said.

"Yeah, because you can't drive," she shot back.

Tate only grinned at her, then stepped over to the fridge and opened it. He closed it a moment later and said, "I'm going to go shower." He pinned her with a look. "You be good tonight."

"Good?" She scoffed. "I'm always good, Tate."

"No kissing."

"No kissing?" Ruby laughed and left the kitchen. "He's my boyfriend, Tate. I can kiss him if I want to."

"But I don't want to think about you kissing him."

"Then don't."

Tate sighed like he needed to blow all the air out his lungs and refresh it all with his next breath. "Can you just tell me you're going to be good?"

She faced him and saw the frustration and pleading on his face. "Okay," she said. "I'll be good tonight."

"Thank you." Tate spoke in one of the softest voices she'd ever heard, and he took off his cowboy hat and hung it on the hook beside the back door. "I'm going to go shower."

"You're okay?"

He'd been able to shower himself for a while now, but sometimes getting dressed taxed him. "I'm okay," he said over his shoulder as he entered the hall and disappeared from her view.

Ruby couldn't stand to be inside while she waited for JJ to come over from the cabin next door. He moved off the ranch next weekend. And that wasn't entirely true, as the Adair property now belonged to Seven Sons. He was simply moving to a different, new part of the same ranch.

She'd driven from her cabin to his new place, and it had taken her fifteen minutes. She had to go off the ranch and out to the highway, then down to another road that led east until she reached yet another highway. Then she went north again, making a turn and going under a sign JJ had told her he'd replace with the Seven Sons branding just as soon as he could.

His house sat down a winding dirt road with plenty of trees, and to Ruby, it seemed like a storybook scene.

But for now, all he had to do was come outside and go next door, and they could have their date. She grabbed her purse and headed for the door. She paused just before stepping outside, taking a deep breath to steady herself.

You've kissed him already, she reminded herself. *This isn't new*. But somehow tonight felt different. It wasn't a stolen moment in the shadows of the barn, or her sneaking next door in the pre-dawn light. It wasn't an accidental brush of lips.

This was intentional.

This was a real date.

When she stepped out into the warm evening air, JJ was trotting down his front steps. He looked as handsome as ever in a clean button-down shirt done in navy blue plaid, his cowboy hat tilted just right, and those worn jeans that fit him like they'd been stitched just for his long legs.

He smiled when he saw her, and the butterflies in her stomach took flight. "Hey," she said, feeling shy all of a sudden. She went down her front steps and met him with a quick hug.

"Heya, Scarlet." JJ walked around the truck and opened the passenger door for her, a gentleman through and through. "You look beautiful." His eyes lingered on her for several moments. "I love this outfit."

Ruby's cheeks warmed under his gaze, and she'd so be breaking her promise to Tate. It hadn't been real anyway. "Thank you."

As she settled in the truck, JJ closed the door and rounded the front to climb into the driver's seat. He glanced over at her, his dark eyes soft and warm. "Ready?"

"Yes, sirree."

JJ chuckled, pulling the truck onto the main road that led away from Seven Sons Ranch. The air between them felt charged with something unspoken, a mix of excitement and anticipation. Ruby glanced out the window as they drove, the open fields stretching out beneath the wide Texas sky.

"Did you see the sunset tonight?" she asked.

"I'm lookin' at it right now," he said as he made the hairpin turn that led them back toward the highway.

She sighed with happiness. "I love it."

"How do you feel about eating outside?" he asked.

Her gaze flew to his. "Outside?" She pinched the thin, silky fabric of her pantsuit. "I mean, is there a table?"

JJ tapped his fingers on the steering wheel, a small smile playing on his lips. "Yeah, I think so."

"You think so? Should I be worried? Are you taking me out into the Panhandle wilderness?"

He laughed. "No, no. It's nothing crazy. Promise."

"Okay," she said, settling back into her seat. She glanced over at him, studying his profile—the strong line of his jaw, the way his hat shaded his eyes. He seemed more relaxed than she'd ever seen him, but he still possessed that quiet intensity, like he had something important on his mind, like he carried something crucial just beneath the surface.

"Tell me something you love," she said. "Besides horses."

"Besides horses," he mused.

"And it can't be coffee," she rushed to add. "Something I don't know about."

He glanced over to her. "Mushroom Swiss burgers."

She grinned back at him as he turned off the main road and onto a lane that boasted a "dead end" sign. It seemed to hold only houses, and Ruby's curiosity about where they'd be dining outside doubled.

"What about you?" he asked. "I know about the chocolate covered cinnamon bears, so you can't say that."

Ruby thought about it while he pulled into the driveway of a pretty, two-story house.

"I'll be right back." He slid out of the truck before she could ask what they were doing there, and he jogged up to the front door and right through it without knocking. This

233

had to be one of his uncles' houses, and Ruby watched the front door while the radio played quietly in the background.

JJ returned only a minute later, now carrying a big brown paper bag with handles. He put it in the back seat with, "This is dinner," and then got behind the wheel again.

The scent of delicious food met her nose, and Ruby twisted to look at the logo on the bags. "Kitchen to go," she read.

"I got what Tate said."

Surprise knocked through Ruby. "You asked Tate what I'd like?"

"He's eaten at The Kitchen with me," he said. "He mentioned something you'd like there last summer, but I couldn't remember what it was." JJ turned left at the stop sign marking their arrival on the south side of town, and went west. He skirted around the town on the same road Ruby had driven with her father and sister, and asked, "So? What's something you really like that I don't know about?"

"Rainbows," she said with a grin.

JJ smiled too. "That tracks, actually."

"Are there a lot of rainbows in Three Rivers?" she asked.

JJ's expression blanked. "About the same as everywhere else, I'm sure."

Ruby grinned at him, then watched as he pulled into the parking lot of a landscaping company. "From the Ground Up," she read aloud. "They don't look open, Jay."

"They're not." He drove through the empty lot and onto a gravel road that led back through mounds of decorative rock, bark, and stones. He passed boulders and a dozen of rows of trees and shrubs. Then a greenhouse.

Finally, he pulled around the back of that and nodded. "We should be able to see the sunset from up there."

Ruby followed his nod to see a three-story building with a bunch of pink and white balloons tied to a pole on top. "We're eating on the roof?"

"If I can figure out how to get us up there." He grinned at her. "I got directions from my friend Link. His aunt owns this landscaping company."

"Oh, of course," Ruby said, trying to keep the sarcasm out of her voice. If she'd learned anything about JJ, it was how well-connected he was around town. He had a lot of friends who ran or worked on ranches, and their network seemed endless.

So endless that her first date with the man of her dreams would be a rooftop picnic surrounded by the beauty that could grow in town, as the sun went down.

He collected their food from the back while Ruby unbuckled and dropped from the truck. Then he checked his phone and led her toward the door on the red-brick building. He entered a code on the door, which worked, and he chuckled nervously as he entered ahead of her.

"Stairs in the corner," he read from his phone, and he glanced around.

"Right there." Ruby spotted them first, surprised they weren't industrial steps, but a wide set of steps that belonged in a residential building. She stuck close to the wall as she navigated over to them, and then she asked, "All the way up?"

"All the way up." JJ's cowboy boots clacked as he climbed, and then Ruby pushed open a door and stepped back outside.

A breeze lifted her hair and filled her lungs with air, and she smiled into the still-waning sunshine.

JJ moved over to a table that had been set with a tablecloth and real dishes in pure white, with silver utensils and ruby red napkins. "What do you think?" He set down the food and turned back to her.

Ruby's heart swelled at the sight of that table, at the cowboy standing beside it. "It's perfect."

He grinned and reached for her. Ruby stepped right into his arms and tilted her head back. "A rooftop dinner, with a sunset."

"I'm earning a ton of romantic points, aren't I?"

Ruby giggled and snuggled into his chest as she turned to face the sunset. "You totally are."

"Tell me something you absolutely will not eat," he said.

"Cooked carrots," she said.

"Oh, that's too bad," he said with a hint of sadness in his voice. "My momma makes the best brown sugar carrots for Thanksgiving every year. I love 'em."

"Well, anything you add sugar to will make it better," she said.

He chuckled again and turned to get out their food. Ruby joined him and took the seat facing the sunset. A moment later, he placed a wide black container with a clear lid on it in front of her. Ruby's stomach growled in response, making her laugh.

"Guess I didn't realize how hungry I was," she said.

"You're in luck," he said. "The Kitchen has huge portions."

"Can I open it?"

"Yeah, sure." He put a plastic cup of sweet tea in front of her, then folded the bag and tucked it away as he sat down.

Ruby gave him a flirtatious look and popped the lid off her container. The glorious sight of meatloaf sat there, with a pile of creamy mashed potatoes, plenty of brown gravy, and the most beautiful asparagus spears she'd ever seen.

"Jay-J," she breathed, her mouth positively watering. "This looks amazing."

He grinned at her and took off his own lid. He had a steak, a mushroom risotto, and broccolini spears. "Tate said you have an old soul, and you've always loved your momma's meatloaf when no one else in the family would eat it."

"He's not wrong." Ruby leaned toward him, hoping he'd meet her halfway and kiss her. He read her cue very well, and he leaned way further than halfway, going so far as to loop his arm around her. He pulled her into him and kissed her, and Ruby suddenly didn't need to eat ever again.

If she could kiss JJ, that would sustain her for a good, long while. His lips knew exactly how to stroke hers, and he tasted like mint and everything warm and wonderful in the world.

He broke the kiss and leaned his forehead against hers. "It's so good to be out with you."

She agreed, and while Ruby didn't usually have a problem getting her voice to say what sat in her heart, right now, she couldn't. She took a deep breath, and JJ straightened. He picked up his knife and fork, and Ruby copied him.

"Tell me why you love the sunset so much," he said.

She considered him for a moment. "It's like—it's God's reminder that no matter how hard the day was, there's always beauty in the end."

JJ looked over at her, his expression thoughtful as his smile slowly transformed his face into a thing of beauty. "That's a good way of looking at it," he said. "I guess I've always seen it as a time to reflect. Think about what I did right, what I could've done better."

Ruby smiled, finding comfort in the fact that they both found meaning in something as simple as a sunset. "I thought you liked the sunrise better."

"I do," he said as he cut the first bite of his steak. "I suppose I do my reflecting then, and I make a goal that I'll do better today than I did yesterday."

"I like that." She scooped up a bite of her mashed potatoes and forked off the corner of her meatloaf to go with them. "So, tell me," she said, her voice playful. "What's something most people don't know about JJ Walker?"

JJ chewed his food as he watched her. He swallowed and went in for another bite. "That's a tough one. I'm not exactly the mysterious type."

"Sure you are," she said. "You're super mysterious, because you don't talk much."

He lifted his eyebrows. "I don't talk much?"

"I mean, compared to Tate." She shrugged one shoulder and cut an asparagus spear in half.

He thought for a moment, that small smile tugging at the corners of his mouth. "All right, how about this—I can't stand peanut butter."

Ruby's eyes widened in mock horror. "What? How can you not like peanut butter? It's practically a food group."

JJ laughed, the sound rich and warm in the evening air. "I don't know. It just doesn't sit right with me. It's Conrad's favorite thing."

Ruby shook her head, still grinning. "Well, I guess nobody's perfect."

They both laughed, and the sounds melded together in an easy, natural way.

JJ's eyes gleamed with curiosity. "What's something you really want?"

"Like, that big dream for my life?"

"Sure," he said. He took a bite of his broccolini, and the fact that he'd eat vegetables made Ruby like him even more, strange as that seemed.

She spread her arms wide, her fork in one hand and her knife in the other. "I want adventure."

"Like, you want to travel?"

"That's one way to have an adventure, sure." She beamed at him. "But adventures come in all shapes and sizes, and I just want my life to be an adventure."

JJ nodded, glanced out at the horizon and went back to his food. Ruby finished her meatloaf and took a swig of her tea. "Okay, a fast round."

"Fast round?"

"Say something—anything—that comes to your mind."

JJ put the lid back on his container too and leaned away from the table. "Okay, shoot."

"One thing you can't do. I'll go first: whistle."

"Snap my fingers."

"What? That can't be true. All cowboys can snap."

He grinned at her. "All cowboys?" He chuckled and shook his head. "I can do it, but it barely makes a sound."

Ruby raised an eyebrow, intrigued. "Okay, now I have to hear this. Go on, try it."

JJ held up his hand, took a deep breath, and then attempted to snap his fingers. The result was a faint, barely audible click.

Ruby burst out laughing, and JJ joined in, his face flushing. "See? It's pathetic."

Ruby wiped a tear from her eye, still giggling. "Okay, okay. So we're both a little imperfect."

JJ smiled at her, his eyes softening. "I think that's what makes life interesting, though. The imperfections."

Ruby's laughter faded into a soft smile as she met his gaze. Something about the way he looked at her made her heart ache in the best possible way. She'd known JJ for years, but in this moment, it felt like she was seeing him with new eyes.

"Tell me more about your plans," Ruby said after a beat,

her voice quieter now. "The Adair property, and what you want to do with it."

JJ's expression shifted, a mixture of excitement and uncertainty combining. "Well, it's a big step for me," he admitted. "I spent a lot on the land, but I'll live there. I've wanted my own place that's not a cowboy cabin. I mean, I'm their boss, you know?"

"Mm, yes."

"And I don't need my parents right on top of me." His tone turned a touch darker. "And I've always wanted to expand into horse breeding. Maybe even longhorn cattle breeding, if things go well."

Ruby heard the passion in his voice. "That's amazing, JJ. You're so good with horses. I think it's a perfect fit for you."

He smiled at her, a little shyly this time. "Thanks, Rubes. I'm gonna do my best not to mess it up."

She scooted closer to him and leaned into his side as he lifted his arm around her shoulders. They faced the now-quickly-waning light, and Ruby liked the way his touch grounded her.

The land sprawled out before them, wide and open, untouched. It was as if she had a blank canvas that held all the possibilities in the world, limited only by what she dared to dream, in the palm of her hand.

The last slivers of sunlight slipped below the horizon, casting a golden glow over the land that felt like a promise, like the beginning of something she couldn't quite see yet, but which she sensed just beyond her reach.

And she wanted it very, very badly.

Chapter Twenty

J J gripped the edge of the mattress as he and his daddy eased it through the front door of the farmhouse. His fingers strained to get a good grip, but the satisfaction of finally moving into his own place overpowered any discomfort. The early-morning air was already warm but not stifling, and the wide-open space of the Adair property—his little piece of Seven Sons Ranch—stretched before him, a promise of the future he'd dreamed about for years.

"Easy now," his daddy said, his voice steady and calm. His father had been the rock of Seven Sons Ranch for the duration of JJ's life, and today, as they carried JJ's new mattress into the house, that steady presence soothed his nerves. It should've felt like a regular move, as JJ had gone back and forth to Amarillo and several different apartments over the past five years, but it wasn't.

His own place. His own house. No roommates.

They maneuvered the mattress down the hallway, past boxes of unopened appliances, dishware, and housewares, and into the master bedroom. The furniture company had delivered everything JJ had picked out yesterday, but that didn't mean it was all where he wanted it.

Good thing all the uncles would be here in the next half-hour.

The bedroom smelled like fresh paint and the faintest whiff of sawdust from the recent renovations. JJ had worked with Uncle Micah on a few things, as his uncle was a master craftsman. He'd built in some bookcases in the office, installed a ceiling fan in the living room and this bedroom, and built JJ an entertainment cabinet for the master that would hold a TV, a gaming console, as well as provide some storage.

"Right there." JJ nodded toward the bed frame, which they'd already assembled in the middle of the room. He and his daddy lowered the mattress onto it, and JJ stepped back, wiping the sweat from his brow with the back of his hand.

His daddy straightened, dusting his hands together as he surveyed the room. "Looks good, son."

"Thanks, Daddy." JJ tried to keep his voice casual, but the pride swelling in his chest refused to be tamped down.

"How's it feel to have a place of your own?" His daddy's voice carried that familiar tone of teasing, but something else rode in it too—something like respect.

JJ glanced around the room, his eyes lingering on the simple furniture he'd picked out. A sturdy wooden bed frame, matching nightstands, and a dresser. All brand new, all his. "Feels good," he said, his voice quieter than he'd intended. "Real good."

His daddy clapped him on the back, a solid thump that nearly knocked the wind out of him. "Well, it looks like you're off to a decent start, that's for sure."

A decent start. JJ smiled to himself as his daddy walked out of the room, leaving him alone for a moment. It was more than a decent start—it was the beginning of something he'd been working toward for years. He'd never wanted to live in the same house where he'd grown up.

One, he still had siblings living at home with his parents. Two, JJ loved his family, but he didn't want his house to be the epicenter of every Walker gathering.

The homestead where Momma and Daddy lived had been that for all twenty-six years of his life, and JJ wanted more of a sanctuary. More privacy.

Plus, he needed the space for the horse breeding program he wanted to start.

He took a deep breath, savoring this moment of achievement before stepping back into the hallway. The house buzzed with activity; his uncles had arrived, as evidenced by the loud voices and laughter coming from the front of the house.

JJ stepped into the living room and glanced into the kitchen. Tate stood there, opening a box he then pulled a stack of plastic containers out of. The red lids followed, and he held them up for Clara Jean. "Where does he want these?"

She opened a cupboard door and looked inside. "I don't

know," she said, and JJ grinned at them as he moved into the kitchen too.

"Just pick somewhere," he said. "I'm sure Momma will go through it all and organize it for me."

"Or Daddy," Clara Jean said. "Put them here, Tate."

"Let me move that lamp," Ruby said, and JJ turned toward the sound of her voice. She darted ahead of Uncle Skyler and Uncle Liam, who each had an end of a couch. "Right here." Ruby grabbed the table lamp and swept it out of the way so his uncles could put the sofa in the right spot.

Ruby caught JJ's gaze with her bright eyes and gave him a quick smile, one that made his chest tighten in that familiar, wonderful way.

"Mugs," Tate announced, and JJ barely knew which way to turn.

"Jay-J," Daddy called from the front porch. "Come tell us where to put this stuff."

He'd been summoned, and he stayed out of the way as Uncle Wyatt brought in the endtable JJ had ordered and Ruby set the lamp on it.

"Don't be liftin' much," Uncle Liam said to Uncle Wyatt, and they started a friendly bickering session that JJ turned his back on as he headed outside.

"What stuff?" he asked his daddy. He'd gotten there early and put sticky notes on all the furniture, so that when his uncles arrived, they could get it where it needed to go. He'd wanted a guest room, so any of his siblings or cousins could come stay with him and have a bed with a fully stocked bathroom, but that queen mattress and boxed springs still sat on the front porch.

Daddy held up a handful of bright orange sticky notes. "The wind foiled your little plan."

JJ snatched the notes from him. "You're kidding."

Uncle Micah and Uncle Tripp stood there, and JJ looked at the top note. "The bed goes in the first room on the right down the hall," he said, and they moved to do that. "This desk goes in the office." He moved over and tried to stick the note down again. It wouldn't stay, and he looked at his daddy.

"Let's get it in the office then."

"Love seat in the living room," JJ told Uncle Skyler and Uncle Liam who'd come back outside. "Uncle Rhett, all of that bedding goes in my bedroom."

"All right," Uncle Rhett said, and he nodded to it at the same time he stepped toward it. Conrad joined him, and JJ didn't have to wonder where his daughter was that morning.

Aunt Evvy had taken her, JJ was sure. Or Grams. Probably both of them, as they planned to cook together all day, so they could bring JJ some food later.

His heart filled with love for his amazing aunts and uncles who'd given up their summer Saturday to come help him.

JJ picked up the end of the desk and waited for his daddy to get into position too. He had no idea what to do with an office, but the room sat right off the front of the house, and when JJ had toured the place, it had held a piano and a couch.

Since he didn't play, and he did need somewhere to keep track of everything on the ranch, he figured he could turn it into an office. And every good office needed a desk.

"There's a chair here somewhere," JJ said.

"Momma's calling," Daddy said, lifting his phone to his ear. He ducked outside as he said, "Hey, baby, what's up?"

JJ glanced around the house, taking in the sight of his family bustling around, helping him settle into his new home. He went back out onto the porch and brought in a couple more boxes that had come from the home goods store, expecting them to hold dishes, or pots and pans, or towels, or something else he needed to actually live in his house. Things his momma had always just owned, but which he had to buy.

A soft laugh drew his attention, and he turned to see Ruby sitting on the couch as she put together a lava lamp. Something played on her phone that she watched for a moment, then went back to the directions for the lamp.

He set down the boxes on the island countertop and picked up the knife someone had left there so he could slice open the box. He watched her twist the base onto the lamp, then go back to the instructions, something in that simple action making his heart open another door for the lovely Ruby Reynolds.

"Mm, I know that look."

JJ looked over to Tate. "There's no look." He cut through the tape on the box and opened the flaps.

"Sure there is," Tate said. "You smile so much more now."

"I just bought a house," JJ said. "It's smile-worthy." In fact, Tate would be singing at the top of his lungs if he were moving into his own house, on his own ranch, today.

"She's good for you."

Irritation spiked through JJ, though he wanted his girl-friend to be good for him. He just didn't want to hear it from Tate, who'd been the biggest obstacle to their relationship for so long.

Ruby glanced up, catching his eye, and smiled. "You okay over there, cowboy?" she asked, her voice teasing.

"Oh, gross." Tate turned away and took a couple of broken-down boxes with him as he left the kitchen and headed for the garage.

JJ's pulse skipped around his body, because he didn't want to be "gross" in front of other people. Since no one else was in the back of the house—even Clara Jean had gone somewhere else—he crossed his arms, a grin tugging at his lips. "Yeah, just enjoying the view."

Ruby's cheeks flushed, but she didn't shy away from his gaze. "Well, if you're done ogling me, you can come help with the rest of this decor." She held up the complete lava lamp. "Where do you want this?"

"My bedroom," he said as he approached her. "I had one growing up, and when I saw it at the furniture store, I just threw it in the cart."

"Must be nice," she said. "To just put anything you want in the cart."

JJ listened hard to the shape of the words, trying to find

the meaning behind them. "Yeah," he said when he couldn't find anything. "It is."

Ruby moved on to the next task—unpacking the towels in the guest bathroom—always a whirlwind of activity, moving from one thing to the next with a kind of effortless grace that made JJ's heart swell with pride. She had a way of making everything feel light, fun—even the mundane tasks of unpacking and organizing.

He and his uncles got all the furniture off the porch and into the place where it belonged, and by the time his momma and his sisters, plus Jason, arrived with lunch, the house had started to look like a home.

"Hey, everyone," Hattie called as she stepped inside, carrying a large picnic basket. "We brought enough food to feed an army."

Momma followed with a tray of sandwiches in her hands. "Y'all better be hungry," she said with a smile. "We've got sandwiches, chips, fruit salad, and lemonade."

JJ's stomach growled at the sight of the food, and he realized it had been hours since breakfast. "I'm starving," he said as he crowded around the island where his momma stood arranging the food.

"This place looks great, baby." She smiled at him, and JJ stepped into her arms for a hug. He loved hugging his mother, and then he backed up, out of the way, and took Ruby's hand in his.

"Food's here," Uncle Rhett called, and that got anyone who hadn't already gathered in the kitchen to come. Uncle

Wyatt arrived last, carrying a hammer in one hand and his phone in the other.

Then all eyes came to JJ. His daddy raised his eyebrows, and JJ dang near jumped out of his skin. "Oh, it's my house."

His uncles chuckled, and JJ looked at Conrad. He nodded, giving JJ the strength and permission to own his house. "It's my house," he said again. "Conrad, will you say grace? Momma and the sibs brought the food, so be sure to thank them."

He grinned at Jason, his only brother, and nodded to his sisters. Then he quickly pulled off his cowboy hat as Conrad did, and everyone closed their eyes in preparation for the prayer.

"Lord," Conrad said, and then he paused. JJ knew he'd been in a mighty struggle with a lot of things lately, but he'd always exuded confidence in such an easy way.

Now, he cleared his throat. "We're so grateful for a good family. We're grateful JJ was able to get this house and the land to achieve his vision for Seven Sons, and we're real glad we're all healthy enough to be here to help him move into it.

"Thank You for this food and those who prepared it. Thank You for blessings that might look like trials. Bless us to employ our faith and humble ourselves to come to Thee as often as we need to. Bless us to be forgiving and kind, and we're glad we have the scriptures to see the perfect example of such things in the life of Thy Son."

JJ could listen to his cousin pray for hours, as Conrad said each word with practiced precision, and he should've been a pastor.

"We love Thee," he said. "Amen."

"Amen," JJ said, adding his voice to those of his family. They looked around at one another, and then Daddy stepped forward.

"Thanks for the food, sweetheart. Thanks for that real nice prayer, Conrad." He picked up a sandwich and took a whole bag of chips over to the dining room table that had literally just been put together an hour ago.

JJ found himself between his father and Uncle Skyler, with Ruby across from him with Tate, Clara Jean, and Hattie. He glanced at her, finding her joy and enthusiasm so contagious.

"You're awfully smiley today," Daddy said.

JJ jerked his attention away from Ruby. "Yeah, it's moving day."

"Moving days are terrible," Uncle Skyler said.

"Maybe if you're hiding a marriage," JJ shot back, as Skyler had moved back to Three Rivers a married man—and no one in the family had known at the time.

Uncle Skyler laughed loudly, and JJ was glad his joke had been taken as such.

"You like Ruby."

"Yeah, Daddy," JJ said as he ducked his head. "That's why I'm dating her."

His daddy nodded, his eyes twinkling with something akin to amusement and wariness at the same time. "And how's that going?"

"Good," JJ said, his gaze flicking to Ruby again. "Really good." He finished up, and he got up to hug his uncles as they started to leave. "Thank you," he said over and over. "Thank you so much."

They loved him so much, and JJ knew that, but it was entirely different to see it, to feel it. The house emptied as Daddy took Momma's basket and trays outside to her minivan, as JJ's siblings followed, as Tate took Clara Jean's hand and said, "I'm gonna go show her the wishing well."

JJ waved them out of the house and turned to find Ruby standing at the back window. "Thanks for coming, Scarlet," he said as he joined her.

"Are you kidding? This place is incredible." She leaned her head against his shoulder. "I can stay to help you hang the curtains and finish with the kitchen stuff."

"Okay." JJ wasn't going to argue with someone offering help. "My grams will bring dinner. Maybe we can have an at-home date tonight."

"Sure," Ruby said. "I just have to check on a few orders this afternoon, so I'm ready to start at your momma's place on Monday." She looked over to him, and JJ took the opportunity to match his mouth to hers and kiss her. She kissed him back, which made his blood run hotter through his body.

When her phone buzzed, she pulled away, breaking the moment. She pulled her phone out and frowned at the screen. "It's Opal and Oak," she said. She looked at him, her brow furrowed, but JJ didn't know what Opal and Oak was.

Something tickled in his memory, and as she swiped on the call, he remembered that was the name of the interior design firm she'd been meant to intern with this summer.

"Hello?" She turned her back on him and paced away. She faced him again, her free arm folded across her body as if protecting herself from the call.

JJ couldn't hear the other side of the conversation, but he could see the way Ruby's expression shifted from confusion to surprise to something else. Something that made his stomach twist.

"Yes, I remember...September? That soon?" Ruby searched his face from several feet away, but JJ certainly couldn't help her.

JJ's heart thudded in his chest as he watched her, his mind racing. September? What was happening in September?

"Okay," Ruby said, nodding now. "I'll let you know. Thank you." She hung up, her eyes still wide with shock as she turned to face JJ.

"Who was that?" JJ asked, his voice steady, but his heartbeat anything but.

Ruby swallowed, her eyes darting away from his. "That was Opal and Oak, that interior design firm I was going to intern with. They have an opening, and they want me to come in September."

JJ's heart sank. September. That was only a couple of months away. And San Antonio was hundreds of miles from Three Rivers.

Suddenly, the future he'd been building in his mind— the one with Ruby by his side—became a little less certain.

Chapter Twenty-One

R uby stood in the middle of the Walker family kitchen, staring at the blueprints and sketches spread across the wide, wonderful, wooden table. She had everything she needed to start—her tape measure, her sketchpad, her notes, and a whole heap of helping hands coming to do demolition today—but her mind lingered somewhere miles away.

The farmhouse sat in silence except for the occasional creak of old floorboards, but even the pure country stillness couldn't settle the storm raging inside her.

Opal and Oak. San Antonio. September.

She ran a hand through her hair, the strands catching in her fingers as she tried to focus. She should be excited about this project. Whitney had given her complete creative freedom to redesign the farmhouse, and Ruby had been thrilled to have the opportunity to add something real to her student portfolio. This was exactly the kind of work she'd always dreamed of—transforming an older space into something new while preserving its history and charm.

But now, with the call from Opal and Oak hanging over her like a dark cloud, everything felt heavy, like a weight pressing down on her chest, making it hard to breathe.

She took a deep breath, closing her eyes for a moment. *It's two months away,* she told herself. *Focus on the farmhouse. One step at a time.*

But she didn't know how to start this project if she couldn't finish it—and there was no way she could finish the whole first floor in only two months. Who would finish the house when she left for San Antonio?

She opened her eyes and stared at the sketches again, trying to force her mind to cooperate. She had a vision for this place—something bright and airy, full of life and warmth, just like the Walker family itself, with the incorporation of the outdoors in the indoor space.

It was a chance to prove herself, to show what she could do. And yet...

Her phone rang, and she jumped, the shrill sound startling in the silent space. She fumbled to pull it out, her heart sinking when she saw the name on the screen.

Opal and Oak.

Again.

She stared at the name for a second, her thumb hovering over the screen. *Answer it,* her mind urged. *See what they want. It could be important.*

But she couldn't. Not right now. Not when her chest felt

like it could cave in at any moment. She turned the phone over and set it facedown on the table, the buzzing stopping as the screen went dark again.

"Ruby?"

She jumped again, her hand flying to her chest as she spun around to see Whitney standing in the doorway, her brow furrowed with concern. "You okay, honey?"

Ruby forced a smile, her heart still racing from the phone call she'd just ignored. "Yeah, I'm fine. Just thinking through the best way to get the cabinets out of here."

"Oh, the boys do that." Whitney stepped into the kitchen and glanced around the room. "They should be here soon." She smiled and looked at Ruby. "I hope this renovation doesn't drive Jeremiah into his grumpy mode."

Ruby wanted to tell her it wasn't a renovation. She was replacing the cabinets, yes, but that was all. Fine, she'd update the flooring in the living room, foyer, dining area, and kitchen too. But she wasn't knocking down walls and rearranging the layout of the house. Once they'd emptied it and taken out the cabinets, then Ruby would have the flooring installed, put in the new light fixtures, and order the furniture.

"Oh, Simone found some pieces she thought would fit your theme," Whitney said. "She wants you to come over and meet with her and Micah. He can build anything you can't find."

Ruby nodded, trying to focus on Whitney's words. She appreciated how kind and supportive JJ's mother had been—how the entire Walker family had welcomed her in like she'd always belonged to them. She'd found a sense of community here, a sense of belonging that she hadn't realized she'd been missing until she had it.

But that sense of belonging was exactly what made this decision so hard.

"Do you need anything from me?" Whitney asked.

Ruby shook her head. "No, I've got everything I need. Just going over the timeline again." She flashed Whitney a smile. "I'll call Simone." Well, she'd text, as Ruby didn't super-love calling anyone.

Whitney smiled, reaching out to give Ruby's arm a soft squeeze. "Well, I trust you, Ruby. Whatever you decide will be perfect."

The words hit Ruby harder than they should have.

Whitney's trust, her confidence, felt like an anchor, holding Ruby here, keeping her tied to this place. But what if she needed to let go? What if she needed to take that leap, even if it meant leaving all of this behind?

Whitney must have noticed the change in Ruby's expression because her smile faded, replaced by a look of concern. "You sure you're okay, honey? You seem a little— well, you're not as bright as you usually are."

Ruby hesitated, the words on the tip of her tongue. She could tell Whitney about Opal and Oak, about the decision that felt like it would press all the oxygen from her lungs.

"Whitney, can I ask you something?"

"Of course," she said as she moved over to the fridge and opened it. She pulled out a diet cola and popped the top, waiting for Ruby to speak.

"I came here to help Tate, because this internship I had lined up in San Antonio had fallen through." She pulled out the dining chair and sat down. The cowboys she'd recruited to come help get the cabinets and furniture out of the house wouldn't be here for another half-hour. She could get through this.

"Okay." Whitney joined her at the table.

"They called over the weekend," Ruby said. "They have a spot opening up in September, and they offered it to me."

Whitney watched her, and Ruby dropped her eyes to the sketchbook. She hadn't even called her parents yet, and they'd certainly give her some good advice too. She'd been thinking about the offer non-stop since it had come in, and she couldn't even remember what the pastor had spoken about in church yesterday.

"Do you want the internship?"

"I mean, yeah, I...did." She whispered the last word. Now? She wasn't sure if she wanted to pack up and leave Three Rivers. Leave JJ. Leave this job behind.

"Why don't you now?"

Ruby didn't want to tell Whitney that she was falling in love with JJ. But she was. She felt wild and young, and perhaps she didn't even know what love was. The words sounded ridiculous inside her own head.

"I won't be able to finish this job," Ruby said. "The internship is unpaid." She blew out her breath and kept going. "I'm dating JJ, and he's pretty solidly here."

"That he is." Whitney studied her for a moment longer, then lifted her soda can to her mouth and tipped her head back, breaking the connection. "I had a very successful baby photography business when I met and married Jeremiah."

"You did?" Ruby perked up, as JJ hadn't told her much about his parents. And why would he? They were getting to know each other, not each other's parents.

"I sure did." She smiled at Ruby. "We had JJ almost immediately, and I have the cutest pictures of him with cabbages and celery."

Ruby lit up like the sun. "I have to see those."

"I'm surprised he hasn't shown you." She giggled and tucked her hair behind her ear. "Oh, wait, no I'm not. He hates them."

Ruby laughed with her, and she *would* be seeing those baby pictures of JJ. Without a doubt.

"Clara Jean came along something like fifteen months later," Whitney said, her smile still in place. "I stopped doing the photography. I stopped working for my family's grocery store. I had little babies—a lot of them—really close together. Did you know Jason and Clara Jean are actually Irish twins? They're only eleven months apart."

"Wow," Ruby said.

Whitney nodded. "Yeah, wow. At the time, I didn't feel wow. I questioned everything Jeremiah and I had decided to do. I simply didn't have time for photography."

"Did you miss it?"

"Yeah, of course," Whitney said. "But I had all these sisters-in-law, and they were having babies too. I did the veggie newborn pics for them." She smiled. "I found ways to still do this eccentric thing I loved." She gave Ruby a beautiful smile.

"You're a smart woman," Whitney said. "Already done with college. You'll figure it out."

Ruby nodded, though she didn't want to figure it out. She wanted someone to tell her what to do. She wanted God to open the doors to the future and show her what her life would be if she picked the internship in San Antonio, and what it would be if she didn't.

If she picked JJ.

"Oh, the boys are here." Whitney got to her feet as the sliding glass door behind her opened and cowboy voices started to fill the house. "Come on in, fellas."

Ruby stood up too, and she took one deep breath after another. JJ broke through the group of men who'd just shown up, and he smiled at her as he neared. "Hey, Princess Scarlet. You wanna go to lunch after this?"

She grinned as he reached her and wrapped her up in his arms. "Do you have time for lunch today?"

"Yeah, and we can meet Ollie and Aurora. You haven't met them yet, and you'll love them."

Ruby nodded, though she really just wanted a quiet lunch with JJ at his house. She pressed her cheek to his. "Can we still have dinner at your house tonight?"

"Absolutely," he murmured in her ear just as Whitney said, "All right, Ruby, we're just waiting on you to tell us what to do."

She pulled away from her boyfriend, embarrassment heating her face when she found everyone looking at her.

She'd asked the cowboys to come in from their ranch chores that morning to help, and she couldn't waste their time.

"Okay," she said as she picked up her notebook. "Steve, Kevin, and Cody, I'm going to have you start to empty the living room. We can put things in the two bedrooms up front, as we're not going to do that carpet until the end of the redesign."

She surveyed the group again. "Lance, Bobby, and Scotty, I want you—oh, and Jeremiah—to take out the cabinets. They're going in the barn behind Skyler's house, and they'll need to be installed over there."

"Where do you want me, baby?" JJ asked.

"You're going to help move stuff out of these main rooms." Ruby hadn't given herself a job, because overseeing eight men —one of whom was her boyfriend and another the father of her boyfriend—already had a trio of knots forming in her stomach.

"All right," Whitney said. "You boys moving things into the bedrooms, let's get going."

People started to move, to pick up throw pillows and lamps, potted plants and end tables. They took them out of the room and around the corner to the bedrooms, which Whitney had prepped.

Jeremiah took charge in the kitchen, claiming, "I put these cabinets in, and they should just come right off the wall."

Ruby loved demo day, especially since it wasn't really a big demolition. She let her indecision and the fear of the unknown get buried beneath the hustle and bustle of removing cabinets and clearing three spaces that all belonged to the same space.

Living room, dining room, kitchen.

With strong, capable men, it sure didn't take long for the space to be empty, with half the cabinets gone. She'd replace the island when the new cabinetry came, and since she hadn't ordered it yet, Jeremiah and Whitney—and Emily and Hattie, Clara Jean and Jason—would have to live without much of a kitchen for a while.

Jason was planning to move into JJ's room in the cabin next to Tate and Ruby, and Clara Jean said she could bring home meals from Wilde & Organic. But Jeremiah loved to cook and entertain, so Ruby wanted to get their house put back together as fast as possible.

Perhaps she could do this in two months, instead of the four she'd outlined.

"All done," JJ announced as Lance and Bobby carried out the last of the cabinets. "My daddy's almost got them up in the barn too." He grinned at Ruby and took both of her hands. "I canceled lunch with Ollie and Rory."

"You did?"

"I could tell you didn't want to go." He pulled her close and started slow-dancing with her. It felt almost a little naughty to do that in his parents' empty house. Anyone could walk in and see that they had zero space between them.

"I don't know what to do about the internship."

JJ held her tight, right against him, his hands big and

warm against her back. "You don't have to decide right now, Ruby. There's time."

"Is there?" She wanted to believe him, but time felt like it slipped through her fingers faster than she could hold onto it. "I don't want to lose this," she whispered, her voice barely audible.

JJ pulled away and looked right at her. "I don't want that either." He closed his eyes and leaned in. "I'm falling in love with you, Ruby."

Pure joy burst through her, and Ruby lifted her hands up to his face and cradled it in both palms. "I feel the same way, and San Antonio feels impossibly far away."

"You've always said you wanted an adventure." He gave her a small smile. "How long is the internship?"

"Four months," she said.

"Done by the New Year," he said. "Easy."

"Yeah," she said. "Easy."

Four months wasn't forever.

But she also knew that if she left, everything would change. They wouldn't be able to see each other every day, wouldn't have these simple moments like this one, slow dancing after a morning of working together.

And she wasn't sure she could handle that.

JJ must have sensed her turmoil because he let her go and stepped back, his expression thoughtful. "You've gotta do what's right for you, Ruby. I'll support you, no matter what."

She stared at him, her heart aching as her mind raced. She felt as if she stood on the edge of a cliff between two canyons, and no matter which way she jumped, she'd lose something vitally important.

She needed to call her momma and get her words to mix up with Whitney's. Or maybe her mom would simply tell her what to do—stay at Seven Sons with JJ, finish falling in love, and build her adventure here with him, or take the internship in San Antonio and open a dozen new doors that could lead her anywhere.

Chapter Twenty-Two

JJ shifted his weight from one foot to the other, his arms crossed tightly over his chest as he watched the workers maneuver the new arch into place. The metallic scrape of the bolts sliding through the frame set his teeth on edge, the sound vibrating through the open space around him. He tried to focus on the task at hand—on the way the arch, with its bold *Seven Sons Ranch* lettering, would stand tall over this new east entrance to the ranch— but his mind kept wandering back to Ruby.

He shoved his hands into his pockets, his fingers curling into fists as he tried to keep his thoughts from spiraling. Conrad stood a few feet away, his eyes squinted against the wind that had kicked up in the last hour. JJ glanced at his cousin, who seemed content to simply observe, offering the occasional nod of approval as the workers tightened the bolts and hauled off the old arch.

"Looks good," Conrad said, his voice carrying over the noise of the truck engine idling nearby.

JJ swallowed hard, his throat dry as the weight of the moment pressed down on him. "Yeah," he muttered. "Real good."

And it felt great too.

"Why are you so grouchy then?" Conrad gave him a smile, and JJ started to relax.

"Feels...big," he said.

"Yeah, but it's not a two-year-old you didn't know about." Conrad clapped him on the shoulder. "The stars are amazing. Maybe I should put something up at the farm with me and Grams."

JJ did love the navy blue stars that somehow shone brightly. One for each of the seven sons, his daddy included. None of them had had seven sons, but the legacy of their family meant something to him, to Conrad, to all of his uncles.

The new arch symbolized something bigger than just a name. All the work JJ had put into the ranch, into this land he'd been living on for a month now, his very future, shone in those stars.

Even as he enjoyed the new arch, he sure wished Ruby stood at his side while it went up. She'd been working feverishly on the remodel of the homestead at the heart of the ranch, because she still hadn't decided if she would take the internship in San Antonio, and she didn't want to leave the house half-done.

The fact that she'd accelerated the timeline at the homestead told JJ she'd be leaving the Panhandle. Leaving Seven Sons. Leaving him.

Tate still couldn't do the work of a fully able-bodied man, but he did work all day long. Stuff JJ had done as a ten or twelve-year-old. He claimed his ribs were better and better every day, and JJ didn't know how to push his best friend into being completely honest. For all he knew, he *was* being completely honest.

His jaw clenched, the muscle there twitching as he fought to keep his emotions in check. He didn't want to think about the phone call Ruby had gotten, or the uncertainty that had crept into their relationship ever since.

"She'll love it." Conrad's voice broke through JJ's thoughts, and he shot his cousin a look.

"Who?"

"Ruby." Conrad's tone came out casually, but a knowing glint sat in his eyes. "You're thinking about her, right?"

JJ grunted, turning his gaze back to the arch as the workers packed up their tools and started loading them into the truck. "I'm always thinking about her."

Conrad chuckled softly. "That's kind of the point, isn't it?"

JJ didn't respond. He didn't have to. Conrad knew him too well, had seen him pine after Ruby for years without ever saying a word. And now that they were finally together —now that it was real—JJ couldn't shake the feeling that it was all slipping away before it had even really begun.

"You talk to her lately?" Conrad asked, his voice still calm, almost nonchalant.

"Yeah," JJ said, though his voice was tight. "We're supposed to have dinner tonight. At my place."

Conrad nodded, his gaze shifting back to the arch. "I meant about San Antonio. I know you talked to her about it when she first got the call. What about now?"

JJ's stomach twisted at the mention of the city. He hadn't wanted to bring it up, hadn't wanted to force Ruby into a conversation she wasn't ready to have. But the truth was, every day that passed without a real discussion felt like a countdown to something he couldn't control.

"She hasn't decided yet," JJ said, the words coming out more defensive than he intended. "I don't need to ask her. Ruby says whatever's on her mind."

Conrad raised an eyebrow, but he didn't push the conversation further. He just stood there, his presence steady and solid, like it always had been. "You can't avoid it forever."

JJ's jaw tightened again. "I know."

The truck rumbled down the gravel driveway, the dust kicking up behind it as it disappeared down the road. Silence settled over the property, broken only by the soft rustling of the wind through the trees and the distant hum of machinery from the other side of the ranch.

JJ stared at the arch, at the bold letters that now marked the entrance to his home. He loved this new plot of land, and he had an appointment with the land surveyor next week to go over where JJ could build the breeding stable, and he couldn't wait for that.

So many things that he'd only held in his mind and

hoped for in his heart were becoming reality, and he let a smile spread across his face as he turned away from the arch. "Let's go get lunch," he said to Conrad.

"I have to pick up Sarina in forty minutes," Conrad said, going with JJ toward the front steps.

"Then you have twenty to eat a sandwich with me and tell me how to get an answer from Ruby tonight."

Conrad chuckled. "Oh, boy. I don't think I'm cut out for that. Remember how I had a daughter I didn't know about?"

JJ grinned at him. "I've heard that. But I feel like I'm hanging on by a thread, and I'm not sure how much longer I can do that."

Later that evening, JJ stepped off the back porch, his boots crunching against the gravel as he made his way toward the barn. He needed to clear his head, needed to get his hands on something solid, something real. His horses could always soothe him in their steady, dependable way, unlike the mess swirling in his mind.

As he entered the barn that he was still trying to make his, the familiar scent of hay and leather washed over him, grounding him in the present. The horses shifted in their stalls, their soft nickers greeting him as he made his way down the aisle. JJ stopped in front of Doc's stall, reaching out to stroke the gelding's nose.

"Hey, boy," JJ murmured, his voice low. "You ever feel like the whole world's spinning out of control?"

Doc snorted softly, nudging JJ's hand with his nose. JJ smiled, the tension in his chest easing just a little. The horse just wanted a treat, but he let JJ stroke his hand down his nose, then his neck, each move seeding another ounce of calmness inside him.

"Lord," he whispered to the equines and the stable. "I don't want to be the reason Ruby doesn't get to have her adventures."

God didn't tell JJ what to say when Ruby arrived, and He'd never really given JJ the right words. His daddy had told him that if he just opened his mouth, the Lord would step in, but JJ wasn't sure that had ever happened to him.

Minnie nickered from down on the end of the row, and JJ grinned down to the more vocal horse. "Yeah, all right." He sauntered her way, enjoying this slow, easy time with his horses. He did give them butterscotch treats, and he'd just said good-bye to them when his phone rang.

Ruby's name sat there, and JJ's heartbeat bumped up against his ribcage. He answered with, "Hey, Scarlet," his eyes set on the farmhouse.

"I'm standing in your house, and you're not." She sounded in good spirits tonight, and JJ's step lightened. The load that had been weighing on his mind for the past few weeks suddenly lifted, and when he took a breath, the air entered the right way.

He didn't know what that meant, but he increased his pace as he said, "I'm on my way in."

"All right." Ruby opened his back door and stepped out onto the porch. It ran along the back of the house, with five or six steps dropping down to a deck before another five or six spit people out onto the gravel path that split the back lawn.

She beamed at him with the golden afternoon sun shining fully on her. "I thought you'd finished with the horses a while ago," she called.

JJ jogged down the path, not really sure why he had to get to her so fast, only that he did. She giggled as he took the steps to the deck two at a time, and then repeated it to get to her. She squealed as he wrapped her up in his arms, and she brought her feet off the ground as JJ lifted her up.

Mm, he really liked this woman. Maybe he loved her. JJ wasn't sure, as he'd never been in love before.

He set her down, glad that she clung to him the same way he did her. "I didn't make dinner."

"Your momma ordered pizza, and she got one for us." Ruby took his hand and led him back inside his own house. "Things are looking *so good* at your parents' place. I'm super proud of the paint color, and the flooring is going to be done on Tuesday next week."

JJ smiled at her back. "That's great, princess."

She flipped open the lid on the single pizza box on the counter, and JJ's stomach growled at the sight of the cheese, pepperoni, and olives. His momma. She knew just what he liked.

He didn't bother with plates, and instead picked up a piece of pizza and took a bite of the tippy, triangle end. After he swallowed, he asked, "How much longer on the house, then?"

Ruby held a piece of pizza too, and she mimed chewing in an exaggerated way, then swallowed and said, "Not sure. Every time I see your dad, he looks at me with this edge in his eyes that says he might fill my cabin with water just to get me to move faster on the redesign."

She gave him a dry look and took another bite of pizza.

JJ could just see that look in his daddy's eyes. "I know that look." He chuckled, took a bite of pizza, and went over to the fridge. He pulled out a bottle of lemonade for Ruby and a can of root beer for himself and leaned against the counter.

He watched Ruby eat and talk about the homestead, the new linens she'd bought that would be here by the end of next week, and then the topic moved to Tate.

"He's doing so much better," she said. "The doctor says he can lift up to twenty pounds now."

"That's great." JJ finished his first piece of pizza and waved to the couch with his second. "Should we sit?"

"Yep." Ruby joined him, and the moment she finished eating, she lay down, extending her feet out toward the end of the sofa as she laid her head in his lap.

JJ played with a tendril of her hair, the quiet peacefulness of this moment something he wanted to extend for a long time. "I'm going to have the rancher's luncheon here in August," he said. "And Finn invited us to his birthday party in a couple of weeks."

"Ooh, you and the luncheon." Ruby grinned up at him. "What are you going to make?"

"Well, I can't cook for ten people," he said. "Despite my daddy's lessons growing up."

"Maybe you could ask your grams to make something."

"Nah." JJ shook his head and finished off his second piece of pizza. "She's real busy with Conrad and Sarina."

"His momma helps a lot too," Ruby said. "Your grandma would do it."

"Sure, she would," JJ said. "Doesn't mean I'm going to ask her."

"So what are you going to make?"

JJ took a moment to think. "Well, I have a slow cooker, and this is a cattle ranch—at least in part. I think I can cut up a few potatoes and carrots and put them in with a roast."

"Mm, that sounds good—except for the cooked carrots."

"Easy to pick out, Scarlet."

She let her eyes drift closed and as JJ gazed down at her, he definitely felt some inklings of love streaming through his heart. He watched her for a moment and then looked out the window and into the backyard.

Everything he wanted sat within his grasp, and yet JJ couldn't get a grip on it. As he sat there, he realized he didn't need to hold things so tightly.

You can't anyway, he thought, the words almost coming from outside himself. His daddy had taught him he couldn't control the weather that came through Texas. He couldn't control the price of cattle.

Heck, sometimes he couldn't even control the way his animals acted, as evidenced by the bulls getting loose and injuring Tate.

He couldn't control Ruby and make her stay with him, and he wouldn't even if he wanted to. He never wanted to cage Ruby, tether her to the ground so she couldn't live her life to the fullest. And while the thought made his heart ache, it also brought a smile to his face.

"Rubes," he whispered.

"Yeah?" She spoke in an equally quiet voice.

"I'm going to miss you when you go to San Antonio."

She stirred in his lap, and he tracked her as she sat up. "I don't know if I'm going to go."

He reached up and took her face in the palm of his hand. "Yeah, you are. And it's okay. It's not forever, and it's the adventure God wants you to have."

She studied his face, her bottom lip quivering. "But...."

He smiled softly at her. "There's no *but*, my scarlet princess. How long are you going to argue with the Lord?"

Tears slipped down her face, and JJ pulled her into his chest. "Hey, I'm going to be right here. That's the best part of all this. You know right where I'm going to be, and it's here, at Seven Sons Ranch."

All he had to do was hope and pray that she'd come back when she was done having her adventure.

Chapter Twenty-Three

Tate gritted his teeth as he pushed himself up from the chair, his ribs on the right side screaming in protest. Just when he'd been getting better too.

He pushed his breath out, irritated on top of frustrated on top of angry.

He hadn't had sharp pain like this in weeks, and the doctor had told him he could lift more weight. "Not that much," he muttered to himself as even the simple act of lifting his foot to take a step caused a sharp, stabbing pain to radiate from the front of his body around his ribs to the back.

He sucked in a breath, something he'd done so much since arriving on this ranch. He hated that he still loved this place, and that his normally bright personality had been dulled by a single moment and an errant bull.

He just needed more coffee. That would perk him up enough to have dinner with Clara Jean.

As he poured himself a cup, he wondered if he should even try to fake it. Maybe he should dump this liquid caffeine down the drain and break up with Clara Jean the moment she walked through the door.

Heck, he probably should've texted her. Then she wouldn't have spent money on something at the grocery store where she worked, wouldn't have spent time heating it up, and wouldn't waste more time and energy on him.

"You've been kissing her too much and for too long to break up with her with a text," he told himself. That got him to stir in a spoonful of sugar and lift his mug to his lips.

He didn't want to break up with Clara Jean at all.

The rich aroma of the coffee filled his nostrils, a small comfort in the midst of his frustration. He took another sip, letting the warmth spread through his chest, trying to focus on that sensation instead of the constant throb in his side.

A knock at the door made him turn, but he stayed right where he stood. Clara Jean. "Come in," he called, his voice rougher than he'd intended.

She entered the cabin full of radiance and joy. The bright smile lighting her face made him smile despite his bad mood. "Hey, cowboy." Her voice sounded like a summer breeze, and she closed the door behind her, sealing the two of them in the small space together. "You haven't eaten, have you?"

"I always have room for a second dinner," he said.

She slid the foil-covered pie plate she'd brought onto the countertop and eased into his personal space, one hand lightly resting against his chest as she tipped up to kiss him hello.

Tate loved the shape of her in his arms, in his life—and he knew he wasn't strong enough to end things with her.

She settled back on her feet and smiled at him. When he didn't return it right away, hers faltered. "You had a bad day."

He shook his head when he should've nodded, but Clara Jean understood what he meant. He looked away, the tension in his muscles infecting his vocal cords to the point that he couldn't speak.

"What happened?"

Tate's jaw clenched. He didn't want to talk about it. Didn't want to admit how useless he felt, how scared he was that he'd never heal completely. But Clara Jean had a way of drawing things out of him, whether he liked it or not.

"I tried to lift a half-bale of hay today," he said, his voice barely above a whisper.

"Tate."

"It's twenty-five pounds."

"The doctor said twenty."

Tate knew that; he'd heard the doctor too. "I couldn't even get it off the ground." He brushed by her as much as he could with his body in the condition it was.

"Tate, it'll be okay." She reached out and tried to grab his arm.

Her words, meant to comfort, only fueled the fire of frustration burning in his chest. "I'm sick of healing," he snapped, jerking away from her touch. "I'm sick of being treated like I'm made of glass. I can't even do my job, and your family is paying me to sweep hallways and write numbers in a book. It's ridiculous."

Clara Jean took a step back, hurt flashing across her face. "I—no one cares what you do."

"Thanks for saying it out loud."

"That's not what I meant."

Tate knew exactly what she meant, but how he'd taken it could also be true. No one cared what he did.

She pulled the aluminum foil from the pie plate to reveal a toasty brown chicken pot pie, her movement swift and somewhat angry. Tate went back into the kitchen and opened the cupboard to get down a couple of plates.

She opened the drawer with the large kitchen utensils and took out a serving spatula; he got out two forks. Clara Jean served him a big piece of chicken pot pie, the steam rising into the air as she did, then repeated the process for herself.

Tate carried both plates over to the small table, and Clara Jean opened the fridge to get out a bottle of hot sauce and the pitcher of unsweetened tea she'd made last night.

When she settled at the table with him, neither of them had spoken another word, and the tension in the cabin had only doubled. At the same time, Tate recognized and enjoyed the routine they'd built between each other as they got dinner on the table.

"Thank you for the food," he said.

Clara Jean nodded at him, her fork poised perfectly in the air, a chunk of chicken and crust on it. He knew that look, the way she paused, all of it. "You just need to give yourself more time to heal," she said.

Time. That was all anyone ever said. *Give it time.* But time was slipping away, and Tate felt like he was standing still while the world moved on without him.

He told himself not to snap at her. She'd lived a very charmed life, and that wasn't her fault. Maybe it made her a touch naive and maybe he found that adorable. He certainly didn't want her life to be hard or for her to know hardship and pain as intimately as he did.

But those things keenly reminded him of why he'd started thinking they shouldn't see each other anymore.

He took a breath, not sure he could push the words out. Her eyes widened, because they'd spent a lot of time together this summer, and while Tate intellectually knew he couldn't truly know a person inside and out in only three months, he did know a lot about Clara Jean.

"You're going to break up with me," she said, falling back in her seat.

"I should," Tate said.

She folded her arms. "Why?"

Tate picked through his chicken pot pie to get a forkful of peas. "Where do you see this going, Clara Jean?"

"Well, I know relationships end in only one of two ways." She was way too smart for her own good, Tate knew that. "We break up or we get married."

"Married?" His eyebrows rose. "And then what?"

She blinked. "I don't know. Family? Life?"

Tate shook his head. "And where do you see us doing

that, Clara? Here? This tiny little cabin in Cabin Row, with all of your daddy's other hires?"

"No," she said in that stubborn way she had when she got her defenses up.

"Then what?" he pressed, his dinner forgotten now. "I can't provide anything for you, CJ. Can't you see that?"

She looked away. So she knew. "I don't care about that."

"Oh, you'll care when your momma and daddy sit you down and say, 'Enough, Clara Jean. Tate's a nice man, but he's not for you.'"

Her dark eyes came back to his, full of anger. "I don't care what they say."

"Yes, you do."

Her strong bravado fell, and that only made Tate's heart twist all the way around so that it settled backward in his chest. "I don't want to break up with you."

"I don't want that either," Tate said. "But CJ, I can't give you anything you're used to. I came here to work for your daddy so I could save up and buy my own place. And let's say I manage to do that somehow. It'll be years before it actually happens, because I can't actually work a ranch the way it needs to be worked. I'm incapable."

There. He'd said it all, and he actually did feel a bit better.

"You think I'm a spoiled rich girl."

"I do not." He gave her a sharp look and picked up his fork again. "I think you're used to a certain lifestyle, and I will never, ever be able to give you that."

"I have money."

"I know you do." And he hated it. "It only makes me feel weaker, CJ. Not better."

"I—"

"A man wants to take care of a woman," he said. "Not because she needs him to. Not because she's weak or spoiled or whatever. But because that's what makes us feel like men."

She leaned forward in her seat and covered his hand with hers. The warmth of her skin seeped into his, and he just wanted to give her the world. He wanted to let go of this fear and frustration that had been eating at him for three solid months. But the doubts lingered, a persistent whisper in the back of his mind.

"What if I never get better?" he asked, his voice barely audible. "What if this is as good as it gets?"

"I would love you as-is," Clara Jean whispered.

Tate sucked in a breath and looked at her. Those beautiful eyes to match such a sunny spirit. "Clara Jean," he said in a warning voice.

"Tate Reynolds, you listen to me real good."

"Yes, ma'am," he whispered.

"I'm going to tell you the same thing I told my momma last week."

"Okay," he said into the silence she let filter in after her statement.

"I believe in the power of love," Clara Jean said, her throat moving as she swallowed. "And I believe that life doesn't have to be perfect, with big, beautiful homesteads and gently waving grassy fields, for it to be absolutely beautiful."

Tate believed that too, but money also didn't grow out of those fields, and groceries didn't just show up on front porches—unless the whole town knew they couldn't pay their bills and had dropped something off as an act of service.

"I believe that when two people are in love, they can weather really violent storms." Her hand over his tightened. "And it can make a tiny cabin like this a palace, and it can heal broken ribs, and it can give a man the confidence he needs to build the future he wants for his wife."

Her eyes blazed, and Tate fell a little bit more in love with her then.

"You told your momma all of that?" he asked, the words scraping his dry throat.

Clara Jean smiled and shook her head, then pulled her hand away. "No, I told her that I was falling in love with you, and it didn't matter if you worked for Daddy for the rest of your life. I'm literally running a small-town grocery store and planting vegetables for a living. It's nothing special."

"It's amazing." Tate surprised himself with the tenderness in his voice. He reached out and grabbed the edge of her chair, then tugged. But with his ribs as injured—and re-injured—as they were, he couldn't pull her closer.

Clara Jean did him one better and got up, took the two steps to him, and slid onto his lap. "Okay?" she whispered as he pulled in a breath and held it, as if that alone would preserve his ribs.

"Yeah," he said tightly. "CJ?"

"Yeah?" She brushed his hair back off his forehead, her touch so feminine and so wonderful.

"The only future I care about is one with you in it," he whispered. "I'm sorry I get inside my head sometimes."

She gave him a small smile. "So you don't want to break up." She wasn't truly asking, and Tate chuckled under his breath.

"No," he whispered. "I don't want to break up." He touched his mouth to hers, the expected and familiar jolt of pleasure filling him. He thoroughly enjoyed kissing Clara Jean, and he did believe in love the way she did.

"I will work hard to get better," he said. "For you."

"No." Clara jean folded herself into his arms and leaned against his chest, making him feel strong enough to hold her there. "You'll work hard to get better for you. Not me."

"So no more lifting hay bales."

"Not right now, no," she said. "You'll refrain now, so you can do it later." She lifted her head. "Okay, baby? Promise me."

When she spoke in that throaty, sexy voice, Tate would promise her anything. "I promise," he whispered just before he kissed her again. He wanted to believe that her folks would allow her to marry him, and that she could truly be happy with him, whether they lived in this tiny cowboy cabin forever or whether he could somehow, someday, afford a place of his own and turn the farmhouse into a palace for her.

Chapter Twenty-Four

C lara Jean Walker wiped her hands on her apron and reached for another Ambrosia apple to complete the pyramid. She'd spent the last half hour arranging them just-so, making sure each one was nestled securely without risking a collapse that would send fruit rolling all over the floor.

Most people probably didn't aspire to work at a grocery store, but Clara Jean loved it. She spent half her time out in the fields, checking the crops that produced the watermelons, the tomatoes, the lettuce and potatoes and carrots that they sold here in the store.

These apples came from the orchards here in Three Rivers, and Wilde & Organic bought produce from multiple farms and ranches in the area. Her aunt still managed all of the ordering and receivables in the store, but Clara Jean would take it over one day.

The store had been her second home for as long as she could remember, and Clara Jean had worked multiple positions within it. Today, she stocked the produce section with what they needed to make it through the weekend shopping spree, but she could help customers find anything they needed in any aisle too.

She moved over to the herbs, which she'd harvested plenty of that morning, lovingly placing them into the plastic containers her aunt also managed to keep in stock. She twisted and picked up several containers at once, noting she'd done a good job with the stickers today.

Aunt Patsy had been relentless when Clara Jean had first learned how to do the herbs, but she was a pro now.

"Hey, Clara Jean," a woman said, and she glanced up to a friend and co-worker, Maria.

"Oh, hey," she said, leaving the cart with produce to give the sandy blonde a quick hug. "How was your date last night?"

"Oh, my shooting stars," Maria gushed. "Tomkins is *so* cute, and he took me on that starlight hike. Have you done that?"

"A couple of times," Clara Jean said with a smile. Not with Tate, though once he was fully healed, Clara Jean fully intended to take him all over town and do all the things she'd loved about growing up here.

Maria told her all about the date while she helped her get the rest of the herbs out and along the shelf. That done, Clara inhaled deeply, the scent of basil filling her nose.

The public address system beeped overhead, and Clara

Jean's mind tuned in. Sometimes she was needed up front, and she couldn't just zone out as she thought about her own sweet cowboy boyfriend.

So it was that she held three lemons when a man's voice filled the grocery store with, "Howdy, folks. We have a real treat for y'all today at Wilde and Organic."

Clara Jean knew this voice instantly, though it felt like two of her worlds colliding.

She glanced toward the front of the store, half expecting to see Tate standing there, though she knew he had to be in the upstairs administrative offices to be speaking into the PA that went through the whole store.

No, she thought. He could be at any register too, including the customer service desk or the floral department back here by the produce. She spun that way, but didn't see him.

He didn't speak again, and maybe Clara Jean's ears had played a trick on her. Maybe it had been Jason speaking, about to remind customers of the sale on strawberries or the new shipment of organic honey.

"There's a real pretty young woman who most of you know—at least I'd be shocked if you didn't know her."

Clara Jean's pulse picked up speed, and she glanced around to find the few customers in the produce section stalled.

"See, I'm in love with Clara Jean Walker."

And she knew then for certain the voice speaking belonged to Tate Reynolds. Tears filled her eyes, because she couldn't believe this was happening.

Maria giggled, drawing her attention, and Ruby turned toward her, feeling shocked right down to her toes. And Maria was recording her.

"If you see Clara Jean, could you give a cheer? A whoop? Something to let me know where she is, so I can find her too?"

No one in the produce section said anything for a couple of moments, and then Maria cupped her hand around her mouth and called, "Yeehaw!"

A couple of others whooped and started to clap, and that brought more customers out of the other aisles and over to the produce department. It flowed into the bakery, and Clara Jean surveyed the employees and her fellow co-workers as they came out to watch this as well.

Oh, she was going to kill Tate—right after she kissed him.

She took a deep breath and turned in a circle, catching sight of the meat department workers grinning like fools, and then—her momma and daddy.

Her legs became jelly, and she reached out to grab onto the freestanding stand that housed all the bananas.

"Right here, love," came over the speaker system, and Clara Jean swore she heard an echo of the voice closer to her, non-amplified. "Behind you."

She turned and faced the back of the store, her eyes immediately going to the corner where the fresh flowers waited for customers to pluck them up and take them home.

Tate stood on the counter there now, the phone that broadcast his voice throughout the whole store—and the parking lot—in his hand as he grinned at her. JJ stood only a few paces away, his arms folded and his perfectly grumpy cowboy look on his face.

"I love you, sweetheart, and I know I don't have much more to offer you than that." He held up his free hand, something pinched between his thumb and forefinger. "Clara Jean Walker," Tate said, his voice steady but full of emotion. "Will you marry me?"

Time seemed to stop in that moment, the world narrowing down to just the two of them. Clara Jean's heart felt like it might explode as she stared at Tate, at the ring in his hand, at the love and hope and vulnerability in his eyes.

She opened her mouth to speak, but no words came out. Her mind raced, her heart thudding wildly in her chest. She wanted to look over to her momma and daddy to get their reaction, but they'd obviously known about this proposal. They wouldn't be here otherwise.

Maria tracked her as she started forward, almost outside her body as she heard whispers and giggles but couldn't place where they'd come from.

She reached the counter and looked up at the diamond in Tate's hand. She had no idea how he'd bought that, and while she'd started to confess some of her feelings to him a week or so ago, and he'd said lovely things to her in return, she hadn't been expecting this proposal.

"Clara Jean?" Tate asked, his voice soft but steady. "What do you say, honey? Will you marry me?"

Clara Jean blinked, her mind whirling as she tried to process everything. "Yes," she whispered, her voice barely audible. Then louder, stronger, she said, "Yes, Tate. Yes, I'll marry you."

The room erupted with cheers and congratulations as the customers clapped and Maria let out a whoop of excitement. JJ whistled through his teeth, nearly deafening her, and Tate took a few seconds to get down off the counter, his face only flickering with pain for a single moment.

Then he appeared in front of her, his smile wide and glorious and handsome as he slid the ring onto her finger. She looked at it with wonder, and then up to him.

"I love you," he said. "I know this is—"

"I don't care." She shook her head. "It was wonderful." She stretched up and kissed him. "I love you too."

Tate didn't kiss her for long, and he grinned down at her, his eyes twinkling with joy and mischief. "Well, that's good, because I just made a real big fool of myself in front of half the town."

Clara Jean laughed again, the sound light and full of happiness. "You're crazy, you know that?"

Tate's grin widened as he leaned down and kissed her again, his lips warm and soft against hers. "Crazy about you," he murmured against her mouth.

"Congratulations, you two."

Clara Jean turned into her mother and flew into her arms. Yes, she'd told her mom she was falling in love with Tate, and yes, both of her parents had been concerned.

Momma said nothing as Daddy shook Tate's hand. Maria said, "I got it all on video. I'll send it to you."

"Thanks." Clara Jean stepped out of her momma's arms

and back to Tate's side, carefully avoiding JJ's gaze. Funny how all of their relationships had come to light only a handful of weeks ago, and now she was engaged to his best friend.

She'd have to talk to him eventually, and she would. She absolutely would.

But for now, she just wanted to admire the diamond ring on her finger and revel in the weight and warmth of Tate's arm around her waist.

Chapter Twenty-Five

Mitchell Glover stood on the gravel driveway outside the homestead at Shiloh Ridge Ranch, his heart pounding in a rhythm that was both familiar and strange. The wide expanse of pastureland stretched out before him, the same way it had for decades, yet everything felt different. Maybe because *he* was different. After almost a decade on the East Coast, learning, growing, and becoming the man he was now, it sure felt amazing to come home to Shiloh Ridge Ranch, Three Rivers, and Texas.

The ranch hadn't changed much. The same sprawling land, the same sky that seemed to stretch on forever, and the same smell of earth, hay, and horses. But Mitch had. He wasn't the unsure twenty-four-year-old who had left Three Rivers to attend Whispering Pines in Virginia. He was thirty-three now, with two advanced degrees in deaf studies and interpretation under his belt.

Champ, his copper-colored cocker spaniel, sat at his feet, tail wagging gently as if sensing the change in the air. The dog had been his constant companion for the past couple of years, alerting him to the world around him, from doorbells to sirens to even someone calling his name. Champ had never let him down, and for that, Mitch was grateful. He knelt down, scratching the dog behind the ears, feeling the reassuring warmth of his fur.

It felt good to be home, and Mitch wondered what storm his daddy had cooked up behind the door. Uncle Ranger and Aunt Oakley lived in this house, but they willingly gave it up for whole-Glover-family gatherings on a regular basis.

Here, or True Blue, the barn down the road that had hosted dozens and dozens of events for Mitch's family.

He signed, *Let's go*, to Champ, and he started toward the front porch with his backpack over his shoulder. He squinted against the mid-afternoon light glinting off the huge front windows.

The ranch hummed with life, and Mitch could only imagine the sounds it might make. The energy of it coursed through his bloodstream, reigniting the original excitement Mitch had felt at coming home for a surprise visit.

In the end, he'd told Link, and Link had promised to "be discreet" about getting everyone to Uncle Ranger's for dinner tonight. How he'd done that, Mitch still didn't know. But he didn't doubt Link could do it.

He'd returned to Three Rivers a few times over the years, mostly for holidays or family events, a wedding or a graduation. But this time was different. This time, he'd come home for good, ready to start the next chapter of his life. He had a dream—one that had been growing and developing in his mind for years—and now, with his education behind him, he was ready to turn that dream into reality.

A school. Not just any school, but a place for deaf children and teens to learn, grow, and feel understood. A place where they wouldn't be the odd ones out, where their language—*his* language—was the norm. And maybe, just maybe, it would be a place where hearing people could learn to understand the deaf world better too.

The thought filled him with a mixture of excitement and trepidation. He had the vision, the drive, but he knew the road ahead wouldn't be easy. Building something like this in small-town Three Rivers was going to be a challenge, especially when most people here knew next to nothing about deaf culture. But if there was one thing Mitch had learned over the years, it was that nothing worth doing was ever easy.

A flicker of movement caught his eye, and he turned to see Link approaching from the stables, a wide grin plastered on his face. His cousin hadn't changed much in the years Mitch had been away—still tall, still broad-shouldered, still sporting that same easygoing nature that made people feel like his best friend.

But something else shone through in Link's demeanor now. Responsibility, maybe. Maturity. Or maybe just the fact that Link had now fathered two boys of his own.

Mitch loved Link to his core, but he noticed the way time had a way of making boys into men, and men into ranchers.

You're here, Link signed as he drew nearer, his hands moving with the ease of someone who had been signing for years. He had learned sign language when they were kids, back when Mitch first came to the Glover family, and he'd never stopped learning. Heck, he'd even taught his wife and kids to sign too, simply so they could all communicate with Mitch.

I made it, Mitch said, a smile tugging at his mouth.

Link arrived, his mouth an open smile as he laughed. Mitch had no idea what it sounded like, but the joy seemed to punch him in the chest. He hugged him tightly, feeling the vibrations from Link's chest as he definitely laughed right out loud.

He stepped back and asked, *This is all you've got?* and reached out and snapped the strap on Mitch's backpack.

I have a suitcase in the car. Mitch indicated the SUV he'd rented at the airport. He'd had his daddy come pick him up in the past, but neither of his parents knew he currently stood on the ranch.

I have the end cabin ready for you. Link grinned at him. *They'll probably come out in the next thirty seconds. I told them I had to run and check on something in the stable and to wait for me.*

Mitch grinned at the huge, two-story house, such fondness sliding through him. *I give them sixty seconds.*

He loved his enormous family, and he never got overwhelmed by the noise. He'd live here on the ranch and help with a few chores while he worked on finding a suitable piece of land for the academy he wanted to build. He'd gone around to several parcels a few years ago, and since then, Mitch had filled a couple of notebooks with sketches and plans.

A lot has changed, he said to Link. *But a lot hasn't too.*

Link gave him a smile. *You'll get back into the swing of things.* He lowered his hands, then pulled his phone out and checked it. His fingers flew again as he said, *Misty says she can't keep them contained for much longer.*

Let's go then. Mitch hitched his backpack tighter like he was going into battle, and the front door opened before he'd taken a single step.

Link's oldest spilled out of the homestead, a bundle of movement and excitement. He waved both hands, and Champ put his paw on Mitch's leg to indicate his name had been spoken. Yelled, more likely.

Mitch grinned at the child and hurried forward now as more people started to exit the house too. He crouched down and braced himself for Diesel's arrival, the three-year-old's mouth moving, moving, moving, as he ran toward Mitch.

He caught him up, stood, and tossed the boy into the air. He caught him on the way back down and laughed with him as the little blond boy giggled and giggled.

He looked up as he sensed more movement around him, and Mitch quickly passed Diesel to his daddy so he could hug Uncle Ward. Everyone talked at the same time, and while not all the Glovers possessed the same level of sign language skill as Link, they could all say hi. They could all hug. Mitch could feel and feed off their happiness to see him.

Where's my daddy? he asked Misty as she finally embraced him. She carried her and Link's second son in her arms, gave him a quick hug, and stepped back to say, *On his way in.*

Mitch's mother wasn't here either, but he beamed at Aunt Etta, who had also learned a lot of sign language and had always been extraordinarily good at talking with him. She had both of her twins with her, and Mitch felt like he barely knew them. They'd only been seven years old when he'd left for the deaf college back East, and surprise ran through him when Nash said, *Your momma went to get more whipped cream for the cakes.*

She'll be back in a few minutes, Nellie said, her signs better than her brother's.

Pure love filled him, and to his horror, tears filled his eyes at the way Aunt Etta had taught her kids sign language. It was such a big deal to be able to communicate—and had been Mitch's life-long struggle. He didn't want others to go through what he had, basically being starved of language, which was why he wanted to open his academy here in town.

Link touched his shoulder and indicated that they should all go inside, and Mitch followed him to get out of the late July sunshine. He watched the couples around him and how they worked together, how Link and Misty could communicate with just a look.

He admired them and the way they worked as a team, raising their boys and building a life together. Mitch had always imagined something similar for himself, though, if he were honest, he had always pictured himself with a hearing woman. Someone who could bridge the gap between his world and the hearing world.

Being immersed in the deaf community had opened his eyes to the possibility of a different kind of future. He had dated a few deaf women during his time at college, and for the first time in his life, he had felt truly understood. There were no barriers, no misunderstandings, no need to constantly explain himself. It had been incredibly freeing.

But that was Whispering Pines, Virginia. This was Three Rivers. And as far as Mitch knew, he was the only deaf person in town.

For now.

He let the Glovers sweep him into the homestead and under the arched doorway with the family name carved into it. The kitchen, dining room, and living room expanded from there, where Mitch picked up a piece of pre-cut cake and found a spot on one of the bigger sofas. He couldn't hear the conversations around him, but he could read lips, and he watched the teens talk about an event in town this weekend.

What's that? he asked Flint, who was Ward's son.

They filmed a mechanic here, he said, and that made no sense to Mitch. He glanced over to Ollie, but he hadn't been looking at Flint.

"What?" he asked, but he didn't sign it.

Mitch signed to him—*They filmed something here?*—but Ollie looked away and called for someone. Who, Mitch didn't know, because he couldn't see Ollie's whole face. Familiar frustration filled him with having to figure out ways to get and give the information he needed.

And people forgot all the time that he had to be able to *see them*, or he couldn't understand what they said.

In the deaf community, all of this was so much easier. Everyone knew to make eye contact and face who they were talking to. He didn't constantly have to remind everyone around him that he couldn't hear. In that moment, Mitch doubted his choice to come back to Three Rivers more than he ever had.

Link came around the couch, his mouth moving. He asked Flint what they'd been talking about, and the teenager turned away from Mitch to tell him. Then Link met Mitch's eye. "They filmed a movie here," he said, speaking it with both his voice and his hands. "And it's premiering this weekend. They're showing it in the park on Saturday night."

Ah. Mitch nodded and forked up a bite of his cake. He'd just put it in his mouth when Champ put both of his paws on Mitch's knees. He looked at his beloved cocker spaniel, whom he'd trained from a puppy, and then looked over his shoulder to find his father—the wonderful Cactus Glover—had entered the homestead.

Their eyes met, and Daddy asked, "What are you doing here?" with his hands and mouth.

Mitch handed his cake to the closest person, got to his

feet, and then climbed right over the back of the couch as his daddy laughed and opened his arms to him. Mitch grinned and grinned as he said, *Surprise,* and then stepped into his daddy's brilliantly strong arms.

When he stepped back, Daddy was already signing. "Your mother is going to be so happy to see you. How long are you staying?"

Mitch beamed at his father. *We should wait until Momma gets here.*

His phone buzzed in his pocket, and Champ pawed his leg again. He pulled it out and looked at it, surprised to see he'd missed a text. Champ always alerted him and he kept the vibrations on high, and Mitch wondered if it had come in while he'd been driving.

He had one text from Jerry Bozeman about a new listing in Three Rivers, and this newest one from a woman named Willow Bentley.

Mitch, everyone here at Bloomton Construction loved the proposal. We'd love to have you into our offices to talk. When are you available?

Mitch's breath caught in his throat. He looked up and turned his phone toward his father's inquisitive expression. Daddy's eyes flew from right to left and back again as he read, and then he met Mitch's eyes again.

He started to laugh, and Mitch had no idea what others heard when he did that. He didn't much care. He'd never spoken, as he hadn't grown up with any deaf services at all. His mother had taught herself—and him—sign language from books and then the Internet.

He'd been so deficient going to Whispering Pines, and he hadn't even known it. His resolve to make sure no other children had to grow up the way he had hardened as he hugged his daddy for the second time. When they parted this time, Mitch's hands flew.

She's my contact at Bloomton, he said. *I gave them the final pitch and proposal for a massive—like, huge—construction grant to help me start the academy.*

Better tell her you can come in anytime, Daddy said.

He looked down and stared at the message, his mind racing with possibilities. If he could get help with the construction costs, he'd be that much closer to taking the deaf academy that lived in his head and making it bloom in real life.

He quickly tapped out a response that told Willow he could come at her earliest convenience, and then he shoved his phone back in his pocket.

Champ had his paw on Mitch's calf again, and he looked around, trying to find who'd said his name. Daddy had turned slightly from him, and he spoke with Uncle Bear and Uncle Ward.

Mitch could read lips, and he smiled at Uncle Bear as he said, "That's great, Mitch."

So Daddy was telling them about the construction grant. Mitch had worked on it for a couple of months, and he'd had his father, Link, and Uncle Preacher go over it with him and for him. Then he'd asked a lawyer friend from his History of Deaf Community class, and *then* he'd turned it in.

As he stood there, very much a silent island among so

many Glovers, Mitch could only smile and thank the Good Lord Above for His help in bringing him to this very spot, at this very time.

Oh, how he'd missed the energy at Shiloh Ridge Ranch, Three Rivers, and his family.

And while he missed his place inside the Deaf community, it sure was good to be home.

Chapter Twenty-Six

Henry Marshall stretched his legs out in front of him, the porch swing creaking beneath his weight as he rocked gently back and forth. A slight breeze rustled the leaves of the oak trees surrounding the homestead, offering some relief from the summer heat.

But he'd wanted to give his wife a break, and Wrangler was being tough to wrangle today. Henry had taken his eight-month-old son and put him in the back of his truck and driven him to town and back. The little boy had fallen asleep within the first ten minutes, and Henry had been back at Three Rivers Ranch, on his parents' front porch, for about that long too.

He glanced down at the blond boy sleeping in his arms, smiling at his son's chubby cheeks and sweet, peaceful breaths. Despite the endless demands of Lone Star on both him and Angel, and the pressure of fatherhood, and the commute they endured each day with Wrangler strapped in the back seat, moments like this made the early mornings and crying episodes all worth it.

The weight of Wrangler in his arms grounded him, a reminder of the blessings he'd been given, even when things had been so uncertain for him for so long. And who would've ever guessed that he would have the first grand-child for his momma and daddy?

Not him, that was for sure.

The screen door behind him squeaked open, and Henry glanced over his shoulder to see Angel stepping out onto the porch, a soft smile on her face as she saw him. She'd braided back her long, blonde hair while he'd been gone, and her bright blue eyes sparkled with the same energy that had drawn him to her from the start.

"How's he doing?" she asked, her voice gentle as she came to sit beside him on the swing.

"Out like a light," Henry whispered, shifting his arms slightly to adjust Wrangler's position. "It's so hot." Sweat drenched his body, mostly because Wrangler was dead weight and another warm body cuddled into Henry's at the end of July.

"I can take him and go put him down in the bedroom."

Henry nodded, sliding their sleeping son into his wife's arms. Wrangler grunted and sighed, but he didn't wake, thankfully. Wrangler had never been easy to settle to sleep, and they'd both experienced plenty of sleepless nights over the past few months.

Becoming a father had changed him in ways he hadn't

anticipated—softened him, maybe, but also strengthened him. Something about holding his son, about knowing he was responsible for this little life, gave him a new kind of resolve to be the very best man he could be.

"Your daddy lit the grill five minutes ago," Angel said as she went back inside.

Henry blew out his breath. "Okay," he said. His parents had established a Sabbath Day luncheon on the second Sunday of every month, and they'd invited all of their kids and spouses and friends to come. Paul and Brielle lived here on the ranch, in a house that Henry had spent plenty of evenings and weekends helping his daddy, uncle, and brother build.

He looked to his left, where the house sat right next door to Momma and Daddy, and a prayer started in his heart immediately. "Bless them to be strong," he murmured. The pastor that morning had already given a great sermon about giving over trials and burdens to the Lord to carry, but Henry understood how hard that could be sometimes.

Paul and Brielle had been married for longer than he and Angel, but God had not yet blessed them with a baby. Henry knew his brother and his wife desperately wanted a son or a daughter, but he couldn't pretend to know the pain of not receiving that righteous desire in his life.

He and Angel had not had to try very hard to have Wrangler, and he tore his gaze from his brother's house and looked past the dirt road in front of the house and over to his aunt and uncle's house.

Well, his cousin and her husband lived there now—

Libby and Rusty Jackson. They didn't have children yet either, and Henry thanked the Lord for that.

"Henry," his momma called, and Henry pulled himself from the heat waves and his thoughts and got to his feet. He loved the Sabbath Day now, as it gave him a chance to slow down, to spend time with family, and to enjoy the simple pleasures of life on the ranch. This one, his own small farm, or Lone Star when he and Angel went to visit her parents.

He pulled open the screen door and entered the glorious air conditioning. Paul and Brielle had arrived at some point, and they laughed with Daddy and Rich, who both stood in the kitchen getting lunch ready. His momma had never let her boys wear cowboy hats indoors, but she'd apparently given up on enforcing that rule, as both Daddy and Paul wore their hats.

Henry had hung his by the back door when he'd arrived with his family, and he had no plans to go out in the after-noon heat again today, so he didn't need it.

"What are we having for lunch?" he asked as he approached the festivities in the kitchen.

Paul grinned over to him, and Daddy said, "Sausages with peppers and onions." He had an array of red, green, and yellow bell peppers all sliced up and ready to go on a piece of aluminum foil. "I'm going to go put these on. I want them nice and soft."

He crinkled up the edges of the foil to make a faux tray, and then he folded it in half and took it out onto the back deck, where the grill stood.

Rich, Henry's youngest brother who'd just graduated

from Amarillo State, salted a big bowl of potato and pea salad, then ripped off a long piece of plastic wrap and sealed it over the top. He stepped over to the fridge as Brielle said, "Grab the sausages too, please." She pushed the buns closer to Henry. "You can slice those."

"Giving me the safe job," Henry said with a smile. He could cook if he had to, but he didn't enjoy it and he didn't make elaborate meals.

"You'll be using a knife," Brielle said. "Not sure that's so safe." She grinned at him, and Henry sure did like her.

Henry untwisted the tie keeping the buns fresh and took them all out of the bag. Angel joined him and gently took the serrated knife from him just as he'd finished the second one.

"Did he go down?" he asked.

She nodded with a smile. "Hopefully, we can eat without him waking up."

"I can take him if he does," Momma said. In the next moment, she sniffled, and everyone looked at her. Everything in the house paused. Then Daddy came back in with a loud bang, the way Daddy did so many things.

That gave Momma a chance to turn away from everyone, and Angel exchanged a glance with Henry. He knew why his momma's emotions had spilled over, and he also knew she'd contain them as quickly as they'd come.

She'd told him how much Wrangler looked like her daddy and Henry's grandfather. They'd named him Frank Wrangler Marshall and used his middle name, simply to honor Granddad, especially now that both of Henry's grandparents had passed away.

Momma missed her parents on the best of days, and while she loved Wrangler with every cell of her being, she really wished her momma could've met him in this life.

Life had a way of moving forward, even when it felt like the world should stop, and Daddy looked at Momma's back and asked, "What did I miss?"

"Nothing." Momma turned around, her eyes completely dry and her voice absolutely normal. "Libby and Rusty are coming over." She put her phone on the corner of the counter and took in the food there. "What else do we need?"

Daddy watched Momma like a hawk, then took a breath and surveyed the rest of them. "I'm going to put the sausages on, then we'll warm the buns at the last minute."

"Salad's in the fridge," Rich said.

"Paul and I brought cookies." Brielle unwrapped a stack of paper plates, and she obviously came over a lot more than Henry and Angel did.

"So we'll be ready in about ten minutes," Daddy said.

Angel finished slicing the buns, and she put them on a tray for Daddy to take out when he needed to.

"All right," Momma said. "Rich, get the drinks out of the fridge, and let's circle up about Finn's birthday."

Henry smiled, because his parents had always called their boys together to "circle up" when they had something to talk about, brainstorm, or reveal.

"I don't have a present for him yet," Momma said. "I need to know what y'all are getting him so I don't duplicate."

Rich put a case of Ruby Red Fresca on the counter and turned back to the fridge as he says, "I got him a gift certificate to Lower's meats. Then he and Edith can get something they want."

Henry nodded, because he'd love a gift card where he could pick out the best brisket in the state.

"His parents got him a new saddle," Daddy said. "I know that."

"We're here," Libby called as she walked in the side entrance to the house, the one that Henry had used the most growing up, because he parked in the driveway, and it was the easiest way inside.

"Libs." Momma went to greet her with a hug, stalling the conversation.

As they made their way back to the island where everyone had gathered, Henry looked at Paul. "I don't have anything for him yet either," his brother said.

"We got him that cheddar cheese and caramel popcorn he likes," Angel said. "The huge tin of it, half-and-half."

"Special-ordered it from that place with the Christmas tins," Henry said. "They have birthday stuff too."

"What are we doing?" Libby asked, glancing around the room.

"Finn's birthday," Henry said. "What we got him. Momma needs ideas."

Libby's eyes flew to Momma. "You know what would be perfect?"

Daddy ducked back out onto the deck to check the food, and Libby continued with, "Sheep."

"Sheep?" Momma asked at the same time Henry, Angel, and Brielle did too. They looked at one another and started to laugh.

Libby giggled too, and then nodded. "Yeah, sheep. Finn has wanted some for a while, and Rusty knows a guy who's selling his farm, and it includes a small sheep herd."

"Define 'small,'" Momma said.

Libby looked over to her husband, her eyes searching his. "Rusty?"

"I'm texting him," he said. "Not many, I know that. He's got a small farm down the lane from my family, and—nine." Rusty looked up. "He's got nine sheep."

"What do you do with sheep?" Momma asked, looking at Henry and then Paul.

"Finn and Edith love animals," Paul said. "I could totally see them adding sheep to their farm."

They had horses, a couple of dairy cows, a whole herd of beef cattle, chickens, a few goats, dogs and cats, and Finn raised a pig every year and held a pig roast in the spring.

"How much for nine sheep?" Momma asked.

"We're buying sheep?" Daddy asked as he entered the house with a tray of sizzling sausages and the aluminum foil filled with softened vegetables.

"Not for us," Momma said. "For Finn."

"Does Finn even want sheep?"

"He'd love them," Libby said.

"A thousand bucks." Rusty looked up from his phone. "And Libby and I can go get them when we go for my mother's birthday."

Henry volleyed his attention back and forth between Libby and his momma until Daddy said, "Can we pray and sit down to eat? We can talk sheep then just as easily as now, and the food is ready."

"Yes," Momma said, folding her arms. "Let's pray."

Henry put his arm around Angel and brought her closer to him as he closed his eyes and bowed his head. Then a squawk came from down the hall. "I'll get him," he murmured as Paul started the prayer. He strode down the hall as Wrangler really started to get worked up. He didn't like being alone—so much like Henry—and he hadn't slept nearly long enough either.

But Henry ducked into the room to find his son standing up in the crib. "Look at you, buddy. Standin' up." Pride beamed through him, though Angel wouldn't like Wrangler pulling himself up in the crib. The boy babbled and squealed, his smile bright as Henry reached for him.

"Come on, bud. Grandma wants to hold you." Henry barely recognized his life it had changed so much in recent years, but it was so, so good. "Thank you, Lord," he murmured as he left the bedroom.

He didn't think life would always be blue skies and red roses, but Henry believed it would always be good if he continued to turn to God in all things.

Chapter Twenty-Seven

Conrad leaned against the wall in the barn at Three Rivers Ranch, arms crossed, watching the flurry of activity before him with a mix of fondness and discomfort. The air buzzed with the sounds of laughter, chatter, and the occasional burst of music from the speakers set up in the rafters.

A few kids chased each other around the open area where Conrad assumed there would be dancing later, their shrieks of joy blending with the hum of cowboy conversation.

Happy birthday, Finn, he thought, thinking of the two birthdays of his daughter's that he'd missed. Three, really, as he hadn't been there for her birth either.

An inexplicable flash of anger roared through him, something fairly uncharacteristic for Conrad. He simply felt too many eyes on him, though everywhere he looked, no one seemed to care about him at all.

His sister currently held Sarina on her hip while she talked with JJ, Alex, and another cowboy named Brandon. Elaine didn't date a whole lot, but Conrad wasn't sure why. No one in his family had gotten married yet, though now with Clara Jean engaged, the Walkers would finally have a wedding.

JJ held hands with Ruby across the barn, and they stood talking to Beau Peterson, the foreman here at Three Rivers Ranch.

"You can't hide in the shadows all night," Dawson Rhinehart said as he joined Conrad and handed him a can of cola.

"I'm not hiding in the shadows." Conrad popped the top on his cola, the snap-hiss so satisfying. "And I can't stay all night. I have to get back to my grandmother and put my daughter to bed." Sometimes just hearing himself say the words "my daughter" made him marvel.

This was one of those times.

"Did you eat?" Dawson asked.

The barn, decked out in colorful banners and strings of lights, provided shade from the scorching late July sun outside. Inside, the Ackerman's had misters running from the ceiling, with fans trying to move the cooled air about. Long tables held a buffet of food, from barbecue ribs to burgers to grilled cheese sandwiches. Potato chips, potato salad, potato skins, potatoes, potatoes, potatoes.

Finn loved potatoes.

Conrad took a swig of his soda and shook his head. "Not yet."

"Come eat," Dawson said. "My niece is here too, and she's wearin' a look about like you are." He gave Conrad a quick smile, and Conrad went with him to get something to eat.

Along the way, he paused beside Elaine. "You okay with her?"

"Just fine," Elaine said with a quick smile. It faded quickly as she looked over to Clara Jean and Tate. "If I have to listen to Clara Jean talk about that *fake* diamond one more time...."

Conrad glanced over to his cousin, surprised at the irritation in his sister's voice. "She's just excited."

"She acts like that ring is real."

"Laney," Conrad said, and that got his sister to look at him. She was a triplet and the only girl in their family, and she could hold her own. Boy, could she hold her own. She glared at him with dark eyes and asked, "What?"

"Be nice," he said, repeating something his daddy had told them all as they'd grown up.

Elaine turned her back on Clara Jean. "I just need to move."

Conrad took his daughter from Elaine. "Go get something to eat."

"Oh, there's Joelle." Elaine leaned in closer. "The rumor mill is buzzing that she went out with Preston Miles last weekend."

Conrad looked at the pretty woman a couple of tables

away. Joelle Stockton had grown up out here at Three Rivers, and she was a few years younger than Conrad. She had honey-blonde hair, plenty of freckles, and the brightest blue-green eyes he'd ever seen on a human being.

But when he looked at her, he could smile. Sure, he could admit she was pretty. But she did nothing to stir anything romantic inside him. "So?"

"So, she's dating again," Elaine said. "You should ask her out."

Conrad scoffed right out loud. Sarina gripped the collar on his shirt, pulling it out of place, and he gently removed her hands from the fabric. "Leave it, baby."

She looked up at him with the biggest, most beautiful brown eyes. "Da-da-dad."

He grinned at her. "Yep, let's go get some dinner." He nodded toward the long buffet table. "You first, Laney."

"Fine," she said, marching over to the end of the table, where she picked up two plates. "I'll get yours."

"Thank you," Conrad said softly, and he trailed behind his sister as she got their food. Conrad felt like he was forever trailing behind someone. The moment he turned from the buffet, he saw Dawson waving his hand above his head.

He pointed to the empty seats at his table, where he sat with his wife and small son. And his very pretty niece, April.

Conrad didn't know what game Dawson was playing, and then he reminded himself that Dawson Rhinehart didn't play games. He wouldn't try to set Conrad up with his niece, so he waded through the tables to where Dawson sat with his family.

"Hey," he said as he looked at the spot next to April. "I'm okay to sit here?"

"Sure, whatever," April said.

Dawson cleared his throat in an exaggerated way, and she glared over to him and folded her arms. "I was nice. I said yes."

"You made it sound like he'd be a complete idiot to sit next to you." Dawson gave her glare right back to her.

April had just graduated from high school a few months ago, so she was one-hundred-percent too young for Conrad, which was great, because he wasn't looking for a girlfriend.

Beside him, Elaine sat down and put his food on the table in front of him. Then she put a chunk of cheese on the table in front of Sarina. His daughter dang near jumped out of his arms as she dove onto the cheese, and his arms tightened around her so he wouldn't drop her.

"Whoa, tiny," he said.

"Can I hold her?" April asked, reaching for the little girl.

"Sure," Conrad said, because he'd only known about his daughter for a couple of months, and he had a lot of family to share Sarina with. His momma seemed to want her all the time, as did Grams. Conrad didn't complain, because he was so far out of his element as he learned how to take care of a two-year-old child.

April settled Sarina on her lap and picked up a piece of cooked pasta from her plate that she hadn't eaten yet.

Conrad started to eat, feeling more like an outsider than

he had in years. Normally, these gatherings were a highlight for him—a chance to catch up with old friends, swap stories, and enjoy the camaraderie of the ranching community. But today, he felt like he'd been sectioned onto a slide and put under a microscope.

It seemed like people didn't know how to act around him. Maybe they felt sorry for him, or maybe they just didn't know what to say. Either way, the weight of their unspoken questions hung in the air, thick and suffocating.

"Can we sit here?"

Conrad looked up to find Link and Mitch Glover standing there. They'd fill the table, and Conrad nodded as Dawson said, "Yeah, of course."

The two cowboys sat, and Conrad nodded over to them in hello. He didn't know sign language, as Mitch was probably eight years older than him, and outside of the rancher's luncheons, Conrad had no reason to interact with Mitch.

He'd heard the man had returned to Three Rivers, to Shiloh Ridge, and that certainly seemed to be true.

An obnoxiously loud beep filled the barn, and then a woman's voice came through a megaphone. "It's time for presents and cake," Kelly Ackerman, Finn's mother, said.

The conversations in the barn died out as all attention went to her. "Then we'll turn on the music and have our dance." She smiled around at everyone who'd come to celebrate her son's birthday.

"You gonna dance?" Dawson asked.

"Doubtful," Conrad said, his gaze skating past April.

He finished eating as Finn unwrapped gloves, a puffy

vest from his wife, a huge package of almond M&Ms from Link, a new saddle from his parents—boy, that was nice.

Conrad admired the light brown leather with perfect trim, and his heart warmed as he watched Finn hug his parents. This party had brought out kids, teens, people Conrad's age in their twenties, and the older generation too.

His momma and daddy had come, for crying out loud.

The Ackermans were definitely pillars of the community, and Conrad supposed the same could be said for his family.

"...at the grocery store," Clara Jean said, her voice right behind him. He scooped up a bite of pasta salad and ate it as Elaine stiffened beside him. "It was *so* sweet, and we're planning to get married next spring."

"Don't," Conrad muttered as Elaine got to her feet.

But she did.

"Clara Jean," she barked.

"It's actually an oval-cut setting," Clara Jean said, as if she hadn't heard Elaine say her name.

Conrad ducked his head and looked out of the corner of his eye to see Clara Jean holding out her left hand for someone to examine the diamond. Then Elaine's hand covered Clara Jean's and curled into a fist.

"Enough," she hissed. "There's more going on at this party than your engagement."

Clara Jean looked at Elaine with wide, round eyes and yanked her hand out of Elaine's grip. "She asked."

"Elaine," Conrad said, his voice too soft to really get his sister to listen.

"Everyone okay here?" JJ asked, arriving on the scene.

Conrad got to his feet too, ready to leave the party though Finn had just opened a new pair of cowboy boots.

"I'm just sick of hearing Clara Jean brag about her engagement."

"What's going on?" Tate was the last person who Conrad wanted to join the conversation.

"Nothing." He stepped in front of Elaine while JJ glowered at her. "Laney, this is not the place for this." He spoke in a barely audible voice, and his sister didn't seem like she'd back down.

"And now we need to go outside for our final gift," Kelly said into the megaphone, and Conrad pressed his eyes closed as his ears rang with the loudness of her voice.

"Let's go," JJ said, guiding Clara Jean and Tate past Elaine and Conrad. Their eyes met, and Conrad didn't quite know how to communicate with JJ about the situation.

Elaine might be a little jealous; Conrad wasn't sure.

"She's holding her hand out so that every light in here catches on that ring," Elaine said, definitely loud enough for everyone to hear.

"Elaine," Conrad chastised. Thankfully, Tate, Clara Jean, and JJ just kept walking. He turned his back on them and glared at his sister. "You're going to regret that. You'll just have to apologize later."

"I hope when I get engaged, I'm not that annoying."

"You're irritating me right now," Conrad muttered. "Let's go see what Finn could possibly get that requires us to go outside."

He followed his cousins outside, a blip of his own jealousy moving through him as Tate pulled Clara Jean close to him and placed a kiss on her temple. Conrad was happy for them—truly he was—but it was hard not to feel like he was standing on the outside looking in. Everyone seemed to be moving forward, finding their place, their person, while he was still trying to figure out what it meant to be a father.

While he was still struggling to get back to a place where he could hold his head high, where he could feel clean before the Lord.

He sighed as he left behind the cooler interior of the barn. The distinct sound of bleating sheep met his ears, and Conrad could barely believe his eyes as several sheep got unloaded from a trailer.

"These are for me?" Finn asked. He glowed like the stars on a dark night, and Conrad chuckled. He and Edith had an amazing cattle ranch that also functioned a little bit like a hobby farm.

"Hey, Conrad."

He looked over to Joelle and gave her a smile. "Howdy, Jo."

She didn't seem too happy, and Conrad swallowed. He'd never really had much trouble talking to women, even if he was a little quieter. Being quiet wasn't the same as being shy.

"I am so sick of everyone talking about me," she said, still not looking at him. She wore a bright red sundress that fluttered in the slight breeze, and she did smile out to the sheep as Finn whooped and went to hug his aunt, who'd gifted them to him.

"Will you dance with me?" Jo's eyes skittered over to his and away again. "It's not a big deal. I don't like you or anything, but I just need everyone to stop talking about me and Preston."

He grinned at her. "You make such a strong case," he teased. "I don't like you at all either."

Jo huffed out her breath. "You know what I mean."

"Or maybe if we dance," he said, watching some of the younger kids start to play with the sheep. Someone had washed them up nicely, and Conrad didn't believe for a second they'd stay that white for very long. "It'll just ignite the rumors. Then people will be like, "Oh, that Jo. She's so over her ex-fiancee, and now she's dating a whole bunch of people.""

She scoffed, but Conrad couldn't stop smiling. He'd known her for years, and she'd always been friendly with him, maybe even flirtatious at times. Conrad had never really thought much of it. He'd been too focused on the ranch, on family, and now, on Sarina.

"You dance with me, and they'll just talk more," he said.

"Well, you need something to make you look less broody."

Conrad chuckled, shaking his head. "I didn't realize I was looking broody."

"Oh, you're definitely broody," she said with a grin she didn't give directly to him. "I am too, so it would never work between us."

"Totally wouldn't," he said.

"You need someone like Glory Rose," she said, completely surprising him.

"Glory Rose? Glory Rose Glover?"

Jo looked at him then. "Yeah, she wants to dance with you too. You up for it?"

As Conrad looked at her, he realized she'd come over to ask him to dance with her friend. His heartbeat thumped painfully in his chest. Of course he knew Glory Rose— everyone in town knew the Glovers.

"I'm too old for Glory Rose."

"Five years." Jo shrugged. "It's not that big of a gap."

Conrad didn't know how to respond to that, so he glanced around as people started to move back into the barn. They had to walk right past him, and his eyes caught on Glory Rose as she went by with her cousins Gunnison, Fawn, and Wilder.

Conrad knew them all, and he knew the way Glory Rose tucked her hair behind her ear and smiled in his direction meant she liked him.

"She's made of cotton candy," Jo said with some measure of disgust. "The real life of the party."

"I'm not throwing any parties," Conrad said, tearing his eyes from the dark-haired beauty. Yes, she was pretty. Absolutely she was.

But did he want to dance with her? Go out with her? Start dating?

He had no idea. He felt underwater all the time now that he had Sarina to consider and care for.

Everything had changed. His priorities, his focus—it was

all different now. He wasn't just a single cowboy anymore; he was a father. And that meant everything else had to take a backseat.

"So I'm telling her no?" Jo asked. "I don't want to do that."

"You're the one who came over here and started this," Conrad said.

Jo looked at him, really searching his face. "We can't dance if you don't dance with her."

"I don't—" He cut himself off before he said something rude. "I'll dance with both of you," he said. Then maybe he could go home.

She nodded, and with that, she turned and walked back into the barn, leaving Conrad alone once again. He watched her go, feeling a strange mix of relief and guilt.

He had to go back inside too, because he couldn't have April babysit his daughter all evening, and he sat down beside them with a, "Thanks, April. I can take her."

"Can I just hold her?" she asked with hopeful eyes. "Then I won't have to dance with anyone, and my uncle won't glare my face off, because I'm not dancing and my parents won't eye me warily because I am."

Conrad could just see Dawson doing that, and he started to laugh. And laugh, and laugh.

And it felt so good. Conrad felt like he was shedding some of the scales that had prevented him from growing, and it felt so freeing.

"Yeah," he said. "You can hold her. I have two dances to

get through, and then we're going home. I can give you a ride if you want."

"Really?" She searched his face and nodded. "Okay, I'll text everyone so they know."

He got back to his feet, trying to decide if he should dance with Jo or Glory Rose first. Glory Rose stood on the edge of the dance floor, swaying slightly, and Conrad had his answer.

As he walked toward her, he muttered, "Some help here, Lord, would be great."

She turned toward him as he touched her elbow, and Jo was right—everything about Glory Rose was made of sunshine and sugar. "Hey," she said brightly.

He indicated the dance floor. "You wanna dance with me?"

"Yes."

As he took the first step off the sidelines, Conrad felt like he was doing so much more than that. He was finally moving forward after being stuck for such a long time.

Chapter Twenty-Eight

J J Walker stood at the edge of the freshly mended fence, his gaze sweeping over the rolling pastures of Seven Sons Ranch where his horses grazed. His personal horses, of which he owned seven. And next week, when everyone went back to school, he'd load up with his daddy and go to a horse auction to potentially get more.

They could house them in the current stable until the construction on the new one finished.

"If you find any you want," he reminded himself, though JJ wanted to buy every horse he came in contact with. But for this, he wanted specific stock, something he'd have to remind himself of again.

The sense of ownership he felt over this part of Seven Sons Ranch still baffled him a little bit, and it definitely made his chest puff out in pride. At the same time, he tamped that down, because he could easily have been born and raised in a family like Tate's, and he'd have nothing.

JJ swallowed, because he expected Tate to show up for lunch at any moment, and JJ needed to stop admiring his pastures and get back inside. He started walking toward the farmhouse, which he'd hired someone to paint. They'd be here next week while he and Daddy drove to Oklahoma to look at horses.

The land beneath his boots represented a piece of his future, a future that, if things worked out the way he'd been praying they would, Ruby would be part of.

His heartstrings tugged as Ruby stepped out onto the porch of his house, her shiny hair catching the sunlight and glinting with that hint of red he loved. She'd been helping him all morning, setting out the tables and chairs, ensuring the drinks got put in the fridge and that he had enough ice for today's luncheon, and making sure the food from the local diner got laid out just right.

She'd chatted with him about their friends, Clara Jean and Tate's wedding, the topics the ranchers might bring up, even ribbing him a little about whether or not Finn would show with his new sheep in tow.

Ruby had a way of making everything feel lighter, easier, and yet lately, every moment with her felt heavy with the unspoken. She was still here physically, but her mind lingered hundreds of miles away in San Antonio, where her next adventure waited.

He couldn't ask her to stay, though. He had made peace with that much. But it didn't stop him from wanting her to fit here, to belong in his world. She sure seemed like a small-town girl, and JJ had been thinking through the adventures he'd had that summer—and there were plenty. But Ruby hadn't had much in the way of excitement, other than the remodel on his parents' house.

No wonder she wanted to go to San Antonio.

He'd just reached the bottom of his front steps when he heard the growl of a truck behind him. Ruby gave him a soft smile, the kind that always made his heartbeat skip and dance. "Link, Dawson, and Mitch are here," she said as he climbed up to her. "Guess I better make myself scarce."

None of the wives attended the rancher luncheons, but Ruby knew his friends. "You could stay and say hello," he said. "I think Finn's bringing Edith anyway. He doesn't want to leave her so far away for too long."

She shook her head, a laugh escaping her lips, though it didn't quite reach her eyes. "This is your thing, JJ. I'll just be in the way." She leaned into his chest and pressed a quick kiss to his lips. "I have tons to do at the homestead anyway."

"All right," JJ said as she stepped out of his arms. "There will be lots of leftovers. You're coming back for dinner, right?"

"Yes, sirree," she said, then she skipped down the steps and stopped to talk to the Glover cowboys and Dawson as they got out of their truck. She got in her car and swung around as Finn, Henry, Paul, and Libby drove onto the property. JJ expected them to have Alex with them, as he lived north of town too, but the fifth spot in the truck sat empty.

"Howdy, fellas." JJ grinned at Link, Dawson, and Mitch as they came up to the porch. He signed a quick hello to Mitch, which was about the extent of his sign language capabilities. But Mitch could read lips, and Link could interpret for him. "How are the Southern ranches?"

"Still owl-free," Link said.

"Duke wants me to arrange everything for Market Day," Dawson growled. "So if you don't have a topic today, JJ, I volunteer that one."

JJ blinked at him. "Wow, Market Day?" His daddy handled all of that, including scheduling the trucks, getting drivers, making the appointment at the weigh station, and more. He couldn't even imagine taking that on, and he swallowed. Dawson had a few years on him, and JJ didn't doubt he could do it.

Dawson nodded and turned as voices spilled out of the truck, all of them seeming to talk over each other. They were all related, and JJ smiled as he came to hear their argument.

"...just saying that there is no way—no *way*—that Don is going to lose a single game this year." Finn shook his head at Henry, who simply shrugged.

"Who cares about football?" Libby asked, and Paul sucked in a breath. "It's high school football in Texas."

"Yeah," Paul shot back. "It's high school football in Texas." He gaped at her like she'd grown an extra head. "Tell her, Finn."

"I've tried to tell her before." Finn started up the steps, and he looked at JJ, a smile coming to his face. "This place is great, Jay-J."

"Yeah," Henry said. "Real nice."

"Thanks." JJ shook Finn's hand and pulled him into a hug, then did the same to Henry, Paul, and even Libby. "No Edith today?"

"She's coming with her brother," Finn said. "They had to stop at the feed store for a second."

"Head on in," JJ said. "Air conditioning works real good."

Only Conrad, Alex, and Edith hadn't arrived yet, so JJ followed his friends back inside, his heartbeat racing beneath his ribs. He wasn't sure why. Probably because he'd never hosted the rancher luncheon before. He didn't have a wife to help him make the meal. He hadn't planned and carried out dinner and game night.

He'd been a college student until very recently, and now he felt thrown into the deep end of adulthood, both on the ranch side and the personal side.

But the great thing was, JJ liked it. He was tired of living a student life, and he wanted to open new chapters and doors for himself.

"I ordered from the diner," JJ said as he joined the others in the kitchen. "Ruby helped me get all the dishes out and cleaned up." He took in the oversized dining room table, which he and Ruby had put the leaf in to make room for everyone.

"Wow," Dawson said as he turned and looked at the table. He moved over to it and ran his fingers along the pale green table cloth Ruby had chosen. "This looks like you're hosting Thanksgiving dinner." He turned and raised his eyebrows at JJ.

"It's all Ruby," he muttered. "She's an interior designer." The bright white plates suddenly seemed too formal, and JJ pulled the lids and foil off the food. "I ordered beef tips and mashed potatoes. Gravy." JJ swallowed, because his friends had eyes and could see the food for themselves. His family went over the food before every big meal, a practice that drove JJ to the brink of insanity; he didn't need to do it here.

"Hey, hey," Conrad called from the front of the house. He strode through the living room toward them, his daughter in his arms. "I had to bring Sarina. Can I put her down in your guest room?"

He barely waited for JJ to say, "Yeah, sure," before he ducked down the hall, talking in a low voice to the little girl.

"Edith's here," Finn said as he looked at his phone. "Be right back."

A cry came down the hall from where Conrad had gone with Sarina, and JJ turned toward the sound, because it was so foreign here in his house.

"He sure is in over his head with that baby," Dawson said.

JJ's eyes flew to his. "Is he?"

"I think he's handled it pretty well, actually," Libby said, a note of coolness in her voice.

"I wouldn't even know what to do," Link admitted, his hands flying with every single thing said, whether he said it or not. "I'm barely keeping my head above water as it is."

Mitch's hands moved too, and Link nodded. "He asked

if that's Conrad's daughter. I guess I never told you about it." He stopped speaking out loud, but he continued to talk with his hands.

Mitch's eyes grew round, and he looked toward the mouth of the hallway as Conrad appeared again. He did seem flustered and flushed, and he entered the kitchen and went straight to the sink to wash up.

"Sorry I had to bring her," he said. "Grams forgot she had a hair appointment today, and I didn't want to miss your first luncheon."

"Will she be okay in there?" JJ asked. He'd put a queen-sized bed in the guest room, not a crib.

"I put her in the closet," Conrad said, which caused more than one person to suck in a breath, including JJ.

"You what?" Dawson asked.

Libby wore pure worry in her eyes, and JJ wanted to jump to his cousin's defense. He had no idea what he'd do if a former girlfriend of his showed up with a two-year-old he'd not known about.

"The closet is a smaller space," Conrad said as he reached for the towel hanging from the handle of the oven. He faced everyone, finally cluing in that they thought he'd gone crazy. "It's not like I chained her in there." He glanced around at everyone. "She's fine."

"What do you mean you put her in the closet?" Henry asked. "Because my wife would kill me if I put Wrangler in a closet to sleep." He exchanged a glance with his brother, but Paul didn't have children and therefore didn't comment.

Conrad's eyebrows drew down. "She does better in a

small space than a big bed. She won't sleep in a crib, even, and I've downsized her to a playpen and then a bassinet."

"This is just getting weirder," Dawson muttered.

JJ wanted to tell him to be quiet, and he didn't know why Dawson had decided to judge Conrad. Finn, Alex, and Edith came through the front door, the three of them talking, which stalled the conversation in the kitchen. JJ exchanged a look with Dawson, who held up one hand and said, "Sorry. I don't know the situation."

"I don't think she had much space to sleep in Dallas." Conrad glared at everyone and folded his arms. "None of you know her."

"Who doesn't know who?" Edith asked, her eyes flying around the group as she joined them. "Wow, it is tense in here."

"She has her favorite blanket and a stuffed otter," Conrad said. "I can put her down anywhere with those two things, especially if the space isn't that big. It's not like I closed the door on her. "

"I'm just going to go check on her," Libby said. She peeled away from the group before JJ could even think.

"I don't need you to do that," Conrad called after her. But she didn't stop, slow, or come back.

"What's goin' on?" Alex asked.

"Nothing," Conrad growled, and JJ's pulse vibrated strangely in his body. "You know what? I don't have to be here." He glared at everyone, with Dawson getting the longest stare. He blinked and looked at JJ. "Can I take some food or will that have everyone talking about me too?"

"You don't have to leave at all," JJ said.

Conrad's face held a shade of red that couldn't only be because of embarrassment. "Yeah, I do." He took in the meat, potatoes, the green beans, and the brownies. "She'll sleep for a couple of hours, and I'll be back to get her." He turned his back on everyone else, none of whom said anything, and faced JJ only. "Is that okay? She's a good baby, JJ, and she missed her morning nap. You won't even know she's here."

"It's absolutely fine," JJ murmured. "You don't have to go. Don't go."

Conrad turned around again and glared at everyone as Libby returned. "She's fast asleep," she reported.

"Thank you so much for clearing me," Conrad said dryly. He normally didn't cause a problem at all, but JJ heard the hurt in his tone. "Y'all have a good luncheon."

"You're leaving?" Finn asked.

"I'm not staying with people I thought were my friends," Conrad said. "But who are secretly judging me and talking about me and my lack of parenting skills behind my back." His chest billowed out as he took a big breath. "No, I have no parenting skills, okay? And if you think for a second that I'm not already beating myself up for every decision, every second of every day, you're wrong." He scoffed, gave everyone one more glare, and turned to leave.

"I guess I thought I had a place here, and it sucks that I don't."

"Conrad," JJ called after him as his cousin yanked open the back door and stalked out. Helplessness filled him, but JJ couldn't let him leave like this. "Grab a plate off the table," JJ said as he went after him. "Get something to eat. I'll be right back, and I'd love to talk about who needs what for the upcoming harvest, and Market Day."

With that, he ran after his cousin in pure silence.

"Conrad," he called again, but the cowboy in front of him strode with all the power he possessed in his long legs. JJ jogged to catch up, and when he did, he swallowed, tried to catch his breath, and begged the Lord for the right thing to say.

"I just want to be alone," Conrad said. "Go away, JJ."

"No," he said. "I don't want you to be alone."

"I'm not wanted here."

"Yes, you are."

Conrad threw him a glare. "Well, I'm not goin' back. Everywhere I go, I'm embarrassed. I do my best to keep my head up, keep my mouth shut, take care of my own business." Every word he said became more and more animated, and Conrad never got like this. He spoke softly, with plenty of power and meaning.

"The last place I thought I'd have to feel so...so *stupid*, so humiliated, was here. With them." He gestured wildly back toward the farmhouse, which didn't feel as safe as it once had. Conrad came to a stop, and he drew in deep breath. "Listen, just go back, okay? It's your house and your luncheon, and I didn't mean to ruin it."

"You didn't ruin it."

Conrad's stomach growled, and JJ just wanted to take care of him. He couldn't even imagine the pain his cousin had endured. "I'm going to call Emily and have her bring you some food." He raised his eyebrows, a clear challenge for Conrad to argue with him.

He didn't, and instead, he started to nod really fast. "Fine." He sniffled, and that broke JJ's heart right in half. "I'll be back for Sari in two hours."

The luncheon's only went for ninety minutes, so he had plenty of cushion where he wouldn't run into anyone from their group.

JJ grabbed onto Conrad and held him tight. Conrad stood stiffly in his arms and then sagged into him as he started to cry. JJ gritted his teeth and held on, his own emotions lashing through him too.

Just as quickly as Conrad had broken down, he stitched himself back together. He stepped away from JJ and ducked his head, using his cowboy hat to hide his face. "I'll...be back." The words ground through his throat as if they were made by rusty nails.

He walked away again, this time with a touch less anger in his step. JJ watched him until Conrad ducked into the main barn, and then he exhaled and turned back to his farmhouse. Mitch Glover stood there, but JJ didn't have to worry about him overhearing anything he'd said.

JJ sighed, looked left and right for some reason, and then headed back to his house. He did have to host the luncheon today, and he needed to eat to make it through the rest of the afternoon.

He joined Mitch on the deck, then they went up to the porch, where the other cowboy opened the door for JJ. He flashed him a smile before ducking inside. "Sorry, guys," he said.

"No, I'm sorry." Dawson got to his feet. "I didn't mean anything by it. Of course Conrad is doing the best he can." He threw a nervous look to the others. "I've already texted him."

JJ nodded, his jaw tight. "Nothing to be done now," he said as he picked up one of the two remaining plates and moved around the island to the food. "What were y'all talkin' about?"

"I was just about to make an announcement," Paul said, and JJ glanced up at him. The man cleared his throat and wiped his mouth with one of the light gray cloth napkins Ruby had carefully folded and put at each place. "Brielle and I have been talking about fostering, maybe even adopting. We're still in the early stages, but it's something we're praying over."

"Wow," Finn said.

Alex nodded heartily. "It's good to have options."

"I think she feels like she's doing something," Paul said, scooping up another bite of beef tips and gravy.

Libby covered his hand, a kind smile on her face. "That's great, Paul. You and Brielle will make great parents to any child lucky enough to end up with you."

Paul nodded, his expression thoughtful, his eyes full of vulnerability. "It's a big decision, but we both feel like it's what God's calling us to do. We'll see what happens."

JJ admired Paul's faith, his willingness to step into the unknown. It was something JJ had always struggled with—

trusting that things would work out, even when the path ahead felt covered with mist. He supposed that was what faith was all about, but it didn't make taking that first step any easier.

The conversation shifted again as JJ took his seat at the table, this time with Link nudging Mitch and saying, "Your turn, buddy. Tell them."

Mitch grinned and then his hands moved quickly as he signed, as he glanced around the table as if they could all read his fingers and gestures that fast. JJ had no idea what he said, and thankfully, Link could keep up and translate.

"Mitch just secured some *major* funding for the construction of his deaf academy. He's actively looking for the right piece of property here in town to get started."

"No way," Finn said, the last of the tension finally easing out the window. "That's amazing, Mitch."

"Completely amazing," Dawson said, both with his voice and his hands. He grinned at Mitch, but the action fell away from his face quickly, and he darted a look over to JJ filled with guilt.

JJ didn't want that, but he didn't want to bring it up right now. "That's huge, Mitch," JJ said, catching his eye for a moment before Link started signing for him. "You're gonna change a lot of lives with that place." He grinned at them, waited for more personal news, and when it didn't come, he said, "All right. What are y'all doing to prep for the upcoming harvest?"

* * *

A couple of hours later, JJ rocked back and forth in the chair on the front porch, Conrad's beautiful daughter cuddled into his lap. Ruby made the arc around the curve in the road that led back to his house, and he lifted his head in a single, slow, cowboy hello nod.

Ruby grinned like a golden retriever when she got out of the car, a blue pastry box in her hand. "Look at you with that little girl." She bounded up the steps and collapsed into the second rocking chair with a sigh. "Thanks for sending Emily with the food. Conrad came over and ate with me and Tate."

JJ nodded and murmured, "Thank you, Ruby." He leaned his head back and reached for her hand. "How's it going over at the homestead?"

"Good," she said. Her smile flickered and fell from her face. "I have to tell you something." She pulled her hand away from his.

After the day he'd had, JJ simply looked at her. He was fairly sure he already knew what would come out of her mouth, and he waited quietly while Ruby's hands twisted around one another and she studied her fingernails.

Then she opened her mouth and said—

Chapter Twenty-Nine

"I signed the internship paperwork about an hour ago."

Ruby immediately pulled in a breath, because those words had been choking her for the past sixty minutes.

"Mm, I figured you'd be doing that soon." JJ didn't sound upset, and Ruby chanced looking over to him. She sure liked seeing him cradle little Sarina while he held a toy for her to play with. She did, flipping the beads and buttons and flaps on the brightly colored item.

The sight should've made Ruby smile, maybe even laugh at how JJ—a man who claimed to know nothing about babies—had so effortlessly become a safe harbor for this tiny girl. But instead, a knot twisted tighter in Ruby's stomach, pulling her in two directions at once.

Her words seemed to have disappeared into the breeze that rustled in the big trees that stood guard over this land. This late afternoon reminded her of a slow, summer day growing up, and Ruby had always loved Texas. The smell of freshly mown alfalfa carried through the air, mixing with the scent of JJ's leather gloves and Sarina's clean baby powder goodness.

JJ gave her hand a gentle squeeze, his grip firm and reassuring, as if he could sense the storm brewing inside her. Maybe he could. JJ had always been more perceptive than he let on—quiet and observant, noticing things about her that no one else ever did. Like the way he knew when she'd come to town without her contact case or solution, without even her wallet. He was so steady, so constant.

"I have to be in San Antonio on September sixth."

"Okay," JJ said.

"Will you—?" Ruby's breath shuddered through her lungs, and she couldn't get the words out. How could she ask him for more than she already was.

"Hey, princess?"

"What?

"Scarlet, look at me, okay?"

Ruby took a breath and looked up. It took her another moment to look over to JJ. He gave her a soft smile full of kindness and love. He nodded at her, and Ruby really wished his lap wasn't occupied, because she'd like to sit there.

"Will you help me move on the 5th? It's Labor Day, and I know you're super busy here, but I figured you could drive down with Clara Jean, and Tate could come with me, and then the three of you could make the journey back here." Then she wouldn't be alone on the five-hundred-mile drive to San Antonio, and JJ wouldn't be alone on the way back.

"Of course," JJ said. Just like that. Like he could leave everything and everyone who relied on him and make a thousand-mile-round-trip without a problem. For her.

She flipped open the pastry box and looked inside. "I got you a raspberry fritter." She lifted it out of the box and extended it to him. He released her hand to take it, and Sarina caught sight of it and perked up.

"Jay, Jay, Jay," she said. She didn't say much else, and JJ pinched off a piece for her and gave it to her. He took a bite and gazed out over the front yard and road as well.

"My contract ends on December fifteenth," she said.

"How many weeks?" he asked.

"Fourteen."

JJ didn't say anything for a long moment. The only sound came from the creaking of the rocking chair and the distant hum of the world beyond them. Ruby could feel the weight of his silence pressing down on her, making it harder to breathe.

"You know what?" he finally asked. "I'm going to make a paper chain, and every week, I'll rip one off and send you a picture."

Ruby blinked at him, sure she hadn't heard him right. "A paper chain?"

He grinned at her fully now, something JJ didn't do very often. "With the secrets my momma has told you about me as a boy, I'm surprised you don't know about the paper chains."

Ruby picked up a square doughnut and peered through the hole to him. "Do tell."

He chuckled as she took a bite, and then he said, "When I was a kid, it took me a while to grasp the concept of time. I was forever askin' my momma how long until Easter, how long until Christmas, how long until we could go to Grandma's."

"You questioned your momma relentlessly?" Ruby wasn't sure she believed him. "That doesn't sound like you."

"I didn't become a super grump until high school," he said good-naturedly.

Ruby burst out laughing, and JJ smiled over to her and took another bite of his fritter, then gave another small piece to Sarina.

"Anyway," he said. "She'd tell me, but I didn't understand the concept of a week. So we made paper chains, and every week after church, I could rip off another ring. Then I knew how long it was until whatever I was waiting for."

Ruby nodded, charmed by this story. By this place. By him. "So you'll wait for me to come back?"

"Are you going to come back?"

"I'd like to," she said. "I don't want to break-up with you." She stuffed a huge bite of doughnut in her mouth so she didn't blurt out too much.

"Things change," he said simply. "Opportunities come up. You might find something in San Antonio that makes you want to stay longer."

She got the glazed goodness down and shook her head. "No," she said firmly. "I'm coming back. I want to be here, with you. Tate's here, and he and Clara Jean are going to live here. I'm just leaving for a little while, not forever." She couldn't stand the thought of saying good-bye, and she'd already determined she wouldn't.

"Well, I'll make a paper chain, and we'll text and talk and stay in touch," he said. "And just see what happens."

Ruby's chest tightened. She wanted to scream at him, to make him understand that she wasn't going to leave him behind. That this was just a temporary thing—a stepping stone in her career. But deep down, she knew he was right. Things did change. And as much as she wanted to come back, she couldn't predict what the next few months would bring, just like she hadn't foreseen what had transpired this summer.

She glanced down at Sarina, still playing peacefully with her toy, and her heart ached. What she wanted became crystal clear: A life here, in Three Rivers, with JJ. Family, and this farm, and his family. This small-town community, with loads of adventures she hadn't even experienced yet.

But she also wanted to prove to herself that she could do more, be more. That her struggles throughout college meant something. That she could take care of herself if she ever needed to. Her parents had taught her that, and Ruby didn't want to just throw away everything she'd done and learned.

With JJ at her side, though, she wouldn't have to work. She knew that. Surely he knew it too, and perhaps he wondered why she needed to do this.

"Jay," she said, and he popped the last of his doughnut

in his mouth as he looked at her. "You know why I have to do this internship, right?"

He swallowed quickly. "Tell me."

"My daddy's a farmer," she said. "And he got hurt once when I was, oh, gosh, about ten, I guess. No, that's not right. Tate was only ten, so I must've been like, six or seven."

JJ simply waited patiently for her memories to sift themselves into the right place. When they did, she said, "He couldn't work the farm, and Tate was too little to help. My momma had nothing she could do to earn money for our family, and we were so, so poor."

He'd finished his doughnut, and he reached over and retook her hand in his.

"She went back to school to finish her teaching degree, and Daddy had to hire out hands. Now, sixteen years later, they just paid off the last of the credit cards they'd used to keep our family afloat during that time. And they taught us all that we needed to have an employable skill."

"Mm."

"We didn't have to go to college, but we had to have something we could do to earn money, because life is not even. It has bumps and mountains and valleys, and my momma and daddy wanted us to be able to provide for ourselves if we had to."

JJ let a few seconds of silence press between them, and then he said, "No wonder Tate wants his own farm so badly."

"It's ingrained in us," Ruby said. "I may never have my own interior design studio. I might do this internship and never have to work another day in my life. But I need the experience just in case. And when I get back to Three Rivers, I already have a plan for what I want to do."

"Am I part of your plan, Scarlet?" he whispered.

"You're my whole plan," she said.

"I'm falling in love with you," he said. "I will wait as long as you need me to wait. I will come visit when you need me to come visit." He gazed at her with those intense dark eyes, with so much of that love he'd spoken of clearly there. "And whatever you have in your plan, I will do whatever I can to help you achieve it."

Ruby nodded, tears pricking her eyes. "I'm falling in love with you too." She might've already done that, but she wasn't sure. With so much going on, Ruby hadn't slowed down enough to truly examine how she felt and ask God if JJ was the one-and-only for her.

Before she could say anything more, the porch door creaked open and Conrad stepped out, his expression weary but relieved. He gave them both a small smile, though it didn't quite reach his eyes. "Hey," he said.

"Da-dad," Sarina said, perking right up. She reached for him, making small, urgent noises until he swooped past Ruby and plucked his daughter from JJ.

"Hey, my girl," he murmured, hugging her and sweeping a kiss along the girl's cheek. "Were you a good girl for Uncle JJ?"

"She's an angel," JJ said with a smile. He made no move to get up, and Conrad gave him a look, glanced at Ruby, and then back to his cousin.

"Thanks for watching her. I really appreciate it." His brow furrowed slightly as if sensing the tension but choosing not to comment. "I'll get out of your hair. See you later, Jay-J. Ruby."

"'Bye, Conrad," she murmured. Ruby watched as he carried Sarina down the steps and toward his truck, her head resting on his shoulder. The sight tugged at her heart. Conrad had been through so much lately, and yet he was still pushing forward, still doing his best to make things work for his daughter. It made her wonder if she possessed the same kind of strength.

When Conrad's truck rumbled off down the driveway, leaving them alone again, Ruby turned back to JJ, her hands twisting nervously in her lap. "I don't want you to think I'm choosing my career over you," she said softly. "That's not what this is."

"I'll try not to think of it like that, then."

Ruby nodded, the truth out between them now.

"I don't want to hold you back," he said.

She looked up sharply, her breath catching in her throat. "You're not. You're the only thing keeping me grounded."

He shook his head, his eyes full of sadness. "I don't want to be your anchor, Ruby. I want to be your partner. But I get why you need to fly right now." He squeezed her hand. "Really, I do."

Tears welled up in her eyes again, and this time she didn't bother trying to blink them away. They spilled over, running down her cheeks as she got up and took the two steps from her rocker to his. He opened his arms to her, and she settled in his lap and let him wrap her up tightly against that perfect cowboy chest.

"I don't want to leave you," she whispered. "But I don't know how to stay either."

"You don't need to stay," he assured her. "I'm not going anywhere, and I promise I'm okay with this choice you've made."

Ruby simply curled into his chest and listened to the steady thump of his heart beating. Everything about JJ calmed her, and as she sat with him, she had the very distinct thought that he could be her ultimate adventure.

"Can I help you make your paper chain?" she asked.

JJ tightened his hold on her, making her feel safe and oh-so-wanted. "Of course, Princess Scarlet. Of course you can."

Chapter Thirty

JJ stared at the stack of construction paper in front of him, his fingers flexing as if the mere act of cutting it would somehow make everything more real. The red paper sat there on the brand new kitchen table in his parents' house, mocking and yet unassuming.

To him, it might as well have been a ticking clock. Ruby had already scribbled the first few dates on the strips, neatly spaced out to count down to December fifteenth, and then she'd gotten a phone call about the light fixtures she needed to complete the living room here at the homestead.

"Fourteen weeks," he muttered to himself, then glanced into the kitchen where his momma and sisters worked to dish up ice cream.

Fourteen paper rings.

Fourteen pieces of his heart that would shed when Ruby moved in a couple of weeks. Fourteen pieces he'd have to find and fit back into his chest before she'd be back in Three Rivers, back in his arms.

His stomach tightened as he looked over to the scissors. He didn't want to do the cutting or gluing. He just wanted to eat the cookies and ice cream his sisters had made, and he glared over to them, silently willing them to hurry up.

The sliding glass door slid open, and Tate walked in while he laughed with Daddy. That sight made JJ's heart lift at least a couple of inches, as Tate would be part of the family before the bluebells bloomed next spring. No one would ever be good enough for Daddy's daughters, JJ knew that, but Tate sure was trying.

And Daddy did like him, so that was something.

"Hey." Tate pulled out the chair next to JJ and sat down. His eyes sought out Clara Jean, who said, "I'm taking the toppings over to the table." She glanced around as Daddy pressed a kiss to her forehead. "Where's Jason?"

"The man's lost his mind," Daddy grumbled, and he and Momma exchanged a glance.

"What does that mean?" Clara Jean asked. "Is he coming in or not?"

"He's talkin' to Betty Glover," Daddy said in a loud voice. "With a foolish smile on his face."

"Betty's a nice girl," Momma said, giving Daddy a sharp look. "Be nice."

"I like Betty," Clara Jean agreed as she plunked down a small Mason jar of homemade hot fudge, a bottle of butterscotch sauce, and another jar of caramel. Uncle Liam made the best ice cream and all the toppings, and the fudge and caramel had come from him.

Hattie slid a plate of miniature cookies onto the table, and Emily added bowls and spoons. JJ pulled the paper chain supplies closer to him and cast a look toward the front hallway, where Ruby had disappeared.

It should've felt normal. Comfortable, even. But nothing had felt normal since Ruby had signed her internship paperwork. He heard Ruby's voice in the other room, laughing about something. He closed his eyes for a moment, letting the sound of her laughter wash over him. He'd miss that. He'd miss everything about her.

He suddenly didn't want to sit here doing nothing, and he picked up the scissors and then a piece of red construction paper. He cut the heavier paper into strips, his movements slow and deliberate.

"Jay-J, you're cutting them too thick," Clara Jean said, leaning over his shoulder to inspect his progress. "They're supposed to be uniform. You know, like a real chain." She leaned over and touched her lips to Tate's. "Hey, baby."

He grunted in response but didn't adjust his cutting. He also didn't want to be between his sister and her fiancé while his heart got cut and made into a paper chain.

Clara Jean was always precise about things like this, but he couldn't bring himself to care about the width of the paper strips right now. What did it matter? They'd all be ripped off and thrown away anyway.

Clara Jean sighed and sat down beside him, grabbing a new sheet of paper and cutting smoother, thinner strips.

"You know, you're acting like she's leaving for the other side of the world," she said gently. "It's just San Antonio, JJ. You can visit."

"I know," he said, his voice low.

But it wasn't just about the distance. It was about the uncertainty. Would Ruby come back to him after everything? Or would San Antonio swallow her up, offering her a life so full of new opportunities that she'd forget about the quiet routines of Seven Sons Ranch?

He wasn't a fool. He'd seen it happen before. People left small towns like Three Rivers, and sometimes, they didn't come back.

JJ dropped the scissors down with a thud. "I don't want to do this."

Tate swept the scissors into his hands. "Let me."

JJ growled and glared at his best friend, then caught Ruby as she came flouncing back into the kitchen. He worked hard to clear the frustration and grumpiness from his face before she could see it, but he wasn't sure he succeeded.

He forced himself to look away, and he reached for a glue stick, as if that had been his goal all along.

"Ice cream," Momma said as she set one metal bowl in front of Tate and JJ. "That one's cheesecake, boys. This one is vanilla." She put another bowl fresh from the machine further down the table. "Girls, come sit down. Jeremiah, you too."

Ruby looked at Tate and then JJ and then Clara Jean. "I'll move," JJ's sister said, and she got up and went behind JJ to the other side of Tate so she could sit beside him, and so Ruby could have her spot at JJ's side.

"Got it worked out?" he asked.

"Yeah." Ruby sighed. "The truck got delayed due to those weird ice storms in Minnesota." She looked at JJ's chunky strips, her eyes widening. "This is how you make paper strips?"

"I've already been lectured about it," JJ grumbled as he half-rose to get himself a bowl. "You want some ice cream, Scarlet?"

"Yes, please," she said.

"Vanilla or cheesecake?"

"Cheesecake."

JJ dished it up while Ruby quietly folded his errant strips in half and slid them under her leg. She took the new ones from Tate and rewrote the dates on them while JJ added butterscotch and caramel to his cheesecake ice cream, then dropped a handful of mini oatmeal cookies on top.

He gave that bowl to Ruby and then duplicated it for himself. "Tate?" he asked.

"Vanilla, with everything, buddy." He grinned like he'd just won the keys to a brand new truck.

JJ glared at him and frowned as he went down to the other end of the table to get the ice cream. "Who else can I serve?"

Clara Jean blinked at him, and Emily said, "We did this for you, you know. You could be nice about it."

JJ swung his attention to her, pure surprise coursing through him. Emily was the peacemaker of the family, and she never said anything against anyone else. "You're right. I'm sorry."

His emotions stormed through him, but he picked up another bowl. "Clara Jean? Cheesecake or vanilla?"

"Cheesecake, please, Jay-J."

He served everyone at the table, including his parents, and then he re-took his seat. Tate had finished cutting the strips, and Ruby currently had at least half of them looped around into chain links, the colors alternating from blue, to yellow, to white, to red.

"Looks great," JJ said, and he looked around at his family gathered there. His throat narrowed, and JJ couldn't even get melted ice cream down it. He cleared as much from it as he could and met his father's eyes. Daddy tilted his head to the side, his dark eyes blazing with questions, with energy, with encouragement.

"Hey, uh," JJ said. "I want to—thank you so much for...." He waved his spoon around, a drip of cheesecake ice cream flying a few inches and landing on the table. "For this. For making the cookies and ice cream. For helping me and Ruby with the paper chain."

"I'm making one for Christmas," Hattie said. "Did you know there's only seventeen weeks until then?" She gazed around at everyone, deadly serious.

"Wow," Daddy finally said in a deadpan, and for some reason that tickled JJ's funny bone. He let loose with a laugh, so grateful it cleansed the worry and darkness from his soul.

The sliding door opened again and Jason ducked into

the house with a, "Sorry, I'm late. Oh, good, there's still cookies." He avoided both Momma's and Daddy's eyes and went to wash up in the sink. "Conrad's coming over. He said he's pretty mad no one told him about the ice cream party."

"I did tell him," JJ said.

"I was there," Ruby said. "He did tell him."

"I'm sure he was joking," Jason said as he squished himself in between Hattie and Emily. "Can I sit here?"

"Looks like you already are," Emily said with sharp edges in her voice, once again surprising JJ.

"What's with you?" he asked his sister, and Emily blinked at him. Her face turned red, and oh, JJ had hit on something.

"Maybe I'm just having a bad day."

"Now you've started it," Clara Jean said just as Momma piped in with, "Why are you having a bad day?"

"No one ever asks JJ that," Emily said as she leaned over her ice cream bowl. Her hair fell down around her face, and she used that as expertly as JJ could use the brim of his cowboy hat.

"She doesn't have to say," JJ said. "It's fine." He smiled at Clara Jean and Tate, then Ruby, Hattie, Jason, Emily, Momma, and Daddy. "I love you guys. Really, thank you for being here tonight."

They'd had plenty of real and serious conversations in this spot, around an older version of this same table. Sure, Tate and Ruby were new additions to the family, but they belonged just as well as JJ's siblings.

"We love you too, Jay," Emily finally said into the

silence. She drew a deep breath pressed her eyes closed. As they came open, she said, "All right, I have to tell everyone something."

Beside him, Ruby drew in a breath, and JJ dropped his hand to her lap so he could hold her hand. She'd only been here for the summer, but she should definitely get to see how his family did things.

"Speak, then," Clara Jean said.

"Speak," JJ seconded, and he grinned at his sister.

Emily nodded, her dark eyes wide. "I applied to the cosmetology school in San Antonio, and I got my acceptance letter today." She skipped looking at Daddy and instead focused on Ruby, of all people. "The next round of beginning classes starts October first, so I'll be in the city with you, Ruby."

"October first," Daddy said, with a whistle coming after it. "You don't give your daddy much time to get used to the fact that you'll be gone." He smiled at Emily, but Daddy wasn't joking. He had an enormous heart, and he loved every one of them so, so much.

"I can send my boxes back with JJ and Clara Jean," Ruby said, finally joining the conversation. She smiled at Emily, who grinned back at her.

Emily had not moved out yet, and she'd turned nineteen at the beginning of the year. JJ admired her for going as far as San Antonio, and he said, "Congrats, Em. That's great."

"And you won't be alone there," Clara Jean said. "Since Ruby will be there."

JJ wanted to tell his sister that Ruby wasn't part of their

family, not really, but he held back the words. So many changes were coming to their family, to Seven Sons Ranch, and while JJ normally resisted such things, as his siblings grew up, met people they'd fall in love with, and made their own way in the world, change was inevitable.

And they were good changes.

As the conversation picked up again, Ruby leaned her head against his bicep, and JJ looked at her. "You okay, Scarlet?"

"Yeah."

"Should we start going through your stuff, so Clara Jean can bring home the boxes you need?"

"Yeah, let's do that."

JJ suddenly wanted to be alone with his girlfriend, and he got to his feet and moved over to hug his momma. "Thank you, Momma. We're gonna go look through what Ruby has to move soon."

"Okay." Momma stood and hugged him tightly. "You two be good."

JJ heard her hidden message—*don't just go back to her cabin and kiss*—so he said, "Okay," and then he said good-bye to everyone as he ushered Ruby out of the house.

Once free from all their eyes, JJ took her hand and walked with her through the evening heat to the cabins. The moment they entered the shade of the big tree on the back edge of the property, JJ pulled Ruby closer and kissed her.

She giggled against his lips, and his whole world expanded, billowing out and out and out until he could see his future—and it definitely had Ruby in it.

He broke the kiss. "God will bring you back to me," he whispered as he moved his mouth to her jaw and then her neck. "Because we're meant to be together."

Ruby breathed out and pressed into him. "You think so?"

"I know so," he said as he lifted his head. "Now, come on. I promised my momma I wouldn't just sneak away to kiss you."

Ruby smiled at him. "You did? When?"

But JJ simply laughed and pulled her against him, both of them stumbling as they walked clumsily in the direction of her cabin. *Lord,* he prayed as everything inside him sobered again. *Please bring her back to me.*

Chapter Thirty-One

R uby stood in the center of her cabin watching as Tate flipped pancakes at the stove. She'd been living here with him for just over four months now, and he'd be fine without her.

As much as she didn't want to admit that, it was true. Besides, he wouldn't be alone here, as his fiancé lived here, with plenty of cowboys in the cabins next to this one. And JJ had said Tate could come live with him if he needed to. Tate had said he didn't need to do that, and that only caused a pinch of worry inside Ruby.

Everything seemed to be doing that right now, and she got herself to move into the kitchen. "I'll get the syrup heated up."

"Sure," Tate said easily. "They'll be here soon, and we'll get you loaded up after breakfast." He smiled over to her and stepped down to check on the pan where the sausage links sizzled.

Ruby had been packing for a little over a week now, and she'd finished fifteen minutes ago, after showering and packing up the last of her toiletries. Everything she owned seemed to fit so neatly into cardboard boxes and suitcases, yet the weight in her chest felt anything but neat. It was a jumbled mess of emotions—excitement, fear, and a deep, gnawing ache that only grew with every item she'd packed.

She pulled out the maple syrup, popped the top on it, and put it in the microwave. She set the butter on the table, along with a stack of plates and forks, pausing when the front door opened and JJ and Clara Jean walked in.

"...just saying that of course she's not going to say no," JJ said. "It's your wedding, and Momma's gonna do whatever will make you happy."

"Then booking the Starlight Gallery should be no problem," Clara Jean said, but she wasn't teasing or even happy.

"You're missing my point," JJ said.

"Which is?"

He glanced over to Ruby, who understood a brother-sister dynamic better than most. "That there will come a point where Momma *will* say no, and you don't want it to be on something you truly want."

"You just said she'd give me whatever I wanted." Clara Jean arrived in the kitchen, and she said, "Hey, Ruby."

"Hey." She hugged her. "You toured the gallery? How was it?"

"Incredible," Clara Jean said at the same time JJ said, "Expensive."

"It's not like Momma and Daddy can't afford it." Clara Jean rolled her eyes, which only made JJ turn a shade darker in his demeanor.

"Have you met our father?" JJ muttered. Then he looked at Ruby, brightened, and said, "Hey, princess." He swept into her personal space, kissed her cheek, and put one big warm hand on her back. "You ready for this?" he asked, his voice soft but steady.

Ruby let out a shaky breath, her fingers fidgeting with the buttons on his shirt. "I think so. I mean, I'm excited, but...." Her voice trailed off as she struggled to find the right words. *But what?* That she was terrified? That she didn't know if she was making the right decision? That leaving him felt like tearing out a part of herself?

JJ reached out and took her hand, his rough fingers warm against hers. "Looks like Tate's making breakfast."

"And it's done," Tate said. "Hey, baby." He smiled at Clara Jean and kissed her solidly on the mouth. "I'm not dishing anything up. We can pull it out of the pans."

"I feel like I'm in college again," JJ said dryly.

"Why dirty a plate that'll just hold pancakes when the pan's doing that just fine?" Tate honestly looked confused, and he picked up a plate and turned toward the stove. "Here, sissy." He stood at the stove and put pancakes and sausage on plates for everyone, joining them at the table last.

They crammed everyone in, but no one seemed to want

to talk about anything. Ruby would be driving her car, they'd load whatever she couldn't fit in there into JJ's truck.

"Are you driving?" she asked, breaking the silence in the cabin.

"I'm going to drive JJ's truck at first." Clara Jean looked over to him. "Right?"

"You or Tate," JJ said, barely looking up. "I'm riding with Ruby."

It was almost a straight shot south from Three Rivers to San Antonio, and it would take them eight hours without stops. But Ruby had planned lunch in Abilene, and she wouldn't be able to go for hours without stopping to use the bathroom.

"Remember, we're stopping for lunch at the Burger Spot," Ruby said, though she'd told everyone before.

"We're leaving at the same time," Tate said.

"You like to drive fast," Ruby said. She'd only eaten one of her pancakes, but she didn't want the other. She offered it to JJ, who slid it onto his plate and kept eating.

Ruby got up and took her plate to the kitchen sink. She didn't want to sit here any longer. They had a long drive ahead of them today, and she just wanted to get this show on the road. Literally.

"I'll get my suitcase," she said. She'd seen the bedroom where she'd be living, and she didn't want to have to unpack tonight if she didn't feel like it. So she'd packed what she needed to sleep and then start her internship in the morning. She could then go through her boxes as-needed, without being rushed or over-tired.

In her bedroom, Ruby stood still for a moment, taking in the small room filled with bags and boxes. Fine, the room wasn't filled. She really only had clothes, shoes, books, and knick-knacks, plus a lot of pillows, a couple of sheet sets, and a record player.

It would probably take fifteen minutes to get everything out into the vehicles, and Ruby drew in a deep breath as she heard boots coming her way.

She turned to find Tate coming into the room. "You just want the suitcase with you, right?" he asked as he reached for the handle of it.

"Yes," she murmured.

"Don't get too far inside your head," Tate said, and then he left the room before Ruby could ask him what he meant.

"Everything?" Clara Jean asked.

"Not the bed or bedding," Ruby said. "Or the desk. Everything else."

Clara Jean picked up a box and turned to leave. Ruby did the same, because she knew what Tate meant. She couldn't stand here and worry, get too deep in her thoughts, and not do something. The work needed to be done—move the boxes, load the car, make the drive.

She could worry about the good-bye later.

When the last box got loaded, JJ closed the tailgate on his truck and turned to her, wiping the sweat from his brow with the back of his hand. "You ready?"

Ruby glanced back at the cabin, her heart squeezing painfully in her chest. She knew she'd be back to visit—Thanksgiving wasn't that far away—but it didn't feel soon enough. This place, this ranch, had become her sanctuary, and leaving it felt like leaving a piece of herself behind.

She turned back to JJ and forced a smile. "Yeah. I'm ready."

JJ stepped forward and pulled her into his arms, holding her tightly against his chest. "You're going to do great, Ruby," he whispered into her hair. "You're going to knock 'em dead."

She held him back for only a moment, mostly because Tate sat in the driver's seat of JJ's truck, and he started the engine with a mighty roar. She smiled up at JJ and said, "Can we stop and get a soda before we get going?"

"Sure thing, Scarlet." He smiled back at her, and then went around to the passenger seat of her car.

Ruby got behind the wheel, started the car, and looked over to JJ. "To San Antonio."

"To San Antonio," he repeated, and Ruby backed away from the cabin, turned, and left Seven Sons Ranch.

"Eggs, yogurt, milk, strawberries, bread, and butter," Tate said.

"I've got the whole list," Clara Jean said. "We'll be back in a bit." She grabbed onto Tate's hand and pulled him away from where Ruby and JJ stood in the kitchen of the apartment Ruby had been assigned. She lived with three other women, and they each had their own bedrooms.

She'd only met one of her roommates, a brunette named

Esther, and she'd been given a couple of cupboards in the kitchen.

"This here?" JJ asked, because he wanted to make sure she was set up before he left. He, Tate, and Clara Jean had a hotel that night, and her brother had just left to get groceries for her.

Ruby blinked, trying to focus, but it had been a long day. "Yeah, wherever," she said. "I'm going to go—" She hooked her thumb over her shoulder and down the hall.

"I'll finish here," JJ said, and Ruby turned and walked away from him, her chest vibrating in a strange way. "Then I'm going to order pizza," he called.

"Okay," Ruby called back. Her room sat at the back of the hall, on the right, and she ducked into it and pressed her back against the wall. The light switch dug into her skin, and she sucked in a breath in an attempt not to cry. She wasn't even sure why her emotions teetered so close to spilling over. She'd moved out before. She'd lived with complete strangers before. None of this was new.

Leaving JJ is, she thought, and Ruby opened her eyes as the sexy scent of her boyfriend's cologne entered the room.

"Hey," he said softly, and Ruby stepped into his arms. To her great relief, her eyes stayed dry though she didn't want to let go of the very solid form of JJ. She needed him to stay upright, and she couldn't imagine him leaving her alone in this apartment tonight.

He stroked her hair and said nothing, and Ruby sure liked the silence between them. She liked that it felt comfortable, and she liked that she could stand in his arms and be completely understood.

"Come lay down," he murmured. "It's been a long day, and Tate and Clara Jean won't be back for a while." He led her over to the bed, which she'd stripped and remade with her own sheets, pillows, and comforter, and she climbed all the way over to the wall.

JJ lay down beside her and drew her back into his arms. She pressed into him and kissed him, her lips soft against his, but the kiss wasn't like the ones they'd shared before. This one held all the things she couldn't say, all the emotions she was too scared to voice. It was a kiss that said *I love you*, even if the words hadn't been spoken yet.

He didn't kiss her for too long, and she curled back into his chest to listen to his heart beat. After several minutes, each one calming her further and further, JJ whispered, "Do you want a salad with the pizza?"

"Yes, please," she said.

"Blue cheese dressing," they said together, and she sure liked that JJ didn't have to ask her anymore. He knew her favorites, and she loved how he took care of her. She wasn't sure she was in love with him, but her heart did hurt.

"Okay, pizza's ordered." He lowered his phone and pressed his cheek to the top of her head. "It's not good-bye, Princess Scarlet."

"What is it, then?"

"It's just—see you later."

Ruby did like that, and she sighed as she relaxed for the first time that day. She breathed in deeply, then let the air slide out of her mouth. "Okay, then," she said. "I'll see you later."

JJ chuckled, and Ruby smiled despite the heaviness of the situation. She shifted in his arms, and JJ sobered as he looked down at her. "I sure do like you, Scarlet." And he kissed her again—definitely saying good-bye and see you later and maybe, just maybe, even *I love you.*

Chapter Thirty-Two

JJ tightened the girth strap on his horse, Hickory, his fingers moving with the same practiced precision he'd used a thousand times before. But today, the action felt mechanical. Hollow, almost. He patted the horse's neck, the familiar warmth of the animal beneath his palm grounding him a little. Hickory nickered softly, nosing at JJ's shirt pocket, which usually contained a slice of dried apple or two.

"Not today, boy," JJ muttered, shaking his head with a faint smile. "You can't have apples every day, bud."

Hickory wanted them, but JJ wanted a lot of things he couldn't have.

Since Ruby had moved, the rhythm of his life had shifted. It wasn't that he didn't know how to function without her—he'd spent years working this ranch, doing these same tasks, without her around. But now that she'd been here, now that she'd become part of his every day, her absence felt like a gaping hole. One he couldn't quite figure out how to fill.

He ran a hand through his hair and glanced toward the horizon, where the sun dipped low, casting shadows over the pastures. The horses grazed peacefully, their tails swishing lazily as they wandered near the fence that separated them from the new boarding stable, which had finally been started.

JJ turned back to Hickory, sighing as he adjusted the bridle. "Let's go," he said, his voice low in the quiet afternoon. He mounted the horse in a fluid motion, his body moving automatically into the familiar rhythm of riding. The soft clop of hooves against the dry earth filled the air as he guided Hickory toward the fence line, where a section had come loose the night before.

His ranch had never been in better shape, because the only way JJ knew to stay sane was to work from dawn until dusk. Then he'd go to his parents' house so he didn't have to be alone. Or Conrad's, where Grams would feed them dinner and tell stories about their daddies growing up.

Anything to stay busy, keep his mind off Ruby, pass another day.

He'd ripped off two paper chains now, with a third coming up in only a few days. The remaining twelve chains hung by his back door, and JJ smiled at his girlfriend's handwriting on the paper before folding it and putting it in one of his kitchen drawers.

"Let's move a little faster, Hick." He prodded the horse

into a light trot, focusing on the gait of the horse. Hickory had come to Seven Sons with another couple of horses, and JJ was training them to work the cattle. He hadn't bought any breeding stock yet, because he didn't have his facilities ready yet.

Hick kept his head in the right position, and JJ sure enjoyed riding this horse. He possessed a gentle yet powerful spirit, and he'd be a great herd leader if JJ could get his other horses on-board. They definitely had a pecking order, and Hickory wouldn't be a jerk to the other equines.

JJ tensed in the saddle and moved the reins just-so, and Hickory came to a stop in only a few steps. He'd be able to cut cattle out of the herd just fine, and JJ would take him out into the fields in a couple of weeks to bring the cattle in for the round-up.

He took Hickory around the whole pasture, noting that the mare and the gelding he'd brought to the ranch at the same time as Hickory fell into motion behind him. JJ made it back to the gate, and he dismounted and ran his hands down Hickory's neck.

Firefly and Hazel, Hickory's pasture buddies, crowded in close, and JJ smiled as he found himself in the midst of these gentle creatures. He knew not everyone liked horses, but he sure did, and he didn't feel unsafe or worried the way Emily sometimes did around equines.

"All right," he said. "I'll get you guys cleaned up and watered, and then you can spend the evening out here." He did just that, taking care of his new charges, and then he started working in the barn to get it back to perfect. He cleaned the tack he'd just used and put it away; he swept the grass out of the aisle; he went out to feed and water the chickens.

He kept his phone on his person, but it didn't chime or buzz or vibrate. By the time he exited the barn, the sun had started to arc toward the west, and JJ's stomach growled. His gaze drifted toward the house, and he needed to mow his lawn. Maybe he should do that right now.

He could still picture Ruby standing on the front porch, her hair catching the light as she grinned at him, teasing him about something or calling that she'd brought something to eat. She always made him laugh, even when he'd had a bad day and *wanted* to be grumpy.

He needed something to drink, and he headed for the house, though he didn't want to stay there. He trudged up the steps and into the house, where he washed all the way to his elbow, then scrubbed cold water and soap into his beard and across his face.

He dried everything, the distinct thought that he needed a dog here with him. His father had several ranch dogs, and two that came into the house as family pets. JJ needed some of his own, then he wouldn't have to come home alone.

He filled a water bottle with ice and water from his fridge and stood at the counter while he drank and texted.

JJ to Conrad: *Do you know where I can get a dog?*

Conrad: *You need to talk to Cactus Glover. I can get his number from Glory Rose.*

"Glory Rose, huh?" JJ wondered aloud.

Conrad: *Are you coming for dinner tonight? Grams*

made white chicken chili and cornbread, but I can bring it to you.

JJ didn't know what he wanted to do. Part of him just wanted to stay home, put a movie on, and fall asleep on the couch. He never really watched a lot of TV, because there was always work to do on the ranch, and when he wasn't doing that, he'd been doing something with his family.

But now, when he wasn't as integrated into the western side of the ranch, where all of his aunts, uncles, and cousins lived, JJ could spend a quiet evening at home if he wanted to.

You know what? Conrad texted. *I'd like to get out of here today, so can Sari and I come crash on your couch tonight?*

Any night, JJ said. *What's going on there?*

More leaking pipes, Conrad said and he didn't have to explain more. *And Chloe's been asking for pictures of Sarina a lot lately, and I don't know what it means.*

JJ's heartbeat thumped oddly in the back of his throat. *What does it mean? Do you think she'll come back and want to take Sarina back to Dallas?*

I have no idea, Conrad said. *And I really don't want her to do that.*

Maybe you need to talk to a lawyer.

I'm talking to Grams about it.

Grams had earned her law degree and passed the bar only about twenty years ago, but she'd never really practiced. She'd helped people in the neighborhood with contracts and minor squabbles between neighbors here in

Three Rivers. She could definitely counsel Conrad on the best thing to do to protect Sarina, to protect himself.

She's helping me with the paperwork to make sure I have sole custody and the courts on my side, so Chloe can't just show up whenever she wants and demand to take Sarina back to Dallas—or wherever she is—with her.

Smart, JJ said, because he had no good advice for his cousin. Conrad sounded semi-angry too, and it took a lot to get him riled up, so that told JJ how stressed he was too.

Come whenever, he told Conrad. *If you can't, that's okay too. I know how to feed myself.*

Church Sunday? Conrad asked.

Absolutely. JJ would be able to help with Sarina, and then he could rip off another paper chain and be one week closer to having Ruby back in his life physically.

* * *

JJ pulled into Conrad's driveway and flipped his truck into park. The front door opened before JJ could get out, which was probably best, as he'd left the ranch a little past the time he should've. Conrad herded his little girl outside, then pulled the door closed behind him.

He picked up Sarina and jogged down the steps to his truck. He reached over the back and into the bed of the truck and lifted up a car seat. "Hey," he said as he opened the back door on the passenger side. "I just gotta get this in, and we can go."

"Sorry I'm late," JJ said. "I have fences that need fixing, and I had to move my animals before I left."

"It's fine," Conrad said. "I had to redress Sari after she spilled her breakfast down the front of her dress, and we just barely finished." He twisted and picked up his daughter. "Okay, Sari, in you go, girl."

He buckled his daughter into the car seat, then swung into the truck and exhaled. "Okay. Let's go."

JJ navigated them the few blocks to the church, and the lot had filled up enough that he bypassed it and went straight to the overflow parking. People still walked inside, and the clock hadn't ticked to ten yet, so they hadn't missed the beginning.

Still, he took the first spot he found, and he and Conrad moved with purpose to get Sari and her bag and head inside the chapel. JJ led the way, and he paused to find a place for the three of them. He could've sat with his parents and siblings, or Conrad's parents, or any array of aunts and uncles.

"Over here," Conrad murmured, and he led the way to the right, moving down a few pews to an empty one. He entered first and settled his daughter down while JJ took the spot on the end. He hated feeling rushed, and he took a couple of breaths to calm down and find his center. He wanted to find the rest the Sabbath Day had offered him as a younger man, and he inhaled the familiar scent of polished wood and old lady's perfume.

Conrad picked up Sarina and held her on his lap while he held a book with brightly colored farm animals in it. JJ smiled, watching her for a moment before turning his attention to the front, where Pastor Willa Glover now stood, a glorious smile on her face as the sun's rays came through the stained glass window behind her.

Strong, steady, and filled with a deep, abiding faith that resonated with JJ, Pastor Glover told personal stories that taught gospel principles at the same time. JJ respected her, even if he didn't always understand everything she preached. She had a way of cutting through the noise and getting to the heart of things, and JJ needed that today.

"Welcome," Pastor Glover said. "We're going to start our services today with a musical number from the Glover family." She beamed out at everyone. "They'll be our choir today as well, and I've been tasked with thanking you for allowing my family to hopefully invite the Holy Spirit to be here with us through music."

The Glover cowboys filed up onto the stand, along with their wives and children. They reminded JJ so much of the Walker clan, with lots of brothers, older teens, younger ones, and some young adults as well. Lincoln and Misty, but not Mitch, went up onto the stand.

Willa herself sat at the piano and waited for the Glovers to get into position. Then she started to play, and the Glovers had clearly practiced, because they all swayed to the right and then the left, not a single one of them going the wrong way.

Their voices spanned the range from high to low, and they'd all been blessed with some measure of musical talent. They sang a song about redemption, and it did exactly what

Pastor Glover had wanted—it brought the spirit straight into JJ's heart, touching him and calming him further.

Another pause came while the Glovers found seats up behind the pulpit, where Willa adjusted the microphone and took a deep breath.

"I love autumn," she said, speaking with her mouth and her hands, as her son was home and couldn't hear her, and JJ settled back into the hard pew, ready to receive what she had to give.

"Jay-Jay," Sarina said right out loud, and JJ reached over absently and took her from Conrad. He kept the books and toys, and held a goldfish-shaped cracker in his hand near Sarina, who snuggled back into JJ.

"The season represents the end of one of the busiest times of the year. To me, it's the culmination of so much hard work. An entire year's worth of income for most farmers and ranchers around here. If our summer isn't kind to us, we have a hard fall."

JJ had never thought about autumn like that, but Pastor Glover wasn't wrong.

"I love seeing the hard work of spring and summer pay off in autumn—it reminds me every year to acknowledge that God has a time and a season for everything."

Something pricked at JJ's heart, sending a chill through his whole body. He breathed in slowly, trying to hear and learn what the Lord wanted him to hear and learn.

"We live in a world that's always in a hurry, always pushing us to move faster, to achieve more, to get what we want *right now*. But the Lord's timing is not our timing. His plans are not always our plans." Pastor Glover glanced down at something on the pulpit. "When I first met my husband, we had just started to spend time together when I got a call about my son.

"I had to leave suddenly, and I had no idea when I'd return to town, if I'd be able to return at all. I told Cactus nothing, and I'm sure he wondered what had happened to me, where I'd gone." She glanced over to her husband, and JJ did too. He simply watched Willa with love shining in his eyes, and oh, how JJ wanted what they had in his life.

"It was a struggle," Pastor Glover said. Her hands kept moving, but she paused vocally. "I didn't know how to parent an amazing child like Mitch, and he'd been through so much in his life, living with me, then having to go with his dad, and then living with a foster family for a couple of days until I could get to him after his father's arrest."

Her voice pinched and tore as she fought her emotions, and JJ was fully invested now. Pastor Glover usually had ultimate command of her emotions, and JJ felt his swaying wildly all over the place too.

"We returned to Three Rivers, because Patrick was here," Pastor Glover said and signed. "I needed the support, and when I finally went back to Cactus, I suddenly had a son I hadn't told him about.

"Our relationship reminds me of autumn. Of God's timing. I'm sure he was frustrated at times, wanting things to be different, to move faster. I'm sure many of you feel like that right now, sitting here."

JJ sure did, and he pulled in a slow breath as he tamed his emotions back into their boxes.

"God's timing often doesn't match up with what we want or expect," Pastor Glover continued. "Think about Abraham and Sarah, waiting for the child God had promised them. They waited years—*decades*—for that promise to be fulfilled. And in their waiting, they had moments of doubt, of frustration, even of trying to take matters into their own hands. But God's plan was always in motion. His timing was perfect, even when they couldn't see it."

JJ's throat tightened. He didn't want to be like Abraham, waiting decades for Ruby to come back to him. He didn't want to doubt, to try and force something to happen before it was time. But the waiting was so much harder than he'd imagined.

"But here's the thing, my friends," Pastor Glover said, her voice softening as she looked out over the congregation. "God's timing isn't just about waiting for the right moment. It's about *trusting* in His plan, even when we don't understand it. It's about surrendering our desires, our timelines, our *fears* to Him and believing that He not only knows *what* is best for us, but *when* is best for us."

JJ swallowed hard, his gaze dropping to the top of Sarina's head. She gummed a cracker, oblivious to the amazing sermon happening around him. He looked over to Conrad, who actually wiped his eyes.

Surrendering his fears. Trusting God's plan. Somehow, exercising his faith had always been the hardest for him. He liked to be in control, to have a plan, to know what was coming next. And then, he went to work. Daddy had taught him to go to God, and then go to work.

And Pastor Glover wanted him to wait, watch, and trust.

"When we trust in God's timing," she said. "When we let go of our need to control everything, we find peace. We find hope. We find the strength to keep going, even when the waiting feels unbearable."

JJ closed his eyes, a prayer forming in his heart. *Lord, I don't know what You have planned for me and Ruby. I don't know if she's the one You've chosen for me, but I love her. I love her so much, and I don't want to lose her. Please, help me to trust in Your timing. Help me to surrender my fears to You and to have faith that You'll bring her back to me if it's Your will.*

The silence in the church felt heavy, but not in a bad way. It was a comforting weight, a reminder that he wasn't alone in this. That God was with him, even in the waiting.

JJ opened his eyes and glanced over at Conrad again. His cousin gave him a soft smile and smoothed down his daughter's hair. JJ wondered if Conrad felt the same pull, the same need to trust in God's timing with everything going on in his life.

"So today, I invite you all to lay down whatever burdens you've been carrying. Whatever fears, whatever doubts, whatever you've been struggling to control—give it to God. Trust in His timing, and know that He will guide you through whatever you're facing."

JJ let the words sink into his heart and mind. He needed to trust in His timing. Lay down his fears. Exercise his faith.

He could do that. He *had* to do that, for his own sanity. He couldn't keep holding on so tightly to the fear of losing Ruby. He had to trust that if they were meant to be together, God would bring her back to him.

In His own timing.

"So as autumn continues to descend upon us, think of all you've been able to accomplish this spring and summer as you reap your harvest. That harvest can only happen at a certain time of year, and God has determined that time. It represents hours and days and months of hard work and waiting, and that's why autumn is one of my favorite seasons —because it reminds me that waiting for something is not an idle activity. It's a necessary part of our spiritual growth."

As the service ended and the congregation rose to sing the final hymn with the Glovers, JJ found himself singing with more conviction than he had in weeks, maybe months.

As the final notes of the hymn faded and JJ passed Sarina back to her daddy, JJ whispered a prayer under his breath, his heart steady and sure for the first time in a long while. "Lord, I trust You. I trust Your timing. And I trust that You'll bring Ruby back to me when the time is right."

Chapter Thirty-Three

R uby stood in front of the floor-to-ceiling window at Opal and Oak's sleek, modern office, trying to focus on the breathtaking view of the San Antonio skyline. The city stretched out before her, a dazzling array of high-rise buildings, bustling streets, and twinkling lights just beginning to flicker to life as dusk approached. The hum of the city pressed in on her constantly here, a far cry from the quiet, wide-open spaces of Three Rivers.

Her fingers absentmindedly tapped against her phone as she stared at the towering skyscrapers. In her other arm, she clutched a thick stack of sketches she needed to review and sort for tomorrow's meeting. But she couldn't focus on layouts or color schemes. Even the big client presentation she had next week only got her attention for about fifteen minutes before her mind wandered back to the ranch.

Right now, JJ was probably finishing up his evening

chores, maybe riding Hickory out to check the fences or finishing up in the barn or meeting with the construction manager on his new stables. "No," she murmured. "He had that appointment at Lone Star with Henry and Angel."

They owned an enormous boarding stable closer to Amarillo, and seeing as how JJ wanted to have a stable where he housed a lot of horses, he wanted to see how they ran things. He wouldn't be boarding, but breeding, but he'd told her he wanted to draw from their expertise in dealing with a lot of animals coming and going quite often.

Ruby had wanted to go with him, of course, but she'd simply encouraged him and told him to call her afterward.

She pictured him in the saddle, the way his hands moved confidently over the reins, the way his dark eyes softened when he looked at her. The memory of his arms around her, the warmth of his embrace, made her chest ache. She missed him more than she'd ever thought possible.

When she'd first arrived in San Antonio, the excitement of the city had been enough to distract her from the heaviness in her heart. The bustling streets, the restaurants, the galleries—it had all been new and thrilling. But now, a month into her internship, the initial excitement had started to fade, and the reality of the distance between her and JJ had set in.

"Should've made your own paper chain," she murmured, not for the first time. She had nothing to mark the weeks away from JJ, and a couple of days ago, he'd sent her a picture Tate had taken of him ripping off Week Four's chain. There had been evidence of bread bowls and soup, and Ruby had nearly burst into tears at the thought of JJ entertaining her brother, Clara Jean, Conrad, and others with dinner when she couldn't be there.

She'd never felt so lonely.

It was a busy kind of loneliness, one filled with meetings, deadlines, and late nights at the office. But no matter how busy she was, no matter how many new experiences she had, this nagging feeling stuck with her. A terrible feeling that she was missing something.

She'd thought the internship would fill the void, that the thrill of working at a prestigious design firm would be enough to keep her mind and heart full while separated from JJ. But the truth was, it didn't. As much as she loved the work, as much as she felt proud of herself for making it to this point, it wasn't enough. And that scared her.

With a sigh, Ruby turned away from the window and set down the portfolios on her desk. The open-plan office behind her sat quietly, most of her colleagues having left for the evening. Only one other woman remained, working diligently at her computer and sending a click through the silence every few seconds.

Ruby glanced at the clock—almost seven. She needed to head back to her apartment soon if she wanted to eat dinner at a reasonable hour.

But instead of packing up, she sank into her desk chair, pulled out her phone, and scrolled to Simone Walker's text string. She'd started talking to Simone, JJ's aunt, as she'd worked on the remodel at the homestead. Simone took old furniture and restored it. She found everyday and farm objects like barrels and made them into beautiful, custom pieces that she sold at fairs and festivals—and now online too.

She had a she-shed in her backyard, and Ruby could still feel the wonder and awe she'd felt when she'd gone there for the first time.

I showed your sewing-desk-vanity to my boss today, and she absolutely loved it. Ruby smiled as she typed out the text and sent it. *She wants it, so can you mark it sold, and I'll get you the purchase order tomorrow?*

Oh, I'm so glad! Simone sent back. *I'll send you an invoice, so you can put that number in your system. I'm just picking up Laurel from her acting class, so I'm not home, but I'll do it before I go to bed.*

No rush, Ruby said, though Jill, her boss, did like to have invoice numbers matched up with purchase orders. Ruby could add it at any time, though.

What are you going to do with the vanity?

One of our clients right now is a wedding venue, Ruby said. *They're redoing their brides' and grooms' rooms, and they want it for one of their bridal rooms.*

Perfect! Simone sent a smiley face too, and Ruby stared at her phone, her neck starting to ache from how she had it bent.

She sighed and looked up, the darkness covering the city quickly now. She worked in an unpaid internship position that included her housing, but she still had to eat. She couldn't afford to get dinner on the way home every night, but she really wanted a bag of tacos or a cheeseburger tonight.

Tapping quickly, she moved over to her bank account to check it. Her parents couldn't afford to help her very much, and Tate had told her to let him know if she needed a little something extra. She hadn't done that yet at all, but the state of her bank account made her heart leap up into her throat.

Without second-guessing, she tapped to dial her brother. His line rang once, then twice, and Ruby fretted that she might be interrupting him and Clara Jean.

Then he said, "Heya, Rubes. What's up?"

Just hearing his voice made her explode to her feet. She didn't call JJ very often either, because it was easier emotionally to text instead.

"I hate to ask," she said, her voice choked. She heard it in her own ears, and she hated that Tate could too. "But could you send me twenty bucks? I'm still at the office, and I just want a bacon cheeseburger from Whattaburger."

"Sure," Tate said easily. "Clara Jean and I are picking up dinner from the grocery store right now. I wish there was a Whattaburger here." He chuckled like he didn't have a care in the world, though Ruby knew he did.

"Thanks, Tate," she said.

"Yeah, sure, sissy." He paused for a moment. "Okay, I sent it. What else?"

"What else?" she repeated.

"You could've texted me to ask for a few dollars," he said, his voice turning quieter than before. "What else is going on? You sound a little nasally."

"I'm okay," Ruby said as she paced over to the windows again. "I just feel a little down tonight."

"Are you still at the office?" He sounded surprised. "You are. Ruby."

"I know," she whispered. "I just—"

"You said you'd go home at a normal hour," Tate said, a frown in his voice. "Am I going to have to start checking your pin every evening at five and then texting and insisting you go home?"

"No," she said.

"Okay." He sighed like she'd caused him a lot of worry. "Well, go home now. Get your burger, and text me when you're there."

"Okay," she said again, feeling very much like the younger sister she was. "Thanks, Tate."

"Love you, Rubes."

"Love you too." The call ended, and Ruby did return to her desk and pack up her things this time. "Bye, Tara," she said to the other woman in the office, and Tara said she'd see her tomorrow.

Ruby rode the elevator down to the lobby, and as she stepped out onto the street, her phone chimed with JJ's notification sound. Her heartbeat pivoted in her veins, and a smile touched her mouth before she could even lift her phone.

I don't want you to argue with me, JJ had said, and that made Ruby pause and blink at her phone. "Argue with him?"

Then her cash app chimed out a *cha-ching!* noise, signaling that she'd gotten a payment.

She didn't even have to tap to see it. *JJ Walker has sent you money!*

Her chest hollowed instantly. She called him, and his line rang and rang and rang. Irritation buzzed through her like an errant fly dive-bombing her every few seconds, because he'd just had his phone. Obviously.

She tapped to open the cash app, because she could pay for her burger from it or transfer the money to her bank account.

Her eyes widened as she stared at the amount he'd sent. "No." Her fingers shook as she tapped—stabbed, really—to call him again.

I can't talk this very second, he sent. *I'll call you back.*

She looked up, disbelief running through her. She didn't actually think JJ would call her back, but she continued her walk down the street to her car. She didn't have to go far, thankfully, and she swung by the Whattaburger only a couple of miles from her apartment.

She'd eaten all of her French fries by the time she pulled into the parking lot, and she took her burger inside to finish her dinner there. "Hey," she called to the apartment, because Lori usually came out to say hello, and Brynn sat on the couch with her lap desk and an open folder.

"Hey," she said in return. She whipped her glasses off her face and smiled at Ruby. "Ooh, you got Whattaburger."

"I should've asked if you wanted anything," Ruby said as she slung her bag onto the recliner. "I'm sorry."

"I wouldn't make you buy me something," Brynn said. "I used my coupon for that free slice of pizza at Italiano's." She smiled at Ruby as she went into the kitchen.

"Did I hear Whattaburger?" Lori asked as she arrived in the kitchen.

"Sorry," Ruby said, regretting bringing in the brown bag. She should've eaten it in the car too.

"I'm ordering it," Lori said, her phone already out. Her daddy sent her money all the time, as he worked as a lawyer in Los Angeles. She had tons of money, and she would've bought everyone in the apartment Whattaburger. "Do you want anything, Brynn?"

"I can't," Brynn said, shooting a nervous glance to Ruby.

"Of course you can," Lori said, looking up. Her eyes widened as she looked at Ruby too. "Nothing—you don't have to buy us dinner, Ruby."

"I had to call my brother and ask for money to get this," Ruby said. "So I'm sorry I can't get dinner for everyone. I would if I could."

"And I can," Lori said with a smile. "So...Brynn?"

"I'll take the chicken fingers meal," she said. "Thanks, Lori."

"I'll text Esther." Lori went into the living room and sank onto the couch too. "Anything else, Ruby? Maybe a chocolate shake?"

Ruby wanted to say no, especially with the amount of money JJ had just sent her. But she said, "Sure, Lori. Thank you so much." She sat at the table and unwrapped her burger. She'd just taken her first bite when her phone rang.

JJ's name sat there, and Ruby stared at it for a long moment, not sure why she didn't dive onto the device and answer the call.

She took another bite of her burger, trying to figure out what to say to him when she spoke with him. She couldn't have the conversation in front of her roommates either, and Ruby cast a quick glance over to Lori and Brynn. Then, as her phone stopped ringing, she tapped out, *I'm eating real quick. Call me in ten minutes?*

Okay, JJ said, and she was honestly surprised he'd called her back at all. He said he would, but still. As she took another bite of her burger, she realized she was making him wait for her again.

He seemed to do that a lot, always there, steady and dependable. And here she was, hundreds of miles away, chasing a dream that didn't feel nearly as fulfilling as she'd thought it would.

As she sat there and listened to Brynn and Lori giggle about something on their phones, Ruby finished her bacon cheeseburger and worked through her feelings for JJ.

And she knew in that moment that she'd fallen all the way in love with him.

She got to her feet, her heartbeat pounding, pounding, pounding in her chest. Surely the whole apartment would hear it, but neither of her friends looked at her. "I'm gonna sort my sketches in my room," she said.

"I'll bring you your shake when it comes." Lori tipped her head back and smiled at Ruby as she walked behind the couch.

"Or text me, and I'll come get it." Ruby smiled at her too, grabbed her bag from the chair, then quickly escaped to her bedroom. She stripped off her slacks and blouse and stepped into her pajamas, a sense of relief at the cooler fabric sliding along her skin.

She didn't want to work tonight, and she tucked herself into bed with her bag still zipped closed. She wasn't sure how many minutes had passed since she'd texted JJ, but her phone rang—and his name sat there again.

She swiped on the call this time. "Hey," she said, her voice not quite as chipper as it would've been at lunchtime.

"My scarlet rose," he said, a new nickname for her. "You sound tired. You okay?"

Ruby let her eyes drift closed. "I am tired, but I'm also okay." She wanted to tell him she loved him, that no matter where life took her, no matter how far she went, her heart would always belong to him.

Tears pricked at the corners of her eyes as she tried to find the next thing she needed to say. "You can't just send me a thousand dollars."

"I think I can," he said. "Because I did, and it went though just fine."

"Jay."

"Scarlet."

She sighed, not wanting to fight with him, not when he spoke in that hard, unyielding voice.

"I asked you not to argue with me," he said quietly, and that was somehow more dangerous than if he'd shouted. "I can't stand the thought of you down there, begging Tate for a few dollars to buy dinner. Not when I'm here, with so much money I'll never spend it all." He took a breath, as that was a lot of words for JJ to string together and say out loud.

"So, please, my princess. Do not argue with me on this."

"Okay," she whispered, her throat narrowing as her emotions surged. "Thank you, sweetheart."

"And if you need money—or anything else—I want you to call me, not your brother."

Ruby's eyes fluttered open at the intensity in his voice. "You're—are you jealous?"

"Absolutely, I am," he said. "I want to take care of you. I sent Tate his twenty bucks back."

"JJ."

"Don't argue with me on this," he said. "Your brother is saving for a farm of his own, and I don't need the money. In fact, what I need is to feel like you need me. Like he needs me. Like I can do something for the two of you."

The way he spoke told Ruby he wouldn't accept anything but what he'd done, and she didn't want to argue with him. "Okay," she whispered. "I'm sorry."

"Don't be sorry. Just call me next time."

"Okay," she said. "I wish you were here to eat cheese-burgers with."

He chuckled, his mood swinging in the opposite direction now. "Me too, Scarlet. Me too."

Ruby took a deep breath, feeling a little drowsy now that she'd eaten and heard JJ's voice. "Tell me what you're doing for Halloween," she said. "Or about Conrad's court hearing.

Or how Market Day went. Just...talk to me, Jay. I just want to lay here and listen to your voice."

Maybe she'd said too much. Maybe the way she felt had come out in those words. But as JJ started telling her about what his family had planned for Halloween and his role in it, Ruby didn't care what, if anything, she'd just admitted to.

As he laughed, Ruby smiled and vowed the next time she saw him in person, she'd tell him she loved him. Right out loud.

Chapter Thirty-Four

Conrad snuggled his sniffling daughter against his chest as he checked out with the receptionist. "This is the prescription?" he asked, looking at the square of paper he'd just been given.

"No, sir," the woman said. "Doctor Leeds sent that straight to the pharmacy at Wilde & Organic. Should be ready by the time you get there." She tapped the paper. "That's the referral to the hearing specialist to do the assessment for Sarina." She smiled at him. "And then you've got one there for the Intervention Specialist team at the hospital. They'll want the results of the hearing test first, so I'd schedule there and then call over to the IS team."

"Okay." Conrad swept the papers off the counter and into his pocket. "Thank you." He did his best to smile at the woman, because she knew his momma. Everyone did, it seemed.

He wasn't sure he pulled it off, and he caught the sympathy in the receptionist's eyes as he turned to leave the doctor's office.

He stepped out into the brisk afternoon air, clutching Sarina close as she continued to fuss against his shoulder. The cool breeze brushed against his neck, a refreshing contrast to the warmth of the clinic just behind him. He could feel the weight of the papers in his pocket, reminders of the journey ahead, and for a moment, he let himself breathe, allowing the chaos of today to ebb away.

"It's going to be okay, Sari," he murmured softly, planting a kiss on the top of her head. Her unruly curls tickled his chin, and a small smile played on his lips despite the anxiety swirling in his gut. He shifted Sarina a bit to look at her face, her little nose scrunched up in distress as her pretty eyes shone at him with unshed tears.

They'd had to take some blood inside, though Conrad still wasn't sure why. So many things had come at him in recent weeks, and he reminded himself that this was how fathers acted. His daughter barely spoke, even when he showed her pictures of animals and asked her what they said.

She seemed to be able to hear just fine to him, but he was no doctor, that was for dang sure. So if the pediatrician his momma had helped him get into wanted to send Sari for a hearing test, Conrad would do it. If he had to go to an "intervention specialist clinic" because his daughter wasn't three yet, fine. He'd do it.

He tucked her closer, and she finally seemed to calm,

her small fingers curling around the collar of his shirt as she snuggled closer.

And at the grocery store, he'd get the chocolate ice cream with peanut-butter-stuffed footballs he loved, and once Sari went to bed tonight, he'd decompress with the miniature donkeys and a cold treat.

Sarina had been fussy all morning, insisting on wearing her rain boots even though the sky was as clear as one of those fancy glass paperweights Grams collected. She'd refused every breakfast option he offered, finally settling on dry cereal—which she then spilled all over the kitchen floor. So now, he'd run out of milk along with his patience, and he'd had to come in from the farm early to get her to the doctor.

He walked past the back of a red hatchback just as the tailgate started to rise. It took his overwhelmed brain a moment to catch up to the fact that he was going to smack right into that, and instinctively, he turned to his right to protect Sarina.

He grunted as his shoulder and bicep hit the hard metal of the car, and then he started to stumble as he moved forward and backward at the same time. He couldn't drop Sarina, and Conrad ended up crashing his right hip against the corner of the car where the cargo area started.

And he sat down hard there just as a gorgeous brunette rounded the corner of the car on the driver's side. "Great gravy and grits," she said, her eyes wide. "Did I hit you?" She looked past him as if there'd be more pedestrian casualties. "I'm so sorry, I didn't see you, and I—" She cut off when her eyes truly met his for the first time.

At least the first time that day.

"Hullo, Glory Rose," Conrad said, his heart thumping hard. Too hard for this simple altercation with a hatchback gate that had lifted and clipped him in the shoulder slightly.

So hard, because Glory Rose had her hair clipped back on the sides, but it otherwise tumbled over her shoulders in long, dark ringlets. She wore makeup that made her an absolutely stunning woman, and Conrad wasn't sure he'd ever seen her with such bright red lips or that dark makeup around her eyes that made her seem older and more beautiful than ever.

She wore a black pencil skirt that accentuated her curves, with a white fluffy blouse made out of a fabric Conrad had never seen before. She carried a folder in her hands that she tossed down as she stepped closer.

"Are you hurt?" She easily took Sarina from him and held the baby, and Conrad wasn't sure why that was so hot either. He'd danced with Glory Rose at Finn's birthday party, two months ago now. He hadn't called her. Hadn't asked her out on another date—heck, a simple dance at a friend's birthday party was *not* a date. She'd been all smiles and laughter—pure flirtation—while he'd tried not to trip over his own feet.

Conrad blinked, his brain scrambling to catch up. He cleared his throat, suddenly very aware of the fact that he was wearing the same shirt he'd slept in last night. "I'm fine," he said, his voice coming out a bit rougher than he intended.

She smiled, and it was like the sun decided to shine only on him, even though they stood outside with plenty of October sunshine everywhere. "Where did you get hit?"

"My arm," he said, automatically reaching toward his bicep.

"It's your lucky day." She passed Sarina back to him. "I just finished up my nursing program, and I could look at it for you." Her eyebrows went up, and Conrad somehow found himself nodding numbly.

Glory Rose edged closer, the scent of pure goodness mixed with flowers and tangerine met his nose, sending his hormones into a frenzy. For a moment, Conrad forgot they stood out in the open of a parking lot. He forgot about the milk he needed, and the prescriptions, and the chores waiting for him back at the farm.

All he could focus on was the way Glory Rose's eyes sparkled when she laughed, and how her presence seemed to fill the space around him as she checked his arm and deemed him fine, if a bit bruised.

"So," she said, tilting her head slightly. "How've you been?"

Conrad hesitated, unsure how to answer that. How could he tell her that most days, he felt like he was barely holding it together? That between raising Sarina, managing the farm, and trying to figure out what the future held, he sometimes forgot what it felt like to actually breathe?

"I'm managing," he said finally, offering her a small smile. "It's been a little crazy, but we're getting by."

Glory Rose nodded, her expression softening. "Well, if

you ever need a break, I'm a pretty good babysitter." She winked at him, and Conrad's heart did that stupid flip-flop thing again.

He opened his mouth to respond that he did *not* want her to be his babysitter, but before he could, Sarina turned into a luge participant, her body going rigid from shoulder to sole, and he dang near dropped her as she shrieked in his arms.

"Dad-down," she said, which was about all she ever said. He got to his feet, which somehow appeased Sarina, and Conrad glanced at Glory Rose, feeling that strange tug in his gut again. Something about the way she looked at him—like she saw more than just the tired father or the rancher who was barely keeping his head above water—made hope soar through his body.

Sari put both hands on his face, forcing him to look away from Glory Rose. He couldn't believe he could feel anything for Glory Rose Glover.

"Dad-down," she insisted.

Glory Rose stepped back to give them room. "She knows what she wants." She smiled at the little girl as Conrad bent to set her on her feet before he humiliated himself completely.

He kept hold of her hand and straightened. "Yeah, she's a lot like her mom in that way," he said, the words slipping out before he could stop them.

Glory Rose's smile faltered just a little, and Conrad cursed himself inwardly. Why did he have to bring up Chloe? It wasn't like he was still hung up on her—he wasn't.

He was just trying to figure out how to move forward. And that was hard when he had a constant reminder of Chloe in the form of a two-year-old who looked at him with her mother's eyes.

"I didn't mean to—" he started, but Glory Rose waved him off.

"It's okay," she said, her smile returning. "You don't have to explain."

Conrad nodded, grateful for her understanding but still feeling like an idiot. He glanced down at Sarina, who was now content at his side, and then back at Glory Rose. "So, what brings you here today?"

"I'm interviewing here," she said, a hint of pride swelling her shoulders an inch or two taller. "And my daddy didn't even call in a favor." She grinned at him. "So, I'm counting it as a win."

Conrad had parents who could—and would—call in favors all the time, so he understood completely. The Glovers were old blood in Three Rivers, which sent a bolt of panic through him. No way she'd want to be with him, the now-single dad with a daughter that had come without a wedding first.

"Then I have to get to the grocery store," she said. "We're having a family barbecue tonight, and I got roped into picking up the ingredients for my famous salsa."

He raised an eyebrow. "Famous, huh?"

She grinned. "Well, famous within the Glover family, anyway. If you're lucky, maybe I'll save you some."

Conrad hadn't been out with anyone in a while, but he

recognized flirting when it came his way. He chuckled and shook his head. "I'll take your word for it."

She stepped closer, her eyes locking on his. "Or I could save you some, stop by the farm, and you could try it for yourself. It's not too hot, I promise."

Everything felt absolutely on fire, and Conrad didn't dare breathe just in case the air singed his lungs. The invitation hung in the air between them, heavy with implications. Conrad's pulse quickened, and he suddenly felt like he stood on the edge of a cliff, looking down into something he absolutely wasn't ready for.

"I...I don't know," he said, rubbing the back of his neck again, feeling himself take a giant step back when he wanted to fling himself off the edge, parachute or no parachute. "I've got a lot going on with Sarina, and the ranch, and—"

"Conrad," Glory Rose said, cutting him off. "It's just chips and salsa. No pressure."

He exhaled, feeling the tension in his shoulders ease just a little. She wasn't asking for anything more than his company. And maybe that was something he could give her. Maybe he didn't have to figure everything out right now. Maybe he could just take things one step at a time.

He glanced down at Sarina, who had crouched down and was picking at something on her shoe, then back at Glory Rose. "What time's the barbecue?"

Her smile widened. "Six o'clock. Fair warning, it's outside."

"It's warm still," he said.

"Supposed to rain this week." She glanced up, but the gate blocked the view of the sky.

"I don't know if I can come tonight," Conrad said. "I had to come in early for an appointment, and—but—uh—if you wanted to stop by, we could have chips and salsa on the front porch."

"Tomorrow?" she asked. "Salsa's always better the next day, after all the flavors have had a chance to marry."

Conrad nodded, a strange mix of excitement and apprehension boiling in his gut. What would he tell Grams? And JJ? He saw them both every evening, and he didn't want to lie. He absolutely wouldn't do anything to put more distance between him and God.

"See you tomorrow," Glory Rose said, giving him one last smile before she reached into the back of the car and picked up a small box. "Wish me luck with my interview."

"You'll crush it," he said, getting out of the way so she could close the gate.

She did that, then gave him another grin before heading for the doors. Conrad watched her go, his heart thudding in his chest. He glanced down at Sarina, who had taken off her shoe.

"Nope, baby." He swooped her into his arms, grabbing the shoe as he did. "You've got to wear those."

She disagreed, but Conrad kept her in arms as he headed to his truck. Now he just had to figure out how to tell Grams and JJ about a front-porch chips and salsa date with Glory Rose Glover.

Chapter Thirty-Five

M itch sat at the wheel of his truck, his hands resting lightly on the steering wheel as he stared out at the sprawling expanse of land before him. Fifty-eight acres, give or take. The land sloped gently, dotted with clusters of trees in every direction, and at the far end, a large, luxury home stood like a sentinel overlooking the property. It gleamed like dark wood gold in the distance, its wraparound porch and tall windows giving it a timeless, elegant feel.

The realtor had called it a "Southern charmer," and Mitch could see why. It looked like something out of a movie, with a wide porch and perfectly manicured lawn.

Out of the corner of his eye, he saw Link's truck pull up beside him, kicking up a bit of dust as it came to a stop. His cousin climbed out, stretching his long limbs before making his way over to Mitch's window. Link rapped his knuckles on the side of the truck, his grin wide and easy.

"What do you think?" Link asked, mouth moving as his hands did, and Mitch opened the door and stepped out, holding the door for Champ to jump down beside him.

Mitch didn't answer right away. Instead, he rounded the truck's hood to stand next to Link, his eyes scanning the property, trying to see it for what it could be—not just what it was now.

In his mind's eye, he could already picture the academy. A place where deaf children from all over the region could come to learn, to grow, to find their community. He imagined classrooms filled with the soft rustle of hands moving in conversation, the hum of learning and happiness that didn't rely on sound.

This dream had taken root in his heart years ago, back when he'd first realized that Three Rivers didn't have the resources it needed for deaf children. He'd been lucky—his step-father had made sure of that. But not every deaf child had the same support. Not everyone had someone willing to learn sign language alongside them, to be their voice in a world that often didn't know how to listen.

Not everyone had unlimited funds to get hearing dogs, tutors, and interpreters.

Mitch wanted to change that.

He signed slowly, his movements thoughtful. *It's perfect.*

Link followed his signing easily, nodding as he glanced toward the house. He turned back to Mitch before saying, "Yeah, it's a good piece of land. Flat enough to build on, but with enough character that it won't feel like just another development. Plus, that house could be something special for you."

Mitch smiled slightly. The house had drawn him to the property, he could admit that. The manor could serve as the administration building for the academy, or maybe even a dormitory for faculty who needed it. He didn't want to limit himself by his own imagination, his own thoughts.

I don't need something special, Mitch signed, his lips twitching into a smile. *I just need it to be functional.*

"It can be both," Link said.

Mitch didn't respond to that, not because he didn't agree, but because it felt too big to think about. It was easier to focus on the logistics—on the land, the buildings he needed, the fundraising that still needed to happen. He could worry about the personal stuff later. For now, he needed to make sure this property could really be the home of the academy he'd dreamed of for so long.

They started walking, and Mitch took in a deep breath of the late October air. The Glovers would have their annual family dinner, meeting, and Angel Tree decorating in just a few days, something they did on the last Sunday of October year after year.

He desperately wanted to have a slide in the presentation that showed his progress on building out his dreams. Link didn't say anything, and Mitch enjoyed the silence in a way he never had before. He lived with it in perpetuity, and at times in the past, Mitch had found himself in tears over not being able to hear.

Thirty-three years of absolute silence felt so unfair

sometimes, but Mitch had been trying to see more positives than negatives, trying to thank God for his blessings instead of focusing on what he lacked.

Mitch thought of the layout of the land, with white fences running down the left-hand side of the road and guarding what would surely be emerald-green fields when watered and taken care of properly. He took out his phone and started recording, so he could show his parents the land and tell them about the potential for renovation, for more buildings, for parking lots, all of it.

He had water rights here, and this land sat on the east side of Three Rivers, off the highway that ran north and south and connected the southern ranches to the luxury home suburb where Wyatt Walker lived with his family. Uncle Preacher had once gotten in a terrible accident on this highway, but this property sat further south than that.

It wasn't the most ideal location, as people coming to the academy would have to go all the way around the town of Three Rivers to get to it.

But wow, the space out here...Mitch took a deep breath and felt the power of the earth, of the heavens, of God, fill him from top to bottom.

When they reached the house, Link stopped and turned to face Mitch, his expression more serious now. "So, what do you think?"

I think this is amazing. Mitch turned and looked back the way they'd come, scanning his phone across the enormity of the entrance road to the property. At least four dormitory-like buildings could fill the space across from the pasture, and the fully formed facility bloomed to life in his mind's eye. His throat tightened, because he couldn't quite believe this was happening. But standing here, looking at the land, the house, the endless possibilities, it felt real. More real than it ever had before.

Link clapped him on the back, his grin returning. *I think so too. This is going to be an absolute God-send for people.*

Mitch swallowed hard, his hands stilling at his sides. He hoped what Link had said would come true. He didn't want to just build a school. He wanted to build a community. A place where kids like him—kids who had grown up feeling different, feeling like the world wasn't built for them—could find a sense of belonging. He wanted them to know that they weren't alone. That there was a place for them, a place where they could thrive.

They went up the steps to the porch, and Mitch ran his hand along the railing, the smooth wood cool beneath his fingers. The house seemed to be in good shape; the previous owners had clearly taken care of it, and though it was larger than what he'd need for just himself, it could serve as a multi-purpose building for the academy, with offices for himself, for teachers, for administrative personnel.

Just as he reached for the front doorknob, Champ nosed his calf from behind. Mitch just wanted to get to the back of the house and see if the land back there would support another of his ideas—a community education center for the deaf and hearing alike.

But now he paused and looked down at his dog. Champ raised up on his back paws, his nose pointing at his back pocket, and Mitch pulled his phone out. He'd gotten a text, and the light must've alerted Champ. He tapped and swiped to open his device as Link entered the house ahead of him.

His pulse accelerated as he saw the text from Lacy Hayes. *I just submitted my final paperwork, Mitch. I'm looking forward to hearing from you.*

A slow smile filled his face, because Lacy's video submission had been some of the best sign language Mitch had seen. She was a hearing person who'd been studying sign language in both the US and the UK, and she'd been interpreting for the state of Texas for five years now.

He'd recruited her to come teach at his academy, something he really hadn't been sure he'd be able to do. He couldn't imagine why anyone would want to leave their current job and come to this small town in the Panhandle to work for him.

For an academy that wouldn't open until at least next fall.

Next fall was the goal, whether he could provide on-site housing or not. But Mitch really wanted to provide on-site housing. So maybe not next fall. Maybe almost two years from now.

But he wanted key faculty to start with him in the New Year, so they could develop a sign language and deaf studies curriculum for all ages, from toddler to adult.

He dang near fell down at the very thought. Developing the curriculum alone would take more than two years, and he needed someone like Lacy at his side to do it.

And he didn't need to review her final paperwork.

Great, he tapped out to her. *I'll get it approved when I get back to my computer.*

He hesitated for a moment, because he wanted to share this place with someone besides his cousin or his parents. *I think I found the perfect place for the academy,* he told Lacy. *Finally. I'm getting pictures and video, and I can show it to you later.*

That's great news! she said, and Mitch did like her positivity.

Mitch glanced out at the land again, his heart swelling with a mix of excitement and fear. He knew it would be hard. He'd faced hard before. Growing up deaf in a world that didn't understand him had been hard. Learning to navigate a world that wasn't built for him had been hard.

But he'd done it. And he'd do this, too.

The inside of the house impressed him just as much as the outside. High ceilings, hardwood floors, and large windows that let in plenty of natural light. It was more than Mitch had expected, and he could already see how the space could be transformed into something functional yet welcoming.

He toured the house behind Link, his mind racing with ideas. The kitchen could be turned into a communal dining area for staff. The upstairs bedrooms could be converted into offices or guest rooms for visiting teachers. And the large living room could serve as a meeting space or lounge for small groups of students.

By the time he stepped out onto the back porch, Mitch

couldn't quite get a full breath. Nothing was perfect, but this house had gotten really close.

Link straightened from where he leaned against the deck railing when Mitch joined him. *So?* he asked. *Final thoughts?*

Mitch took a deep breath and surveyed the land behind him. Farmland, yes. With two sheds to the left, probably for storage or equipment, a bigger, more industrial metal shed beyond that, likely for tractors and other big machinery.

A barn crowded in close to the edge of the backyard, and a stable jogged next to it, with fencing between. Another paddock. More pastures.

Plenty of room for a community-center-esque building.

He grinned over to his cousin and said, *I'm going to buy this place.*

Link clapped him on the back, his smile blinding. *Heck, yes, you are.*

Mitch laughed, sure Link was doing the same. He settled against the railing the way Link had been a few moments ago, a sense of peace settling over him. For the first time in a long time, he felt like everything was falling into place.

Will you hold my phone so I can call my momma? Mitch handed his phone to Link, then tapped to dial while he held it up. He couldn't contain his grin, so he wore a semi-maniacal look when his momma connected the video call and signed, *Howdy son.*

She took one look at him, and her eyes sparkled like diamonds. *The house is nice, it looks like.*

Real nice, he said. *But it's the land here, Momma. It's perfect for an academy.*

So do you want me to call Jerry? she asked.

Having his hearing parents make phone calls on his behalf made everything easier, so Mitch nodded. *Would you?*

Absolutely, Momma said. *Daddy will want to see it. I want to see it.* She smiled as her hands dropped down. *Will we be able to come take a tour?*

I don't see why not, Mitch said. *Ask Jerry, but no one's living here right now.*

I'm going to make the call, and then I'll put in one of those pizza casseroles.

Mitch laughed, wondering what the sound of his voice sounded like. He felt it vibrating and moving through his throat, his nose, his chest. Then he signed, *I think a pizza casserole is the perfect way to celebrate the purchase of this property, Momma. Thank you.*

She wore her excitement on her face, and her signs flew as she said she was going to tell Daddy, call Jerry about putting in an offer, and *then* put in the pizza casserole. Mitch said, *I love you*, and she signed it back just as the call ended.

Link handed back his phone, and Mitch sighed as pure joy pulled through him. He looked over the land again, then met his cousin's eye. *This is a huge endeavor.*

Sure is. Link nodded toward the door, and they went back through the house to get to the front porch and down to the dirt lane again.

When his boots hit the ground at the bottom of the steps, he looked over to Link. *I can do all things through Christ who gives me strength.*

Link slung his arm around Mitch's shoulder, and Mitch sure was glad he hadn't had to come look at this property alone. He'd never really done anything in his life alone, unless he wanted to.

You sure can, Link said, and Mitch appreciated the vote of confidence. *The real question is, can you eat two dinners tonight? Because I told Misty about this place, and she's already making the fried chicken sliders you love....* Link lifted his eyebrows as a final punctuation mark to his statement.

Mitch laughed again, and he paused and hugged Link, wishing he could tell him in a loud voice, "I can eat two dinners tonight," because he loved his cousin, his wife, and their boys.

Since he couldn't use his voice, he pulled away and nodded. *I'm dying for two dinners tonight.*

Chapter Thirty-Six

J J paced over to the front windows and looked out again, probably for the fifteenth time in as many minutes. He could check his phone to see where Ruby was. The last time he'd done that, she'd been passing Shiloh Ridge, which meant she should be here any minute.

He'd torn off the eleventh paper chain two days ago, and JJ simply wanted to *see her*. In the flesh. Touch her, hold her, kiss her.

He turned away from the glass that showed him an empty driveway and strode back into the kitchen. He didn't think she was stopping by to see Tate or Clara Jean before she came here, and if she did...

JJ swallowed. Surely she wouldn't. Surely she was as anxious to see him as he was her.

He picked up the blue velvet box containing the diamond he'd bought three or four paper chains ago.

Liz Isaacson

"Is this a bad idea?" he muttered to himself, asking the Lord as well.

When he'd first come in off the ranch, in one of the sourest moods he'd ever been in, he'd flopped down next to his daddy and said, "I'm in love with her, and I'm dying."

His father had chuckled, which had only stoked the ire inside. When he'd seen that his laughter was not going over very well, Daddy had quieted right down and said, "Well, maybe you should ask her to marry you."

Of course, JJ had been thinking about marrying Ruby, but he hadn't even told her that he loved her. They talked a little bit about their future, but really, everything had been put on hold until December fifteenth. Now, only three and a half weeks until then, JJ wasn't sure what Ruby would do come December sixteenth, and if he asked her to marry him, everything could be blown wide open.

"That's what you want," he told himself.

Conrad had joked with him and said that JJ wouldn't last four minutes without telling Ruby that he loved her, but JJ had rolled his eyes and said he wasn't going to do that. Now he wasn't so sure.

He flipped open the lid of the ring box and took in the diamond, the sparkling gem inside. He'd gossiped with his sisters to find out what Ruby liked. Then he and Conrad had gone to the jewelry store here in Three Rivers and bought the ring. JJ couldn't even imagine the gossip flying through the rumor mill this past month, and thankfully, he didn't live inside that space too often, and Ruby wasn't in town at all.

422

His stomach felt tight, like someone had stretched it like a drum. He snapped the lid shut and turned toward the front door just as someone rang the bell. His pulse went wild, stampeding through his veins as the door opened and his glorious, beautiful Scarlet Princess poked her head inside.

"JJ," she called, and then she saw him. She froze in the open doorway, her smile absolutely radiant, and JJ swept off his cowboy hat and threw it as he whooped and ran toward her.

"You're here," he said, needlessly, sweeping right into her personal space and pulling her into his arms.

Nothing had ever felt so good as the warm press of Ruby against him. She held him too, her chest rising and falling a little too fast to be normal.

JJ almost let go so he could ask what was the matter, and then he realized she was crying. He held her tighter, stroking one hand down the back of her head and through all that silky, reddish-brown hair.

"Hey," he said softly, very aware of the clock ticking. He so wanted to prove Conrad wrong and yet comfort Ruby in the best way possible. "It's all right," he said. "You're okay. You made it."

She nodded against his chest, her grip around his waist tight enough to let him know not to let go. So JJ stood there in the late November air and held the woman he loved, so many things flying through his mind and threatening to come out of his mouth.

"I have missed you so much," he said, his lips right at her

ear. He took a breath and added, "You smell so good." He touched his lips to the soft spot of skin right below her earlobe, and then skated them down even further, pure fire raging through his veins.

"I didn't even realize how lonely I was until this moment," he whispered, and he knew that he was about to lose to Conrad. "You make everything brighter in my life. Without you, the stars have no shine, and the sun is dark. I *need* you, Ruby Reynolds."

JJ hesitated for half a second, then pushed through his fear and said, "I love you, Scarlet."

Her hold on him lessened, and he released his grip on her so they could pull apart a little bit. She looked at him with watery eyes, wide and filled with wonder.

"You do?"

"With everything I am," he said, smiling at her. "I'm in love with you, and I've been working on some plans that I'd like to run by you."

He pulled back even further, his hand dropping to hers as he pulled her out of the doorway so he could close the door and show her what he'd been working on for the past few weeks. He got the door closed and had taken a couple of steps toward the kitchen counter where he'd left that navy blue velvet box in plain sight when Ruby dug in her heels and stopped.

"Wait," she said.

He turned back to her, hoping he could block the view of that ring box and that he could get it off the counter before she saw. He wanted to propose, but once all of his uncles had found out that he was in love with Ruby and was going to ask her to marry him, they told him that the proposal had to be, quote, "really good." And JJ had been stressing about it since.

He certainly couldn't just flash the ring box and say, "Oh, by the way, I bought you a diamond. Will you marry me?"

"What is it?" he asked, searching Ruby's face. He couldn't believe he hadn't kissed her yet, and he cradled her face in both of his hands and said, "I've got to kiss you hello. Can it wait?"

She nodded, and JJ grinned as he leaned in to kiss her. The moment his mouth touched hers, JJ got confirmation that asking her to marry him was the absolute right thing to do. He couldn't survive without her, and he kissed her like the cowboy in love that he was.

She kissed him back pretty fervently, and JJ felt every stroke power through his gut and down to his toes and back. She broke the kiss, and while JJ had taken everything he wanted from her, he still felt like he needed more.

She said nothing as he leaned his forehead against hers, so he asked, "What is it?"

"I just..." She ran her hand up the front of his shirt and gripped his collar. "I just need to tell you that I love you too."

JJ sucked in a breath as he lifted his head, shock and delight twining together inside him.

"You do?" he asked, echoing what she'd said.

She grinned at him and said, "I really do."

JJ tipped his head back and laughed, a joy like he'd never experienced before filling him, overflowing and filling again as it ran through him. As he sobered, he couldn't erase the smile from his face, and Ruby's seemed permanently etched on her mouth too.

"Well, that might make my plans a little bit easier," he said.

"Can I kiss you hello?" Ruby asked, in her half-shy, half-coquettish way, and JJ said, "Absolutely."

After getting their hellos properly out of the way, he led her to the kitchen counter, where he grabbed the navy blue box in one hand. As he rounded the island, he opened a drawer and tossed it inside, tapping the folder he'd prepared with his other hand.

Ruby looked from the folder to him and back to it.

"What's in that?" she asked.

"Did you drop Emily off at the homestead?" he asked.

"Yes," Ruby said.

"And you're driving back together, right?"

"We were planning on it," Ruby said. "On Sunday, after I go to church and rip off your paper chain for you." She gave him a smile that JJ simply wanted to kiss away and hold in his pocket forever.

"I want to come live in San Antonio with you," he said, just blurting it right out.

Ruby's eyes widened. "Well, I don't know...." She stammered, and JJ realized what he'd just said.

"I mean, not *with* you," he amended quickly. "I'm gonna stay with Emily in her apartment, and then I'll be able to see you after work every day. And we can throw away this blasted paper chain." His tone turned a touch dark as he spoke the last few words, and he reminded himself to stay hopeful and bright.

Relief washed over Ruby's face. "Oh, you're gonna stay with Emily?"

"Yeah," JJ said. "I talked to her about it. Her landlord said it's fine if I'm there for less than a month. Otherwise, I have to sign a lease."

Ruby reached for the folder and slid it out from underneath his fingers. She flipped it open and scanned the page. "So this is your plan to move to San Antonio for three weeks?"

"Right," he said.

She lifted it up and gave him a flirty look over the top of the folder before she looked at it again. "You're gonna drive back with us on Sunday. Wow."

JJ said nothing, because he wanted her full reaction to come out first.

"You're gonna stay with Emily, on her couch, and you'll drive her to work, so you can use her car." She looked at him again. "And you think you can survive three weeks without your truck?"

"For you, Ruby," he said quietly. "I can do anything for three weeks, except not see you every day."

She immediately lifted the folder a little higher, a sniffle coming from behind it. JJ reached out and gently pushed it down so that he could see her.

"You don't have to hide from me, Scarlet," he whispered. "If you don't want me in San Antonio, just say so. But know that you'll be killing a cowboy, and you'll have to live with that on your conscience."

She grinned, her eyes flooding the room with a sparkle that landed on him and held. "Well, I can't be killing cowboys."

JJ chuckled. She flipped the folder closed and laid it on the counter. "I don't really see why you need my permission to do this," she said.

"Of course I do," he said. "What if...." He trailed off, unsure how to finish. "What if you really like being alone at night? What if you feel pressured to leave work earlier than you want to because I'm there? What if I'm smothering you? What if you had a plan for the fourteen weeks, and I'm blowing it up on week eleven?"

He paused long enough to take a quick breath. "I just want you to be happy, Ruby."

She stepped closer, and JJ slid his hand along her waist. "I want you to be happy too, JJ," she said.

"Being with you makes me the happiest," he said. "I suspected it before you left, but it didn't take long to know it for real after you'd gone. I'm sort of a mess without you, Scarlet. I want you in my life every day, every day, every day."

Ruby wore the softest, sweetest smile as she said, "I want that too."

"So will you approve the plan?" JJ asked.

Ruby opened her eyes and looked at him. "The plan is approved, Mister Walker."

JJ tilted his head back and called, "Yeehaw!" to the ceiling before he kissed Ruby again.

Chapter Thirty-Seven

R uby entered her apartment with a bag over one shoulder, a backpack on, and her briefcase in hand. She'd been rushing for the past couple of hours to finish up a meeting and then get all of the emails sent for the contracts before she could come home.

"I'm so sorry I'm late," she said.

JJ looked up from his phone. He sat on the couch in her apartment, a pure cowboy god in blue jeans, cowboy boots, and a black-and-white plaid shirt, his dark cowboy hat tilted just so on his head.

"You're fine," he said.

Ruby dropped all of her bags, shrugged out of her backpack, and laid it all in the recliner across from him. "Is anyone else home?"

A slow smile curved his lips. "They all went out," he

said, and he carried something in his voice that told Ruby he'd made sure they'd be here alone tonight.

She'd had a fantastic Thanksgiving week and weekend with him in Three Rivers, and he'd come back with her a week and a half ago to San Antonio. He drove his sister to her aesthetician classes every day so that he could use her car. JJ had shown up at Ruby's office with lunch some days, donuts and coffee on others, flowers on still others—always with his charming smile and his handsome good looks.

She loved him more and more every day. As she sank into the couch beside him, and he put his arm around her, she looked up at him and said, "You're pretty perfect, you know that?"

He chuckled and shook his head. "If I were perfect, sweetheart, dinner would be here already."

She laughed too and then asked, "How far out is it?"

He picked up his phone and glanced at it. "Still seven minutes."

"Wow," she said. "Seven minutes off. I don't think we can be together anymore."

He grinned at her, and she grinned back, and then he kissed her hello in that slow, country boy way he had that made her bones melt, her muscles sag, and her heart know that this man loved her.

"Did you get my text?" she whispered, and then she kissed him again.

"Yes," he murmured, barely pulling away far enough to do so. "And I'll do it, Ruby. I'll do whatever you want. I absolutely should meet your parents as your boyfriend."

She nodded. "I think so too."

"You've told them about me, though, right?"

"Absolutely, I have."

He exhaled, straightening his hand, his thumb stroking along her elbow. "Talk to me, Scarlet: When do you think you'd like to get married?"

They'd talked generally about marriage in the past couple of weeks. Of course, JJ had a ranch he lived on, and he lived alone in an empty house. So of course, Ruby would move in there with him.

It sure seemed like God had opened the storybook and filled out all the blanks at the end, and then provided a way for Ruby to move through the pages until she could get to her happily ever after.

"It'll be hot in the summer," she said.

"The Glovers have an air-conditioned barn," JJ said. "It's called True Blue, and they rent it out to anyone. My family's known theirs for decades. I'm sure they'd let us use it if it's available."

"Yeah," Ruby said, though she wasn't sure if she wanted to do that.

"Where are Clara Jean and Tate getting married?"

"This place in town," JJ said. "It's called the North Hampton House, and it used to be our church. About fifteen years ago, they built a new one, and they sold that one to someone who runs it as an events center."

"Okay," Ruby said. "This might be kind of silly, but I'd like to get married at Seven Sons." She leaned away from his chest and looked up at him. "What do you think about that?"

"Exactly what you just said—it'll be hot outside in the summer," he said. "And it doesn't really cool off until like November."

"Yeah." She sighed, leaning back against his side, because she couldn't imagine waiting almost another year to become his wife. Of course, he hadn't asked her to marry him, and she had not seen any diamonds yet, though she had told him and showed him some pictures of the types of rings she liked.

And another year would make her twenty-four before they got married, and maybe then her parents wouldn't freak out that she and JJ were too young.

"Something to think about," he said as he got to his feet. "Food's here."

He went to the door to get the food from the delivery driver. Ruby could hear them talking, but she couldn't focus on the words. As JJ returned to the couch and put the bags of food on the coffee table in front of them, she said, "I don't want to wait until November to get married."

"We can get married anywhere," he said. "I just want to marry you. I just want to be yours."

JJ looked at her, barely tilting his head enough to see her past the brim of his cowboy hat. "Maybe July or August," he suggested. "I don't think my mama will mind if we're a few months away from Clara Jean's wedding."

"Will Clara Jean care?" Ruby asked.

"I'll talk to her."

She reached for the bag and undid the knot at the top. "What did you get?"

"Your favorites," he said, and he let her pull out the cashew chicken, the snow pea chicken, and the orange chicken.

She grinned at all of them as she opened the flaps on the white Chinese containers, then turned to him. "You got all chicken? Where's your Szechuan beef?"

He got to his feet and said, "Let me get some forks," instead of answering her.

She opened the second bag and pulled out the egg rolls, the pork pot stickers, and there sat JJ's Szechuan beef.

Ruby could eat with chopsticks, but she didn't super love it. She opened the rice containers to find he'd gotten one of the ham-fried rice and one of the white, as he liked plain rice better than she did.

Ruby had taken a couple of bites of the snow pea chicken before she realized that JJ had not returned from the kitchen, and it shouldn't take that long to grab a couple of forks and come back. In fact, it should have only taken twenty seconds.

She twisted, and she asked, "What are you doing?"

She got to her feet and sucked in her breath as she saw that every surface in the kitchen—the countertops, the dining room table, the top of the fridge, the stovetop—all held ruby red roses.

JJ turned from the back door that led out onto a small deck and then down to a playground. He'd somehow replaced the door with a wall of roses, and Ruby's blood raced through her veins as she took in the additional vases and tin cans filled with them.

He picked up one single rose from the countertop as he came to stand beside the island. Ruby's heart thundered through her chest, the sound of a thousand horses galloping over dry ground in her ears.

"I love you, my Scarlet Princess," JJ said. "I've loved you in secret for a long time, and I love you more and more every day, and I promise to find ways to keep falling in love with you for the rest of our lives. You want to be mine, and I want to be yours, and I can't wait for us to start our lives together at Seven Sons Ranch."

He held up the rose, his smile absolutely dazzling. "Will you marry me?"

A smile burst onto Ruby's face, and she didn't even think before she gasped out, "Yes!"

JJ reached over to the table and picked up a blue velvet box. He dropped to his knees in the kitchen and said, "Come a little closer, Scarlet."

She walked over to him as he popped open the top of the box. She looked down at the ring and said, "Oh," in a soft, wonder-filled voice.

"You're my Scarlet Princess," he said, lifting the box. "So I thought a ruby would be fitting."

She gazed at the bright red gem in the box, sitting on a silver band, what she suspected was white gold, as that is what she had told JJ she liked. The ruby had been cut into a diamond shape, and it had five diamonds flanking it on both sides. This thing had cost him thousands.

And tears rushed into Ruby's eyes.

"You were so far away," he said. "I'm not sure I heard you. Will you marry me?" he asked.

"Yes," she said in a loud voice, squealing as he laughed, took out the ring, and slid it on her finger. Ruby dropped to her knees in front of him, grabbed onto his face, and kissed him.

"Yes, I'll marry you."

"So I guess I'll meet your momma and daddy as your fiancé," he said. "And not your boyfriend."

"I guess so," Ruby said.

"It's going to be fine," Ruby said a week or so later, though her nerves assaulted her as well. "You're making me more nervous than I already am."

"I've met your parents before," JJ said in a grouchy voice. "I'm not sure why I'm so worked up."

"Probably because you were Tate's best friend," she said. "And they didn't think that you'd fall in love with their daughter."

"I'm a good guy, though, right?" JJ asked.

Ruby laughed as she looked over to him and found pure worry in his eyes. "JJ, you're a billionaire. My parents should be thrilled that you want me."

Sometimes Ruby still couldn't believe it, but one glance down at the giant red gem on her hand told her otherwise. "They're going to love you."

"I think they already love me," he said, looking away out the passenger window. They were almost to Lubbock and almost to the turnoff to get to her family farm. "I need them to love me *for you*."

"They will," she said, reaching over and curling her fingers between his. "Why wouldn't they?"

"Because you're really young," he said.

"So what?" Ruby said. "I went to college for four years, then I lived in Three Rivers, then I went to San Antonio by myself. It's not like this is the first time I ventured outside of my house."

"Yeah, I know," he said, and then he fell silent.

Ruby let him disappear inside his head, because sometimes she needed that. And he would pull her back. Then she would do the same.

When they arrived at the farm, they were staying with her parents for a couple of days before continuing to Three Rivers, where she would move back in with Tate, enjoy the holidays, and then start with Micah and Simone as their interior designer in January.

She made the required turns and put the miles under the wheels until she came to the family farm where she'd grown up. To her knowledge, JJ had never been here because he'd only been an hour from Amarillo State, and he'd always gone home for every holiday and summer to see his family and work his own ranch.

"This is it," Ruby said, her voice pitching up a little bit. "Golden Acres."

"Golden Acres," JJ read as they went under the arch. "I like that."

"Do you?" Ruby asked.

JJ looked over to her. "Sure. Why not?"

"I don't know. Feels a little cliché to me."

She grinned at him. JJ did give a chuckle, which hopefully would loosen him up.

"Tate's bringing Clara Jean home for Christmas," he said.

"Yeah," Ruby said. "She told me."

"Do your parents think it's weird that siblings are marrying siblings?"

"I don't know what they think," Ruby said. "They haven't said that. And besides," she added, "it's not weird." She glanced over at him as she rumbled over the dirt road that led back to the farmhouse. "Do your parents think it's weird?"

"I don't know," he muttered. "They haven't said that."

"Right?" she asked.

"No."

"Then it's not weird," Ruby said.

She pulled up to the house, and her mother and two younger siblings spilled out of it before she even put the car in park. She started to laugh, secured the car, and jumped from it. She loved her family, and for her mother to be home in the middle of the day on a Thursday meant she'd taken the day off from teaching, and that was a big deal.

Ruby ran toward her and up the stairs and right into

their arms as they all called to her, "Hello!" and "Welcome home!"

She did a three-way hug, as she exclaimed over how tall Ben had gotten, and Natalie asked her how the drive was, and Mama explained that her hair had gotten way too long and needed to be cut before the holidays.

They'd always talked over one another, and Daddy and Tate had always called them "squabbling chickens" when they did. Somehow, through the squabbling, she heard the sound of a car door closing, and she turned to welcome JJ to the farm and to her family.

She ran down the steps to meet him at the front of the car, and she took both of his hands in hers, and said, "Come on," like she had the most amazing thing in the world for him to see.

She led him up the steps and said, "Mama, Nat, Ben—this is JJ Walker. He's the man I'm going to marry."

* * *

Oh, JJ and Ruby. Their road wasn't exactly straight, but it was perfectly precise! I'm so happy they found their way to each other in Three Rivers.

And keep reading for the first two chapters of the next book in the series, THE COWBOY WHO SPOKE SOFTLY, featuring the single dad, friends to lovers - GLOVER and WALKER saga - with Conrad and Glory Rose!

Sneak Peek! The Cowboy Who Spoke Softly Chapter One:

Conrad Walker pulled up to his parents' house, deep gratitude instantly striking through him as he drank in the colorful banners, streamers, and balloons that had taken over the entire front porch.

"Oh, my goodness, Sari," he said. "Look at Grandma's house."

His daughter was turning three this week, and Conrad had decided to have a family birthday party on the weekend so that his aunts and uncles and cousins could attend. Her late February birthday meant that everybody had school and work, and since this was the first birthday that Conrad had gotten to celebrate with his daughter, Sarina, he'd wanted her to have his entire family there.

Truth be told, Conrad needed his whole family with him as well. As the gratitude drove deep through him, it left a hole for the guilt to fill. He shouldn't have asked his mother to host the party here. He should have done it at his own house so that she wouldn't have to clean things up afterward. Not only that, but he certainly didn't deserve such an amazing party for his daughter, the daughter that no one had known about until last summer—not even him.

Just as quickly as the guilt chased the gratitude, Conrad was able to reason it away. He'd been working on making things right between him and God for a long time, even before he found out about Sarina, as he knew he'd done some things wrong in his past that he needed to repent of—whether those things had produced a baby or not. And in this case, they had.

He thought of his ex-girlfriend and how she might be feeling this year not having their daughter with her. So he got out of the truck, and before he moved to the back to get his little girl down, he snapped some pictures of the house so that she could see how much his family loved Sarina.

Then he turned his attention to the back seat, where Sarina giggled and kicked her legs to get out of the seat.

"All right," he said with a chuckle. "Come on, let's go see what she's got."

"Boon boon," Sarina said, and Conrad would take that, because his daughter didn't talk very well or very much. He'd been taking her to an early childhood behavioral specialist for the past couple of months. When he read her books with dogs and frogs and pigs and cats, now she said all of the animal noises. She'd always called him "Dad," but now she called Grams "Gams," too, and he was pleased with the progress she'd made in her speech.

He set her on her feet, and she ran laughing toward the house. Conrad's heart filled with joy too, and he took a picture of his little girl running toward the house so he could send it to Chloe too.

He knew things between him and Chloe were irreparable. Had he known about the pregnancy in the beginning, he probably would have married her. But since he hadn't, she'd left town and hadn't told him about their child. She hadn't wanted him, and that hurt Conrad, but he'd been over her by the time she came back into his life with a little girl bearing all the Walker features, from eyes to nose to chin —all of *his* features.

He jogged to catch up to his daughter as she took the steps one at a time, both feet on each one before she went up to the next. The door opened, and his daddy came out, already bellowing, "Happy birthday, Sari!"

He carried an enormous stuffed sloth that made Sarina freeze and then shriek, "Sloth! Sloth!" She pronounced it with an "F" sound at the end instead of "TH."

Daddy laughed and scooped her up off the top step and into his arms. She grabbed onto his face and laughed as he tickled her with his beard and pressed kisses all over her face.

"How are you, my darling girl?" he asked.

Sarina started to talk as Conrad ran up the stairs too. He caught a few words like "Gams" and "balloon," but not much else. When Daddy looked over to him to interpret, Conrad just said, "Yeah, Grandma and Grandpa got you a lot of balloons, didn't they, baby?"

His mother came out onto the porch too, carrying a purple balloon in her hand with a matching tie that she put around Sarina's wrist. She took the little girl from Daddy, already talking to her about cake and presents and how she was going to be the best three-year-old in the world as she took her back into the house.

Chatter and laughter leaked out of the house before Momma closed the door behind her. Conrad knew he and Sarina were the last to arrive. In fact, he'd staged it that way on purpose, so that he didn't have to greet everyone as they came in. He could simply greet everyone once as he arrived.

"How you doing, son?" Daddy asked.

Conrad turned his attention to his father. "Just fine," he said, his voice somewhat guarded.

He used "just fine" all the time, because he was just fine.

How's the farm?

Just fine.

How was church today?

Just fine.

How's Sarina doing with her potty training?

Just fine.

Okay, that last one wasn't really true, and Conrad had given up the endeavor until she turned three. He'd been reading books on how to potty train for the past couple of months, and he'd simply started too early. But he didn't have to get into specifics when he said "just fine," because in reality, everything was just fine—even if he still struggled some days, even if he couldn't get the mini donkeys to come into their pens at night, even if Grams continued to get older and older, and Conrad worried about the day she might not wake up.

"Sure," Daddy said, clearly disbelieving. "Tell me what's in your head."

He gestured toward the door with one big hand. "It's my daughter's third birthday," he said. "And the first that any of us get to celebrate with her."

"Yeah," Daddy said, almost an implied *And?* at the end of that, as if it was no big deal.

"I don't know," Conrad said. "I feel stupid."

"Why?" Daddy asked.

"You know why," Conrad mumbled. He didn't have to articulate it again. "Let's just go inside."

"Wait just a second," Daddy said, and he moved over to step right in front of Conrad, blocking him from entering the house. He slid his hand along the side of Conrad's neck and to the back of it, holding him there, making him feel loved and valued, but also making it so Conrad couldn't look somewhere else.

"You're a good man, Conrad," Daddy said, pure emphasis in his voice. "You have got to stop believing otherwise."

"I don't know how," Conrad told his father.

"You still seeing that therapist?" Daddy asked.

Conrad nodded. "Every couple of weeks."

Daddy dropped his hand. "So keep doing that. And I think maybe it's time you went back to God and asked Him where you stand."

Conrad ducked his head and looked at his boots. "He knows I need to know," he said. "Why do I have to ask too?"

"I don't know," Daddy said. "But sometimes we do. And maybe if you ask Him how you're doing and where you stand with Him, He'll be able to let you know what I can see —that you're good, that you've repented, that you don't need to beat yourself up about Chloe, about Sarina, about any of it, anymore."

Daddy reached out, put a gentle hand under Conrad's chin to lift it up. "It's time to be done with all that. You're forgiven."

Conrad ached to be forgiven, and he nodded, because his emotions had coiled tight and knotted in his throat to the point where he couldn't speak.

Daddy once again dropped his hand, and Conrad hated that he'd caused any turmoil for his parents at all. Of course, they hadn't known that he'd been sleeping with Chloe. He hadn't told anyone about that, but when Sarina showed up in his life, everyone had found out, and everyone judged, no matter what they said and no matter how they acted.

Conrad had worked through that with the Lord, and he'd learned that everyone had to deal with what he'd done in their own way, that it did have consequences for more than just him and Chloe and Sarina, that sometimes people needed space to grieve or process, that sometimes people needed to talk it through.

Sometimes it took a long time, and sometimes it took no time at all.

Conrad had been eternally grateful for his cousin JJ, who seemed to work through whatever he needed to in a matter of minutes before he'd arrived at pure acceptance of Conrad for who he was in the moment and who he could be in the future.

His parents, particularly Daddy, had taken longer. But as Conrad looked at his father now, he distinctly knew that Daddy loved him, wanted the very best for him, and had worked through any conflicting feelings about Conrad being a single dad who'd never been married.

He yearned for that knowledge and acceptance of himself, and he determined that he would pray. He would kneel down and pray that evening and ask God what else he needed to do, if anything, to be made whole and to be forgiven completely.

He nodded. Daddy did too, and then he turned to open the front door.

"Oh, there you are!" Aunt Ivory said. She and Uncle Tripp lived just down the road on this same lane. "I was just coming to get you. Evvy wants to do the cake and presents right now."

"Yep," Daddy said. "We're coming." He went in the house without a backward glance at Conrad.

Conrad gave a tight little smile to his aunt, who pulled him into a hug and said, "I love you, buddy," the way she had when he was a little boy, a tween, and a teenager.

Conrad had always loved being a Walker, and he had loved his aunts and uncles and all of his cousins growing up. So he hated that things between them had been strained and silent and just so different since Sarina had come into his life—come into all of their lives.

But now he melted into his aunt's embrace and said, "I love you too, Aunt Ivory."

The interior of the house had been transformed completely into the set of a tiny girls' wonderland, pink and purple and all the shades in between. Balloons, decorations, banners, gifts, and more had been thrown everywhere. Conrad barely knew where to step, as Momma had set up chairs and tied balloons to every single one, almost creating a maze through the living room to the back of the house in the kitchen, where an enormous three-tiered cake sat on the counter, done in bright pink-bubblegum frosting.

Sarina sat on the counter next to it, and Momma lit the chunky candles as Conrad and Daddy moved through the house to join the party.

"Daddy!" Sarina called. "Cake!"

"Yeah," he said in a bright voice. "That's a big cake."

His mother wouldn't look at him, and Conrad had already decided not to give her a hard time about anything she chose to do for the party. He'd asked her to host it, and he'd told her she could do whatever she wanted. He wasn't going to now criticize that she'd maybe gone a little overboard.

He reminded himself that Sarina was her first and only grandchild, that none of her kids had gotten married yet, and that she simply wanted to pour out her love on Sarina.

And by extension, on you.

That thought entered his mind in a voice he didn't

recognize, and as Momma lit the last candle, Conrad realized God had just spoken to him.

His mother's enthusiasm and exuberance for this party wasn't just for Sarina. It was to show Conrad that she loved him, supported him, and accepted him. And everyone's attendance meant they did too.

"All right," Momma chirped. "We sing first." She looked around at everyone.

Since they'd celebrated many birthdays over the years in the Walker family, they all took a big breath and then started singing "Happy Birthday to you..." in tandem.

Conrad tried to join in and found he couldn't. His emotion surged up and down and back around, and he couldn't get his voice to come out of his throat. He also couldn't hold back the tears, and instead he let them stream down his face as first JJ came to stand next to him, then Easton, and then Austin, and then Elaine.

He loved the triplets with his whole heart, even if Elaine could be a little sassy sometimes. Right now, she stood in front of him as if she could protect him from the eyes of his aunts and uncles and cousins, and if they had anything to say to him that wasn't one hundred percent perfect and positive, they would have to go through her first. Elaine had always been a fierce friend to everyone around her, including Conrad, and he loved her so very much in that moment.

The song finished, and JJ stepped in front of him and turned his back on the party. Austin did the same, and Elaine handed him a tissue over their broad shoulders.

Easton completed the barrier between him and everyone else as he wiped his eyes, and then he smiled as the room erupted in cheers because Sarina had gotten all three candles blown out on her cake.

"What are you doing tonight?" JJ asked, his voice quiet and yet somehow heard among the crowd.

"Going home," Conrad said. He glanced over to Easton.

"I think the five of us should go out."

Conrad blinked at him, because JJ knew full-well he had a three-year-old daughter he had to take care of.

"I'll ask your mom if Sarina can stay here tonight," JJ said, and he turned and walked away before Conrad could say a single word.

"It's a good idea," Austin said, his voice low and somehow set on growl as well. "Let's just go get burgers and wings and hang out."

Conrad wanted to tell him that single dads didn't get burgers and wings and "hang out." But Elaine muscled her way into the spot that JJ had vacated, and she said, "Yeah, let's do that. Maybe you guys can help me meet a man."

Conrad blinked at her, surprise running across his face. "What happened to you telling us to stay out of your business?"

"I'm a little dumbfounded myself," Easton said.

She glared around at all of them, cocking her hip and folding her arms, looking so much like Momma when she did. "I'm allowed to change my mind," she said. "Surely you guys know some single cowboys our age."

Conrad did, yes, and his brain blitzed through who he could possibly set Elaine up with.

JJ returned and said, "She said she'd love to have her."

"I'm gonna call Beaumont." Elaine stepped out of the circle, once again before Conrad could protest or accept what she'd said. He found himself being swept along by this tidal wave of Walkers that he loved so much. He didn't know how to stop them. He wasn't even sure he *wanted* to stop them.

Thankfully, his phone chimed, and he looked down at it to get away from their gazes. He turned his back on them as he saw Glory Rose Glover's name flash across his screen.

What are you doing tonight, cowboy? she asked. *My uncle just gave me two tickets to the stargazing taste testing tonight. Maybe we could go together.*

Conrad had been flirting with Glory Rose for months now, and he'd asked her out a time or two. They'd even set up dates, and then somehow it had always fallen through.

In this moment, he spun back to his cousins and sibling and held up his phone.

"Glory Rose just asked me out," he said.

"Great," JJ said without missing a beat. "You should go out with her. I know you've been trying for a while."

"It's for tonight," Elaine said, a touch of surprise in her voice.

And Conrad already had a babysitter.

Austin, ever the level-headed one, said, "You should go, Conrad. We can do our thing another night."

"Yeah," JJ said.

He looked at Easton and raised his eyebrows. His brother read the text and then grinned at Conrad. "If Glory Rose Glover was offering me tickets to the stargazing taste test, I'd have already said yes."

That caused several people to laugh, including Conrad, but his thumb still hovered over his phone, and he turned his phone back to him, still wondering what he should say to her.

"Oh, give me the phone," JJ said, and he swiped it out of Conrad's hands before he could protest. His thumbs flew over the screen, and then he shoved the phone back at him and said, "There, you have a date. Now come enjoy your daughter's birthday."

Sneak Peek! The Cowboy Who Spoke Softly Chapter Two:

Glory Rose Glover stood in front of the full-length mirror in her bedroom, tilting her head as she scrutinized the outfit she had carefully chosen for the night. The sweater hung down a little too far on the right, and she pulled it back left. At least these dark-wash jeans hugged her legs just right, but she second-guessed the ivory-colored sweater with the criss-cross fabric in the front that then hung down past her hips on the sides.

It wasn't too fancy, but she wasn't the neatest eater—and tonight's date with Conrad included a taste test. She'd definitely be eating, maybe even saucy, Texas-type ribs or wings.

She tucked a lock of her long, dark hair behind her ear, her fingers brushing the silver hoop earrings she had decided to wear. A smile tugged at the corners of her mouth as she thought about the man she'd be seeing tonight.

Conrad Walker was quiet, sure, but something about

him intrigued her. Something that drew her in like a moth to a flame. Something that scared her a little, because Glory Rose sometimes ran out of things to say too.

"He's not like the other cowboys around here," she whispered to her reflection. "He's different."

And that difference had her heart doing little flips in her chest every time she thought about him. She had been flirting with him for months now, and while they had danced around the idea of going out, life always seemed to get in the way. Either his daughter needed something, or something had blown up on his farm, or Glory Rose had a family obligation.

But tonight?

"Tonight is so going to be different."

A knock on her bedroom door startled her from her thoughts, and she turned to see her cousin Fawn poking her head into the room.

"How's it going in here?" Fawn asked, her voice full of teasing as she scanned Glory Rose's outfit. "You look like you're about to go on a first date with a really hot cowboy or something."

Glory Rose rolled her eyes, but she couldn't help the grin that spread across her face. "Don't make me more nervous than I already am." She turned back to the mirror, her gaze locking onto Fawn's as her cousin came closer. "What are you doing tonight?"

Fawn was only a few months younger than Glory Rose, and they'd grown up next door to one another here at Shiloh Ridge Ranch. Their daddies were brothers, and Glory Rose leaned into Fawn as her cousin put her arm around her. They'd been best friends for a long time, so when it came time for them to move out, they'd moved into together.

Yes, still here on the ranch, but into one of the cabins just north of the Top Cottage, where Link lived with his wife and family.

Uncle Bear and Uncle Ranger had both fully retired from the ranch work now, and Lincoln—Bear's oldest son—and Wilder—Ranger's oldest, and Fawn's older brother—both ran the ranch now. There were so many Glovers living and working here, and Glory Rose and Fawn were just two of them.

And really, Glory Rose didn't work on the ranch. She just lived here, as she had a nursing job down in town, at a pediatrician's office. Fawn, however, had earned her vet technician certificate, and she worked with the animals here at the ranch.

She wanted to become a vet, but she hadn't quite pulled the lever yet, as it would take her away from Shiloh Ridge, away from Three Rivers, away from all the Glovers. And Fawn was very much a homebody. She still sometimes drove the five minutes down the road to sleep at her momma's, as they got along so well.

Right now, Fawn reached up and swept her fingers through her own dark hair that fell in waves over her shoulders. "What am I doing tonight?" She sighed. "Helping Pearl Jo with her application to the Animal Science major? Probably that. It's due soon, and I don't have anything better to do."

Glory Rose stepped out of the side-hug and sat on her bed to pull on her boots.

"You're going with the sweater-book look," Fawn said.

She looked up to her. "Not a good combo? It's February."

"It's really cozy."

Glory Rose glanced down at her outfit again, a flicker of doubt creeping in. "I don't want to look like I'm trying too hard, Fawn. We're going stargazing, not to some fancy dinner."

"But it's Conrad Walker, and you've been pining after this guy for months now."

"I have *not* been pining," Glory Rose protested, though her cheeks flushed. That could be because she couldn't get this blasted boot to go on. She pulled harder, which allowed her to focus on her feet instead of Fawn.

"Oh, please." Fawn's laughter filled the room. "You've been talking about him non-stop. Conrad this, Conrad that. *He's so quiet, you guys, but he's got these dreamy eyes. He texted me back, but he didn't say much. What do you think that means?*"

Fawn grinned as Glory Rose finally got the boot on and looked up to her. "And don't even get me started on his daughter. You're practically in love with her, and you've only met her a handful of times."

Glory Rose huffed, got her second boot on easily, and stood. She crossed her arms over her chest and glared at Fawn. "I'm not in love with anyone, okay? I just—I think there's something special about Conrad. He's been through so much, and I like that he's grounded. He's not like all the other cowboys around here who just want to have fun and flirt."

And Glory Rose needed some excitement in her life. As one of a great many dozens of Glovers, and since she didn't play a role here on the ranch, Glory Rose often felt overlooked in her own family. She wondered if Conrad did too. He had a lot of cousins, aunts, uncles, and siblings too.

Maybe that was why Glory Rose wanted to get to know him better. Maybe they could create a space for each other where they were each the most important.

"Who's flirting?" Pearl Jo asked as she appeared in the doorway. She scanned Glory Rose down to the boots and back. "You look amazing." She glanced over to Fawn. "What's going on tonight?"

"Our girl Glory Rose here has a date with the one-and-only Conrad Walker." Fawn grinned at her, and Glory Rose's face heated again.

Pearl Jo looked like she'd just come in from the stables, with mud on the cuffs of her jeans and her hair still braided back. Her eyes only got wider as she stared at Glory Rose.

"Stop it," Glory Rose said, and she brushed her hands down the front of her sweater. "Settle a debate for us. Good sweater or too blah?"

Pearl Jo settled her weight onto one foot and cocked her head to the side. "It's seriously cute. Not my style, but perfect for you."

Glory Rose threw a *so-there* look over to Fawn. "Perfect for me."

Liz Isaacson

"You've always been very good at being yourself," Fawn said with a laugh.

Glory Rose smiled over to her and pushed her hair over her shoulder. "I hope that doesn't come back to bite me tonight."

"Why would it?" Pearl Jo reached up and started to release her hair out of its braid. "I stink. I need to shower."

Glory Rose could've agreed with her, and she had teased Pearl Jo about the...certain smell she brought back to their cabin in the evenings in the past. Tonight, the doorbell rang, and all three of them gasped.

The chime died after only a moment, as the battery needed to be replaced. The higher-pitched bell sank into a low buzz in a way that seemed like the sound was melting.

"That's him," Glory Rose whispered, her heartbeat suddenly a sprint through her veins.

Pearl Jo grinned, rushed toward the window, and peeked through the blinds. "Oh, it's definitely him, all right. And he's looking all cowboy-cool in his jeans and jacket."

"I'll get it," Fawn said, stepping past where Glory Rose had frozen.

Glory Rose took a deep breath, smoothing her sweater down one last time. "The sweater is really okay, Pearl Jo?"

Her cousin turned toward her. "Absolutely." She came over and pressed her cheek to Glory Rose's. "I'm too stinky to hug." She grinned as she stepped back. "Now, I'm going to go get an eyeful of Conrad too."

She left before Glory Rose could tell her not to do that, and Glory Rose stayed where she stood. Pearl Jo had a double name like her, and she was the oldest daughter of her daddy's other brother—Uncle Ace. She was definitely more outdoorsy than Glory Rose, and she wanted to earn degrees in animal science and agronomy. With the rotational ranching Glory Rose's daddy had incorporated here at Shiloh Ridge, the agronomy would be particularly useful at maintaining their crops.

Voices filtered back to her from the front of the cabin, as it wasn't a big space. Glory Rose had her own room, but she could barely take three steps in it. The bigger bedroom across the hall housed Fawn and Pearl Jo, and Glory Rose had never minded the smaller living space.

Her pulse sped even more as she took a deep breath and stepped out of the room. Only a couple of strides put her in the kitchen, and her gaze shot to the front door. Conrad stood inside the house, standing at least a head taller than both of her cousins.

Everything about him made Glory Rose's cells sing. His height, his broad shoulders, his dark hair under that deep, black, midnight cowboy hat. He wore a black leather jacket too, and Glory Rose's hand shot out to steady herself against the fridge beside her.

He held a small bouquet of wildflowers, and the sight made Glory Rose's legs feel like toothpicks that were unable to hold her upright.

His eyes came to hers, and his whole countenance brightened. "There she is."

Fawn and Pearl Jo turned toward her, but Glory Rose couldn't move. Fawn gestured at her with a low hand, and

Glory Rose somehow got her feet to walk her closer to the door.

"Hey, Glory Rose." Conrad's voice came out soft and a little shy. "These are for you." He held up the brightly colored wildflowers.

Glory Rose's smile widened as she took the yellow and orange blooms from him. "Thank you, Conrad. They're beautiful."

He nodded, his eyes lingering on her face for a moment before he cleared his throat. "You ready to go?"

"Yeah, just let me grab my jacket." She turned and reached for her coat, a soft blush creeping up her neck as she felt Conrad's eyes on her.

She handed the bouquet to Fawn, who said, "I'll put these in a vase for you."

"Thank you, Fawny." She gave her cousin a quick hug, then started to put on her jacket.

"Let me help you." Conrad's deep voice tickled all through her, and Glory Rose could scarcely believe this was even happening. She couldn't feel his skin as he helped her put on her jacket, but when their eyes met, pure lightning struck the cabin, struck her vocal cords hard enough to make her mute, struck so deep in her heart, she hoped Conrad could feel it too.

He blinked a couple of times, then reached for her hand with one of his while turning to open the door with the other. He led her outside into the cool February air. The sky had already darkened, and a shiver ran down her spine. Not from the cold, though. Oh, no. More like nerves, excitement, and the way she felt completely unsure of what to expect from the night.

Her skin sizzled from where it touched his, and he adjusted his grip on her fingers. "It's good to see you," he said.

"Yeah," she said, feeling completely foolish afterward. Why had her tongue tied itself into a knot? She'd never had a problem talking to boys, and now that she'd become an adult, men. She'd danced with this cowboy last year at a birthday party and had never run out of things to say.

But now, her mind had gone completely blank.

She glanced up at Conrad, her heart doing somersaults in her chest. He didn't say anything, just gave her a small smile as he opened her door for her.

"Come on, Glory Rose," she muttered to herself as he rounded the hood to get behind the wheel. As he got in, she asked, "Who's got Sarina tonight?"

Conrad started his truck and adjusted the air vents as he said, "My mother."

She nodded, not sure why her insides felt like they'd been encased in ice.

"We had a birthday party for Sari this afternoon," Conrad said. "So she just kept her."

Glory Rose looked over to him. "Oh, is it her birthday?" Her pulse broke through the band of ice around her heart. "Conrad, we didn't need to go out on your daughter's birthday."

He rumbled down the tree-lined lane to the main road on the ranch. He glanced up toward the Top Cottage and then made the turn, the big blue family barn now on his left. "It's not her birthday today," he said. "It's actually on Wednesday, but I wanted everyone to be able to attend a party." He cleared his throat, and Glory Rose wondered if he had more to say.

But he didn't go on.

"Okay," she said. "Good." She immediately started thinking about what a little girl would like. "And she'll be three?"

"Yep."

So what would a three-year-old like? Glory Rose had grown up with a lot of children around her, as her daddy had four siblings and seven cousins, all of them living right here at the ranch—or very close to it. She could talk to Aunt Etta and find out what a three-year-old girl would absolutely love, and she started planning to stop by Conrad's farm and drop it off on Wednesday.

"So where are we going?" he asked. "I'm assuming out into the hills, maybe?" He turned to go past the main home-stead and under the arch announcing the arrival at Shiloh Ridge Ranch. "Stargazing won't be in town, right?"

"Oh, right." Glory Rose dove into her purse to get her phone, and she tapped to get to the email her uncle had sent her. "This says...." She looked up and out the windshield. "We need to go to the Kingman's abandoned farm. It's that road—"

"Right up here," Conrad said with her.

"I know where it is." He flashed her a smile that made

her stomach flip. "My cousins and siblings and I got in so much trouble at the Kingmans."

"Did you now?" Glory Rose tucked her phone away. "Doing what?"

"Oh, me and JJ would make up stories about how the barn was haunted," he said with a chuckle. "Then tell all the younger kids about them, make them go out there when it was dark, that kind of stuff."

"I'm surprised my family didn't buy it ages ago," Glory Rose said. "They tend to do that—buy up land around Shiloh Ridge to add to the ranch."

"Yeah," Conrad said. "JJ did that last year with Seven Sons."

"It's not a bad expansion strategy."

"Maybe your daddy didn't think you guys had enough people in your family to take on the extra land." He threw her a smile that rose higher on the right than the left.

Glory Rose realized a couple of beats later that he was teasing her. *Flirting* with her. She burst out laughing, because no one would ever call the Glover family small.

"Must be right down here," he mused as he bumped along the dirt road. He drove a nice truck, and while he didn't always have a lot to say, Glory Rose liked his steadiness. She liked how safe she felt with him.

He pulled up next to another truck in the designated parking area, and he peered out the windshield. "The wind is not going to be kind tonight."

Glory Rose looked too, and sure enough, the light tree limbs she could see blew and blustered around. "I guess the tasting is here," she said, though she had no idea what kind of tasting someone could put on at an abandoned ranch. The barns and stables here surely didn't have commercial kitchens in them.

Strings of fairy lights had been hung from the single pole in the lot, casting a soft glow over the area, and leading along a path, and as Glory Rose watched, another couple walked that way. "Looks like we go along the lights." She cast a quick look over to Conrad, who nodded.

Then he twisted, reached into the backseat, and pulled a blanket over the seat. "I brought this, just in case."

Glory Rose opened her door and slid from the truck, the reach of the fairy lights and a couple of floods on the corner of the barn not reaching that far into the night. The air entered her lungs in a cold way, but Glory Rose hunkered down into her coat and took in a long, deep breath of it. "It's so beautiful here," she said.

"Isn't it?" Conrad joined her, once again securing her hand in his. "Should we walk through the creepy buildings, trusting that those fairy lights aren't going to lead us to our deaths?"

Glory Rose looked at him, sure she'd find that glint in his dark eyes that would tell her he was joking. But she didn't find it. "You really think this might be nefarious."

"I can just see the headlines now," Conrad said. "Tourists and locals alike get lured to abandoned ranch and slain." He chuckled then, and Glory Rose relaxed. "I'd send up a drone to see what I was walking into, if it were up to me."

"Do you have a drone in your truck?" she asked.

He looked over to her. "No, ma'am, I don't."

"I'm twenty-three years old," she said. "You don't need to call me ma'am."

"What should I call you?"

"What do you mean?" Glory Rose stepped toward the pole with the lights, taking Conrad with her.

"Well, JJ calls Ruby by a bunch of cutesy nicknames. Maybe, I mean—maybe...." He trailed off, and Glory Rose sure enjoyed the flush that stained his cheeks. In the dimmer, yellow light, it almost looked orange.

"I love the stars," he said.

Glory Rose smiled as warmth spread through her chest. "Me too. There's just something about the night sky that makes everything else seem smaller. Like all the worries in the world just fade away."

Conrad glanced at her, his expression softening. "Yeah. Just like that."

Around the corner of the front barn, the lights led them to a square of sorts—an open area surrounded by four buildings. A long table had been set up at the back of the barn, covered in trays of appetizers, desserts, and warm drinks. Glory Rose's stomach rumbled as the smell of freshly baked bread and roasted meats filled the air.

"You hungry?" Conrad asked, a small smile tugging at the corner of his mouth.

"Starving," Glory Rose admitted with a laugh. "I don't know if we just dive in, or what." She glanced around and found a woman taking tickets. "Conrad." She nodded in the direction of the woman, and he took her that way.

They got in line to show their tickets, and Glory Rose pulled them up on her phone from the forwarded email from Uncle Bear. The woman looked at her phone and then her. "These are Bear Glover's?"

"Yes, ma'am," Glory Rose said, because this woman was at least as old as her mother.

She didn't scan the tickets. "This is an invite-only event."

"Oh." Glory Rose didn't know what to say.

"We curate our menu to those who RSVP."

"Uh." Her heartbeat accelerated, because she didn't know how to handle this situation. A crying, squirming baby, sure. She could soothe the infant enough to get the child to cooperate. But this? Uncle Bear hadn't told her anything more than this was a stargazing taste test.

"That's okay," Conrad said, stepping in front of her. "We don't feel like dying tonight anyway."

The woman looked at him, and her name snapped into place in Glory Rose's head. Camille Burke. "Dying tonight?"

Conrad gave her a swift smile. "Come on, Glory Rose. We'll go grab dinner somewhere else." He backed up a step and then turned, taking Glory Rose with him.

She went with him, expecting him to take her back to the truck. Instead, he walked along the buffet at the back of the barn, the scent of sweet-and-spicy barbecue sauce taunting her.

"Conrad," she hissed as they moved further and further from the lit square.

"Come on," he whispered, his hand firm around hers as he moved between the barn and a stable.

"Where are we going?" she whispered back, a thrill of excitement pulsing through her. In two more steps, she'd be alone in the dark with Conrad Walker. Her eyes adjusted with every step, and she could make out shapes now.

He rounded the far corner of the stable and paused, only darkness back here. "We were promised stargazing, so stargazing we will go."

"But...." Her protest faded as he grinned down at her, his face inches from hers. "Are we even allowed?" She drew in a deep breath of him, the scent of his cottony skin, his leather jacket, his woodsy cologne.

"We make our own rules tonight." His lips brushed her earlobe, sending a shiver down to her toes. "So come on."

Where is he taking her? What is going to happen on this date?! I can't wait to spend time with Conrad and Glory Rose - a union of Walker and Glover!

Preorder your copy by scanning the QR code below with your phone!

Liz Isaacson

The Cowboy Who Came Home: A Second Generation in Three Rivers Ranch Romance™ (Book 1): He's been serving in the military for a decade. She's been quietly grieving a devastating loss. When Finn and Edith reunite in small-town Three Rivers where they grew up together, can their second chance romance provide hope, healing, and the happily-ever-after they both crave?

Scan this QR code with your phone to see this series in eBook, audiobook, large print paperback, or regular paperback:

Be sure to check out the other three series set in the beloved town of Three Rivers too!

Meet the cowboys who started it all at Three Rivers Ranch! Scan the QR code below with your phone to check out this complete series.

Scan this QR code with your phone to see and order this series in eBook, audiobook, large print paperback, or regular paperback:

1. Second Chance Ranch
2. Third Time's the Charm
3. Fourth and Long
4. Fifth Generation Cowboy
5. Sixth Street Love Affair
6. The Seventh Sergeant
7. Eight Second Ride
8. The Ninth Inning
9. Ten Days in Town
10. Eleven Year Reunion

Seven Sons Ranch in Three Rivers Romance™ Series

Meet the cowboy billionaire brothers at Seven Sons Ranch! Scan the QR code below with your phone to check out this complete series.

1. Rhett
2. Tripp
3. Liam
4. Jeremiah
5. Wyatt
6. Skyler
7. Micah
8. Gideon

Shiloh Ridge Ranch in Three Rivers Romance™ Series

Become a Glover Lover by reading all the Glover Family romance & family saga at Shiloh Ridge Ranch! Scan the QR code below with your phone to check out this complete series.

1. The Mechanics of Mistletoe
2. The Horsepower of the Holiday
3. The Construction of Cheer
4. The Secret of Santa
5. The Gift of Gingerbread
6. The Harmony of Holly
7. The Chemistry of Christmas
8. The Delivery of Decor

About Liz

Liz Isaacson writes inspirational romance, usually set in Texas, or Wyoming, or anywhere else horses and cowboys exist. She lives in Utah, where she writes full-time, takes her two dogs to the park everyday, and eats a lot of veggies while writing. Find her on her website at www.feelgoodfiction-books.com.

www.ingramcontent.com/pod-product-compliance
Lightning Source LLC
Chambersburg PA
CBHW020516110726
47899CB00004B/1134